T0267846

FORGET ME NOT

THE ROSENHOLM TRILOGY
VOLUME 2

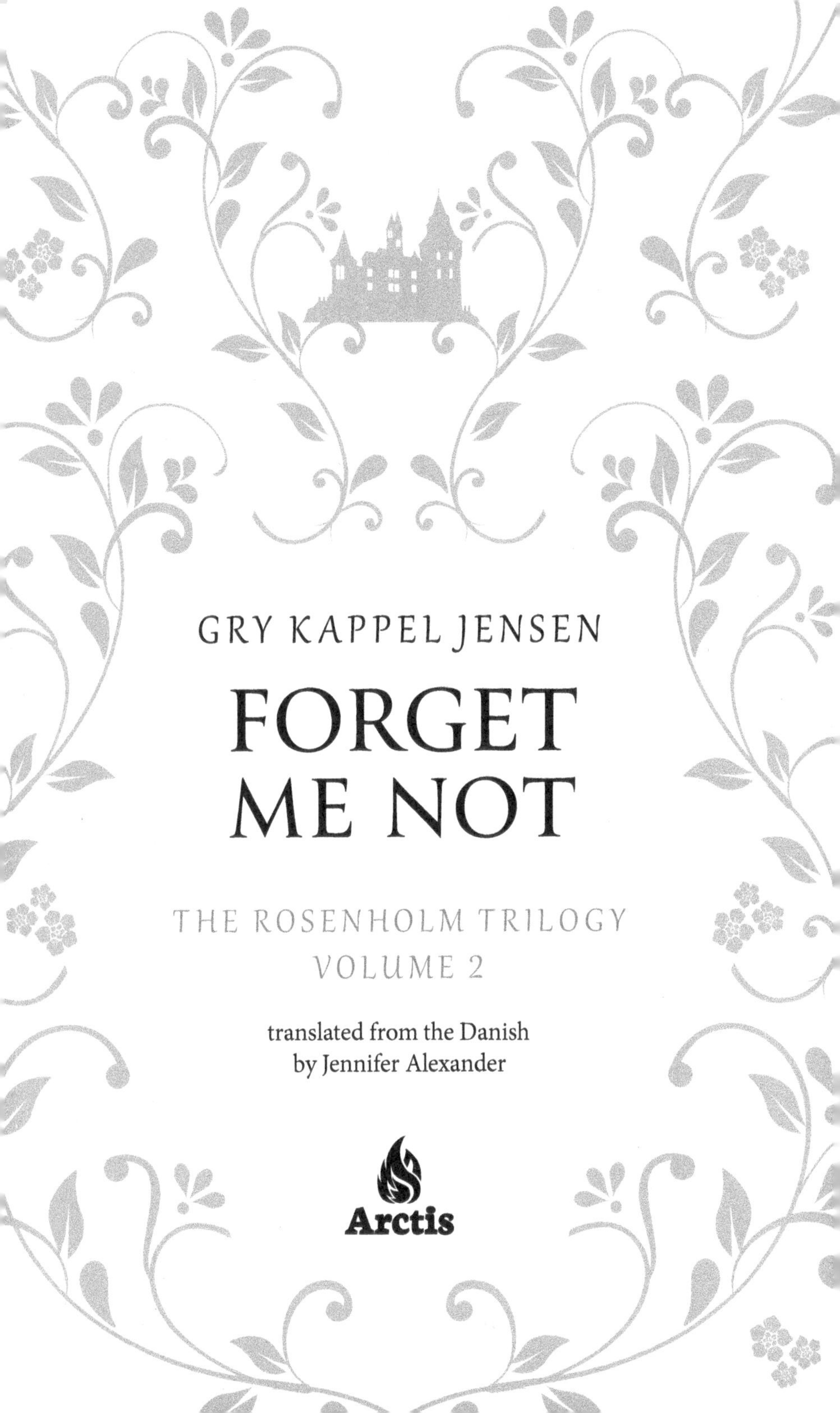

GRY KAPPEL JENSEN

FORGET ME NOT

THE ROSENHOLM TRILOGY
VOLUME 2

translated from the Danish
by Jennifer Alexander

Arctis

This translation has been published with the financial support of The Danish Arts Foundation.

W1-Media, Inc.
Arctis Books USA
Stamford, CT, USA

Visit our website at www.arctis-books.com

1 3 5 7 9 8 6 4 2

The Library of Congress Control Number: 2024931436

ISBN 978-1-64690-013-8
eBook ISBN 978-1-64690-613-0

The quotation on page 243 is from the short story "The Blue Eyes"
by Karen Blixen, in *Winter's Tales*, 1942,
taken here from *Dansk I Dybden*, Gyldendal.

Printed in Germany

PROLOGUE

I loved it when you played with me back then, when we were children. The way I remember, it was always summer and there were flowers in the tall grass: you pushing me on the swing, me laughing skyward, and you laughing as you pushed me higher and higher, over and over, until darkness fell.

It was only later I came to hate you. I hated you so deeply that in the end, I wished you were dead. But when you disappeared, everything just got worse. It was always all about you. It didn't help one damn bit that you died.

PART 1.
SUMMER

Red Rose
"I will love you
forever."

Floriography, or the language of flowers,
originated in Europe in the Middle Ages but was used
widely in middle class circles in the 1700s and 1800s.

JULY 27TH
8:15 A.M.

Malou

Malou cleaned out the sink and dried it off with some toilet paper before placing the items along its edge in the order she would use them. First she let her face cream sink in a little before applying the primer. It was much easier that way to get the foundation and powder set just right. Before starting on her eyes, she took a brush and accentuated the contours of her face, cheekbones, and slender nose with a subtle shading. She thought about eye shadow, but in the end added only a touch of highlighter to her brows before penciling them in. She chose the liquid eyeliner, two layers of mascara, and pink blush. She could pass for at least twenty, surely?

She pulled her straight blond hair into a tight ponytail and put on a white shirt. If she wanted to be taken seriously, she needed to look serious too. Maybe the red lipstick?

As she let herself out of the bathroom with her makeup bag tucked under her arm, she heard a noise from the kitchen. Her mother stood leaning over the table.

"Go get some sleep, Mom," Malou said wearily. Maybe she'd gotten up and started drinking again. Maybe she hadn't been to bed at all.

Her mom straightened up and turned toward her, still supporting herself with one hand on the kitchen table. She scrunched up her eyes and looked at her for a moment.

"You look cheap with that lipstick on," she mumbled.

"Go to hell!" Malou said, and turned away. She slammed her bedroom door and locked it behind her. "Go to hell," she whispered. "Go to hell."

She stood still for a moment in the middle of the floor. Then she put down the case, with all its neatly organized contents, on the bedspread and took off her shirt so it wouldn't get stained. Before, she wouldn't have been able to resist the urge to open her desk drawer, where the razor blade still lay. She didn't use that anymore, but she still needed to feel strong. To feel in control. Powerful. Magic meant power in the ancient languages. They'd been told that at school by Birgit Lund, Rosenholm's former principal. And that had been what convinced Malou, more than anything else, that she wanted to practice magic.

She let her eyes rest on the elbow crease of her arm, where the skin was so thin that the veins were visible, like blue-gray rivers on a map. *Blood is your source of power.* She needed it today. She focused her gaze and concentrated. She felt a prick on her skin, the pain not unpleasant. Slowly it appeared. First a small blue mark under the skin, then getting clearer, turning red, until finally blood pushed through the skin and lay, like a perfect, tiny pearl in the joint of her elbow. She closed her eyes. *You can do it. This is important!* The summer holidays would soon be over and she could get back to Rosenholm. Her school, which had been her home and which she missed, despite everything that had happened. Despite not having kept her promise to the young girl who was murdered at the school many years ago and whose death had never been explained. The girl's ghost had sought them out, and Malou had sworn to her that they would find her killer. *Just hold on, Trine. We haven't forgotten you.*

She opened her eyes and studied the small drop of blood. Then she lifted her arm up to her face and licked it clean. She had a quarter of an hour until her train, but their apartment faced the back entrance to the station and she should still be able to make it. She let herself close her eyes for a moment longer, before checking there were no traces of blood anywhere. Then she stuck a skin-colored adhesive bandage over the wound and put her shirt back on. She checked how she looked in the mirror and nodded to herself before unlocking her room and leaving the apartment without saying goodbye.

She had to run the last stretch and got up the steps just as the train to Copenhagen came in. There were no seats free, so she went into the bathroom instead. Her reflection looked pale in the scratched mirror, which distorted her face. Her mouth was far too red. *Ugly.* She found a tissue in her bag and started to wipe the lipstick off but only ended up smudging it beyond the edges of her lips. *Shit!* The sense of peace from before was now gone, and outside someone was trying to open the door.

Malou took a deep breath, straightened up, and looked her mirror-self in the eyes. "To hell with them all," she whispered. She looked in her bag for her concealer and dabbed a thin layer around the lips where the skin had gotten reddish from the smudged lipstick and her rubbing so hard. Then she took out the lipstick and slowly and carefully reapplied it, despite someone knocking insistently on the door.

JULY 27TH
9:30 A.M.

Chamomile

Chamomile pulled down the attic ladder. It made a loud creaking noise. Her mom was still sleeping, but Chamomile didn't care if the noise woke her.

A shower of dust and plaster fell as the door yielded, and she was able to climb the narrow ladder. Up here, it smelled dusty and old and it was dark, but not pitch black. Light broke through the ancient thatched roof revealing the leaky gaps where snow drifted in over the winter. The attic was not very tall, but at the center, under the rafters, she was able to stand upright, and she walked barefoot over the uneven floorboards toward the hatch at the gable end. The window was wooden, nobody having thought to fit an actual glass pane. She tried to open the hatch, but it held fast and only gave in after a little kick. Light spilled in together with a rush of fresh air and the fruity smell of ripening corn and damp grass. She wiped her forehead with the back of her hand and savored the feel of the cool morning breeze. It was warm up here already, even though it was still early morning. She looked around her. The place was full of boxes, packed old furniture, suitcases, and plastic bags. Where should she start?

She found some boxes with her name on them. *Toys* was also written on one. *Girl's clothes, 2 years.* Chamomile had no interest in things from when she was little. She wanted to find the boxes from *before* she was born. Maybe there'd be something that could tell her more about him. Photos, letters, or a gift from him, maybe? Her mom kept everything, after all.

She dug out one box that was tucked right under the eaves. It had water damage and dents and looked as if it had been moved many times. *Notes* was written on it. She dragged it out onto the floor and opened it. Exercise books, ring binders, multicolored plastic wallets. She rummaged aimlessly in the box, but gave up, resolutely tipping all its contents onto the floor instead.

She recognized her mom's handwriting on lots of the documents. An essay on the Nordic gods' use of euphoriant plants, an exercise on devil's nettle and its many beneficial properties, an endless number of tightly scribbled pages with notes taken in lessons. This was from her mom's time at Rosenholm. It seemed she had been a conscientious student. Chamomile never managed to take such thorough notes. She rummaged through the papers a little more, reading a sentence here and there. At the very bottom of the pile she found a book. No, it was a school diary from her mom's final year. She felt her heart thump as she flicked through it. Her mom's handwriting filled every page. Chapters they had to read, book titles, deadlines, friends' birthdays. Here and there, her mom had drawn in different plants, noting underneath what they could be used for. Each time Chamomile came across one of these small drawings, she took time to study it. *Blue anemone (for problems with the liver or heartburn—NOTE: poisonous in their raw state!), pilewort (for wounds and blisters), starflower (for the relief of respiratory illness and rheumatism).*

Chamomile also noticed her mom had marked some pages of the diary with a small star in the top right corner. Sometimes she had written underneath. *The old mountain ash,* one showed. *The attic* under another.

She was just about to flip the diary closed and throw it back in the box when she discovered something stuck inside the plastic wallet covering the diary. It was a class photo. Her mom was sitting right in the middle, laughing. They were uncannily alike, Chamomile had to admit it, with the same rosy cheeks. A plain leather purse hung around her mom's neck, and she wore a small silver leaf on a chain. She still carried both the purse and the silver leaf, and Chamomile wore an identical chain around her neck. Suddenly she was irritated to no end by the fact they were so alike. Her mom must have been pregnant when that photo was taken. Had she been happy, or was she laughing to hide how she really felt? Was she in love? Or had she already decided that Chamomile's dad should not be a part of her life?

"So this is where you are?" Her mom stuck her head up through the hatch. "What are you up to?"

"Looking for answers," Chamomile said, and rummaged further in the pile.

"Hey," said her mom, climbing the steep ladder to the attic, "I know you're angry with me, but those are my things." She placed a hand on her hip. Her summer dress was two sizes too tight. "You have no right to rummage around in there."

"I don't care," Chamomile stated. "You can't tell me anymore what I have the right to do."

"Miley . . ." Her mom sat down beside her and started to put the papers back in the box. "Was it wrong of me to tell you?"

"You should have told me a long time ago. And what about *him*? Didn't you owe it to him to tell him you were pregnant?"

Her mother stopped refilling the box and looked her in the eyes. "No, you know what, I don't think I did. We were finished and he wasn't interested anymore. It was me who was pregnant, it was my choice."

"But it was *his* child too! You didn't make me on your own!"

Chamomile's mother sighed. "Maybe it was a mistake, but I wanted to make a little family of our own. You and me. We didn't need any man. It was hard, facing it all alone, but we did it. And actually I am quite proud of that. You were a happy child growing up. You really were always so happy." She reached over to take her hand, but Chamomile pulled hers away and stood up.

"You can forget that," she sneered. "I'm done with being your good little girl."

"Chamomile . . ." Her mother's voice trembled, but Chamomile didn't care. She shouldn't think she'd get away with it so easily.

"What do I say to my friends? And what about *him*? Do I tell him?"

"I don't know. Only you can make that decision," said her mother, lowering her gaze. "I understand that it must be difficult."

"Difficult?!" Chamomile's voice was hoarse with rage. "I'll tell you what's difficult: understanding how you could let me start at that school without saying anything to me!" She turned and climbed down the ladder, leaving her mother behind in the warm, dusty loft. She would never forgive her. To think that she had allowed Chamomile to go to Rosenholm for a whole year without telling her that every single day, she'd be crossing paths with her own father.

JULY 27TH
10:00 A.M.

Malou

Malou walked purposefully toward the counter. *It's just a case of acting like you belong here.* The Royal Library. It wasn't how she'd imagined it. She had thought of a formal old building, like Christiansborg Palace or the Round Tower or something like that, but instead her GPS led her to this modern block of glass and black. The Black Diamond.

"Are you looking for a study desk?" the woman at Information asked.

"No, I need to look at some microfilm."

"Microfilm? That's up in the East Reading Room," the woman said pointing up to the next floor.

Malou nodded and followed the signs up the escalators until she came to another counter and an elderly man with interesting-looking hair: bald on the top but long at the sides.

"I have an appointment with someone called Anders."

"Wait here a moment," the elderly man said, and disappeared. He returned with a younger man, still in his twenties.

"You must be Malou?" He smiled and held out his hand. "Good to meet you. So, as you'll see, I've pulled out the film rolls for you. It's this way."

"Thanks for helping me," she said, and gave him her most winning smile.

"Of course, that's what we're here for. Although, truth be told, we don't normally tend to look up the newspapers for people, but I was really curious when you told me about what you were looking for on the phone. And it's all part of an assignment?"

Malou nodded confidently. "Yes, I decided to write about the case when I heard this old story about a girl who disappeared."

"It's real 'true crime', isn't it?" He smiled. "I got totally hooked on your mystery too. And it was a big help when I got the right name to search for." He led her over to a row of large screens. "These are the microfilms, which have all the old newspapers saved on them. When you put them in the machine like this, you can read the text on the screen. The vast majority nowadays are digitalized, it's only these older years that are not. But if you don't mind, let me first show you what I found myself. You can sit down here."

She sat in the chair in front of the screen and looked on while Anders showed her how to insert the film. It soon appeared before them: *Zealand Times,* January 1, 1989.

"I couldn't find anything in the national papers," Anders said, leaning across her to work the machine. "At first I thought a case like that would surely have made the tabloids, but there was nothing. Then I looked at local papers instead. And then I got something. We just have to go forward to the spring." He started turning a dial, and soon the newspaper pages were flying across the screen. "Whoa, I've gone too far. Back a little. There!" He stood again. "I don't mind saying that I'm really proud of finding that."

She was quick to give him another smile and nod in acknowledgment. "Good job!"

"There might be more, so I thought that you could look through the rest of the years yourself. Let me know if you need any help, okay?"

Malou thanked him once more and turned to the screen. There, from a black-and-white photo in the bottom right-hand corner, Trine laughed out at her.

Teenage girl missing from school

Nineteen-year-old Rose Katrine Severinsen, known as Trine, was reported missing two weeks ago. She was last seen on Friday, April 29, at the boarding school she attended. "We have reason to believe that she ran away from the school following a fight with her parents," said Mogens Pedersen of West Zealand Police. "The fight was about a boyfriend, and the missing girl had threatened to run away from home with this boyfriend. We do not suspect any crime has been committed, but we are, of course, very eager to talk with the missing girl."
The girl was brought up in Kalundborg with her parents and younger sister, but in recent years has been living at her residential school. She is described as being 5 feet 4 inches tall, of average build, with longish auburn hair. Please report any sightings of the girl to West Zealand Police Force.

Malou read the text over two times. Then she studied the photograph again. *The most recent photo of Rose Katrine Severinsen, who disappeared from her school two weeks ago,* the caption read.

Trine was smiling, face turned to the camera. She had not been alone when the photo was taken, but had her arm around somebody who had been cut out of the picture. Who was Trine's boyfriend? And who was with her in that photo originally?

JULY 28TH
4:30 P.M.

Victoria

Victoria watched as ripples of cotton candy clouds drifted slowly across the sky and over her parents' large white house and well-tended garden. The sun flickered through the branches of the apple tree, and the only sounds she could hear were the distant hum of traffic and a pigeon's repetitive cooing.

"Is the silent spook at home?" Benjamin buried his face in the crook of her neck and shoulder, giving her goose bumps, even in the summer heat. "Or could we maybe go up to your room?"

"Do you mean Trine?" She propped herself on her elbows and looked down at him, lying on the grass.

"No," he said, and pulled her down again. "The other one. The tall, pale one."

"Kirstine? Hey, you're so mean. You can't go calling her that." Victoria sat up. "Kirstine lives here now, of course she's home. Actually, I should ask her if she wants to come down to the garden too."

"No, leave her be." He pulled on her arm to get her to lie down again.

"You need to be nice to her. Kirstine is the coolest girl I know," Victoria said, pulling her arm back. She remained sitting cross-legged and picked up a scarlet petal from where the English roses had scattered onto the grass. Their perfume was strong.

"I know Kirstine is cool," Benjamin said. "Didn't she save my life, after all? That *is* pretty badass. But I also think she can be a strange creature. She never says anything. Just sits and stares."

"Kirstine is not that good at small talk. And she's got boyfriend trouble."

"What? Kirstine has a boyfriend? Who?"

"You don't need to sound so surprised! She's not with him anymore, and I'm afraid I can't say who it is. *Classified information*, you know? But you need to be kind to her. She doesn't have it easy. Her parents don't want her living there, and I sometimes worry she feels like a third wheel when you're here."

"She *is* a third wheel!"

"Stop it. We could easily hang out, the three of us."

He turned to her with a wry smile. "That sounds really exciting, sure."

"Stop it, you're such an idiot." She gave him a playful shove.

He sat up and leaned in to whisper in her ear. "The truth is, I'd prefer to be with you alone. In fact, that's all I really want at the moment. Lie here in the grass, just you and me . . ."

"Victoria! Come here! Juliet's made lemonade with real lemons!" Her two younger brothers ran out the door to the garden, down the steps and over the freshly cut lawn, which the gardener, on her mother's orders, kept manicured like a golf course. "It was super sour, so we've put more sugar in. Come and taste it!"

Benjamin closed his eyes and leaned his head on her shoulder, giving a sigh.

"Come on," she said, and pulled him up. "You heard it yourself. There's super sour lemonade."

Their large kitchen was in absolute chaos, with lemon peel scattered on the big whitewashed kitchen table and the floor around it, a spilled bag of sugar in the midst of it all. It looked as if the twins had been helping their beloved au pair, Juliet, in the kitchen. She was in the middle of washing the juicer, which was also freshly messy.

"Taste it!" said Harald, holding his glass out right up in her face, while he and his brother, Niels, studied her carefully with their big brown eyes.

Victoria took a big gulp. "Mmm, really tasty!" she said. Both boys' faces lit up with a great grin. "But now you need to help Juliet clean up, okay?"

The smiles disappeared in an instant and they both turned to face Juliet, who stood at the sink.

"Away you go," she said, and waved them off, before grabbing the broom to start sweeping up lemon peel.

The boys sped triumphantly into the living room, shouting to Benjamin as they went to come on and get beaten by them at *FIFA*.

"Maybe later," he shouted after them, shaking his head.

"You spoil them," Victoria said to Juliet.

"It's easier without their help," she said, and shrugged.

"What's going on here?"

Victoria turned. Her mother stood in the doorway. Her light silk blouse complemented her bronzed skin and the glossy, dark hair, which Victoria had always pestered her to be allowed to brush when she was little. Her mom kept her stilettos on as she set her bag down and inspected the chaos of the kitchen.

"I'll clean it up," said Juliet evenly, without letting on that she was surely equally as surprised to see Victoria's mom home so early.

"I've invited people for drinks and they'll be here in two hours," her mom said. "I want the boys to have eaten before then."

"No problem." Juliet smiled.

Victoria often thought that Juliet must have developed a really thick skin since being with them for such a long time. Her mother's icy stare always washed clean over her. Victoria would have loved to have that ability.

"But I can see we have guests already?"

Victoria knew that her mother's tolerance was being tested to the limits, in that she had invited her roommate from school to live with them over the summer, and without talking to her parents about it first. Kirstine mostly kept herself to her room, and her mom seem to have accepted it. (Victoria did wonder if her dad had even noticed they had someone staying with them at all.) Benjamin, though, was something her mom had yet to get accustomed to.

"I was just going," said Benjamin, looking her mother directly in the eyes.

"You don't need to do that," Victoria said feebly.

"I do, I've got something to take care of. I'll see you tomorrow, okay?"

He gave her a quick kiss on the cheek and squeezed around her and out into the hall. The front door closed behind him.

"I don't understand what you see in him," her mom said as she took a bottle of water from the fridge.

"You don't know him," Victoria said.

"I've heard about him," her mom said, then took a sip. "And going by what I have heard, it's quite hard to comprehend how he's the one you've gone and fallen for. They say he's broken off contact with his family?"

"You shouldn't believe everything you hear," Victoria said defiantly, though she still avoided her mother's gaze.

"You should think about yourself a bit more, Victoria. You've only just gotten over your first, unfortunate romance."

"It's been over a year now, Mom."

"I'm just worried about you, that's all."

"Are you?"

"Of course I am. You're my daughter, after all." Her mom placed her hand lightly on her cheek. "I'm going up to get changed. You and Kirstine can eat with the boys, okay?"

Victoria watched her as she strode elegantly up the stairs in her high heels. If she had dared, she would have asked if it wasn't more the family's reputation that her mother was actually worried about.

In less than an hour, the kitchen was spotless and Juliet had even whipped up a meal of fresh pasta with homemade pesto sauce while Victoria had made a salad. She went upstairs and knocked.

"Kirstine, dinner's ready."

The tall, serious girl sat on her bed with her legs curled under her and her phone in her hand. She didn't look up as Victoria came in. "Malou found an old article. And an address that could be Trine's childhood home. She's asking if we want to go with her."

Victoria sat on the bed beside her. Benjamin was right that she was very pale.

"Look." Kirstine held up her phone.

"*We do not suspect any crime has been committed . . .*" Victoria read aloud. "So Trine was reported missing, but nothing more."

"They thought she had just run away with a boyfriend," Kirstine said. "That's also why we couldn't find anything in the papers about her murder."

Victoria let her finger swipe down on the phone's screen so that the article disappeared and was replaced by Malou's messages.

"What if her parents still live here," she said, pointing to the address that showed up. *Solvangen 11, Kalundborg.*

Kirstine turned to face her. "Exactly. Maybe they don't even know that she's dead. Maybe we're the only ones who know that she didn't run away but was killed."

Victoria wet her hands and ran them through her dark hair as she studied her reflection in the bathroom mirror. The window was open and she could hear blackbirds singing from the old pear tree in the clear evening light. The sound of birdsong mingled with the murmur of civilized chat and clinking of glasses drifting up from the library, as her parents insisted on calling that room with the ugly old oil paintings and chesterfield sofas. *So fake.* It was not civilized in the slightest when it came down to it. It was all about wealth and power and the family honor, and they spared nothing in their pursuit of more power and more money. Even so, she found it so difficult to go against their ways.

Victoria glanced at the clock and thought about writing to Benjamin. Juliet was in the middle of tucking in the twins, and Kirstine had gone to bed early. Victoria was not tired herself, but on the other hand she certainly didn't feel like having to exchange niceties with her parents' guests, so she stayed upstairs.

She blew some loose strands of hair from her face. She needed a haircut, but she hadn't gotten around to it and now the summer holidays were nearly over. That was not the only thing she should have done either. Her face glared back at her guiltily from the mirror. She should have told him about it—she had promised herself she would tell him. So why hadn't she just done it? She'd had enough time. Long, lazy summer days at the beach. Long summer nights, when she had snuck out to the garden to where he waited for her under the fragrant jasmine. But she hadn't said a thing. Because she knew how angry he would get. Also Trine had abandoned her and they'd gotten no further in their search for her killer.

Victoria turned the tap on again; steam rose from the warm water in the sink, and her breath was suddenly visible in the mirror. The temperature had dropped to freezing. The hairs stood up on her arm and she closed her eyes. Was it possible Trine noticed that Victoria had thought about her? Was that why this was happening? It still scared her, but it wasn't the same gripping fear as before. It was better to meet her with open eyes. *Face your fears.*

"Trine?" She opened her eyes. The white shadow was visible in the glass behind her. It gave her a start, even although she'd expected it. She turned around. "Hi, Trine."

It was not a girl, but the impression of one. A white shadow.

"We didn't forget you," whispered Victoria. "We're going to go visit your home where you lived as a kid—argh!" She gasped as the shadow moved toward her like a blast of chilly wind. Her legs buckled under her and she fell heavily to the ground. She gasped desperately for breath, struggling to draw any down into her lungs. *Don't panic, don't panic.* The fear almost overwhelmed her, but Victoria forced herself to breathe. Slowly, her heartbeat stilled. *She's gone away again. Everything is fine.*

She got up, the warm water still gushing into the sink. She turned off the tap and rested her hands on the edge. The mirror was all steamed up, and there in the condensation she read:

Will I just meet you at the station?

Yeah. I get in around 20 after

Great, see you!

AUGUST 2ND
2:11 P.M.

Kirstine

The train station was opposite Kalundborg's old, abandoned ferry terminal, and as they stepped off the train they were met by a blast of wind. The air was warm and damp and smelled of seaweed. Still, Kirstine was glad to have slipped away from Victoria's big white house with its many rooms and elegant furniture. She was ashamed to admit that she hated being there. It had been really sweet of Victoria to invite her to live there, now that her own parents wouldn't have anything to do with her. She grimaced just thinking of that trip back to Thy, where she ended up having to turn on her heel again after only a brief exchange of words with her mother at the front door. Her mother hadn't even asked her in or offered a drink of water. Kirstine should be grateful to have somewhere to live, but the truth was, she didn't feel comfortable at Victoria's. There were so many unspoken rules she didn't know, and those were so different from the rules back at her home. At home, you were expected to duck your head, hold your tongue, and do what you were told, but in Victoria's family you got asked about a whole lot of things: your career plans, family relationships, your interests and views on politics and culture, and all manner of other things. And Kirstine never managed to answer in an acceptable way. Victoria did all she could to smooth things over. She was fun and intelligent and always upbeat, but her mother was never happy. On that front she reminded Kirstine a little of her own mother.

"Look." Victoria pointed. "There's Chamomile!"

A red-haired girl with round cheeks and a big smile stood waving enthusiastically to them. She was wearing a white summer dress with a broad skirt and a tie around her middle that accentuated her waistline.

"Hi, guys!" She gave them both a kiss. "It's so great to see you. Wow, Kirstine, you've really lost weight."

Kirstine could feel herself blushing under Chamomile's stare. "I don't think so," she mumbled.

Chamomile threw a knowing look at Victoria. "Well, maybe it's just those shorts that are very slimming. How are you?"

"Good," she said. "I've been living at Victoria's."

"That sounds really cool. I miss you guys so much. My mom is starting to drive me nuts."

"Is Malou coming?" asked Victoria.

"She should be arriving on the bus from Slagelse anytime now."

They sat on a bench and waited until the bus turned into the station and Malou was one of the first to step out, dressed in short cycling shorts. At the ends of her long brown legs, a pair of new sneakers gleamed white in the sun.

"Hey!" Chamomile jumped up and gave her a big hug.

Malou smoothed her hair and gave both girls a hug.

"So," Chamomile said. "What do we do next then, Ms. Detective?"

"Well, let's see if we find anything at all," Malou said, and checked the maps app on her phone. "We need to go this way, in any case. The house is supposedly in a block of older houses."

"Where did you get the address?" Victoria asked as they started to walk.

"I got the local history archive to check it for me. Trine's surname was linked to this address, but they couldn't say if the family still lives there. It's something to do with some data protection rules, and they said if we wanted to know, we'd have to go there ourselves. It may be the house was sold to some other family years ago, but I think it's worth checking it out."

They left the station and headed up toward the town.

"How crazy, though, is that thing with the *Say Sorry* message?" Chamomile said to Victoria. "Did you find out what it means? Is it us who should say sorry?"

"I don't know," Victoria said. "That was all she wrote."

"Maybe Trine is angry at us for not finding her murderer yet. Maybe that's why she thinks we owe her an apology?" Chamomile said.

They continued upward, crossing a more or less empty pedestrian street with a sweets shop bedecked in huge ads for ice cream cones, and other treats, then entered an area of large old houses. They were somewhat similar to the houses where Victoria's family lived, except that these were a little smaller and looked much more run down. As they progressed up the hill, the houses got even smaller in size.

"Solvangen. This is it," Malou said, and pointed into a street on their left. "Number 11."

They stepped forward. The front gardens were laid with small gray pebbles, broken up only by occasional evergreen shrubs, stone planters or pots with flowers peeking out, and outside there were balance bikes and baby strollers. Somebody had drawn a cycle path on the pavement in different colors of chalk.

"Is this it?" Chamomile looked in toward a whitewashed house with windows that had been recently replaced.

"No, that's number 9," Malou said. "It must be that one there."

There was a high hedge and, behind it, a house in the same style as the rest of the street. But while those clearly had young families with kids living at them, this one seemed abandoned. The house was painted in an indeterminate, muddy shade of flaking paint. The window frames were dark brown, and behind the glass thick blinds hung, hiding everything from view. On top of that, the windows were so blurred with condensation that it was, in any case, impossible to see in.

"There's nobody living here," Victoria said. "That house has been empty for a long while."

"Maybe Trine's parents were the last people to live there?" Malou said. "I vote we go into the garden and try to have a look inside the house from there. Maybe we can even break in and we might find something that will help us."

"Like what?" Chamomile said.

"I don't know, something or other that could lead us to Trine's boyfriend, maybe," Malou said. "When women are murdered, it's often their partner who's behind it. The most dangerous thing you can do as a woman is actually to be in a relationship with a man. It was in the paper that Trine had planned to run away with her boyfriend. But instead she was murdered. If we find the boyfriend, we might also find her killer."

"But don't you think someone would already have discovered if there was a lot of prints and clues in there?"

"Maybe they didn't search properly," Malou said, and shrugged. "Come on, we came all this way, after all."

Malou went first and the others followed hesitantly after.

The entrance was screened by a tall fence with a gate in it that led into a small paved yard between the house and a dilapidated shed. Tall weeds had grown up between the slabs, and they could see over to a garden that was a mishmash tangle of long grass, flowering thistles, and huge trees, some of which had died off. Kirstine closed the gate behind them. It was very quiet, as people were presumably on vacation or had gone to the beach because of the good weather. Not a sound came from the street or from the other gardens.

Malou knocked on the door. It was dark brown, with a large, thick pane of yellowish glass, impossible to see through. They waited. Kirstine shivered despite the summer warmth, and she had a weird feeling in her stomach, as if she was getting sick. Was this really a good idea?

"Hello there!" Malou shouted, and knocked once more. Then she tried the handle. It was unlocked. "Come on," she whispered, and pushed the door open.

The hall was dark, with brown cork walls and a colored stained-glass window that let in very little light. It smelled old and damp, like a neglected summer house. Cobwebs hung like garlands from the ceiling. They passed from the hall into the living room. The yellow rays cutting through the gap in the dark curtains fell onto old, lonely looking pieces of furniture. A dark-green-and-orange-striped sofa, a worn armchair in the same fabric, a brown dining table with four chairs, the faded spines of books on a bookcase. The floor was covered by a thick light-brown fitted carpet. The pile was thinner where the house's residents had walked fixed paths: kitchen door to dining table, dining table to sofa. An old-fashioned push-button telephone sat on a small table by the window. It was still plugged in at the wall.

"Wow, it's like going back in time," Chamomile whispered.

"Not one single thing has been changed since this house was abandoned. Can you feel Trine?" Malou looked at Victoria.

The dark-haired girl closed her eyes and crinkled her brow in a concentrated frown, all the while clutching the silver skull she wore around her neck—a symbol that she was a spiritual mage of the Death branch of magic.

"No, she's not here," she said after a moment, and opened her eyes again. "Maybe this isn't the right house?"

"Yes, it is. Look at these photos."

Backed by yellowing wallpaper, there was a framed collage of school photos. They showed two girls who gradually got older. The elder one was a redhead with a big grin, while the younger sister had a darker complexion. She looked, bewildered, into the camera with her large brown eyes. In the last picture in particular, it was obvious that the redhead was Trine.

Kirstine noticed a tingling feeling in her body. It wasn't pleasant, and she felt dizzy. Maybe it was the heat? Had she forgotten to drink enough water today?

"Look, that's the one from the article." Malou pointed at another photograph. Unlike the one in the paper, it was in color, but it was the same photo of the smiling Trine. Someone had cut it in the middle and put the separated half up on the wall.

Kirstine felt a wave of nausea and her vision flickered.

Tick, tick, tick . . .

Two girls ran from the kitchen into the living room. The redhead came first and the other hurried behind, but couldn't catch up with her.

She shook her head, but the flickering images came back into her vision.

Tick, tick, tick . . .

"Kirstine, are you okay?"

"How many times have I said not to run in the kitchen!"

"Trine, wait!"

"Kirstine, you look like you are about to faint." Chamomile laid a hand on her arm.

Kirstine felt as if the ground was rolling under her feet. "I don't feel so good . . ."

Tick, tick, tick . . .

"What's going on? Kirstine?"

She tried to focus and not give in to the dizzy feeling that threatened to pull her from reality and back to a time long gone by. She should stay here. There was something here she needed to pay attention to. Something important.

"The clock . . ." Kirstine pointed up to the wall. Beside the photos there was an old wall clock. The pendulum swung from side to side along with the tick of its hands. "It works."

"Yes, I can see that," Chamomile said, worried. "Oh, Kirstine, you really don't look so good . . ."

"No, I mean there's someone keeping it going," she insisted. "A clock like that needs to be wound. Someone is still living here . . ."

Bang!

A loud bang made them all start.

"What was that?" whispered Victoria.

"The door! Let's get out of here!" said Chamomile.

They ran out into the hall. The inner door was shut and Malou grabbed the handle.

"It's locked!" she said, trying the door in vain.

"It can't be," Chamomile said, pushing Malou away and grabbing the handle. "I can't get it open!"

Tick, tick, tick . . . The clock's ticking now felt like a pulse, pounding at her temples. They needed to get out now.

"Stand back, all of you," Kirstine said. The others hesitated for a mere fraction of a second before stepping away.

"*Hagalaz!*"

The rune caused the door to burst open, and they ran out into the sun.

August 15, 88

Dear Little T,

Things are going great with me—we reached the South of France. What a journey down here. We caught the train in Paris. It was overcrowded and people were packed in the aisles like sardines with their suitcases and whatever else they had with them, too. Eventually we found a tiny little space on the floor to sit down. It was in the aisle of a goods car! If we wanted to stretch our legs, we had to stand up. It was a looooong night!

We're camping and it's so beautiful here—but really H-O-T!!!!

We live on baguettes, tomatoes, and canned tuna—it's all we have money for, but who cares about that as long as we're having a good time, right?

I hope that Mom and Dad don't take it out on you because of how I took off. I know you're angry at me, but I just couldn't take you with me. You can be sure I miss you though! When you're old enough, we could take the train around Europe together? That would be So fun. (But don't say anything to the olds!) I'll be back in a week, and I promise you I'll make everything alright again.

Until then, take care!!

Lv xxx

Trine

August 23, Rosenholm Academy

Dear second and third years,

Welcome back to the new school year at Rosenholm Academy. Registration for second- and third-year pupils will be on September 4, and your classes begin the following Monday.

In consultation with the management team, it has been decided that I, the undersigned, will take up the post of school principal, following Birgit Lund's resignation from the post prior to the summer holidays. As I will continue to teach alongside my duties as head, Zlavko Kovacevic will act as vice principal.

Besides these changes, everything else will continue as usual, and the school's code of conduct remains the same. Boys and girls are not allowed to mix socially, and so on. Should you have any doubts about anything, please see me.

Please find timetables and study plans included with this letter. Books can be collected from the resources store on Monday between 2:00 and 4:00.

With best wishes for a good year of successful learning,

Jens Andersen

Jens Andersen
School Principal

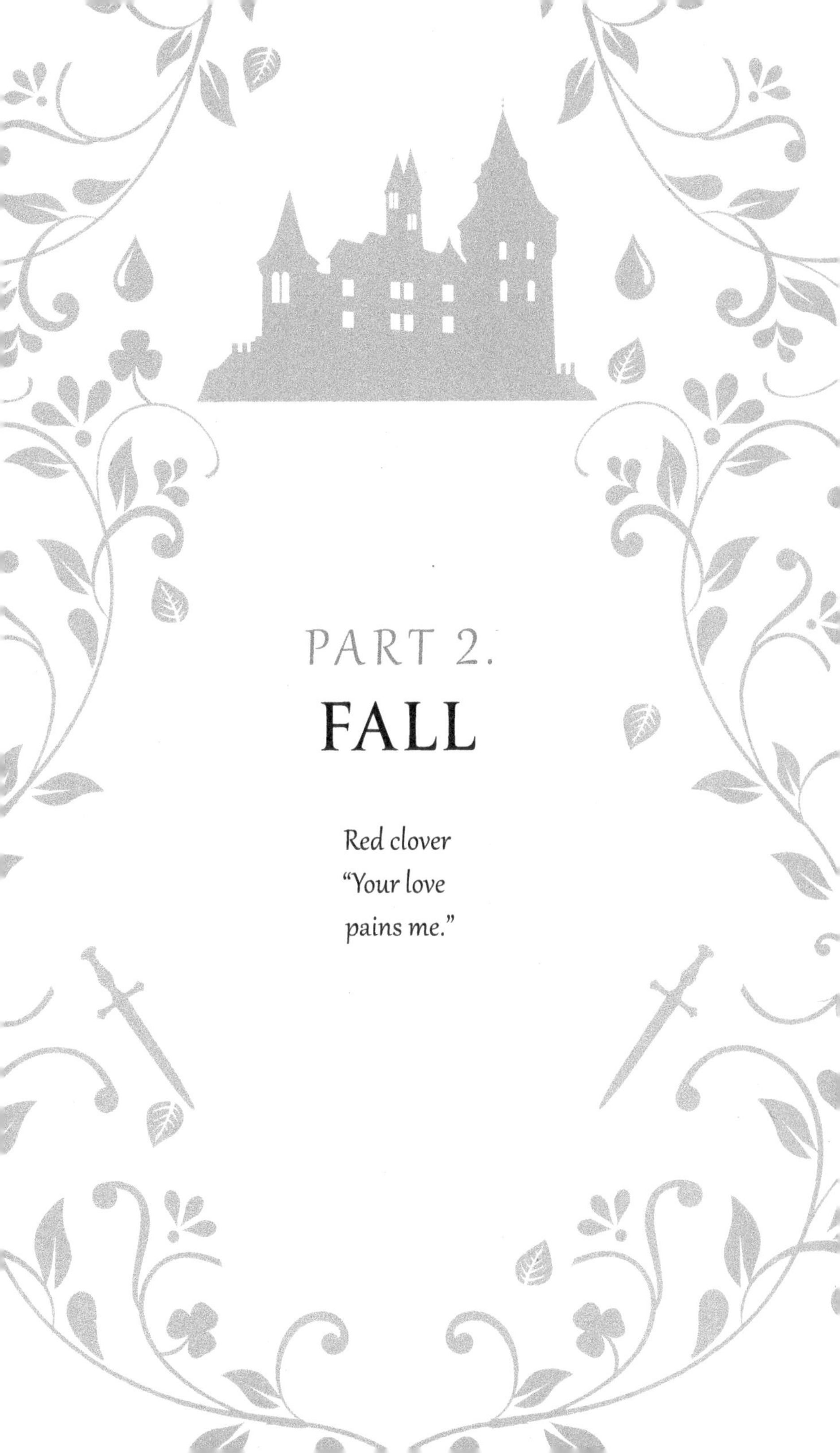

PART 2.
FALL

Red clover
"Your love
pains me."

SEPTEMBER 4TH
10:00 A.M.

Chamomile

Chamomile pulled the wheeled pink suitcase (an ill-judged apology gift from her mother) along the narrow street that led up to Rosenholm. Even on an overcast day like today, the castle was a beautiful sight, nestled as it was with its white towers and proud spires amid the sloping, recently harvested fields. Late-summer flowers on the grass verges gave off wafts of milfoil, tansies, and blossoming clover. Chamomile had worried that her return to Rosenholm would be tainted by the dreadful things Vitus had put her through at the end of last term, but the sight of the white building caused only a pleasant, expectant buzz to run through her. It was something else that was making her anxious, and it had a whole lot to do with the secret her mom had finally decided to let her in on.

Chamomile upped her pace, wanting to get there before it started to rain. The wind was messing up her hair when she'd made an effort to do it nicely, and now she could hear thunder rumbling ominously in the distance. Soon heavy drops were raining down on the scene.

When she finally reached the little courtyard at the castle, she was soaked. She remembered how she had sat pressed up to the windows last year, studying the older students as they arrived at school and greeted one another in the courtyard. There was no such chance for the new first years now as the courtyard was empty, everyone rushing straight into the impressive great hall to shelter from the rain.

"Chamomile!"

Despite her dripping-wet clothes, she was immediately pulled into a group hug with a gang of girls from her own year. The sisters Sara and Sofie gave her a big welcome, and she was happily surprised to see Anne with them all too.

"Welcome back!" Anne smiled and gave her a kiss.

"You're here? That's great!" Chamomile said.

"Yeah. Strictly speaking, I don't belong here, but I thought it'd be okay if I scooched over and said hi. I'll go in a minute."

"How are you?" Chamomile asked.

"I'm good. It's a bit weird, obviously, that I can't hang out with all of you, but luckily I've got some really cool roommates."

Anne had been assaulted by Vitus the year before and had missed so much teaching that she had to repeat a year. But Chamomile was relieved to see that she seemed happy.

"Good that you're here," Victoria said in a low voice, once Chamomile had gotten past the first round of hugs and found the other girls from her dorm. "Malou is already planning some more excursions."

"Come on! We have to visit that house again," said Malou, who had clearly arrived before the weather turned, her blond hair still dry and glossy and perfectly styled in a tight bun. She glanced down to the other end of the hall where the boys stood. Chamomile followed her look. Students generally complied with the rule about not mixing—at least, they did when they were being observed, as they were now. "In that living room it was like nobody had touched a thing in the last forty years. We could find something there that could tell us something."

"But the door . . . We got locked in," Kirstine said.

"It was the wind that blew the door shut, and we just panicked," Malou said. "There was nobody there. The parents may well be dead."

Kirstine fiddled nervously with her sleeves. Chamomile noticed that one of the seams was split and her top was frayed.

"Somebody had wound the clock," Kirstine said. "Or else it wouldn't have been working . . ."

"Maybe it's an especially long-life clock?" Malou said.

Their conversation was interrupted as the students all started finding their seats. The school's new principal would be giving a little welcome speech, apparently.

Soon three men stepped into the hall, and Chamomile felt a nervous fluttering in her stomach. Jens was flanked on one side by Zlavko's thin form and on the other by the hulking Thorbjørn with his huge beard. The principal himself was, as always, dressed in black, which complemented his suntanned complexion and silver-gray hair.

"Welcome back," they heard, in Jens's slow, deep voice. Despite the fact he only reached shoulder height on Zlavko and Thorbjørn, he had an authoritative air that quickly made everyone fall silent. "As the new principal of this school, it is a pleasure to see you all again for a new session here at Rosenholm Academy. For our third-year students, this year will be a real chance to get deeper into your main subject, but it's also important that you second years, from the very beginning of the school year, start to think about what you might specialize in. When spring comes, you will do your second-year assignment, which must be defended before a teacher and an examiner. Of course, I shouldn't need to remind third years that their year closes with decisive examinations. I expect a high standard of you all."

When Jens was done talking about exams and assignments and demands and expectations, the students were finally allowed up to their dorms. Chamomile threw herself onto her bed in relief, leaving her unpacking to some other time. It felt good to be back. Different, but good. She let her gaze wander over the wall where she had stuck up various pictures and notes. A photo of her with her mom, who was laughing aloud. They had taken the picture themselves, and it looked a bit like a photo of the same person, caught mid-laugh, but taken twenty years apart. Momentarily, Chamomile thought of tearing it down, but then she let it stay. Beside that was a photo of Malou, Victoria, and Kirstine, taken at the park. She also had a poster of Danish herbs, which her mom had given her, and a postcard Malou had given her with the slogan *Inspirational quotes suck!*

"Oh, so there you are! I stood waiting for you at the bottom of the stairs!" Malou came in dragging her big, scruffy suitcase, which she heaved onto the bed with a grunt. "What are you doing? Seriously, you're not gonna unpack? You can't just slump there."

Chamomile smiled. "I've missed you, Malou."

**Notice for all second-
and third-year students**

Our initiation ceremony for new students will take place on September 7th. We will meet at the main stairs at 10:45 p.m., where your black robes will be given out. We will then proceed to the old tree as a group.

Welcome!
Lisa

SEPTEMBER 7TH
11:05 P.M.

Kirstine

They walked through the darkness of the forest. A soft rain drizzled down from the trees onto the students' black robes. Kirstine's flapped at her legs. It was too short—or her legs were too long. She had always been the tallest in her class, and that included the boys.

It was only a few months since she had last been here, but everything seemed different somehow. She had been looking forward to getting back to school, but now that she was here it filled her with unease. She gave her head a shake to free herself from her thoughts while she tried to focus on the upcoming ceremony.

She remembered when it was her time: being brought to stand before the old tree and find out which branch of magic she belonged to. *Earth, Growth, Blood, or Death.* She reached briefly for the little silver plow, the symbol for Earth, which she wore on a chain around her neck.

The forest was thick and impenetrable, but Lisa, their Nature Magic teacher, led them confidently and steadily onward until suddenly the forest opened up and the students entered the clearing where the great tree regally stood. Kirstine kept her eyes on the forest floor. The last time she had been here, she had killed a young man. It was a lot to deal with.

The students spread out silently along the edges of the clearing. The foliage offered shelter from the worst of the rain, but the wet moss was cold on her bare toes. She could feel the earth below her while they waited; she could feel the tree. Its roots twisted deep beneath her. *It knows I'm here.*

Then a white shape emerged from between the trees, and behind that, another. The new students in their white robes. A young man was showing them the way. She hadn't noticed him at first in his black robes. Kirstine felt a tight pain in her chest and quickly looked away as Jakob led them on the last stretch. She had been strict with herself about not thinking too much about him over the summer, but now it became clear how the sight of him set her heart absolutely racing. She turned her face away from the new students, away from him. Instead her gaze fell on the great oak, and the rustling of its leaves grew louder, the tree glowing even brighter than she remembered from the year before. A shiver went through her at that sight and she could feel roots moving beneath her. *They're coming closer.*

The white-clad students positioned themselves around the tree, and everyone around her began to recite the words now so familiar to her.

Earth is magic's first branch.
The forefathers' crumbling bones.
Millennia's relics buried.
History is your source of power.

Growth is magic's second branch.
Growth in flora and fauna.
Everywhere in nature around us.
Life is your source of power.

Blood is magic's third branch.
Warm and red. Given or taken.
It flows through man and beast.
Sacrifice is your source of power.

Death is magic's fourth branch.
Those who live no more.
Remembered or forgotten.
Departed souls are your source of power.

The words had a hypnotic effect. Kirstine was invisible in the dark. All those students dressed in black were invisible too and there was nothing but the words. She felt a tingling in her bare toes, as if rising from the earth below and slowly up her body. She wanted to give in to it, to disappear inside it. She scrunched her eyes closed and open again and the sound of the students' chanting disappeared. She could hear Lisa speaking about the different branches of magic, and before her, the tree shone with a silver-like tinge so that the raindrops showering over it looked like crystals falling in the dark. It made everything shimmer before her eyes. Kirstine tried to concentrate on what Lisa was saying. The words were a little different from last time, but her ears were filled with the strange clicking noises coming from below her, from the tree roots. They were close. *Too close.* Something was wrong. It wasn't supposed to feel like this. Kirstine wanted to take a step backward, but her feet were fixed to the spot. She looked down.

Black, wet roots broke through the forest floor and reached up for her like bony hands. She wanted to run, but it was too late. The roots had twisted themselves around her feet and were snaking up her legs. The tingling feeling exploded inside her and became fire.

SEPTEMBER 9TH
7:30 A.M.

Malou

Malou took the timetable from her bag and checked it once more. Nothing had changed since she last looked. Why did Blood Magic have to be the first class on the very first day back after summer vacation? It wasn't fair. It meant she had no time at all to come up with a strategy for surviving this whole thing.

"Does anyone want more coffee? We could squeeze in another cup?" Chamomile had stood up to go to the breakfast buffet. *Again.* Malou shook her head and watched as Chamomile made her way through the tables of bleary-eyed girls eating breakfast. The yellow-painted walls gave the room a cozy, intimate feel that Malou normally enjoyed, but today she couldn't eat.

"Kirstine, want me to get you a roll as well?" Chamomile put her coffee and a cheese roll on the table and leaned in over Kirstine. She sounded like a kindergarten teacher, but Kirstine just shook her head. "A yogurt then? You need to eat something, or you'll pass out like you did at the ceremony."

The initiation ceremony for new students had been cut short when Kirstine suddenly fainted and needed to be taken back to the castle. The next day she'd been back on her feet and unhurt, except for a lump on the back of her head where she hit a tree root when she fell. Ingrid, the school doctor and counselor, put it down to her simply forgetting to eat and drink. Of course that was something Chamomile just couldn't let lie.

"A piece of fruit?"

"Stop pestering her," Malou said. "Maybe Kirstine isn't hungry. Or maybe she can't be bothered to eat, seeing as lunch will be served in a few hours anyway."

"I know why you're in such a foul mood," Chamomile went off again, and this time her kindergarten voice was gone and replaced with her "that's enough now" voice. "It's because you know I'm right. If you hurry up, you can still get a hold of him and say sorry before class starts."

"Why should I say sorry?"

"Because you accused him of a crime he didn't commit."

"Okay. But why should I do it *alone*? We all thought it was Zlavko who attacked Anne."

"Shh," whispered Kirstine, her eyes flicking across to the next table, where Anne was sitting together with her new first-year classmates.

"Still, you were the only one who went and found him in the middle of the night to fling accusations at him," Chamomile whispered. "And now he's just been made vice principal! And you're also the only one depending on getting good grades in Blood Magic."

Oh hell!! Malou sighed. In second year, it was apparently very important that you shone in your main subject, and on top of that, there was the big second-year assignment, which Jens had already harped on about even before the year had properly begun. Chamomile did not need to remind her of these things. She knew full well that her future depended on their moody, malicious Blood Magic teacher. Chamomile belonged to the element Growth, so she was sitting pretty and only had to impress their teacher of Nature Magic, Lisa, who was lovely. *The world is screwed up and unfair.*

"Fine. But if you don't see me again, for sure it's because he's bitten off my head and thrown my body in the moat." Malou pushed back her chair and stood up. "Of course, the most important thing is that I say sorry first!"

She clenched her fists tight as she set off to find the Blood Magic classroom. She paused for a moment outside the door before knocking. She had stood here before, one year ago. Everything was so different, but also exactly the same. She was still at the mercy of Zlavko's caprice. *Here goes nothing.* This was going to be the most awkward and humiliating moment ever.

"Yes?" He was not sitting at his desk as she'd expected, but leaning up against the wall, looking out the window. His dark, glossy hair was pulled into a topknot, high on his head, and he wore a dark, tight-fitting shirt that was buttoned up to the neck. On his belt he wore a sheath with a dagger in it, something Malou hadn't seen on him before.

"So, finally, you came."

She closed the door behind her and took a deep breath. "I owe you an apology." The words stuck in her throat and were almost inaudible. Why should she have to apologize when it was him who had given her a nosebleed?

"Did you say something?" He moved toward her, smiling in a condescending way. He was enjoying this.

"I'm sorry that I accused you." Malou had got control over her voice. She looked him directly in the eyes.

To hell with you.

"I made a mistake," she said hoarsely.

Zlavko studied her face. "Are you aware that I tried to get Birgit to investigate what Vitus had been doing on Christmas Eve? To see if his alibi held up? And that's why I was consequently dismissed from this school?" He came a step closer.

Malou swallowed. "Like I said, I made a mistake."

"It's tactically quite clever of you to come and apologize." He sneered. "But I'm afraid I don't forgive you that easily. I don't think there's any shame in bearing a grudge. The desire for revenge is one of the strongest motivating forces you can find. You'll have to prove to me that you really regret what you did, if you want my forgiveness."

"Go to hell," she said.

He gave a quiet laugh. It was an ominous sound, but Malou had no intention of revealing how it sent a cold shiver down her spine.

"You can start by getting the class ready. I've prepared something really special for you all today. There is a bucket over there filled with ice cubes. If you could please fill those bowls I've set out with ice, I'd be so eternally grateful." He gave her a patronizing smile before turning back to the window again.

SEPTEMBER 9TH
8:09 A.M.

Chamomile

Chamomile squinted at the bowl in front of her, which was filled with water and ice cubes. She looked questioningly at Malou, who was sitting beside her, but Malou just shook her head and looked straight ahead.

"Welcome back to the new school year. You are now no longer beginners in the world of magic, and for that reason, we will be expecting a little more of you." Zlavko stepped away from his desk to pace up and down the length of their tables. "I hope you are all feeling well today, prepared and willing to do your absolute best. We're going to need that! What we are doing today is an experiment in pain."

He pronounced every syllable of the final words slowly and clearly, as if the thought of an experiment that would cause the students pain was a fantastic thing. Seriously, this was what he was pulling out for them in their very first class of second year? He really was too much.

"Shortly, you will place your hand into the ice-cold water in front of you while we record the time that passes. The exercise is to control your blood in such a way that you are able to withstand the cold and pain from the iced water for as long as possible. Okay?"

"But we haven't learned how to do that," objected Sara.

"No, but that is exactly what you are learning now. You can't read about everything—there are some things that you have to experience in your own bodies." Zlavko smiled broadly. "Get ready, I'm starting the timer now!"

Chamomile felt a shudder run through her when she plunged her hand in the ice-cold water. The class fell completely silent.

"The body will quickly react to the potential danger you are now putting it in—that is to say, the danger that you'll get frostbite in your hand, which in the worst scenario can be fatal. But you must overcome the body's signals with your minds; allow the power in your blood to drown out the pain, let it dim the cold."

Drown out the pain? What was he talking about? How did you do that exactly?

"Blood magic can give people supernatural powers: strength, endurance, lightning-fast reflexes, supernatural senses. Those who practice blood magic can learn to overcome hunger, lack of sleep, pain and cold. At the very least, though, all must have a thorough grounding in survival under harsh conditions."

Ouch, ouch, ouch . . . The icy water stung like needles.

"History provides many examples of this. Alexandra David-Néel was a French explorer, opera singer, and writer. And blood mage. She is known for her ability to survive in the extreme cold. In 1924, she became the first European woman to cross the Himalayas in order to reach the forbidden city of Lhasa in Tibet."

Argh! Was the idea that you should concentrate on what Zlavko was explaining while your hand felt like it was being eaten by ants?

"Another explorer who learned to get by in extreme cold was the Dane Peter Freuchen . . ." Zlavko continued, undisturbed by the suffering of the students around him.

Chamomile looked around the class. Was it really only her who felt that this hurt like hell? No, plenty of the others were grimacing or wriggling in their seats. She tried to collect her thoughts around something else, but without success.

Ow! It was getting worse and worse.

"Freuchen undertook many journeys to Greenland, and on one expedition in 1923, he was separated from the rest of the sled team during a snow storm. Miraculously, Freuchen survived. Although one of his feet had to be amputated."

Ach, that has to be enough now! Chamomile pulled her hand out of the water and held it in to her body, moaning. The word *amputated* seemed to have worked as a kind of code, because many of the others also drew their hands back, and Chamomile exchanged a distressed glance with Sara, who looked pale and unhappy.

Zlavko looked at the clock. "Disappointing," he declared. "Not even above the normal average. Of course, that was only to be expected."

Chamomile rubbed at her hand and felt the warmth slowly returning to it. Okay, so maybe she shouldn't become a polar explorer.

"In 1938, Peter Freuchen also founded what became the quite famous Adventurer's Club . . ."

Victoria and a few others took their hands out of the water, and Zlavko took down their times before continuing, "And it was exactly this club that gave me the idea of reviving a good old tradition here at Rosenholm, a tradition that has sadly been long forgotten: that of the student clubs. The student clubs were once an important part of life at Rosenholm. In them, students came together with like-minded peers to challenge and stretch one another."

The last girls took their hands out of the water and Zlavko sighed demonstratively before continuing, "In principle, anyone can request permission to form a student club, student or teacher, and Jens and I have agreed that this year, I will establish a club for the most talented students at the school. Those students who have the ambition to become a little bit more than . . . well, average."

"What does he mean with that?" Chamomile whispered to Malou. "Hey, can you get your hand out of there now!"

Not *all* of the students had removed their hands from the iced water. Malou sat with a dogged expression on her face, staring down into the bowl where her hand still rested.

"You will not be able to apply to join this club, but students who show potential will receive an invitation from me. Various tests will need to be taken before becoming a full member, and as it will be quite demanding, students from first year will not be taken on."

"Malou, give it up now! You've won!" Chamomile said, no longer whispering, so that the rest of the class were now more interested in Malou's immersed ghostly white hand than they were in Zlavko's speech.

"For those who have the ability and the will, the club will also provide a place for the future's most powerful mages to form a community that will give them the best opportunities throughout their careers and their lives."

"Stop it, now, your hand's gonna drop off!"

"Chamomile, what is it you find so important that you think you should sit and talk over me?" Zlavko said.

"It's Malou," Chamomile said. "She's still got her hand in the water!"

"Yes, she certainly does," Zlavko quietly confirmed.

"Isn't it dangerous? Can you not get frostbite?"

"Yes, you can." He smiled. "But perhaps Malou knows what she's doing? Or it could be she is too stupid and stubborn to stop in time. We'll soon find out."

"Is this an approved teaching method?" Victoria asked.

"In case you weren't aware, I am the vice principal of this school, and I do not need to defend my teaching methods to you or to anyone else. A lot of things have changed here, and a whole lot more is to change still." He patted on a knife handle that was sticking up from a sheath in his belt. "The more observant of you will have noticed that our new principal has, for example, lifted the ban on blood mages of a certain rank carrying their ceremonial weapons."

Chamomile ignored Zlavko's childish fixation on his knife and turned to Malou. "Will you please take your hand out now?" she begged. "Zlavko, tell her that she should stop!"

Malou still had her eyes fixed down on the iced water, her jaw taut.

"Pain is relative. It differs in intensity from person to person." Zlavko walked down to Malou and Chamomile's table, where he rested his hands on the edge and leaned in over Malou. Slowly, she lifted her gaze to look him in the eye.

"And there are also those people who enjoy pain," he said, and smiled at her.

"That's enough, now!" Chamomile grabbed Malou's bowl and pulled at it so it tipped over, and the ice-cold water poured out.

Zlavko straightened up and tutted at her in a condescending manner. "You have a talent for drama, if nothing else," he snapped at Chamomile, turning his back on them.

"What did you do that for?" Malou said angrily, holding her hand in toward her chest.

"It's not worth getting frostbite in your hand over this!" Chamomile retorted.

"The lesson is over," Zlavko said, even although there was nearly a half hour remaining. "We'll continue our futile journey toward toughening up you soft and rather pampered young people another day. Make sure you dry that before you go." He nodded toward the water still dripping off the table and onto the floor, then left the class without closing the door behind him.

"Wasn't the plan that you would say sorry to him?" Chamomile asked, as the rest of the class sat gaping at them.

"I did," Malou said. She pushed her stool angrily behind her and went to find a cloth.

"I don't think you did it right, then," Chamomile muttered. "It hasn't worked, in any case."

Hey sweetheart
missing you

Missing you too.
What you up to?

Bored. Thinking about you a bit.
(Just a bit)

Have you started up again?

Yup. Classes started yesterday.
Already had the pleasure of
Blood Magic.

Ah, yeah. How is good old
psychotic Zlavko doing?

More of a psycho than ever before.

Let me know if you have
trouble with him. I'll come over
and bare my fangs!

Might be necessary.
I think he's up to something . . .

SEPTEMBER 11TH
11:30 A.M.

Kirstine

Kirstine sat at the very back of the class. She'd have preferred to sit alone, but Chamomile plonked herself at her side, thumping down the book on Viking Magic that had just been handed out to them in a way that gave Kirstine a start.

"We're going there as soon as we can, right?" Malou said, who was sitting at the next table with Victoria.

"Yeah, I guess we better," Chamomile said, a little reluctantly. "I just think it was so weird there."

"Well, it was definitely weirdly ugly," Malou added, and pulled out her books before turning to Victoria. "Isn't it strange that you couldn't feel Trine there, when that was her childhood home?"

"Yeah, I didn't really get that either . . ." Victoria said, and seemed as if she was going to add something else, but they were interrupted by the arrival of a group of girls.

Chamomile quickly turned and smiled. "Hey."

"Hey," said Sofie, flicking her long dark hair behind her shoulders. "What's all this about us getting a new Norse teacher suddenly? And no explanation?"

"A new teacher?" Chamomile turned to Malou, who shrugged, looking puzzled.

"I don't know anything about that."

Kirstine stared hard at the desktop in front of her. Thorbjørn had told her that news a few days ago, but she hadn't said anything to the others yet. She really preferred to avoid the subject.

"Good morning!" Thorbjørn came into the class looking, as always, like a bear that had lost its way. Too big, somehow, for the classroom.

Chamomile leaned toward her. "Did you know we'd be getting him this year?"

Kirstine nodded.

"Well, that must come as a relief. I mean, that we don't have Jakob, now that you two are over with." Chamomile gave her an understanding look, but Kirstine only shifted her gaze back to the desktop without a smile.

"So, as some of you—those who got my message—will know, I will be teaching your class this year," Thorbjørn said, once the students had all taken their places. "And we—"

"Why is Jakob not teaching us?" Malou interrupted.

Chamomile shot her a warning look and nodded over to Kirstine, as if she were a little child who needed to be treated with kid gloves.

"Right . . ." whispered Malou.

"Yeah, why isn't he?" added Sofie. "We've done so much with Jakob, we don't want to be starting over with any of it, right?"

"No, no, don't worry. Jakob has updated me on everything. You've done a great deal of work on the magic of runes, so this year we'll be working on clairvoyance," said Thorbjørn, tugging a little distractedly at his huge beard, which was pulled together in a short braid. "You'll have heard, of course, about the Viking seeresses, the vølve, who had second sight that allowed them to see both the past and the future. This year we will learn a lot more about their methods, and we will also be trying it ourselves."

"Will we have exams in that?" Malou asked.

"No, but those of you from the Earth branch, you could consider it as a subject for your second-year assignment—it's a really exciting subject," Thorbjørn said, as around him the students softly sighed. None of them wanted to hear another word about that assignment, which was due in spring, in any case.

"When do we get to try clairvoyance?" asked Sara, Sofie's sister.

"Now," said Thorbjørn.

"Now?!" blurted out Chamomile, so loudly it gave Kirstine a fright.

She noticed how she had started to sweat. Since the visit to Trine's house and the initiation ceremony, she'd had a strange feeling that something was different. And not just different. *Wrong.*

"Yes, as I was saying, we're going to jump right in. Now, look at this." Thorbjørn leaned over a leather suitcase he had brought in with him and clicked open its locks. From the suitcase, he pulled a strange-looking instrument. "Does anyone know what this is?"

"A deformed ukulele?" Malou guessed.

"No, it's a lyre. A string instrument, used in the Viking era. Music was a big part of Viking culture—that's something not many people know," said Thorbjørn, letting his fingers run over the instrument, which looked like a plaything in the huge man's hands.

"And we're going to learn to play that?" asked Sofie in disbelief.

"No, I brought this because I thought we could do some singing today."

"Singing?!" Malou blurted out. If Kirstine hadn't felt so sick, she'd definitely have laughed at the sight of Malou's horrified look. "No thanks!"

"Calm down now. Everyone can take part. The Vikings would often sing—and singing was also a huge and important part of the magical work of the *vølve*—the seeresses. Often a seeress would be assisted by several choir girls, who would put her into a trance with their magical singing, so she could make her prophesies and answer the questions people asked her," Thorbjørn explained. "And the song doesn't need to sound beautiful for it to be effective. The Arab explorer al-Tartushi"—Thorbjørn pronounced every syllable of the name slowly and carefully—"visited Denmark back in the 900s and after a visit to Hedeby, he wrote that he had never heard such dreadful singing as he heard here. He thought it was like dogs howling. Who knows, we might manage a little better than that today."

"I wouldn't bet on it," muttered Malou.

Thorbjørn dipped into his bag and pulled out some sheets of paper, which he started handing out. Song lyrics. "I Dreamed a Dream This Night."

"Sadly, we don't know a lot about what was sung in Viking times. It was only much later that people began to write down popular folk songs from outside of church. But there is *this* song, which was transcribed in the year 1300. Why, and what the song means, is a mystery, but this is Denmark's oldest song, and that's why I've brought it here. Do any of you already know it?"

There was no response.

"Well, you'll pick it up easily. I'll sing it through once first. Are you ready?"

Thorbjørn fiddled with the instrument and hummed a little to himself to warm up. A few of the students giggled. Then he began to play. The melody was slow and melancholy, beautiful and dark, and the rhythm felt hypnotic. When he started to sing, it gave Kirstine goosebumps all over.

I dreamed a dream this night
Of silk and finest furs
In a dress so smooth and light
In twilight's fine sun rays
Now, the clear morning awakes

"Wow!" Kirstine whispered, scrunching her eyes tight.

Thorbjørn's voice was warm and rich and he sang so beautifully that the music made Kirstine want to let go of everything and allow herself to sink into the melody and the flickering feeling that was spreading throughout her body. She was slipping away, it was so good. Kirstine took hold of her chair and gripped hard, until her hands hurt.

When Thorbjørn stopped, the class was absolutely silent. Then there was a raucous outburst of applause.

"Who'd have imagined that!" Malou said, and clapped and whistled at full volume.

"Thank you, thank you." Thorbjørn nodded, but his face, or the parts not concealed by his impressive beard, turned beetroot red. "Now it's your turn. But we'll take a volunteer first. The reason for singing is to help the person who is carrying out seid—clairvoyance—to connect with their powers and perhaps even enter a trance." Thorbjørn pulled up a chair and placed it in front of the teacher's desk. "In Viking times, the *vølve* sat in a high seat, a *sejdhjælle*, but for today we'll make do with a chair. Who wants to try? Kirstine, would you like to?"

Thorbjørn looked at her expectantly. *Far too expectantly.* She really hoped Jakob hadn't told him she was good at this kind of thing. Kirstine had real issues with their written exercises, but in practical activities she surprised herself by being one of the best in class.

Kirstine lifted her gaze from the desktop. "No," she said.

Chamomile turned and looked at her in surprise. It wasn't every day that she said no to a teacher, she was well aware of that. But this was how it had to be.

"Oh," said Thorbjørn. "And why not? Everybody must have a try."

"I don't want to," Kirstine said, forcing herself to look at Thorbjørn directly.

"Come on," Chamomile whispered. "You don't need to be nervous, you'll probably be really good at it."

Kirstine shook her head. Thorbjørn shifted from one foot to the other, as if he wasn't sure what to do with himself, it was as if the strongest man in the world had just had an embarrassing little accident.

"Well, okay, you can skip it for today. But everyone needs to try at some point or another. What about you then, Victoria?"

SEPTEMBER 21ST
11:20 A.M.

Malou

Malou gathered her coat in at the neck; the wind was brisk and the sea was topped with frothy, white-crested waves. It was Saturday and the streets were full of shoppers carrying armfuls of bags from the supermarket or the mall.

"Hey, wait up," Chamomile said, giving a flick of her head.

Malou looked over her shoulder, to where Kirstine had fallen behind, the wind blowing her hair back from her face. Malou slowed her pace slightly; Kirstine, however, seemed to have all but stopped. She'd become no less peculiar since the start of the new school year.

"She must miss Jakob," Victoria suggested, as she would, given she did nothing but write constantly to Benjamin.

"You know, I don't really want to do this," Chamomile said, when Kirstine finally caught up.

"It's just a house," Malou said, shrugging. As they walked on, Chamomile linked her arm through Malou's, and Malou didn't pull hers away.

The house looked the same as the last time. Empty and sad. They stood staring at it for a moment, not quite ready to go any nearer.

"Come on," Malou said, and went through the gate. The main door was still unlocked.

"Anyone home? Hallooo!" she shouted, and turned to Chamomile. "See, just an empty house."

Still, it was only with great care that they went in, whispering to one another and trying not to make noise.

"What are we looking for?" Chamomile whispered.

"Anything that has a connection to Trine," Malou said softly. "There has to be something here that can help us understand what happened to her."

They picked their way slowly through the living room. The furniture sat exactly as it had the last time; the clock ticked on the wall between the photographs of the two sisters, the eldest red haired and smiling, the youngest dark haired and serious. Malou paused in front of a dark writing desk. In some way or other, it felt wrong to go through people's private things like this—even if they had perhaps been dead for some years. *Stop letting Chamomile infect you with some weird, childish fear!* There was nothing to be afraid of. She reached out her arm, decisively, to pull out the uppermost drawer. A pale hand grabbed her wrist tightly, making her jump.

"Kirstine," she blurted out, somewhere between a whisper and a gasp. "You scared me!"

"Stop it!" Kirstine whispered. Her serious eyes stared widely. "Leave it alone."

Malou drew back her hand and rubbed her wrist. She thought against asking what was up with Kirstine and instead turned and went into the kitchen. The linoleum squeaked underfoot as she went. A worn scrub brush sat by the sink and the tap was dripping. Genuinely, nothing had been cleared from this house since the last residents moved out. Had the parents died, or had they just moved out and left everything behind as it was? Did the house remind them too much of the daughter they had lost?

"Here are the stairs," Chamomile whispered. "Are we going up?"

A creaking noise made them all jump. Malou spun around. *Shit!*

"What are you doing here?!"

Behind them, in the doorway to the living room, stood a woman. Malou gasped, breathless with fright. Where had she come from?

The woman's face was deeply furrowed, her eyes shadowy, and her long gray hair—almost white, in fact—was split at the ends and hung right down to her bony hips. She wore a checked shirt and a pair of corduroy trousers that were bald at the knees and were tied around her thin body with a blue nylon cord.

"Have you come to see the witch?" she hissed.

"We're sorry we barged in!" Malou blurted out. "We didn't know anyone lived here."

"All the kids know the witch lives here." Her voice was hoarse, as if she hadn't spoken in a long time.

"We're not from around here," Malou said. "We're from Rosenholm." It was a gamble. Any mage would recognize that name, but Malou couldn't gauge the woman's reaction.

She blinked her eyes and studied them. "What is it you want?"

"Are you Trine's mom?" Chamomile asked.

"What?" said the woman, and her voice sharpened. "*What* was that you said?"

"We're trying to find out what happened to a girl called Trine," Malou explained. "She disappeared back in 1989. Rose Katrine was her full name—"

"I know very well what her name is, and in nearly thirty years not a single person has come around here asking about her," the woman interrupted. Her deep-set eyes bored into Malou. "So now I would like to know"—the woman's voice was now ominously low, but suddenly rose so that it gave them all a start—"*what do you want?!*"

Her hair lifted behind her as if she was facing into the wind, and her eyes grew large and dark, irises widening and spreading like watercolor, penetrating the white.

Okay, she *was* a mage. And she was dangerous. Malou's mouth felt dry with fear.

"I'm sorry, we'll go now!" Chamomile said, but the woman stood in the doorway, blocking their way. She lifted her hands to her face, her nails yellow and claw-like. "*What do you want with me . . .?*" she hissed, and slowly pressed her nails into her cheeks.

"You're Trine's little sister," Kirstine said. Her voice was strangely calm. "Trine gave us a message for you."

The woman turned to Kirstine. Her nails had left long, bloody scratches down her face. "Trine?" she snarled poisonously. "Trine has never wanted to talk to me."

"She talks to us," Victoria whispered. "She gave us the message: *Say sorry.*"

"Ha!" The woman sneered angrily. "Should I be saying sorry? To her? Never!" She bent forward as if suddenly in pain. "Get out of here," she whispered, her dark eyes staring at them, none of the white even visible anymore. "*Get lost!*" She collapsed to the floor in the doorway.

"Come on!" Malou grabbed hold of Chamomile and jumped through the doorway. The woman's long nails grasped at her clothes and she screamed as Malou wrenched herself free.

SEPTEMBER 25TH
10:06 P.M.

Victoria

Trine . . . Trine, where are you?

It felt . . . transgressive. Yup, that was the word. It felt as if she was about to overstep some boundary, some decisive barrier, and Victoria was frightened that once she had done it there would be no going back again. As a rule, she put a whole lot of her strength into shutting off, screening herself, keeping them away. *The white shadows.* And now she was in the midst of opening up, summoning them even, in a way that made her feel way more vulnerable than she cared to feel.

Trine . . . are you there?

Since Trine had surprised her in the bathroom at home, Victoria had not been able to contact her. She had thought that Trine might be here, when she started at Rosenholm again, but she couldn't feel her presence at the school either. It felt strange. The dead girl's spirit had become a certain, fixed part of her life. Somehow she had gotten used to her presence, and now Trine had suddenly disappeared. *Why?*

Victoria looked around their little kitchen. Even though she couldn't see it herself, she knew her eyes had gone white and vacant. They were on their way, she could tell. They were drawn to her like moths to a night flame. She gave a start as the figure of a man materialized in front of her, clearly visible. He was old and bent and his fingers were gnarled, as if from years of hard physical toil. His watery eyes pierced into her from his white face. She didn't like the feel of his energy. He had an insistency about him; he came too close, and the way he kept moistening his drooping lower lip gave her the creeps. Victoria was scared he could turn out to be aggressive, but she forced herself to stay calm.

No thanks. Please just move on.

She turned him away in as firm and friendly a manner as she knew how, but the man only backed off a few paces, and his eyes stayed on her, making her uneasy. Victoria tried to turn her focus away from him, but the creepy man seemed to be scaring off the other spirits too. They kept in the background and she could sense most of them only as vague shadows. A thin woman wearing an apron and a headscarf rushed by with a hunted look in her eyes. Soft footsteps ran by to the left of her, perhaps a child. But there was no sign of Trine. Eventually, she gave up.

"I can't get in contact with her," she whispered, looking around at the others, her eyes back to their own brown color. "She's not here."

"It was worth a try," Chamomile said, and smiled at her. "Thanks for the effort."

"Okay, so that was a dead end," Malou confirmed. "Trine can't or won't tell us anything about her. The only thing we know is that the woman who lives in that house is Trine's sister. And that she is also a mage. Maybe she was at Rosenholm too? But we don't even know her name. We don't know anything about her, except that she seems to have totally lost her mind and is quite possibly dangerous as hell."

"We do know one other thing," Kirstine said. "We know where she lives."

"Yeah, well, that goes without saying . . ."

"Maybe we could . . . send her a letter?" Kirstine suggested.

"A letter?" Malou said, raising a single eyebrow with a quizzical look.

"Hey, that's maybe not such a dumb idea!" Chamomile said. "She must have been living there alone all these years, maybe she was just scared, finding us suddenly standing in her house. I mean, we did break in . . ."

"I'd say it was more like she was absolutely batshit, but sure, let's try a letter. She's the only person who can tell us anything about what happened to Trine," Malou said. "Will I write it?"

"No, let me," Chamomile said, and grabbed a pen and paper. "You're not exactly known and loved for your diplomatic manner, are you?"

Malou blinked but didn't say anything and just watched Chamomile, who shifted uncomfortably in her seat as she wrote. At one point she looked up and around her as if she had heard something.

"Can I see what you wrote?" Kirstine asked when Chamomile was finished. She leaned over and mouthed the words as she slowly read her way through. "It's good." She nodded.

"Let's hope she checks her mailbox," Malou said. "And that she decides to talk to us."

"Is there a window open somewhere?" asked Chamomile, giving herself a hug. "I feel like its mega cold in here."

Victoria said nothing but watched as the old man leaned in over Chamomile with a lewd smile, licking his lower lip again and again with his big white tongue.

To Trine's sister,

We're sorry we went into your house. We knocked for a while, and when we didn't hear anything, we figured the house had been abandoned. We would really like to speak to you. We are trying to find out what happened to your sister, Trine, and we think you could maybe help us. Here are our contact details—we really hope to hear from you.

Best wishes,
Malou, Kirstine, Victoria, and Chamomile
(Pupils of Rosenholm boarding school)

Invitation to the Crows' Club

Meeting place: The library
Time: October 8th at 9:00 p. m.

CORVUS OCULUM CORVI NON ERUIT

OCTOBER 8TH
9:00 P.M.

Malou

Malou opened the door and stepped in, with Victoria right behind her. A notice on the big double doors explained that the library was reserved for an evening event to which only invited students were welcome. The mysterious invitation had been placed on her bed a few days before. Victoria had also received one, but Chamomile and Kirstine had not, and Victoria had only decided to go at the last minute, mainly because Malou had pushed her into it.

Inside the library a fire was roaring and outside the fall wind rustled the tall poplars. Deep armchairs had been set out in a half circle between the tall bookcases and many of the seats were already taken. Malou recognized a few third-year pupils, who sat whispering about who could have sent the invitation. So it wasn't only her and Victoria who didn't have a clue what was going to happen.

They sat themselves down in two empty chairs, and Victoria immediately took out her phone, looking like someone who already regretted coming along. A blond boy from their year said a friendly hello to her; they obviously knew each other, and Victoria carefully returned his greeting. He then turned his gaze on Malou and nodded to her. The muted chatter petered out and the pupils all sat and waited, listening to the crackling of the fire and the wind blowing outside.

All eyes turned to the door when it opened. Zlavko. *Of course.* Malou felt her stomach tighten and knot. She glanced at Victoria, but she didn't appear to be the least bit surprised.

"Welcome, everyone," Zlavko said, and Malou could tell he was in an unusually good mood. "Welcome to this informative initial meeting about Crows' Club. Tonight's little introduction will be held here in the library, but thereafter the club will meet at a secret location, known only to members, aspiring members, and me. This evening I will tell you about the club and you will learn how you can become candidates for membership."

He looked brightly around the circle of students. "I've borrowed the name 'Crows' Club' from an old student club here at Rosenholm, a club that was sadly dissolved when modern pedagogical methods were introduced. The club's motto also comes from there. The motto, in Latin, in case you're wondering, is this: *Corvus oculum corvi non eruit.* Is there anyone who knows what that means or has gone to the trouble to find out?"

Malou looked around at the others as the blond boy put his hand up.

"Yes, Louis?"

"It means something like 'a crow will never peck out the eye of another crow.'"

"Correct. A Crow will never attack one of its own. The club's members will always—regardless of any internal disagreements or disputes that might arise—be completely loyal toward one another outside the club. A crow never attacks another crow."

"And what if a Crow does something that's wrong?" Victoria asked, surprising Malou with the critical tone in her voice.

Zlavko turned toward her, his good mood already dissipating. "Who gave you permission to ask questions?" he snapped. "If you think that a member of the club has done something wrong, you can take it up with the individual concerned or with the club leader. Me. But you never stab another member in the back. Understood?"

As Victoria stayed silent, Zlavko looked around the rest of the room.

"Yes, Amalie?"

A tall, dark-haired third year was sitting with her hand raised. "What is the purpose of the club?"

"That's a good question. Anyone who wants to set up a club can do so, as long as they have permission from the school's principal and vice principal," Zlavko said, in a tone Malou found unpleasantly smug. "And you decide yourself what the purpose of it will be. The purpose of this club—the Crows' Club—is to form a community of the best, most talented and ambitious students at Rosenholm, where they can challenge one another to reach their full potential, both in their time here at school and thereafter."

Malou let her eyes wander again over the gathered students. Were these really the best students in the school? And in that case, was she one of them?

"Members of the club will be loyal to one another and support each other in school and in their future careers," Zlavko continued.

"Like a Masonic lodge," Victoria commented.

Zlavko chose to ignore her. "The Crows' Club only takes the best, and a place cannot be solicited, it is only by invitation. If you want to be considered, you must first go through an entrance test, where you can prove your worth. If you pass this test—and, following a suitable trial period, you are still seen as worthy of joining—then you will be offered full membership."

Malou raised her hand. "And it's you who decides who gets to be a member?"

Zlavko smiled that smile that made him look like a hungry predator. "Yes, it's me."

"What do you do in the club?" asked a petite, fair-haired girl with wide, frightened eyes, once Zlavko had given her a nod.

"It's a secret. You need to be a candidate for membership before you can know anything about that. And you are not that yet." Zlavko reached down into his pocket and pulled out a handful of black feathers. "Use the coming fall vacation to think about whether you want to be a member of the Crows' Club. In exchange for your loyalty, you will get an unbreakable bond and some really fantastic opportunities to achieve what you want to in this life. But it requires strength and commitment—this is not for weaklings! If you want to be considered, you should deliver this feather together with a slip of paper with your name on it to my mailbox. In return, you will be given a time for your entrance test. And one last thing: your name should be written in your own blood. A little symbol of the sacrifices you are willing to make to be a member."

Victoria let out an irritated sigh and shook her head. Malou looked around at the others to see their reactions. Amalie's eyebrows shot up under her neatly clipped bangs, and Louis looked steadily at Zlavko.

Community, an unbreakable bond and fantastic opportunities . . . Didn't it sound pretty good? Maybe *too* good? Things always came with a price, and when Zlavko was involved, the price would be high for sure. Malou realized she was still staring at Louis. He had turned away from Zlavko and his eyes met hers.

OCTOBER 15TH
11:05 P.M.

Chamomile

"Are you sleeping?" Her mother stuck her head around the door. "Chamomile?"

Chamomile hid under the duvet. *Just go away.*

Her mother hovered a little at the door, as if unsure whether she should enter. "I just wanted to say I'm going to bed now, too. Sleep well," she whispered, and closed the door behind her.

Finally. Chamomile took out her phone again. She used to love vacation time, but not anymore. The first days of fall break had already been hell: Chamomile hid away in her room, while her mother pitter-pattered about outside her door trying to tempt her out. *Chamomile, I made cinnamon rolls, are you not coming out? Why don't we watch a movie? Do you want to go for a walk? Are you okay?*

She sighed and turned over in her bed. And they still hadn't talked about *it*. The only thing Chamomile's mom had asked was "Have you said anything to him?" Chamomile shook her head. Her mother had seemed relieved, and Chamomile had gone to her room. It would be a long vacation if this was how things kept going.

She checked her phone, but there was nothing new. She kept hoping Kirstine would write soon to say mail had arrived.

Kirstine was staying at school over vacation and had promised to keep an eye on the mail. But most likely, Trine's sister had no intention of contacting them, and they'd need to think of something else. They'd wondered about the old graduates' photos that hung in the corridor behind the library. Trine's class photo was there, but no dark-haired girl with the same surname appeared in the year groups after Trine's. Maybe her sister had never attended Rosenholm. But she was a mage?

Chamomile sighed and switched off the phone, but her room did not fall into complete darkness, not quite. A pale light flickered across the wall. It was coming from the window. She shone her phone light again, heart thumping.

"Is anybody there?" she asked. Slowly she made her way to the window and shone her light out over the garden. Malou's face was pressed up against the paned glass. She had a hat pulled right down over her forehead and a huge grin on her face.

"Happy seventeenth birthday!" she yelled through the closed window, shining the light from her own phone back on Chamomile.

"Malou, you idiot. It's pouring rain!" Chamomile opened the window and Malou crawled in. She was dripping wet. "What's happened? Did you hear from Trine's sister?"

"Not a peep." Malou took off the hat, leaving her soaked hair plastered around her pale face.

"But what are you doing here?"

"I came to wish you a happy birthday!" She held out a McDonald's balloon, dangling from the end of a plastic stick.

"It's not until tomorrow," Chamomile said.

"I know. But I thought maybe I could sleep over here. Just for a night."

"Of course. Are you okay?"

"Yeah. I just had a fight with my mom." Malou avoided eye contact. "Where can I put these wet things?"

"Give them to me, I'll find something dry for you to wear. Did you walk over here?"

"I took the bus to some godforsaken village or other and then I had to walk the rest of the way. My god, you do live way out in the sticks." She took off her wet clothes, teeth chattering.

"Malou, why didn't you call? You'll get sick. Get into the bed to warm up. Can I get anything for you?"

"What about some of that herbal tea with extra herbs in? I would love something hot to drink." She shivered under the duvet.

When Chamomile came back with a tray of tea and crackers, Malou was sitting up in bed, wrapped in Chamomile's duvet and wearing one of her old T-shirts, drying her hair with a hand towel.

"Ah, perfect!" she said, and dived right in to the tea and Chamomile's mom's homemade crackers with thickly spread butter and cheese. "I haven't had any dinner."

"You haven't been to McDonald's?"

"Oh yeah. I forgot about that."

"Malou. How are you, really?"

"I'm fine," she said, stuffing half a cracker in her mouth. "What do you mean?"

"I just mean that you don't exactly go wandering around in the pouring rain for hours to go somewhere to sleep, if everything is fine . . . ?"

"I had a fight with my mom, like I said. You know how it is, right?"

"Do I? I'm not so sure."

"Is it a problem, this? I thought you'd be happy I turned up on your birthday."

"Of course I'm happy. You're always welcome here. And you can also always tell me if there's anything you want to talk about."

"Perfect. I will keep that in mind. Come in under the duvet and drink your tea. You don't have any more of those crackers, do you?"

"Good morning, my big girl. Happy birthday!"

"Mom, it's too early," muttered Chamomile sleepily. "Go away!"

"It's ten o'clock. I've prepared a beautiful birthday breakfast and . . . Oh, we've got guests?"

Chamomile stuck her head over the duvet. "It's Malou. She got here last night after you went to bed. She's going to stay a few days."

"Of course. A very good morning." Chamomile's mother leaned in over the bed to where the top of Malou's head was just peeking out. Chamomile couldn't be bothered getting another mattress out, so they had slept together in her bed. "She's a deep sleeper, isn't she?" her mother noted, as Malou grunted from her dreams.

"Yup, she's always a good sleeper," Chamomile said, stretching. "Plus, she had a tough time getting out here. She walked for hours last night. In the rain."

"Aw, poor girl. She must be hungry then. Why don't you come to the table when you're ready and I'll set up for one more?"

Once Chamomile finally managed to rouse Malou, they went through to the kitchen. Chamomile's mother had laid out a spread for them.

"It's so nice to have a guest," she said. "Now, just help yourself to everything, Malou. There are rolls and crackers, plenty of cheese, and rose hip jam. I've made muffins too; they look wonky, but I think they'll taste okay. Wait! I've forgotten the presents. I'll be right back!"

"She's sweet, your mom," Malou said, sitting down on the low bench, which was draped in warm sheepskins and her mother's home-crocheted rag rugs.

"She's sucking up to me right now, but she's not getting off that lightly."

Malou threw her a questioning glance as she reached across for a roll, but Chamomile only shook her head.

As Chamomile unwrapped her gifts, her mother poured herself a coffee and placed her elbows on the table. "So, tell me this: Are you two a couple?"

"*Mom!*"

"Or how would you put it? Are you dating?"

Malou burst out laughing. "Ah, no. No, I've not been so lucky so far, I'm afraid. But you can always hope." She nudged Chamomile in the ribs with her elbow.

"Mom, seriously? Malou is my roommate. I've mentioned her to you, like, a thousand times!"

"Ah, I'm sorry. I just thought you made such an elegant pair."

The rest of the day passed without any further huge embarrassments. In fact, Malou being around helped ease the tense atmosphere in the old farmhouse. Chamomile's mother left them, more or less, to their own devices, except at mealtimes, when she popped up with all of Chamomile's favorite dishes in honor of her birthday. The weather had brightened and the low fall sun cast long shadows over the stubbly fields. After over-stuffing themselves with pear tart and crème fraîche, they decided to go for an afternoon walk. Malou seemed in no hurry to go home, and Chamomile didn't mention the subject. Instead she pointed out places she had played in when she was little, showed Malou the burial mounds and the edges of the forest, where elder, sloe, wild blackberries, and apples grew.

They turned back to the house, rosy cheeked, and dived straight into the bubbling-hot lasagna her mother had put out on the kitchen table.

After eating, they retreated—full and drowsy—to Chamomile's room.

"Are you sleeping?" Chamomile looked down to the floor, where Malou lay on a mattress. They had watched an episode of Chamomile's favorite series on her laptop, but Malou hadn't seemed especially interested.

"Mmm, not yet," she murmured.

"Do you actually know who your dad is?" Chamomile asked, and hoped that the question sounded sufficiently casual.

"Pfft. He's just some asshole or other my mom brought home once," Malou mumbled.

Chamomile propped herself up on one elbow. "Do you know where he lives?"

"He supposedly lives some place in Jutland, and he has a wife and kids. Poor them."

"Have you ever met him?"

"Hmm . . . a few times, when I was little, but only once that I really remember. It wasn't a great success. I don't think he even liked me. His new wife definitely didn't."

"But don't you ever feel like visiting him again? I mean, you're not curious about what kind of a person he is?"

"Nope. I already know what kind of person he is. A piece of shit, is what he is. And he wants nothing to do with me. Seriously, forget that stuff about your dad. It doesn't matter one bit who the hell a person's dad is."

"It does for me," Chamomile said. "My mom finally told me who he is."

Malou rustled around in the sleeping bag and sat up. "Okay. Who is he then?"

Chamomile hesitated. "He doesn't know it yet. Somehow or other, I feel like he ought to know . . . before I tell other people."

Malou nodded in the darkness. "So are you going to contact him?"

Chamomile sighed and fell back onto her bed. "Maybe. Yes, I will. But I just don't know how you go and say a thing like that. My mom never even told him she was pregnant."

"You could end up mega disappointed. He's probably a piece of shit, too, right, or else wouldn't your mom have told him? If I were you, I'd be happy that I have a sweet mom and I'd forget all about that man who just so happens to be your father," Malou said, and lay back down on the mattress.

"I don't think that I can, though," Chamomile said.

"Well, you'll have to tell him then. But trust me: not everyone is suited to having kids."

Chamomile lay still for a while in the dark. She wanted to ask Malou about her mom, but she didn't dare. Malou always clammed up whenever Chamomile tried to talk about it. Instead she asked about another thing she had had on her mind. "Malou, you're not thinking of signing up for Zlavko's student club, are you?"

Malou didn't answer. Her breathing sounded deep and regular, but Chamomile was pretty sure she was only pretending to be asleep.

MALOU

OCTOBER 17TH
11:30 A.M.

Kirstine

She was startled by a sudden knock on the dorm door. Kirstine paused the movie she was watching and put down her phone. She looked for a sweater to pull on over her slip before she went over and opened the door. It was Jakob. He smiled, a little shyly, as if worried she might slam the door in his face.

"Hi. I was thinking we could go for a walk, if you like. I brought some provisions with me." He lifted a basket up in front of her. A thermos flask stuck out the top, and she could see two mugs and something or other wrapped in a kitchen towel. "Hot chocolate!" he said excitedly, pointing to the thermos, as if this news was too good to keep to himself.

"I'm not sure . . ."

"I thought we could have a chat, but we don't have to. We can also just drink the hot chocolate and come home again . . . if you want. It'd be a crime to let it go to waste now."

Kirstine sighed. One hot chocolate couldn't do any harm. "I need to get some clothes on," she said, suddenly painfully aware she hadn't brushed her hair or her teeth, never mind not being dressed yet.

"I'll just wait," he said with a big smile.

Ten minutes later, after rushing around, toothbrush in one hand, hairbrush in the other, hunting for a pair of clean socks, they set off. They didn't speak until they got down into the park. The weather was lovely and every now and then the sun peeked through the clouds, its light filtering down through the trees' yellow and orange leaves.

"Can we stop here?" Kirstine asked, when Jakob started veering toward the woods. For some reason she didn't feel like walking any farther. A creeping sense of foreboding told her it wasn't a good idea.

"Of course. We can have a seat on that bench there," said Jakob. He began to unpack the basket. He poured hot chocolate into the cups, and then passed her something he took from the bottom. Wrapped in a kitchen towel, Kirstine first took it for rye bread.

"Spiced loaf cake," Jakob said. "My mom's recipe."

"Did you make it yourself?"

"Yes, I did. I'm a man of many talents. Here, you should try it with some butter." He passed her a thick slice with cold butter, and Kirstine took a polite nibble. She hadn't had any breakfast and she was actually pretty hungry.

"Mmm!" She nodded, her mouth full of cake. "It's really tasty!"

"No need to sound so surprised." He laughed.

They sat in silence for a little while, eating cake. Kirstine took a sip of her cocoa. Was he waiting for her to say something? It was him who had invited her. On the other hand, it was her who had broken up with him. Kirstine sighed. The picnic was really sweet of him. But she couldn't simply forget how he had let her down at the worst possible time. Instead of listening to her and helping her find Chamomile, whose life had been in real danger, he had chosen to think only of himself and his dumb teaching job, which he was so scared of losing.

Rosenholm's former principal, Birgit Lund, had figured out that something was going on between the two of them, but when she left the school before the summer vacation, Jakob was given permission to continue as a teaching assistant. Kirstine glanced at him but looked away when their eyes met.

He had kept his job but had lost her as a consequence. She had lost him, too, though.

"Was it you who requested a new class this year?" Kirstine asked.

"I thought it was for the best. The way things ended . . ." Jakob ran his fingers through his hair, the way she knew he did when he was nervous or under pressure. "But I was hoping we could maybe be friends?"

"Friends?"

She watched him carefully. Jakob looked down at his own hands. His eyelashes touched lightly on his cheek. At once, she remembered how they felt against her own skin.

"Yes. I still really like you, Kirstine. And even though it didn't work out being together, maybe we can be friends instead. I miss talking to you . . ."

His cheeks blushed pink under his freckles and Kirstine cursed inwardly at how it made him look so kissable. *Stop it, you traitor of a brain!*

He looked at her, waiting, holding his breath.

"We can give it a try," she said.

"Really? Great! Can I give you a hug? A friends type of hug, of course!"

Kirstine couldn't help but smile. He held her in his arms a moment longer than necessary. Suddenly the fall leaves on the treetops above seemed to start swimming around her; a tingling feeling and a wave of nausea washed over her, and she was, once again, filled with the overwhelming sense that something was very wrong.

Meet me in the park tomorrow night.
By the big poplars.

You're not allowed to
come near the school . . . ?!

I'll be careful nobody catches me.

OCTOBER 20TH
11:12 A.M.

Victoria

"Victoria, can you please tell us what extrasensory perception is?"

Victoria discreetly put down her phone and looked at Jens, who was waiting for her, expectantly. "Um . . . what was the question?"

"Extrasensory perception."

"Clairvoyance?" Victoria tried.

"Yes, that's the name of the subject we are doing right now, so that's a decent guess, but can you be a little more specific?" His annoyance gave her a bad taste in her mouth, as if she'd bitten into something sour.

"Is it to do with feeling things extra strongly?"

Their teacher of Spirit Magic looked at her skeptically.

"I'm sorry, I didn't really get the reading done."

Jens sighed. "Has anyone done the reading for today?"

Chamomile cautiously raised her hand. "Extrasensory perception means that you can pick up on things without using your normal senses."

"That's correct. And what kind of things might that mean?"

"For example, telepathy or seeing auras or . . . what was it again . . . psychometry?"

"And what is psychometry then?"

"The ability to read the history of an object."

"Very good, Chamomile, you've grasped this well."

Victoria gave Chamomile a thumbs-up, and Chamomile smiled back. She was blushing.

"Psychometry is a method of reading information about an object or an object's owner purely by seeing or touching it. It is an age-old custom, but the term itself was established by Joseph Rodes Buchanan in 1842. Yes, Kirstine?"

"If you had a picture, like, a photograph, would you be able to read who was there at the time the photo was taken?" Kirstine asked.

"Hmm, that's a good question. I would say you'd have to be very practiced at psychometry to get anything at all from a photograph. As a rule, we use objects that have been close to the owner—for example, jewelry or pieces of clothing. I—" Jens was interrupted by a loud ringtone.

"Sorry, I have to take this," Malou said, pushing her chair back. "Hello? Yes, one moment!" Malou looked up from her phone. "Come on!" she whispered, signaling with her head.

Chamomile got up hesitantly, and Victoria and Kirstine pushed back their chairs.

"What's going on?" asked Jens.

"Sorry," Kirstine whispered.

"It's an emergency," Chamomile said, and followed Malou.

"Tell me, does it take four girls to answer a phone call?!" Jens asked.

"Moral support, you know," Victoria said, before closing the door behind her.

"Hello, yes?" Malou put the phone on speaker. They heard only the sound of strange, rasping breathing at the other end of the line. "Hello?" she repeated.

"*Is that you, the Rosenholm girls?*" The gravelly voice sounded like it was coming from very far away.

"Yes, this is Malou. Who am I speaking to?"

"*I got your letter. I don't like getting mail.*"

"Sorry. We didn't know how else we could get in touch with you."

"*Ha! Get in touch . . .*" the voice screeched out at them. "*You can come here. But you need to bring something!*"

"Of course," Malou said. "What should we bring?"

The woman took a few heavy breaths in and out before answering. "*Milk. Whole milk! And a fresh loaf . . .*"

"Of course, anything else?"

"*When are you coming?*"

"Oh, I'm not sure yet. When do you want us to come?"

"*Are you coming or not?*" the voice snapped, suddenly sounding even more distant.

"When should we be there?" Malou shouted.

"*You may as well not bother,*" the voice muttered.

"We're coming!" Malou said. "We'll get there as fast as we can. Thanks for phoning!"

The call ended. Malou looked up from the phone. "I honestly never thought she would answer that letter."

"What do we do now?" asked Chamomile.

"We go visit her," Malou said. "What else?"

"Look, Mom! They're going to the witch's place."

"Get in the car. We need to leave, just as soon as I get Lilly strapped in."

"But Mom, look!"

"In your seat, now!"

Victoria gave the boy a wave as he crawled into the back of the car beside his little sister. Then they went in the gate.

"Have you got the things?" Chamomile whispered. Malou held the bag up. They had also brought butter, juice, cheese, sausage, and eggs.

"It should be you in front, Malou," Victoria said. "You're the one who spoke with her."

The door opened after only one knock.

"You're late!" The woman stared at them, her eyes dark but not black. She wore the same clothes as the last time, and it was only now that Victoria noticed how dirty they were. "Did you bring the things?"

Malou quickly passed her the bag.

"Go sit in the living room," she snapped, while eagerly pulling the bag toward her.

"What's your name?" asked Malou, who was the first to sit down on one of the dining chairs.

"Leah," said the woman. Her voice sounded somewhat surprised, as if she herself was amazed to even have a name. Perhaps it had been many years since anyone had asked to hear it.

The room was dimly lit. Leah had taken the bag into the kitchen and Victoria could hear her rip it open in there. She sat down by Malou. The door to the kitchen was ajar, and from where she sat, she could see Leah standing at the table. She couldn't help but watch as the woman opened the egg box, took out one egg, cracked it, and tipped its contents directly into her mouth, a sliver of yellow yolk dripping down her chin and onto her shirt. At that moment, she turned toward them and met Victoria's eyes. She turned her gaze down, embarrassed, as if she had caught Leah in a very private act. Leah picked out the bread, milk, and butter and brought them into the living room, where she sat down opposite Malou and Victoria.

"I don't like you!" She pointed at Chamomile. "You look like her. Sit over there." She pointed to the other room, where the sofa was. Chamomile stood up, unsure. "Go away!" she ordered, taking a big bite of the bread and sticking a long yellow nail into the butter. She closed her eyes as she licked it from her finger. "And you are dangerous," she said, suddenly looking at Kirstine. "Sit farther away from me."

Kirstine shifted over toward the kitchen door, while Leah ate more of the butter, as if oblivious to their presence.

"Is this your house?" Victoria asked.

"Yes. Who else could it belong to? Mother and Father are long dead."

"There's something we need to tell you," Malou said, and cleared her throat. "I don't know if you know, but . . . Trine, your sister, she's dead. She died back in 1989 . . ."

"Well," the woman said, still studying her finger, which was now licked clean of butter.

"Maybe you knew that already?" Malou asked.

"I worked it out at some point. Otherwise, we would have heard from her." She looked up from her finger and directly at Malou. "But how do *you* know about that?"

"We can communicate with Trine—or, with her spirit. Trine was murdered. We made a promise to her to find out who killed her."

"Well, did you now?" hissed Leah. "Yes, Trine was always good at getting people to run around after her."

"It's Victoria here who can speak with Trine," Malou said, but Leah didn't look at her.

"Well, I don't want to speak with her," the woman muttered to herself. "I don't want to, no . . . I don't want to have anything to do with her. All of this is too late."

"Do you know who could have murdered Trine?" asked Malou.

"No." She slurped; she had opened the milk and gulped some from the carton so that some ran down her chin. "She just disappeared," she said, and wiped her mouth with the back of her hand.

"We found an article from back then. It said that Trine had a boyfriend. Do you know anything about that?" Malou took a piece of paper from her pocket and opened it out.

The woman barely gave it a glance. "No," she said again.

"Trine disappeared while she was at Rosenholm," Malou tried next. "Do you know the school?"

"Of course I do!" Leah hissed. "What do you take me for? But I wasn't good enough for all of them, those fine gentlemen and ladies. They threw me out, that's what they did. But it was just as well!"

She leaned over the food again and it seemed she was done speaking. Malou nodded her head urgently at Victoria, as a sign that she herself was on the point of giving up.

"Could we have a look around the house, to see if there is anything that might help us?" Victoria asked.

The woman stopped eating and turned to face her. "What exactly are you hoping for?" she snarled. "Trine disappeared, she's never coming back, there's no trace of her here. You've only come to poke around in my misery, that's what you're doing! And how am I supposed to know that you are telling the truth, eh? Anybody could find that old article. How can I be sure you've really been in contact with Trine?"

"We're not trying to trick you or anything," Victoria reassured her.

"Then prove it!" she screeched. "Call on Trine! Call on her right now, and let me ask something that only she and I can possibly know."

Victoria could feel how her eyes were flickering. "Oh, but I can't. I can't feel Trine right now, she's not here . . ."

"Ha! Well, isn't that unlucky?" the woman taunted her. "Precisely today you sadly just can't contact Trine. Liars! You're lying your way into my home!"

Victoria felt a wave of rage and paranoia coming at her from the strange-looking woman, and she had to do her best not to let it get to her. "We're not lying. I *can* speak to Trine, it's true. Just not right now, I don't know where she is . . ."

"Get out, all of you!" Leah exclaimed, standing up. Victoria waited, partly just to see her eyes go dark again.

"Wait!" Malou said. "Give us your question! Something only you and Trine can know. Something that wouldn't be in any old articles. Then we can get the answer for you and you can see that we are not lying."

Malou held still, hardly even breathing. She'd taken a big gamble, but it worked.

Leah nodded slowly. She sat down at the table again and twisted off a piece of the bread.

"Alright then, let's do it. This is the question you need to answer for me. I am the only living person who knows. What was it that Trine always called me? Answer me that, and perhaps I will tell you a little secret."

10/23/1988

Dear Little T,

Thanks for your letter. I'm sorry to hear there's been such a fuss. I know I promised to come home over spring break, but sometimes I feel like it's better if I stay away.
I used the vacation to do some studying and spend time with some of the others who stayed in school. On Wednesday, the weather was so good, a few of us decided to go and collect chestnuts, like we did back in first grade. Then we sat all afternoon making chestnut animals! Totally dumb, but really fun.
And I also got time to go for walks in the woods with one very special person . . . Can you keep a secret? You can't tell anybody!!! Especially not Mom and Dad, they'll kill me if they find out.

I'M IN LOVE!!!

Do you remember I told you the boys here at the school are complete idiots? Well, I've met one guy who is totally different. He's completely great, but he doesn't know yet about my feelings and I don't dare tell him. Romantic relationships at school are forbidden, but I just have the feeling that he is also mad about me! Cross your fingers for me–I need it, or else my heart might end up in a thousand pieces!

Lv xxx

Trine

OCTOBER 24TH
11:30 A.M.

Chamomile

Chamomile leaned over Victoria and placed her hands on her forehead. She closed her eyes and concentrated.

"Now let the energy flow from your inner core—that part of you the Hindus call Anahata, the heart chakra—and over into your partner." Lisa walked calmly around between them, her voice deep and slow, while the air in the class had a heavy, spicy smell. Their Nature Magic teacher preferred to give lessons in the outdoors, but it was too cold outside now, and instead the students sat around in her classroom on thick carpets and large, colorful silk cushions she had spread out for them. Around them, smoke rose from small dishes where dried herbs were burning. Chamomile could smell lavender, which helped combat anxiety, and she knew that Lisa often used evening primrose to relieve stress and reduce blood pressure. Lisa was walking around the students barefoot, and her deep red silk kimono brushed Chamomile's cheek.

"Good, Chamomile, but concentrate still more on how your energy can flow freely over to Victoria," she said in a low voice, looking at her intensely with her large, dark eyes, before continuing to the next pair.

Chamomile tried to visualize how she was opening her heart to Victoria and sending her peace and positive energy. She knew Victoria was stressed, as she still hadn't been able to contact Trine, and she was glad when she saw how Victoria became more and more relaxed, her breath deepening.

"Malou, what are you doing?" Lisa's voice sounded strangely sharp, and Chamomile couldn't help but open her eyes.

Malou was sitting up straight as a board with one hand on Kirstine's head, while with the other she was typing something or other into her cell phone. Quickly, she tucked it away again.

"Kirstine, can you feel any energy from Malou?" Lisa asked.

Kirstine opened her eyes and looked from Lisa to Malou and back again, alarmed. "Maybe a little?" she tried.

"In that case it was probably a signal from the phone rather than from her. Malou, would you please focus on the task? I think you should swap partners. Victoria, you can try to pass energy to Kirstine, and Chamomile can try on Malou instead. You pay attention, now, to how she does it, Malou."

Chamomile couldn't help but give Malou a wink, which she answered with a kind of grimace that made her look less like an attractive young girl and more like a huffy toddler.

Chamomile put her hands on Malou's forehead, but she quickly noticed that Malou's attention was elsewhere and that she wasn't at all receptive. "Have you decided what to do about Zlavko's club?" she whispered instead, once Lisa was busy at the other end of the room.

"Pah," Malou answered, her eyes still closed but her jaw tense. "I'll give that entrance test a try. If I don't get accepted, then that's the way it's meant to be."

"What about you, Victoria?" whispered Chamomile.

Victoria was sitting, concentrating on Kirstine, who was lying a little awkwardly on a royal-blue velvet cushion. "It's not for me," Victoria said. "I'm not interested in that kind of secret society. All their secrets and ambitions . . ."

"And privileges?" Malou added.

"Yes, that too."

Malou opened her eyes, and Chamomile could feel how all the muscles in her body tightened. "It's also easy to think that privileges are ridiculous when you've been born with them. The rest of us have to fight for them if we want to get a slice of the cake," she whispered between gritted teeth.

"Chill out, Malou," Chamomile said. "Victoria didn't mean it like that. Anyway, maybe you should think about that. People are starting to talk . . ."

"What do you mean?" Malou sat up. This time, several of the others opened their eyes and watched them.

"Well, people say that it's only students from magic's so-called 'dark side' who've been invited. The Blood and Death branches?"

"*Magic's dark side*—what kind of nonsense is that? It sounds like something people said in the 1800s. There's no such difference made between the branches like that anymore," Malou argued.

"No, but some people were saying that," Chamomile muttered.

"Well, that's just total crap," Malou said. "I thought you were above that kind of gossip." She shot Chamomile her signature scornful look, but for once, Chamomile felt she might have deserved it this time. Malou was right, she shouldn't go getting hung up on whatever people were spreading around in the corridors.

"Malou, if you do not want to take part in today's lesson, I think you should leave the classroom." With her hands on her hips, Lisa glared at Malou, who barely hesitated before shrugging, standing up, and marching across and out of the room, door slamming behind her. Lisa sighed and shook her head, before turning to the rest of the class. "Try and settle peacefully again and continue the exercise. We still have a good quarter of an hour left of class."

"Why don't you all go ahead, there's something I need to do," Chamomile said, and waved to Victoria and Kirstine, after Lisa had thanked them for today's lesson.

Out in the corridor, Chamomile went the opposite direction from the canteen, where the others were all heading for lunch. Malou was not the only one with something on her mind at the moment. She couldn't keep on going around in the hope of getting a glimpse of him. She needed to decide whether to tell him or not. It might be for the best to leave it alone, like Malou had said. And that would certainly be the easiest way. He had no idea that she was his daughter, and if she were to say anything, it would change everything forever. She could forget about it, her mother would be relieved, and she herself would avoid being let down if he didn't want anything to do with her.

She was so deep in her own thoughts that she didn't notice him. It was only at the last second that she stopped short before bumping right into him.

"Hey, look out!"

"Oh, sorry. I wasn't paying attention."

Jens nodded, distracted, and was about to carry on down the hall when he stopped dead. "I get the feeling I've been bumping into you fairly often." His gaze, which had been distant and self-occupied before was now suddenly focused, and he scrutinized her as if she were a puzzle he needed to solve. "Is there something you'd like to speak to me about?"

"What? Oh, no," Chamomile mumbled, realizing she was finding it hard to look him in the eyes. In fact, she was having trouble seeing anything at all. Oh no, was she going to start crying? *No, no, no, stop it, you!* That was the worst thing that could happen right now. But what could she do? Chamomile felt the tears welling up. She lowered her head toward the floor and hoped with all her heart that Jens would simply continue down the hall and leave her alone.

"Shall we go up to my office? I have half an hour before my next lesson. Come this way!"

Chamomile searched vainly for an excuse, but in the end, she gave up and trudged up the stairs after Jens, discreetly wiping the tears from her cheeks.

She had never been in the principal's office before, but she knew where it was: above the teachers' corridor in a corner office with a view over the park. Jens opened the door and showed her in with a friendly wave of his hand. The office was enormous, with very high ceilings and a huge desk made of polished dark wood. The floor was covered in thick carpet, which seemed to block out all noise. The wall at one end was filled with books, but it was the other wall that drew Chamomile's eye. It was decked out from floor to ceiling with paintings, drawings, and sketches in all different sizes. They were arranged in a way that resembled a complex jigsaw puzzle, where the white wall only showed as a single white frame around each picture. She stepped hesitantly nearer.

"Feel free to have a closer look," said Jens, gesturing with his hand. "Unfortunately, I myself do not have a talent for painting, but I really love to study artworks—and to own them. Are you interested in art?"

"Eh, yes, I suppose . . ." answered Chamomile, grateful that Jens seemed happy to talk about his hobby. Because as long as he talked, she didn't have to.

"Artists have a wonderful ability to show us things that cannot be said or written in words," Jens told her. "As humans, we are condemned to only ever seeing through our own eyes, but when we look at an artist's work, we get to see the world as he or she has seen it in that moment. I think that's something really special."

Chamomile let her gaze roam over the paintings. Most of them were old oil paintings in thick dark-gold frames, but there were also some black-and-white line drawings and a few Asian-looking illustrations. In that sense, they were very different, but there was a sense anyway that all of them had something in common.

"They are all depictions of . . . ghosts?"

"Yes. Ghosts, spirits, demons, poltergeists, souls . . . That's what I collect, quite specifically: representations of spirits in art. That's my own personal interest, of course. It has always fascinated me how this ability I have might be experienced by others. Through art, I get an insight into that."

Chamomile nodded. She knew, of course, that spirit mages were able to see things others couldn't. But that they didn't necessarily see the same as others with the same ability was something she hadn't thought about before. She stopped in front of a very large painting.

"This is the crown jewel of the collection," Jens said with pride. "It's called *The Nightmare*, and it was painted by the artist Henry Fuseli in 1781. The painting became very famous in its own time, and so the artist painted several versions. The other pictures are on display in museums around the world, but only one single painting was privately owned. I managed to get permission to buy it last year."

Chamomile studied the picture. It showed a young woman draped backward over a bed. She wore a white gown that clung to her body, and squatting on her chest was a repulsive demon-like creature, who stared out toward the viewer.

"That's pretty creepy," she said.

"Indeed. Meeting with the dead can be both an unpleasant and uncomfortable experience. But that can also be the case with the living."

Chamomile nodded. *Oh yes.* She knew all about that. She had the feeling Jens knew that her thoughts would have turned to Vitus and what had happened the year before. Perhaps he thought that was what she wanted to talk to him about? Or perhaps he had already worked it out somehow, perhaps he had known a long time. He was so clever, after all . . .

"I think maybe you're my dad," Chamomile said suddenly, and then immediately clapped her hand to her mouth. She hadn't been planning on simply blurting it out like that. What was she thinking?

"What?" Jens looked at her, astonished. "What did you say?"

Oh no. He had very clearly *not* worked it out himself.

Chamomile took a deep breath. "I think—or I know—that you are my dad. My mom's name is Beate, you were . . . together?"

"Beate, yeah, but . . . Beate has a daughter?" He looked at her, his eyes jumping from her face to her hair, and then it was like something fell into place, as if she saw a glimpse of recognition in his blue eyes. "I think I need to sit down a moment," he said.

To: asl@bib.kk.dk
Re: Missing girl

Dear Anders,

Do you remember me? You were kind enough to help me in the summer when I was looking for information about a girl who went missing back in 1989. I need your help again.
Would you be able to check if there is any mention at all in local media of a girl with the name Leah Severinsen? Or if there's anything on the girl's address? It's Solvangen 11, Kalundborg.

Thanks in advance,
Malou Nielsen

OCTOBER 31ST
9:14 P.M.

Malou

Malou pressed send and pressed the laptop shut. It couldn't do any harm, even though it was still highly unlikely that the pet name Trine had for her sister would ever pop up in the national library archives. But they were running out of options. According to Chamomile, Victoria was feeling miserable about being unable to contact Trine, and Chamomile had banned them from asking any more about it. Victoria didn't seem especially down, though, thought Malou. Maybe if she spent a little less time dreaming about Benjamin's biceps, then she might well be able to find out the nickname.

Malou looked in the kitchenette. The other girls had gotten started preparing an impromptu Halloween party. Chamomile had gotten hold of some pumpkin pie from the kitchen, Sara and Sofie had brought a huge stash of candy, and Anne had also pitched in with some of her first-year friends. They were all dressed up as vampires, with big plastic fangs in their mouths, making it impossible to understand what they were saying.

Suddenly the kitchen filled with people, and Malou overheard a few of the girls debating if it would be too risky to invite some boys as well. She had excused herself on the grounds of a headache, but instead of going to bed, she had packed a small bag with her stuff, and now she saw her chance to leave the dorms without anyone noticing in the middle of the celebrations.

Malou tiptoed down the stairs and along the corridors. All the lights in the school were switched off, and instead, carved lanterns and lamps dotted the rooms, casting a flickering light from their flames. A pumpkin's creepy grimace met her as she crept around one corner. She didn't know for sure where she was going because she hadn't been there before, but it had to be down in the castle cellars somewhere. Malou felt her insides tighten into a knot just at the thought of it. As long as it wasn't right down in the farthest cellar, where Vitus had dragged Chamomile and where all of them had nearly died in the flames. Malou had no desire whatsoever to see that place ever again.

By the entrance to the dining hall, she spotted Zlavko and a few other students. The tall Amalie was there already, and beside her the small, pale girl with big staring eyes. Malou nodded to the others but didn't say anything. After a few minutes, another handful of students arrived. Louis, whose shoulder-length white-blond hair was pulled back in a ponytail, was together with a dark, handsome third-year boy who had a slightly odd twitch in his left eye. Malou also recognized a girl from her own year called Asta.

"That must be all of us then." Zlavko nodded, satisfied. "We're going to be in the old kitchens, underneath the castle. It's this way."

Malou was reassured that the original school kitchen, thankfully, was not down where the oldest cellars were, but instead lay roughly below the dining hall. Under the cellar vaults, the fireplaces were still preserved and the walls there were still covered in soot from when the cooks and kitchen maids of old had prepared all of Rosenholm's food.

The students stood in the middle of the high-ceilinged room while Zlavko went around lighting lanterns hanging along the walls. They could see now that chairs had been set out for them in a circle. In the middle of the circle there was a single chair and a small table. Malou realized how seriously nervous she actually was. They hadn't been told anything about what was expected of them. Only that they needed to show they were worthy as a member of the Crows' Club by demonstrating their magical abilities. Every night for a whole week now she had practiced making water boil. Yesterday, she had succeeded three times in a row, so she felt fairly sure she could get it to work, but would it be enough to impress Zlavko?

"I hope you have all come well prepared," said Zlavko, his voice low but nevertheless filling the room around them. It was as if the sound was being thrown back by the arched ceilings. "Who would like to start? Albert?"

Albert nodded seriously and stepped forward into the middle of the floor. His tics went crazy as soon as the other students were all looking at him, and Malou felt a tinge of sympathy for him, which was unusual for her. Albert exchanged a look with Zlavko, then fumblingly pulled out some objects, which he placed on the table. Then he sat upright on the chair and cleared his throat several times.

"Zlavko will now ask you to take a card, and I will tell you which one you have picked," he mumbled, staring at his own hands.

Card tricks? Okay, that's a bit of a cliché, is it not?

Albert was still for a moment, as if gathering his focus, and when he raised his face to them again, his eyes were white. Malou felt a shiver go through her. She had seen Victoria's whitened eyes plenty times before, but it was still always uncomfortable when spirit mages were "seeing" in that way.

Malou had to admit that Albert's presentation wasn't half as pathetic as she had first expected. The students got the chance to pick different playing cards and roll a die, and every time, Albert knew which card they had or which number they had rolled. They were also then asked to draw something, and he would then tell them what the drawing showed, without seeing the piece of paper. Only on one occasion did he have to give up on guessing—but this turned out to have more to do with Louis's drawing abilities—even when he held his paper up in front of him, nobody had been able to identify what he'd drawn, which was, apparently, a bicycle.

When Albert was finished, applause broke out.

"Well done, Albert," Zlavko praised him. "Spirit mages often make good stage magicians—and good stage magicians are often spirit mages. It is always useful to have an invisible friend who can look over people's shoulders. Tell me, is it the same spirit you call on every time, or are there different ones?"

"The same," Albert answered. "His name is Eric."

"Well, let's say thank you to Eric as well. Amalie, will you take over from Albert?"

Amalie had brought something that looked like a small cooler bag. From it, she took a bowl and a lump of ice, about the size of a mango. Beside the bowl, she carefully placed a black-handled knife—an athame, similar to the one Zlavko carried. As a rule, only trained blood mages were allowed to carry their own athame, but Amalie must be especially talented. Malou leaned forward in her chair, concentrating, determined to observe it all down to the tiniest detail.

Once Zlavko had given her a sign to get started, Amalie resolutely picked up the athame and made a superficial cut in the palm of her hand, just enough for it to begin to bleed. Then she took the lump of ice in both hands. Seconds passed where Malou couldn't see anything at all. Then the first drops dripped into the bowl, stained red with Amalie's blood, and from there it went faster and faster, the water streaming down as the lump between Amalie's long, strong fingers got smaller and smaller. In less than a minute, she had melted the big lump of ice. Then she took hold of the bowl with both hands. Oh no, this was going to make Malou's own number look like a kindergarten show-and-tell.

In no time at all, Amalie got the water to boil, but she didn't stop there. Steam billowed out of the little bowl until it was finally empty. *Shit!* Never mind how well Malou did with making her water boil, her act would still stand out as a total flop. She wondered if there was any way she could manage to sneak off.

"Impressive!" Zlavko nodded in acknowledgment. "Very well done, indeed, Amalie. But I suspected that you would, of course, shine. Take your place again. Iris, your turn."

The pale, little wide-eyed girl nervously stood up and sat on the chair in the middle of the floor. She looked chilled, even though she was wearing a dark-green knit sweater and had a large white scarf wrapped around her neck. She didn't have any props with her but simply sat waiting, her large eyes turned to Zlavko.

"You can start when you're ready, Iris," Zlavko said.

As soon as he had said the words, she shuddered, cast her head backward, and let out an eerie hissing noise from her throat. When she turned back to them, her eyes were white.

For a long time, nothing else happened. The girl sat as if paralyzed, with her eyes uncannily wide. Malou glanced at the other students.

"There are too many of you, I can only use one," Iris said, giving Malou a start, even though she spoke in barely a whisper. "Thank you," she muttered, and stood up from the chair.

With slow movements, she began to unwind the scarf at her neck. It was made of a thick white cotton threaded through with thin golden threads that caught the light of the flickering lanterns. Iris let the scarf unfold. It was long and reached down to the ground when she held it in her outstretched hands. In one sudden movement, she threw it up in the air so it floated down, but instead of landing on the ground, it fell over some kind of form, which suddenly became visible to them all. A gasp went through the students. Zlavko nodded appreciatively but said nothing.

"Okay, whenever you like . . ." Iris whispered.

All eyes were fixed on the form under the white scarf. Slowly, very slowly and weakly, they could hear it. The spirit was singing. It was not singing through Iris, whose mouth was closed. The sound came from the invisible form. A thin, frail voice. It was a sad melody, but Malou felt it was familiar, though the words were hard to catch. *Lay me in the same coffin, lay me in the same grave . . .*

Now it came back to her. It was a kids' song the girls from her old school had always sung when they were going on some trip or other by bus.

As the song drew to its close, the spirit's voice rose, as if it was getting stronger and stronger. Iris's head, on the other hand, sank toward the ground and her slight body looked like it could barely hold its own weight, while the spirit sang with more and more power. When it finished, Iris fell to the floor by the spirit's feet.

"Iris!"

Several of the students jumped up, but Zlavko held them back. Instead he quickly muttered a string of unintelligible words and made a curious sign with his hands, upon which the spirit collapsed and the scarf fell to the ground. Iris struggled to sit up.

"Sorry," she muttered. "That doesn't normally happen."

"You lost control with that spirit," Zlavko said, watching as Iris got to her feet. "It was unlucky, of course, but saying that, it's rare to see a young mage capable of giving a spirit a fixed form and a voice, as we have just experienced. You have a lot of talent, Iris. Go back to your seat."

After Iris, it was Asta's turn. The girl, who Malou knew fairly superficially, didn't have much luck with demonstrating her abilities in spirit magic. Zlavko was clearly disappointed and unhappy with Asta's dubious attempt to tell Amalie's fortune. The students clapped, dutifully, but Asta returned to her seat blushing. Malou was certain that Asta would not get into Zlavko's club on the basis of that performance, and judging by Asta's crestfallen expression, she had realized the same thing. If Malou was lucky, she could at least do better than Asta.

But first it was Louis's turn. He stepped confidently up to the floor.

"I thought we should relive another Rosenholm tradition this evening. Namely, a mages' duel." He smiled, as if he had just announced there would be a box of candy for every student. "And for that, I'm gonna need a volunteer. Don't worry, it's not dangerous at all. I just need someone to demonstrate something on. Albert, could I borrow you?"

“Let’s make it more interesting,” Zlavko interrupted. “Choose a blood mage, Louis. Blood against blood. Malou, you help Louis, please.”

“Perfect,” Louis said, and nodded to her. “I would like to present the beautiful and ancient combative technique of iaijutsu,” he said, addressing the students. And with a slightly twisted smile, he suddenly pulled a long, slim sword out of a sheath that hung at his side, unnoticed by Malou until now in the darkness of the cellar.

“This is called a katana,” said Louis, as he swung the sword gracefully through the air so that it made a crisp swishing sound. “The choice weapon of the samurai. Light, elegant, and as sharp as a razor.” He sounded as if he were talking about a girlfriend he was completely in love with. “Now, my lovely assistant and I will show you how it should be used.” He turned, calmly, toward her.

“To hell with that,” Malou hissed. “I’m just supposed to stand still while you stab me with that thing?”

“No,” Louis said. “You should stand still while I try to *not* stab you with this thing.”

He took the sword in both hands. His expression turned to one of concentration, his pupils widened, and suddenly he sprang toward her while flicking the sword. Lightning fast, he did a series of moves, advancing on her. The sword whistled through the air so close that she felt a light draft on her cheek. She heard the onlookers gasp, but she didn’t dare to even breathe.

Louis’s movements were as fast and elegant as a dancer’s, but that wasn’t what made his display so remarkable. Time became almost elastic around him. Some of his movements happened so unnaturally fast that they seemed like a trick of the eye. In other moments, he moved as if he were underwater. He leaped effortlessly, hung in the air for too long, and changed direction mid-jump. She had never seen anything like it. The only sound came from the swishing of the blade.

Malou stood, statue-like, not daring to move even a millimeter for fear Louis could cut off an ear or her nose with his dumb sword. She had no choice but to stand there like a prop in his performance, and soon it would be her turn to make a fool of herself on the same set with her own pathetic routine. She could feel how the anger rose up inside her like a bubble and swept away the inertia that had gripped her.

Finally Louis finished up his show and bowed elegantly to his audience, as wild applause broke out. But his smug smile stiffened when he looked at Malou.

"Oh, sorry. I might have caught you."

Malou put her hand up to her face. She hadn't noticed anything but now there was blood on her fingers. He'd made a shallow cut in her left cheek.

"I'm sorry," he said, and stepped toward her. "Is it deep?"

The hit came when he was least expecting it and took him so completely off guard that he lost his grip of the sword, which fell to the floor. Malou had punched him on his right shoulder, right on the joint, where the arm is most vulnerable, and she didn't stand waiting for his next move. Instead she circled nimbly behind him and delivered a kick to the back of his knee, so his leg doubled under him. He fell to all fours, but when Malou went to kick him in the stomach, he rolled away. It was like a forward roll played backward, and to her surprise, he landed neatly on his feet with his arms raised in an attack position.

Malou could feel the blood thundering around her body, and she let it. She went with the flow, she didn't think. With a yell, she went for him. He dodged but held off from hitting out again, and she took advantage of the opening and got in with her elbow to his face. He let out a groan of pain and, with one flowing movement, threw her over one hip so that she fell hard on her back. Malou jumped to her feet just as fast as he had. His lip was bleeding. She had wounded him back. It was gushing blood and giving her a power that she didn't quite understand but felt willing to use. He should not go thinking he could get away with humiliating her in front of them all. *My lovely assistant. Yeah, right!*

This time when she attacked, he was ready, and in a flash he sprang aside. She had no chance to register that he suddenly wasn't where he had been standing a split second before. She screamed in anger when he took her down and she found herself on the ground once again. Louis positioned himself over her, poised with a punch to her throat to show he had taken the upper hand. Malou fumed. She didn't give a damn about his stupid gentleman's rules. Maybe he had taken some fancy fencing lessons or something, but she had learned to fight the hard way. When Louis straightened up to take a step back from her, she kicked out, sweeping his feet from under him and delivering a punch in the face and a bleeding nose. He fell roughly to the ground, and Malou stood over him with one foot on his neck.

"Who won?" she panted, leaning some weight onto the foot pressing on his throat.

"You won," he hissed. The blood was streaming down over his mouth. But he was smiling.

To Malou Nielsen

It is my pleasure to inform you that
you have been approved as a candidate for
membership of the Crow's Club.

Kind regards,
Zlavko

CORVUS OCULUM CORVI NON ERUIT

Miss you

Me too

When can we see each other?
Are you going home at the weekend?

No, not this weekend ☹
We've got a mound sit-out
with Thorbjørn

Then I'll come to you!

No—what if you get caught?

I won't. It went fine last time,
didn't it?

. . .

NOVEMBER 14TH
9:05 P.M.

Kirstine

Even as they stood by the stairs, waiting, Kirstine already knew it was a mistake. She shouldn't have come.

"Have you all come dressed for the weather? We'll be sitting out for at least three hours, and they're predicting temperatures around zero tonight." Thorbjørn looked around at them standing in the great hall, wrapped in thick coats, hats, and scarves. Kirstine's fingers were already ice-cold in her mittens, but it wasn't because of the temperature. She was afraid. She had managed to get away with not taking part in the practical lessons so far, but Thorbjørn had made it clear that this evening's lesson was compulsory for all.

"Tonight, we will try out our powers in gravemound sitting, which is an important part of the second-year curriculum. Gravemound sitting is a specific type of seid, and I'll tell you a bit about its history before we leave. In Völuspá, the Prophecy of the Seeress, we learn of a vølve named Heid." Thorbjørn pulled a tattered book out of his pocket and opened it to a page near the beginning:

"Alone she sat out when the lord of gods,
Óthin the old, her eye did seek:
'What seeks to know, why summon me?
Well know I, Ygg, where thy eye is hidden.'"

Thorbjørn looked up at them.

"Here we learn that the seeress is 'sitting out'—a phrase with a double meaning. Literally, she is sitting out in nature, but it can also mean to be in a state of ecstasy. The seeress meets Odin, and the poem is about how, in her ecstasy, she has a vision of both the world's creation and of the world's future: Ragnarok." He closed the book and tucked it tenderly back in his pocket, as if it were a living creature. "When having a sit-out, the usual practice is to sit from sunset to sunrise, present in nature and away from any lights, food, phones or anything else that distracts one's attention. Some people choose to fast first, in order to make the experience more intense. Today we'll make a start by sitting for three hours. As the night darkens and falls, you will experience the natural world around you in a completely different way, and if you are very lucky, you might see a vision, which we can interpret together afterward. Are there any questions?"

Nobody raised their hand, so they headed out through the hall and across the moat. The moon was full and Thorbjørn did not want them to use flashlights, as it would keep their eyes from adjusting to the dark. Quickly, Kirstine discovered he was right. The light of the moon was enough to guide themselves by. The night was clear and still, but cold, and it would take them an hour to walk to their destination: an ancient Viking burial mound, some way down a farm track running parallel to the road. She had never been there before, only heard talk that it was a ship setting—a burial mound marked by huge stones in the shape of a ship. Probably to symbolize the journey between the worlds of the living and the dead.

The girls set off slowly. Some of them chattered and laughed, but Kirstine lagged behind. Despite the beauty of the full moon, her unease kept growing, and the farther from the castle they went, the stronger was her feeling that she shouldn't have gone with them at all.

"Thorbjørn?" Kirstine sidled up to the big man where he was walking, a little behind the gaggle of students trudging along the narrow lane.

"Yes, what is it?" rumbled his deep voice.

"I don't feel too good. I think its best that I go back," she said. "I feel like I may be getting sick."

"Hmm. Are you sure that's the reason?"

"What do you mean?"

"The semester is coming to an end and you've still not really taken part in our practical lessons—every time, there is some new excuse. It's almost as if you are frightened of something or other?"

Kirstine said nothing. She hadn't seen a puddle ahead of her in the dark and felt mud splashing up on her trousers.

"What you went through last year, it was very violent. But you don't need to worry. A sit-out is a calm and meditative activity, where you focus inward. And if you are nervous, we can arrange that you are sitting near me."

"I just don't think it's a good idea . . ." Kirstine tried, but Thorbjørn dismissed her outright.

"Of course you should be with us. It will all go fine. Whoa, we need to turn here."

They continued along a fence and past a birch copse, the white bark glimmering in the night light. Then there they were. This was a small burial ground. Some others reached up to almost a thousand feet in length and were made of hundreds of stones, but this one was much smaller and the years had taken their toll on the site. Many of the larger stones were overturned and lay on their side, almost hidden in the grass. Others still stood like proud old men in the moon's silvery glow. Thorbjørn asked them to find a place to sit around the burial mound, in the woods or in the field. Each should find their own space, so as not to disturb one another.

Kirstine walked hesitantly closer. She felt herself drawn toward those large stones, and under the thin soles of her rain boots there was a buzzing.

NOVEMBER 14TH
10:36 P.M.

Victoria

A white shadow could be seen in among the birch trees in the woods; it flickered black and white. *A spirit.* Victoria looked at it, holding her breath. Was it Trine?

She sat still as it came nearer. No, the shape was tall and wide. It was a man. The disappointment came as a jolt through the peaceful night. Besides Trine, Victoria usually saw spirits only as white shadow, but recently, more and more of them had materialized for her so clearly it was as if they were alive. The spirit now wandering through the forest looked strong and walked like he had a reason for being there. He was pulling something behind him with one hand, but she was unable to see what it was. It was heavy, perhaps an animal slain in the forest. The spirit continued farther into the trees and seemed not to notice her sitting there.

Victoria let out a long sigh, relieved that the spirit didn't seek her out. Perhaps it was because of Trine's absence that she now saw other spirits so clearly; perhaps Trine had somehow been protecting her until now. And now she had disappeared. Victoria did not know why, but the fact was, Trine had abandoned her, and no matter how she tried, Victoria could not make contact with her. Never mind asking her what name she had used for her little sister.

She was torn from her thoughts by a distant growling sound. *Could it be a fox or a badger, maybe?* She stood up and listened. Her legs had gotten stiff and cold from sitting so long. A new sound broke the silence—this time it was somewhere between a growl and a scream. *Something is wrong.* Victoria stumbled out through the forest's edge, and when she reached the muddy field, she fell. The damp earth soaked through her trousers. Close by, a branch snapped. It was Chamomile, who had also come out of the woods.

"What's going on?" she asked.

"I don't know, I think it's coming from the burial mound."

Suddenly, a scream cut through the night silence, this time loud and piercing. *A scream of pain.*

"Come on!" Chamomile started to run and Victoria followed. The thick mud clung to her rain boots.

When they reached the burial mound, they could see the other students gathered around it. In the middle stood a twisted silhouette, lit by a bonfire below. No, not a bonfire, but the grass itself was alight, orange-colored flames flickering around her feet. She screamed again.

"Kirstine!" Victoria wanted to run to her, but somebody grabbed hold of her and held her back.

"We're not to go near. Thorbjørn forbid it!" Malou said by her ear. Now Victoria noticed Thorbjørn standing nearby Kirstine. He was muttering a series of incantations without pause and waving his hands in the air as if he were painting. Kirstine's body was contorted strangely as if in the grip of a painful cramp.

"Why doesn't he do something?" whispered Chamomile.

Slowly, Thorbjørn started to get closer to her, all the while holding his hands up in front of him. Kirstine let out a sound like a low growl, but Thorbjørn pressed on, reciting words louder and louder. When he was almost right up to her, he took a sudden, rapid step and placed both hands on her body. At that moment, Kirstine let out a loud scream. The sound rang out through the night, and Victoria felt pain in her own body, a terrible, intense pain that burned from the inside.

"Let her go!" she cried. "You're hurting her!"

But Thorbjørn held fast, his huge body locked on to hers.

"He's trying to lift her!" Chamomile sobbed. "Why can't he manage to lift her?"

Chamomile was right. Thorbjørn was trying to lift Kirstine, up and off of the burial mound. But it was as if she was nailed to the ground. For a split second, Victoria thought of the mighty Thor of Norse mythology, who couldn't lift Utgard—Loki's cat—because it was actually the Midgard serpent in disguise.

"Aaaargh!" Thorbjørn screamed—noises of both pain and desperation, and then Kirstine came free, or it may have been the earth beneath her that let her go. They tumbled out of the ship setting and landed in the mud.

"Get back!" Thorbjørn grunted. "Don't touch her!" He struggled to his feet and looked for a moment at his great hands, while Kirstine still lay unconscious in the grass. The light from the smoldering grass and the moon revealed his palms covered in huge burn blisters.

"What happened?" cried Chamomile, but Thorbjørn didn't answer, he just gathered Kirstine up in his arms and started to run toward the castle.

Stumbling through the darkness, they followed them.

"Did you hear what she said?" Malou asked, as they hurried away.

"What do you mean?" Victoria said. "I only heard her screaming."

"No, at first she also said something. It sounded like a prophecy."

"But what did she say?" Chamomile asked.

"'Fulfill your promise before the night that leads into summer. Or else she will kill, or else she will die . . .' That's what she said."

NOVEMBER 16TH
7:30 P.M.

Kirstine

Kirstine woke up. It was dark where she lay, but light leaked in at the sides of the door to the hallway. Was it night? She found her phone and checked the time. The movement made her groan in pain. Her muscles ached like a raw wound even though there were no visible injuries on her body, and she felt as if she had been broken into pieces on the inside.

For the first couple of days, she had been in a deep, dreamless sleep, helped on her way by Lisa's herbs and Ingrid's charms. But as they gradually reduced the strong herbal remedies, so, too, had her pain become more and more real.

The door to the bedroom creaked open and Kirstine turned toward it.

"Oh, um, am I disturbing you?" The form filled the whole doorway, blocking most of the light from the room.

"No, it's okay. I was awake," she said.

Thorbjørn went to her bed. He looked flummoxed, for a moment she feared the huge man was going to sit on the edge of it.

"There's a chair over there, if . . ." she said.

"Ah, yes, well, thank you," he mumbled. He pulled the chair to her bedside and sat down.

Kirstine turned on the lamp, which cast a yellow glow on Thorbjørn's serious expression. He now looked even more uncomfortable than usual, she decided. First, she thought that he had mittens on, white ones, but then she realized both his hands were wrapped in bandages.

"How are you?" he asked.

"I'm really tired," she said. "I can't remember what happened . . . ?"

"I only noticed what was happening when you were standing in the middle of the ship setting and it was already burning all around you . . ." His voice broke and he had to clear his throat before continuing, "Kirstine, I'm sorry I didn't listen to you when you said you didn't want to go with us."

"You couldn't have known . . ." she said

"No, but you . . . you knew, didn't you?"

"I was scared that . . . something would happen," she whispered.

"And at the ceremony, when you fainted—that wasn't because you forgot to have enough to drink, was it?"

Kirstine shook her head.

"Will you tell me what happened?"

She turned her face away from him, away from the light. It was easier to speak into the dark. "It was as if the tree knew that I was there. It sounds crazy, but I think the roots were reaching out for me, and when I wanted to run away, I couldn't. That's how it felt at the ship setting as well. I was fixed to the ground, as if I had grown roots myself. And then suddenly it was like I was burning on the inside . . ."

Thorbjørn nodded, as if she were confirming his fearful suspicions.

"I'm going mad, right?" Her voice cracked. "There's something wrong with me. It's because I killed him . . ."

"No," Thorbjørn said gently. "You are not going mad. And it is not your fault, what's happening here. But I think it *does* have something to do with what happened when . . . when Vitus died. And I am afraid you might be in danger. Can you remember what you said, when you were standing inside the ship setting?"

"No . . ." Kirstine couldn't remember a thing, other than the pain and the fire that had burned inside her.

"*Fulfill your promise before the night that leads into summer. Or else she will kill, or else she will die* . . . Does that mean anything to you?"

"No, I don't know what that means. Is it me? Is it me who will die? Or . . . kill?"

"I don't know what your premonition means, and until we know more, we can't rule anything out."

"Why me? What is wrong with me?!"

Thorbjørn took a deep breath and held it for an instant. "That night, at the Spring Ball . . ."

Kirstine nodded in the dark. *That night, that night.* That night, when she killed another human being. She had done it to save her life, but still it had changed her.

"It was me who found you. I don't think you can remember that." Thorbjørn's voice was hoarse and had a vulnerability, which she didn't like, because it felt like pity. She did not want to be the object of anybody's pity. "We had put the fire out in the cellars and the other three were brought up to Ingrid, where she and Lisa took care of them. I couldn't find you," he continued. "So I followed your and Benjamin's tracks through the woods. They took me part of the way, until I could see the glow of the flames.

Benjamin was lying there, seriously injured, and you lay there too, unconscious. And Vitus . . . The fire was still raging . . . He . . . he couldn't be saved."

Thorbjørn stopped for a moment and Kirstine neither spoke nor moved to wipe away the tears running down her cheeks.

"So I took you both back to the castle. When I got back to the clearing, the fire had died out and Vitus was all but gone. Only his hand was sticking up from the ground, and when I got closer, that too disappeared . . ." Thorbjørn's voice was now barely a whisper. "As if it had been pulled down under the tree."

"The tree?"

"Yes. I think the tree took him."

"Why?"

"I didn't know. Back then . . . and afterward, so many things happened. Birgit did not want us to investigate the matter further. But after what happened at the ship setting, I started to look up some old sources . . ."

"Yeah?"

"The great oak out in the clearing is a very, very old and sacred tree. It has been nurtured and celebrated for many hundreds of years. A thousand years ago it was not unusual to make sacrifices to the gods and to holy powers. People would offer weapons, expensive gifts, domestic animals, and horses. And when they really had to, they offered the most valuable thing they had: people."

Kirstine closed her eyes, not wanting to hear any more.

"There are some accounts of how, in Viking times, people would be hanged in the trees that were thought to be the most sacred. It was done to satisfy the higher powers and to get something in return. I believe . . ."

She opened her eyes. "Yes?"

"I believe that the tree has understood it in that way. That you sacrificed Vitus to it. And it accepted your offer."

Kirstine felt a burning feeling in her throat and took a big gulp. "What does that mean?" she whispered.

"I don't exactly know, but I think that the tree has gifted you certain powers, which may become dangerous both for you and for others." He lay a large white bandaged hand on top of hers. "I wish I wasn't telling you all this, but I realized that I have to. Until we understand more about it, you need to be very careful. Don't push yourself too much. Of course, I'll make sure of that during classes, but you must also take care. Don't do anything that might set off your powers. Especially don't . . . fall in love."

Kirstine felt her cheeks beginning to get hot. She knew all too well that romantic feelings turned her magic abilities up by a powerful degree.

"I don't want to have these powers," she said. "How can I get rid of them again?"

"I don't know," he said. "But I am going to do everything I can to sort this out, and until then you need to promise me you'll be careful, Kirstine. I'm frightened that this, in the worst case, could cost somebody their life. Perhaps even yours."

To: coolmalou@gmail.com
Re: Verschwundenes Mädchen

Hi Malou,

Of course I remember you. I hope you managed to do a good assignment—it would be great to be able to read it sometime :) I searched for both the things you sent me. I found nothing at all under the name Leah Severinsen, but I did find an announcement from a local newspaper's crime column referencing that address. It is a strange case, and a little bit unpleasant. The announcement is from November 1995. I have scanned it for you and attached it here.

Kind regards,
Anders

Anders Sahl Larsen
The Royal Library
Christians Brygge 8
1219 Copenhagen K

Kalundborg: Neighbors shocked by double suicide

This Friday evening, police were called to Solvangen 11 in Kalundborg after neighbors had been unable to get in touch with the homeowners for several days. On gaining access to the property, police discovered that both inhabitants, a fifty-one-year-old man and his forty-eight-year-old wife, were dead. Police suspect suicide and have called the incident a family tragedy. The funeral will be held privately, according to the bereaved family's wishes.

November 27, 1988

My dearest Little T,

I feel so sad—I can barely see what I am writing because of the tears! I know you are too little to understand me, but I don't have anyone else to talk to. I don't dare tell any of my school friends for fear they'll gossip. You are the only one I can trust with my secret.

One week ago, I was so happy. Happier than I've ever been before. "He" told me that he loved me, and we kissed—finally! I didn't know it was possible to feel so good.

But then, yesterday, we met and he said that we couldn't see each other because it is too much of a risk. It's totally forbidden at school to have a boyfriend or girlfriend, although lots of kids do it anyway, and I tried to say that to him, but he didn't want to listen.

I'm sure that he still loves me, and I switch between believing he'll change his mind and fearing that this really is the end of us.

I don't know what I should do, LT . . . You should be glad you don't need to worry about love yet, because love really is the most painful thing you can imagine. Love is crap!

Your unhappy sister,

Trine

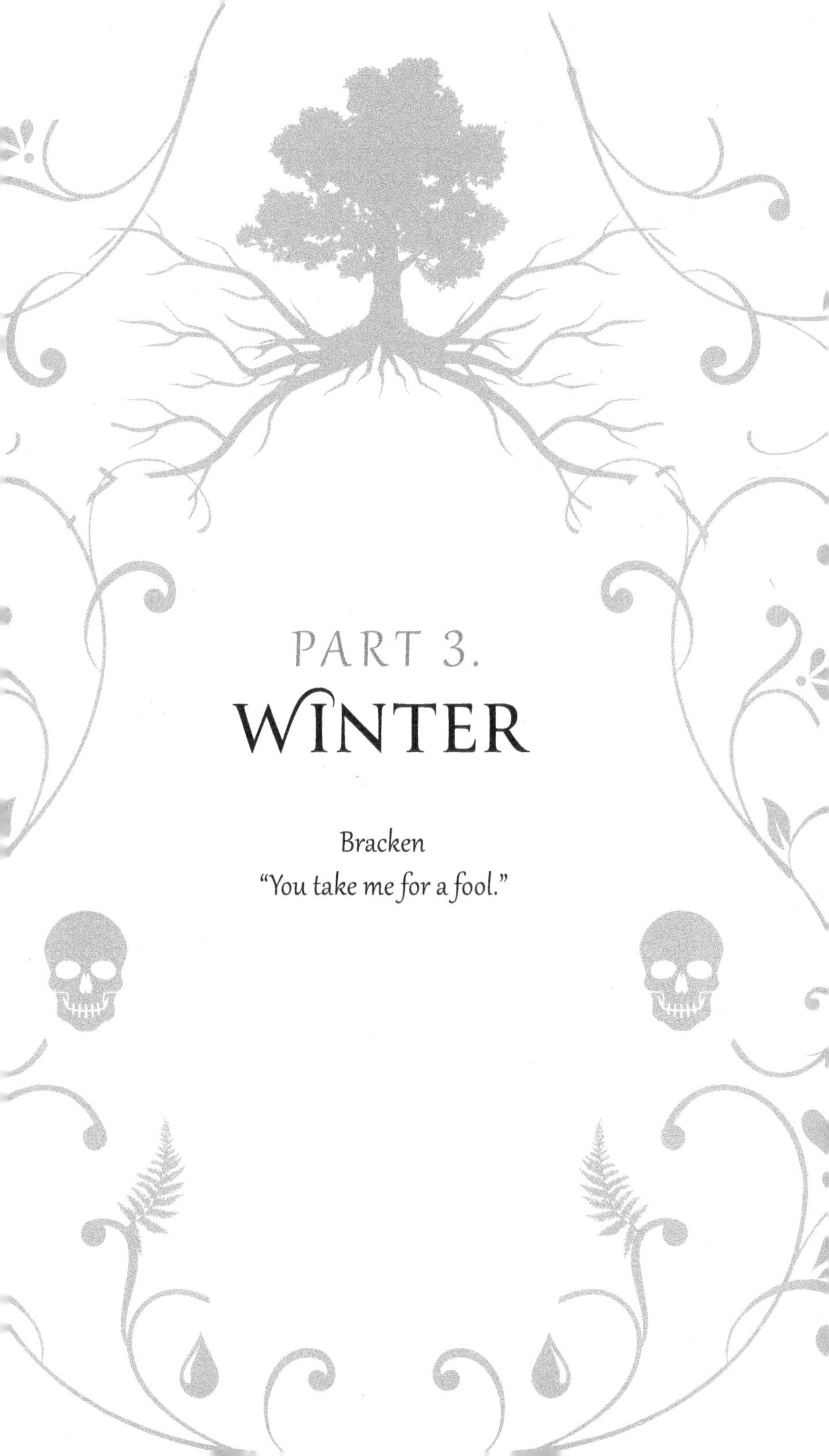

PART 3.
WINTER

Bracken
"You take me for a fool."

DECEMBER 10TH
3:47 P.M.

Chamomile

Chamomile sat in one of the library's deep armchairs, flicking through a book. *Celtic Festivals of the Pre-Christian Era* was written on its brown leather cover. She was looking for a particular section of the book, and when she found it, she read through the text again, scribbling now and then in her notebook. Then she read through what she had written.

Walpurgis Night. The last night of April. Celts and Germanic peoples celebrated the transition from winter to summer. Vigils were held to ward off underworld spirits. People built bonfires, only to be lit using wild fire: fire ignited using the traditional method of rubbing two sticks or branches together. It was later believed that witches met on this night.

She had found the book earlier that day when the whole class was at the library with Thorbjørn, but she had come back to read this again in peace and quiet. Walpurgis Night marked the transition into summer. Chamomile found that a bit strange. Nowadays people think of summer starting in June, but apparently that's not how they saw it in the olden days. She chewed on the end of her pen, before noting down the prophecy underneath what she had just written.

Fulfill your promise.

It was not difficult to understand. It had to be the promise they had made to Trine. The promise to find her killer.

Before the night that leads into summer.

If it meant Walpurgis Night, then it meant before April 30th.

Or else she will kill, or else she will die.

Or else who would kill? Kirstine? It was her who had delivered the prophecy. Or was it her who, according to the prophecy, would die, if they didn't find Trine's murderer? Chamomile made a summary at the bottom:

Find Trine's killer before April 30th or (. . . ?) will die.

She stared at the words. Then she crossed them out. There was still plenty of time; they should be able to manage it.

Chamomile checked her phone for the time, snapped the book shut, and put it back in its place. She had somewhere to be, and she didn't want to be late.

Once she was standing at the huge oak door, she didn't know whether she should knock or just go in. In the end, she did a strange combination of a halfhearted knock and quickly opening the door without waiting for an answer.

Jens's office was empty. Should she go outside again and wait? What if he had forgotten? And what would she say if one of the teachers came along and saw her standing in the hallway outside the principal's office? Chamomile shook her head to cut off the stream of thoughts and instead went over to the massive bookcase where a group of low armchairs sat around a coffee table. She perched on one of the chairs and waited. Luckily, Jens soon came in the door. He backed into the door so he didn't need to put down the tray he was carrying.

"Ah, you're here," he said when he saw her. "Good, good. I was just getting us some tea. And Vibeke from the kitchen has been so kind as to bake us some madeleines. She knows they're my favorite." He laid the tray on the coffee table. On it were a petite silver teapot, white China cups, cake forks, and an ornate dish of small golden cakes in the shape of mussel shells. There were also two white napkins, pressed and starched—or whatever it was you did with those things—so much that they almost stood up by themselves. Jens put his napkin carefully on his lap. His hands were broad and strong, but his movements were elegant as he poured them each some tea, offered Chamomile a cake, and took one himself.

"Vibeke makes them with almond milk and a hint of lemon zest. They really are good," he said, and Chamomile politely bit into one of the perfectly formed cakes, while wondering how exactly her mother and Jens had fallen for one another.

Of course, they do say opposites attract.

They sat for a while without talking. She never normally had any trouble thinking of something to say—her problem was more knowing how to keep quiet. Yet, right now, her mind was blank. She took a big gulp of her tea, burning her tongue, as she noticed that Jens was staring at her. His expression was friendly and curious, but it still felt pretty strange being studied in that way.

"When did Beate tell you that I am your father?" His hesitation before the word *father* was only slight.

"Over the summer," she replied. "I didn't know if I should tell you or not." It ended up sounding like a question.

"I'm certainly glad that you did tell me," said Jens. "I thought I had gotten too old to have children, and then suddenly . . . Can I ask you, have you ever had abilities in spirit magic? It's not so rare for magical abilities to be hereditary."

Chamomile shook her head. "No, in that sense I definitely take after my mom," she said, and touched the silver leaf, which showed she belonged to Growth magic.

"Ah, of course." Jens nodded. "And you don't have any siblings?"

"That's a question I would ask you. My mom only has me."

"I don't have any children," said Jens, and for a moment looked horrified by his own slip of the tongue. "Other than you, I mean," he quickly added.

"So I'm still an only child," she concluded, not quite knowing if she was relieved or disappointed.

Jens took a deep breath, as if considering carefully what to say. "I hope you understand that we will need to keep this a secret. At least for a time. You see, I was a good bit older than your mother, and I was her teacher. It was my first year at the school as a teacher, and if it were to come out, just when I've been made principal, then . . ."

"It's absolutely fine, I haven't told anyone yet," Chamomile said, observing him discreetly. Yeah, he was older than her mother, but he seemed strong and fit, and in no way like an old man. Okay, his hair was a silvery gray, but it was thick and glossy.

Jens topped off their teas once more and took another cake. "It's strange to think how different things could have turned out, if I had known Beate was pregnant when we split up," he commented.

She nodded. "I don't know if I'll ever be able to forgive her for not saying something."

"I'm sure she was doing what she thought was best. Your mother had her own ideas about things, as far as I remember."

"Yeah, that's for sure," Chamomile blurted out.

"But has she been a good mother? I mean, have you been okay?"

Suddenly Chamomile had a lump in her throat. "My mom . . . she's actually pretty fantastic. I had a really great childhood." It was only as she said the words aloud that she realized how true they were.

"That's good," said Jens. "That's the most important thing, after all. You hear so many things."

"My friend doesn't exactly have it easy with her family."

"Really, Victoria?" said Jens.

"Victoria? I meant Malou," Chamomile said, confused.

"Ah, Malou. I don't know her family."

"But you do know Victoria's?"

"Yes, I know them. Or rather, I know *of* them. It can't be easy for her. That's also why I am a little concerned that she might run into trouble."

"Trouble? Victoria? But what is it about her family . . . ?"

"Hmm, I'm worried I may have spoken out of turn," said Jens, wriggling a little in his chair. "I thought you knew . . ." He paused, looking out through the large windows facing onto the park. "I can't really tell you much more—I am still the principal here, even though I am also your dad—but I can say this much: Victoria's abilities in spirit magic are unusually powerful. That's also the reason I offered her extra lessons last year, but unfortunately she stopped coming. I do wonder, now and then, how she is doing."

"She's fine," Chamomile said without hesitating, while picturing Victoria before her, hunched over her phone and her endless messages with Benjamin, or on her way out to a secret date that she thought none of them knew about.

"I'm glad to hear that," said Jens. "And it's good to know she has someone like you to keep an eye on her and look out for her. Friends are so important, not least for Victoria. It can turn out pretty bad if a spirit manages to assert their control over a young spirit mage."

"What do you mean?" asked Chamomile.

"Well, spirits can have all kinds of motives. There may be something or other that the dead person didn't manage to fully realize in life, and they are having difficulty letting go of that. In that case, they try to get the living to fulfill tasks for them. They might even try to make the person commit to a promise."

"A promise? And what happens if you make a promise to a spirit?"

"That is something you should never do," said Jens gravely. "If you make a heartfelt promise to a spirit, you can never break it. The spirit will continue to pester you and drain you of your energy for life, and if you don't do the thing that you promised to, sooner or later, it ends fatally." He looked at her sharply for a moment. "Listen, you're not saying that Victoria has been so silly as to promise something to a spirit?"

"What? No, I don't think so," Chamomile said, suddenly feeling quite hot under the collar. "I just thought it sounded interesting. So there is nothing you can do, if you have made a promise to a dead person?"

"Nothing except fulfilling the promise." Jens rubbed his chin with the one hand, the brush of his stubble making a light rasping noise. "I daresay a victory stone could possibly buy a little extra time. Huge power can be contained in a little talisman like that."

"A victory stone?"

"Yes. Unfortunately they are incredibly rare and almost impossible to get a hold of. But it was just a hypothetical question, was it not?"

"Of course."

At that moment, there was a knock on the door. Jakob stuck his head in. "Sorry if I'm disturbing you, but I was sent up to find you, Jens. We are all ready down in the meeting room. For the teachers' meeting."

"Oh, is that today? I must have had other things on my mind," said Jens, winking at her almost imperceptibly before he got up. "I'm on my way, Jakob. I just need a moment to gather my things. I'll be there in two minutes."

"I'll have to run," said Jens, once Jakob had left. "But let's do this again, soon, shall we? And you can come to me anytime, if there's anything you want to ask me, or if there's anything upsetting you . . ." He hesitated and studied her for a moment. "Will you promise me that?"

"For sure," Chamomile said, and forced a smile. "And thanks for the tea."

To Chamomile,

Thanks for an interesting chat the other day. I think you might find this book quite exciting. It contains some more information on what we talked about (see page 93, under Amulets).

Best wishes,

Jens

THE VICTORY STONE

These are much sought-after and powerful amulets. Their origins are unknown, but in Faroese folktales it is said that the raven hatches its eggs by laying a stone in its nest, a so-called raven stone or victory stone. If one is quick enough and lucky enough, one can snatch such a stone from the raven's nest before the eggs hatch.

A victory stone is known to bestow upon its owner victory in battle and protection against both people and witchcraft. Furthermore, the stone is very powerful during difficult births and was often carried and used by doulas and midwives. Today, victory stones are very rare and only a few known examples can be accounted for.

Dear Crows,

Our first meeting will take place at Zlavko's apartment at 7:00 p.m. on December 21st (before the Christmas party)

CORVUS OCULUM CORVI NON ERUIT

DECEMBER 21ST
6:50 P.M.

Malou

Malou sat on the broad window ledge in her room and looked out. The endless rain they'd had lately had finally eased off in favor of a crystal-clear frost. Her thoughts turned to the prophecy. To what Chamomile had told them about Walpurgis Night and how you should never make a promise to a spirit. But the deed was already done, and now their only chance was to do what they had promised. Find Trine's killer.

She watched Thorbjørn pacing around down below with a lantern, planting torches in the ground. Later, these would light the way for all the students going down to the tent. But before then, there was something Malou needed to get done. She pulled on her boots and went out into the kitchen.

"Do you want to help make decorations? It's getting pretty late if we're going to get the place all festive-looking before Christmas," Chamomile said, who insisted on wanting a cozy Yuletide vibe, even though they had much more important things to think about right now.

Malou sighed. She had been hoping to sneak out without Chamomile realizing. "Is that what you're wearing to the party?" she asked, instead of answering the question.

Chamomile looked up from the wonky garland she was in the middle of gluing together. "You don't like it?" she asked from her seat at the little kitchen table.

Malou didn't answer but just rolled her eyes. Chamomile had spent the best part of December in the same hideous sweater. On its front there was a reindeer with a red pom-pom nose that dangled around the height of Chamomile's belly. It looked ridiculous.

"Take it easy, Grinch. I'll change into some dress or other before the party starts. But you've already changed?" she said as she started cutting out more strips of glossy paper.

Malou was wearing a faux-leather skirt and snow-white sweater, wide at the shoulders and narrow at the waist. It was polyester, but you couldn't tell. "I just have something to do first. I'll see you at the party, okay?"

"Is this something to do with Zlavko's club? Will you come back, though, so we can head over together?" Chamomile asked, laying down her cuttings. She wore an expression that was a tiring mixture of disappointment and reproach, and exactly what Malou had been hoping to avoid.

"I don't think I'll be able to. Just go with the others, I'll see you down there!"

Malou hurried out the dorm and toward the teachers' corridor. The whole school had been adorned with candle-lit red lanterns, pine cones, and festive garlands. *Whose idea was it to hang naked flames and bone-dry branches all through an old building? What would the fire services say to something like that?* Malou sighed. Maybe Chamomile was right and she simply hated anything to do with Christmas.

She found the right door but hesitated before knocking. The last time she'd knocked on Zlavko's door, things hadn't gone so great from there. But how likely is it to go well, really, when you knock on someone's door to accuse them of a crime?

This time it was a different door. Zlavko had gotten a new apartment on the teachers' floor for this year.

"Shall we go in, or just stand outside?"

It was Louis. They hadn't spoken since she had practically broken his nose at the initiation test.

He gave her a wry smile. "Or maybe you were waiting for me?"

He raised his hand to knock, but Malou got in before him.

"Come in," they heard, in Zlavko's unique accent, from beyond the door, which she slowly opened. The apartment was clearly bigger than the one he'd had the year before. She couldn't actually remember what it had looked like. At the time, he had been packing, and all his things had been strewn all over the place. The room they saw now, though, was meticulously neat. A couple of low sofas sat in the middle of the room on either side of a low dark wooden coffee table. An exotic rug covered the majority of the floor and one wall was covered with a silk wall hanging, decorated all over with elegant calligraphic lettering. Perhaps it was Chinese lettering. The writing was red, and Malou couldn't quash the thought it had quite possibly been written in blood.

"Have a seat," said Zlavko, and it sounded more like an order than an invitation. His long dark hair hung loose, rather than in his usual topknot, but thankfully he had on a black woolen sweater—Malou had feared he might be topless, as he had been at last year's Yule party.

Louis sat down on one of the sofas and Malou sat down opposite him, carefully avoiding looking him in the eye.

Shortly after, Amalie arrived together with Albert; after them came Iris and a short girl with dark curls, and then a few more until everyone was accounted for.

"So that seems like all of us," said Zlavko, setting down a tray of elegant, tall glasses on the table between them. "As today is a special day, I think we should start with a toast. Soon we will head down to the tent for one of the year's highlights, the annual Yule celebration. But first it is my pleasure to welcome you to the first official meeting of the Crows' Club." Zlavko opened the lid of a black-lacquered case and pulled out a bottle of gold-colored liquid. He poured some into glasses and offered them around.

"A toast, my little fledgling Crows," said Zlavko, raising his glass. "Think of this as your first step on the path toward greatness!"

Malou tentatively took a little sip. *Euch!* The drink was bitter and tasted nothing like the sweet mead that was served at the Yule party last year. She forced herself to take a drink. The girl with the dark-brown curls started to cough as the drink caught in her throat.

"Yes, it may be a bit harsh to begin with. But you do get used to it," Zlavko said, taking another glug and giving an encouraging nod to Malou. She took a normal sip, all the while striving to keep her expression neutral as the disgusting drink slipped down over her taste buds.

"What is it?" Amalie asked.

"It's my own little mixture. It mostly consists of plum wine, which I brew myself using plums from the castle's orchard. But I also add a selection of herbs. A little of the plant *Banisteriopsis caapi* makes for an excellent wine, if you want to develop your understanding a little. Many South American natives use the same plant." Zlavko held his glass up to the light and looked at the liquid. "I only brew a few bottles each year, but I thought I would share this one with you, to give you the chance of an even deeper experience of the Yule celebration this evening."

Iris looked up at him in fright, much to Malou's annoyance. She was going to great lengths not to give Zlavko reactions of that kind, the kind he so obviously was hoping for.

"Is it dangerous?" the curly-haired girl asked, looking suspiciously down at her glass.

Zlavko smiled, as Malou could have predicted. This was just exactly the kind of thing he loved.

"I don't think so. It is normally quite mild, although this is the first bottle I've opened from the fall batch, and you can never know for sure what it will turn out like without trying it," he said, smiling. "You are all now official candidates for the club, and I expect a great deal of you. I will test your abilities, your loyalty, and your courage. Let's say that tonight's exercise is to share this drink with me, and at the next meeting I'd like to hear about your experiences of the party tonight. I look forward to hearing about it—don't disappoint me!" He looked around at them, one by one. "I hate ordinary people's ordinary stories from their ordinary lives. From all of you, I expect something different."

DECEMBER 21ST
9:15 P.M.

Victoria

The mushy leaves had frozen solid. They crunched underfoot as Victoria slowly made her way farther into the trees. She could hear the distant laughter of students. The ground was covered in frost, so his tracks were clearly visible. What if someone had noticed her sneaking away from the tent and the party, which was already in full swing? Her breath was so visible in the darkness, for a moment she thought she was seeing a spirit in front of her. But here it was quiet. Where was he?

The paw prints continued a little farther, and then she heard what she was listening for. A low growl.

"Benjamin?" she whispered, and the growling noise answered her. The wolf stood on the path up ahead of her. He was bigger than a normal wolf but was no longer an unseemly blend of man and beast. Benjamin's transformation was complete now. The wolf looked handsome. It lifted its ears and bowed its head.

"It's okay," she said. "I want to watch."

The wolf shook itself, as if it wanted to protest, but Victoria stood her ground. At last, it gave in. *He* gave in. The wolf hunched its back like a cat. The fur on its back appeared to split open, revealing the hide below, the fur peeling off the length of its body like an animal being skinned. A lump rose in Victoria's throat, but she forced herself to keep watching. She had heard that transforming could hurt. Now she understood why. The fur disappeared and the wolf was no longer a wolf, but something in between. He panted, standing up on two legs, hunched over. He was naked. She hadn't thought about that. Victoria didn't turn her gaze away; she was unable to stop looking at him. He coughed, straightened up, and turned to face her.

"Curious?" His voice was hoarse. But he was smiling. She could feel his warmth, despite the frosty weather.

For a moment she thought he would come over to her, but instead he ducked into a bush and pulled out a cloth bag. Aha, he had brought clothes with him. She felt a flicker of disappointment and smiled to herself. He must have carried the bag in his mouth. As he was getting dressed, she finally managed to look away and instead looked up at the stars. Music had started up in the tent, its monotonous bass the only sound that reached them out in the woods. It sounded like a mantra, like the deep chanting of a mass, an animal rhythm.

"I've missed you." His breath could be felt on her neck. His lips were soft, his tongue warm. His stubble scratched against her chin and left a prickling sensation even after he had pulled away. He laughed. Inside her, everything was aflame.

"The party's in full swing then?"

"I'd say so."

"Let's just hope they've drunk enough mead for nobody to notice one student too many in there," he said, taking her hand. Now they could hear a melody alongside the drumming. The tent was lit up from inside by a large bonfire, and torches stuck into the dark earth lined the entrance path. He gave her hand a squeeze.

DECEMBER 21ST
9:30 P.M.

Malou

The crowd was jumping to the beat around her, but Malou couldn't hear the music. It had gone quiet and everything was moving in slow motion. Sweaty bodies, laughing faces, mouths that opened too wide, eyes that seemed to slide down cheeks. The tent was spinning too. The slaughtered pig, the blood running from it—her vision was streaked with red. She felt like she wanted to let go, to let herself just fall. As if she was about to lose herself completely in that pulsing, breathy, bloody soup of bodies and sweat. He caught hold of her just before she fell. She didn't know if she was lying in his arms or still standing and had no idea which way was up or down. His eyes shone and grew bigger in his face. He kissed her, and she clung to him as if his mouth was a lifeline, her only way of not drifting off into the open sea. Silence fell, time disappeared. His fingers pressed into her skin, her fingers pressed into his. He was damp with sweat, he was cold, he was burning.

The eyes were black instead of gray. *Shit, shit, shit. Get a grip on yourself!*

Zlavko was standing over her. Was she lying down? Louis still had her in his arms. Zlavko held the knife, covered in pig's blood.

She stood up now. Incredibly slowly, he dipped his fingers into the blood. She watched his hand closely. He raised it up to her face and let his fingers slide over her lips. He smiled at her. A different smile, a new, frightening smile she hadn't seen before. He laughed, his smile split his face into two, a black liquid bubbled up in the hole which had been his mouth until then. Louis pulled her closer again, she could taste him, she could taste the salty taste of blood.

With a bang, noises flooded back, time sped up, and she gripped him, pulling him to her as if she could consume him. Everything shimmered before her eyes, everything burned. She felt his blood coursing inside of him, she knew where it flowed, where it came from: from the aorta, that huge, main artery, through the lung's intricate network of blood vessels, out into his strong arms, and down to his groin. She felt it. And suddenly she had the idea that she could control it.

Frightened, she pulled herself free. He had blood on his mouth. Was it hers? *I need to get out of here.* Malou turned from him, wanting to get away. And that is when she saw her. She turned and disappeared into the crowd straightaway, but Malou had recognized her. And had seen the large knife she held in front of her in those bony hands. It was a blood mage's ceremonial knife, an athame.

Malou had to find her, stop her, and make sure no one got hurt. She squeezed herself through the throng, pushing her way, not caring who she rammed into. Suddenly, she was out in the darkness. She ran, fell, and ran again. The ground seemed to rise up toward her and crash into her side. A thin layer of frost covered the ice-cold mud that took a grip of her, and this time she didn't get up again.

DECEMBER 21ST
10:14 P.M.

Kirstine

Kirstine let the hairbrush glide through her wet hair. What do you do on a night home, alone, when everyone else is partying? Yup, as a teenage girl, sharing a bathroom with three other teenage girls, you take the chance to have a long soak in the bathtub. She didn't mind being alone; in fact, she enjoyed it when the opportunity came up once in a while. Tonight, though, it felt a little empty. Victoria and Chamomile had picked out clothes, accessorized, gossiped about boys. They had giggled, teased each other, and generally horsed around. But Kirstine had to stay in. The Yule celebration was a tribute to the Nordic gods, to Nordic history. It was a celebration to awaken Earth, that power that ran so strongly through her. Thorbjørn had taken her aside and told her it was best that she didn't go. Parties and alcohol were not her thing anyway. But then why did she feel so abandoned nevertheless? Maybe it was only because all her friends were down there in that tent. All the girls, all the boys. The teachers. Jakob . . .

Stop it. There's no point thinking about it. Kirstine pulled on her pj's and sat at the window, wrapped in a blanket. At last year's Yule party, she had been so confused about her own feelings. She and Jakob had argued, but then just after that they had kissed for the first time. Her first real kiss. And now they were supposed to be just friends. Then why did her chest tighten like that, whenever their eyes met? Why did her heart race, whenever he looked at her? And did he feel the same way?

Kirstine had to admit, she enjoyed their little meetings. Jakob could make her laugh. And get her talking. They rarely talked about anything serious, but she enjoyed that too. It felt like a real time-out. She hadn't told him about the prophecy or the inner fire or burning pain she had felt when she was at the ship setting. But at some point she would have to tell him. It could be dangerous for both of them if anything happened between them . . .

Then it was as if the mere thought of it had filled her with unease. Was it her feelings for Jakob that were causing this reaction? Her fingers were tingling, and she thought she heard music from the tent, but it was something else. Something that was pressing in, trying to get her attention. *A vision.* Normally, receiving a vision required her to be in a state that took time, strength, and preparation to achieve. Since Vitus's burning body had disappeared into the ground at the foot of the old tree, they came to her in uncontrolled flashes. She scrunched her eyes tight and shook her head. Images flickered by. *Two girls, hand in hand, spinning around in their light summer dresses. A white tower on a blue sky. The two girls again. Somebody laughing.* The vision changed, becoming clearer and sharper. *A shape lying on the frozen forest floor.*

"*Elgr.*" She whispered the name of the rune, more as a plea for protection than any kind of incantation. The sight lasted no longer than a few seconds, but when it vanished, she was already soaked in sweat. The last part of the vision had been different, and she realized why: It was not in the past. It was the present, or perhaps the future that she had seen. Something had happened down in the woods and she had to go there. Kirstine pulled her winter coat over her pajamas and pulled on her rain boots before running down the stairs. As soon as she stepped outside, she wished she'd grabbed a hat and scarf, too, as it was really freezing now. Torches lit up the path to the tent, but that was not where she needed to go.

She heard the drumming rhythms from the tent clearly now, and they blended with the sound of her own heartbeat. She went down toward the woods. It was quiet, and there were no people in sight. Everyone was at the party. What was she doing? She had told Thorbjørn she would stay in her room, and here she was running around in the pitch dark. Kirstine came to a stop for a moment. She was shivering, her hair had frozen solid around her face, and her sweaty pajamas were cold and clammy under her coat. And she still felt a nagging unease all through her. She had to keep going.

As soon as she entered the forest, Kirstine could feel it. Something waking up. Something reacting to her being there. It moved on the forest floor, whipping and racing around her feet, calling her in one particular direction. The tree.

She forced her feet away from the path and into the forest. She must not let herself be led astray, she must not follow the path being offered to her. She needed to be strong now and show that she could withstand the urge. She stumbled over roots, and branches swished in her face, as if the forest disliked her change of direction. For a moment she thought she could make out black tree roots twisting after her feet in the darkness like huge worms, but they vanished when she looked closer. Where was she? She had lost her way and felt dizzy and tired. She paused and rested her forehead against the surface of a broad tree's trunk.

"Get up!"

Startled, she followed the voice. It was one she recognized.

Zlavko stood over someone lying on the forest floor. It was Malou.

"For God's sake, come on now!" He lifted Malou up in his arms, but her legs buckled under her and she sank back down to the ground. She let out a groan and said something that Kirstine could not hear.

"Pull yourself together!" Zlavko snapped. "What did you see?" He dragged her up again and pulled her roughly along with him, although she fought it.

"No, no, no," she muttered, her head hanging in a strange way, as if she couldn't be bothered to hold it up.

"What's going on here?" It was a male voice.

Kirstine gasped. She had been so paralyzed by the strange scene, she hadn't noticed someone else approaching. Benjamin stepped forward from the trees and stood expectantly before Zlavko. She noticed a hand on his shoulder. Victoria.

Zlavko looked surprised for a moment but quickly collected himself.

"What the hell are you doing here? The Yule celebration is only for current students."

"I'm taking a walk in the woods. Is that forbidden? And what are you doing here yourself?" Benjamin raised his eyebrows and looked at Zlavko, waiting. "What happened to Malou?"

"Too much mead," Zlavko said angrily. "As a teacher of this crowd of idiotic teenagers, it's my sorry duty to keep an eye on any students who can't handle themselves."

"Mead?"

Malou started to sway precariously, and finally Kirstine felt herself react. She darted forward to grab Malou before she fell. Victoria was just behind her.

"Marvelous. Now, it's an official little party we're having," Zlavko said as Kirstine and Victoria each put an arm around behind Malou to support her. Her face tilted backward and the whites of her eyes showed in the darkness.

"I saw her," she muttered. "She was here."

"What? Who?"

"She's babbling," said Zlavko.

"I think Ingrid should take a look at her," said Benjamin. "That's no ordinary high that she's on."

"You keep out of it," Zlavko snarled. "Get her to bed," he said, addressing Victoria and Kirstine. Then he took a step toward Benjamin. "And if you don't get out of here right now, I'll tell the rest of the teaching staff that you've been lurking around the school grounds to meet up with your little girlfriend."

"Hey, take it easy," Benjamin said, and looked Zlavko in the eyes. "You keep your mouth shut about me, I'll keep my mouth shut about you."

"Get out of here." Zlavko's eyes flashed, and Kirstine held her breath. Finally, their teacher turned and marched angrily away through the trees, although not toward the school.

"I better get going," Benjamin mumbled, and took Victoria's hand.

"Of course," Victoria said. "And we need to get Malou back too."

But they both stood there, as if unaware of the other people present. Kirstine sighed. "I can take her the first ways on my own," she said, hopping alongside Malou. "Then you can at least say your goodbyes."

"Are you sure?" Victoria said without looking at her.

Kirstine simply nodded and set off, half dragging, half carrying Malou, who continued her ceaseless muttering of indecipherable words and broken sentences.

After a while, Kirstine paused to catch her breath for a moment. Where had Victoria gone?

"I saw her, she was here . . ."

"What did you say?" muttered Kirstine, setting off again and trying to get Malou over yet another tree root. It seemed like the forest was intent on making their passage as hard as possible, and her arms ached. They were coming to the forest's edge already and there was still no sign of Victoria. She probably still wasn't finished kissing Benjamin goodbye.

"No, not that way. We need to find her. Not that way . . ." Malou rambled.

"We need to get you to your bed," Kirstine muttered.

"We need to find her," insisted Malou. "Leah, she ran into the woods. Kirstine, she had a knife, she'll come after us . . ."

Then she leaned in toward Kirstine and puked in her freshly washed hair.

DECEMBER 21ST
11:40 P.M.

Victoria

"You need to go."

"Two more seconds."

She laughed and shook her head. "We can't do this. You can't come here anymore."

"I don't think I can stay away."

"But now Zlavko knows."

"Don't worry. He won't say anything. Because then he'd also have to explain what he was doing with a semiconscious Malou out in the woods."

"What do you think was going on?"

"I don't know, but keep an eye on her. If she gets worse, you'll get a hold of Ingrid, right?"

Victoria nodded. "Now go."

He bit her ever so lightly on her lower lip before pulling away. "See you."

She stood for a few seconds watching him as he retreated through the trees. Then he was gone. Victoria turned. "Kirstine? I'm coming!"

Kirstine didn't answer. It was so dark. Victoria started walking. She should easily catch up with them because Kirstine was dragging Malou as well, but there was no sign of them. Was she even going in the right direction?

Victoria stubbed her foot on a tree stump and stopped in pain. It was below freezing. Normally, sudden cold came as a warning to her, but this time she hadn't noticed anything until she stood face to face with her.

"*Victoria . . .*"

She jumped in fright. Trine was standing in front of her. More distinctly than Victoria had ever seen her before. Was it the darkness, which highlighted the white figure so strongly? She could recognize the young girl's features from the photograph they had seen at her house. Victoria could see her just as clearly as she could see her own friends. She was not just some strange, oppressive presence who wanted to get her attention. Victoria felt her presence as a real person. And this person was afraid. Ice-cold, light-blue fear mixed with dark-purple sorrow glowed from her like a reverse sun, the cold radiating toward her.

"*Be careful. He must not see us together.*"

"Who? whispered Victoria. The white girl scared her. You should never make a promise to a spirit. Had Trine come to punish her? No, Trine was afraid, not angry. Victoria put out her hand. She wanted to take her hand, tell her that everything would be okay. But you can't hold a spirit by the hand, and Victoria couldn't save Trine. It was too late. Yet it wasn't too late to demand justice for her having died so young.

"We'll still need to find the man who did it. We won't give up, Trine."

Big white tears welled up in the spirit's eyes. "*Come*," she whispered. She turned around and walked off through the trees.

Victoria hesitated for a moment, then followed her. It was hard to say how far they walked. Trine moved unhindered through the woods, paying no heed to branches or thorns that couldn't touch her anyway, while Victoria stumbled breathlessly along. She quickly lost her bearings in the dark. Now and then, the clouds parted from the moon and its white light gently lit the forest floor. She heard the bubbling sound of water and knew at once, without seeing it, where Trine had brought her. The brook at the base of the bluff. The brook, where violets bloomed in the springtime. This was where Trine had been killed. Why was she bringing Victoria here? Trine had showed her all this before. But it was not the bluff that the young spirit was pointing to. She had stopped farther up. Victoria slowly took the last few steps.

"Trine?" she whispered.

The spirit pointed down toward the brook. The water was higher than usual, and faster flowing, so that it had not frozen. Moonlight shone on the water. No, there was also something else . . .

Victoria went right down to the bank, bent down, and dipped her hand into the icy water. It was deeper than she'd expected and her sleeve got soaked. When she pulled her hand back up, she held a silver chain entwined in her fingers.

"What is this?" she whispered.

The white shadow was flickering; Trine was disappearing. Without seeing her lips move, Victoria could hear what she whispered: "*Little Troll.*"

"Trine?!"

"Who are you talking to?"

Victoria slipped the chain into her pocket and turned around. Zlavko stepped out from the dark tree trunks.

"Nobody."

Why was he here? He was bare-chested, but despite the frost, his skin glistened with sweat and his breath was clearly heard in the quiet around them. He had been running. Was he looking for Benjamin? Or her?

"I was trying to get back to the tent, but I got lost in the dark," she said.

"Yeah, that's fairly obvious. You've gone in completely the opposite direction."

She couldn't quite interpret his mood, and that was making her uneasy. He was angry, but also restless, nervous. Was he angry with her? Because she hadn't joined in with his little club?

Zlavko stood for a moment, as if he couldn't quite decide what to do. He rubbed his hand over his face, frustrated. Then he sighed and stood for a moment with his arms hanging by his side. "Come with me," he hissed furiously, and turned toward the castle.

DECEMBER 22ND
2:31 P.M.

Chamomile

Chamomile turned her teacup in her fingertips. The tea had gotten cold without her even drinking any. Kirstine and Victoria also sat quietly with their cups. Before them, in the middle of the little kitchen table, there it lay. The necklace. It was made of braided silver, and on the front there was an elliptical pendant, also in silver. The fastener was broken, as if it had been ripped from the neck of whoever was wearing it. It had no engravings or anything else of note on it.

"Is she still sleeping?" Victoria asked. "Should we try and wake her up?"

"She only stopped puking at five thirty," Chamomile said. "We better leave her be."

Right then, the door to their room opened up and Malou staggered in and collapsed into the fourth chair at the table. "I think I'm dying," she mumbled, and laid down across the table.

"You'll survive," Chamomile said, running her hand down Malou's hair. "But you do smell a bit like death, I'm afraid. Here, drink this, it will help." She poured her a glass of lemonade.

Malou sat up and looked at the glass with suspicion but drank it anyway.

"What happened?" Kirstine asked.

"Zlavko," Malou muttered, and flopped onto the table again.

"Seriously, Malou, what did he give you to drink?"

Malou shushed her and mumbled something incoherent.

"I think you should report it to Jens. I'm sure he'll talk to Zlavko about it. He can't go around poisoning the students," Chamomile said.

Malou looked up. "Sshh, you're talking so loud, my head . . ." She laid her head on her arms again. "I saw all these far-out things. And I think I saw Leah . . . and suddenly it was as if I was out in the woods . . ."

"You *were* out in the woods," Kirstine said. "I should know, I practically carried you home."

"You could have frozen to death," Chamomile said. "If *you* don't want to tell Jens, then *I* will."

"No," Malou objected. "Then Zlavko will think he has won. I'm not letting him have that pleasure."

"Who has won what? There's no competition going on here."

"What's that?" asked Malou, pointing to the piece of jewelry lying in front of them.

Chamomile strongly suspected she was only asking in order to change the subject. "It's Trine's necklace," she answered, nevertheless. "That's what we think, in any case. Victoria found it."

"What? How?"

"We found out you'd left the party. Benjamin saw you leave," Victoria said.

"Benjamin?"

"He stopped by," Victoria said defensively. "Anyway, we came to look for you and found you in the forest. Suddenly, Trine appeared. She was frightened. Something had scared her. That must be why she's been staying away. She led me down to the stream by the bluff. You know, the place she died. And this was lying in the brook. The necklace."

"Has it been in there all these years?" Malou asked, turning the shiny silver chain over in her hands.

"The brook had burst its banks with all the rain. Maybe the necklace had gotten flushed out from wherever it's been hidden away," Chamomile said.

"It must be important, if Trine wanted you to find it," Kirstine said.

"Yeah. If only I knew *why* it was important," Victoria said.

"Should we try and do that psychometry thing? That reading of objects?" asked Chamomile. "Jens said that jewelry is commonly used."

"Whatthehellareyoutalkingabout?" Malou mumbled.

"Reading the object's history. We learned about it in Clairvoyance class."

"Since when did you start listening in Clairvoyance?"

"Let's each try holding the necklace, in turn, and we'll see if we get any kind of a sign," Chamomile said, ignoring Malou's comment.

"Okay," Malou said, and sat up. She reached out for the chain.

"Wait!" Chamomile said. "We can't influence one another. If you sense something, you should write it down on a scrap of paper. We'll only show each other our notes at the very end." She stood up to find paper and pens. "Will you go first, Victoria?"

"No, you go."

Chamomile nodded, took the necklace into her hands, and closed her eyes. She really wasn't sure how this worked, but she tried to open her Ajna chakra and hoped it would help her sight-seeing abilities. She had heard Lisa speak of this as the "third eye," and she knew that this, the indigo chakra, was linked with intuition and having a sixth sense. Surely that was what she needed right now?

The first thing she picked up was a very strong feeling. Passion, maybe? But was it good or bad? Perhaps it was more like a mixture of both. Something that exists between hate and love? After that, a person came forward. Chamomile's breathing quickened when she realized she knew the person. But could that be right? Or had she been distracted by her worries for Malou? The vision was crystal clear, so it would be hard to be mistaken. She wrote something down on her paper and passed the necklace on around the circle.

Kirstine sat for a long time with the chain. Victoria took a few minutes, while Malou barely touched it before scribbling down one word.

"Are we all ready?"

They each turned their pieces of paper and laid them out in the middle of the table, beside the chain. The same thing was written on each one. *Zlavko.*

"Wow!" whispered Chamomile.

"Did you also get love?" Kirstine said.

"And hate. And a revolting amount of desire," added Malou. "It just about made me puke again."

"But does it mean that . . ." Chamomile faltered.

"It was Zlavko who was Trine's boyfriend?" Victoria whispered. "Isn't he far too young for that?"

"Maybe he's older than he looks," Kirstine said.

"Zlavko followed me into the woods. He found me down at the stream," Victoria said. "I thought it was Benjamin he was after at first. Or me. But maybe it was Trine? *He mustn't see us together.* That's what Trine said to me."

"It's Zlavko she's afraid of!" Malou said.

"Maybe," Chamomile said, frowning. "Maybe it really was Zlavko who was Trine's boyfriend. But how can we ever prove that?"

"Leah," Malou said. "She'll know. If she would just talk to us."

"Wait!" Victoria said. "She gave it to me. She told me the nickname. I've only just understood it. *Little Troll.* It was the last thing she said to me."

"Little Troll," Malou muttered, and let her head crash back down onto her arms. "Shouldn't it have been Rumpelstiltskin?"

"So, what do we do now?" Chamomile asked.

"I'll call her and tell her we have the answer to her dumb question," muttered Malou. "And then it'll be her turn to cough up some more information. But first, I need to go lie down a while more."

"Malou?"

She turned around in the doorway. She looked completely washed out.

"Are you sure you won't come home with me for Christmas? My mom says it could be really fun," Chamomile said.

"Thanks for the offer, but I've promised to go home," Malou said. "Oh, yeah, and . . . Merry Christmas," she muttered, then shut the door behind her.

Chamomile sat where she was, while Kirstine and Victoria went through to the turret room. She ought to try one more time to convince Malou. She was far from sure that Malou was telling the truth about her vacation plans. On the other hand, there was something Chamomile needed to deal with while she was home, too. And that would be easier if she was alone with her mother. She had the feeling there was something about this necklace that they were missing. And if they didn't manage to keep their promise to Trine, this task of hers could prove to be decisive.

Chamomile stood up and rinsed out her cup at the sink before heading off to pack her things.

Did you find anything out?

I'm looking into various things,
but I want to be a bit more sure.
Has anything happened?

I've started sleepwalking.
Last night, I woke up already
on the way down the stairs.
I think I was on my way outside . . . ?!

I found the description of a ritual.
Maybe it can help. But it's not without risks.

What is it?

Meet me at my office after dinner.
We can talk about it then.
There's something I need to look into first.

DECEMBER 24TH
7:08 P.M.

Malou

It was pouring rain. Of course it was. Malou hitched her hood over her head and lifted her shopping bag. The look she got from the kid at the checkout still bored into her from behind as she walked away from the register. She must have been the only customer the poor guy had seen all night. And who on earth goes and buys five chocolate rum truffles and a couple of liters of milk on Christmas day, around 7:00 p.m., when everyone in the country is sitting down to their roast pork and gravy? No normal person, that was for sure.

Nobody was around. Pine garlands festooning the street between illuminated shop windows swung in the blustery wind. A Christmas tree had blown over, too, though its lights still shone in the darkness. *What the hell was she doing?*

Chamomile would think it was a really bad idea, for sure. And would definitely be furious if she knew Malou had turned down an invitation to Christmas at her place with nowhere else to actually be. She could have stayed at Rosenholm with Kirstine, but she had said no to that as well. Why, exactly? In the lashing rain, it suddenly became hard to remember why she couldn't just swallow her damn pride and say yes to one of the offers.

The bigger houses had lights in their windows, which were painted with hearts and stars, and there were flowering amaryllis in huge pots. In the smaller homes, Christmas trees lit up rooms of people eating and drinking too much, before unwrapping far too many presents that they had spent far too much money on and nobody really needed. Malou didn't understand why Christmas was so important to people. But she also didn't understand why it had seemed so important to do this, on precisely this night—why she felt she had to wander these deserted streets, looking on all the brightly lit windows and happy families like some spin-off Little Match Girl. *The little chocolate truffle girl. Goddammit . . .*

Leah had told her on the phone to come tonight, but Malou could have said no; she could have suggested another day. Maybe Zlavko was right with what he said that time in the iced-water lesson: Malou enjoyed suffering. Right now that seemed like the best explanation.

She'd reached the house. The windows were dark. What else had she expected? *Christmas tree, a little display of elves, and the Disney Christmas Show? Yeah, right!* She passed through the gate and knocked. Leah opened the door at once, as if she had been standing on the other side waiting.

"What did you bring?" she asked.

"Um . . . chocolate truffles. And milk," Malou said.

Leah seemed to weigh whether chocolates and milk were sufficient for Malou to gain entry to her trash heap of a house.

"There was nothing but a corner store open," Malou said.

Leah muttered something and stepped aside for her. Inside, it was dark and cold and smelled damp. A small table lamp with a gold shade cast a weak light from one corner.

"Merry Christmas," Malou said, her voice sounding strange.

"Ha!" Leah laughed and grabbed the bag from her hand to inspect its contents. "Have you eaten?" she asked, looking at her distrustfully.

"You eat them, I'm not hungry." Malou hadn't had anything since the morning, but there was no way she was going to ingest anything in this house.

This time Leah fetched a large, thick glass from the kitchen and filled it with milk before sitting down at the table to slowly eat one truffle after another, chewing and mumbling with satisfaction.

Malou sat in the seat opposite her. She shuddered. Her jacket was wet and clinging to her, but she was too cold to take it off.

"Why don't you use your heat?" asked Leah, licking the last crumbs from her fingers.

"What?" Malou didn't know what she meant.

"Blood mages don't get cold. You're a blood mage, are you not?"

Instinctively, Malou reached up to touch the little silver droplet hanging around her neck. "Yes."

"So you know how to do it too. How your blood can warm you if you get cold."

"We haven't learned about that yet," Malou said. "Are you one, a blood mage?"

"Haven't learned that yet," mocked Leah, ignoring her question. "Every blood mage should learn that first: keeping yourself alive in the harshest conditions. We may not be worth much, but at least we can do that. Here, give me your hand." She reached her hand across the table, but Malou hesitated. "Nothing will happen to you, you idiot. Come on."

She held out her hand, palm facing upward, and slowly Malou placed her hand into the old woman's. Her long, thin fingers closed tight around hers.

"Ugh, so cold, this little hand." She laughed hoarsely. Her long thumbnail caressed the back of Malou's hand, tracing the paths of the veins beneath her skin. "Now watch." She gripped Malou's hand tight and narrowed her eyes. In the near darkness of the living room, Malou could only just make out how the whites of her eyes began to fill with inky black. The heat came almost at once, a ball of heat, as if scalding tea was running through her veins. It was too much, far too hot. She pulled her hand back, frightened.

"It worked, didn't it?"

Malou rubbed the back of her hand where Leah's sharp nail had left a long red scratch when she pulled her hand away.

Leah laughed softly and inspected her thumbnail again. The tip was red with Malou's blood, and she put it to her mouth with the same look of pleasure you'd expect if it were cream cake.

Malou's stomach heaved and she felt a wave of nausea pass over her. What would have happened if she hadn't pulled her hand free? Leah would surely have cooked her alive and eaten her for dessert, with a side of milk. A ton of milk.

"Did Trine have a boyfriend called Zlavko?"

Leah raised her bushy eyebrows in surprise. "What did you say?"

"Zlavko. Tall, black hair, dark eyes, spoke with an accent?"

"I don't know what you're talking about," she said, and turned her face away, as if Malou suddenly bored her.

"Intolerable smugness with clear psychopathic traits? A blood mage?"

"It doesn't mean anything to me."

"Are you sure? Maybe Trine brought him home one time. Or maybe she spoke about him?"

"Trine never named him." She slapped the glass down onto the table before her impatiently. "Listen, I thought you had something to tell me. If not, you can get on your way again."

"I do. We got the nickname from Trine . . ."

"Ugh, Trine this and Trine that. Everything always has to be about her."

"But the nickname . . ."

"Tell me something about yourself instead."

"What . . . No! You promised . . ."

"You come here, snooping into my life, asking about my sister and my misfortunes, but you won't give anything in return?"

"But—"

"Tell me a secret, something the other girls don't know. Tell me who you're in love with, or who you secretly hate. Tell me that, and then I'll tell *you* a secret."

Malou gritted her teeth. Her first instinct was to get out of there and slam the door behind her. But if she did that, then for sure they'd never get anything out of the crazy hag. She sighed. "Okay. Well . . . at the Yule celebration the other day, I kissed this boy. His name's Louis."

"Did you sleep together?" Leah leaned in over the table. Malou had her full attention now.

"No, we just kissed. I think. It's all a bit hazy."

"Are you in love with him?"

"No, I don't think so. I don't know him . . ."

"Ha! Foolish girl. If you don't know if you are in love, that's because you've never been in love. Just be thankful for that. They say that giving birth is painful—I've thankfully never had the pleasure—but falling in love has to be the worst pain you can subject yourself to."

"Okay, well, that was my secret."

"Why did you kiss him if you're not in love with him?"

"I don't know. One of the teachers had given me something to drink, I wasn't myself."

"I was drunk, I didn't know what I was doing, I'm just a silly, innocent, little girl . . ." Leah laughed scornfully. "So tell me who you hate."

"Him, the teacher who gave me that shit to drink. It's him, the one called Zlavko. Who maybe was Trine's boyfriend?"

Leah narrowed her eyes. "How original, a student who hates her teacher," she hissed. "No, that's no good. Who is it that you hate, secretly? Tell me that, and I'll tell you *my* secret!"

"How long have you got?" Malou's hate list was quite comprehensive.

"Spit it out. Or you can leave."

"My mom."

"A teenager who hates her mom, far too obvious. You've got this in you, come on, try again!"

"Shit . . . Okay, sometimes—not always, but sometimes—I hate Victoria. Because she's got bloody everything. She's the dark-haired one . . ."

". . . the one that can see Trine, right?" Leah smiled, showing her long yellow teeth. She leaned over the table without taking her eyes from Malou's.

She nodded. "And now it's your turn."

"Now, now. Not so fast, missy! First you need to tell me the nickname. What was it Trine called me?"

"Little Troll."

Leah leaned back slowly in her seat. Maybe she had never believed that they could do it.

"I hated that name," she muttered. "Trine was the happy, bubbly one, while I was just a little, ugly troll girl. And she used every opportunity to remind me of it. I was an unhappy child, but Trine couldn't have cared how I was. As long as she amused herself."

"The secret?"

"Ugh, there are so many. A whole life full of secrets and things you can't talk about, things you can never name, never say Trine's name because they'll get angry again . . ."

"Your parents?" asked Malou. "How did they die?"

But Leah paid no attention. "So, so many secrets, and you can only have one."

"Tell me one then," Malou said impatiently.

Leah smiled. "Fine. I still have Trine's letters. I have never shown them to anyone before. Not when the police came, not when the school called, not when he called. Not to my mom or dad, nope—not even to them. But you girls can read them. Maybe there will be something in there you can use. If you bring more food next time you come, then maybe I can find the letters for you."

"Can't I just take them with me now?"

"Not so hasty, you silly girl. Come visit again, and bring the others, and then you can get your letters. If you're willing to give in return. And now, get going. I don't want to talk to you anymore."

"Do you know who Trine's boyfriend was, if it wasn't Zlavko?" Malou tried.

"No more questions and no more answers. Go away."

Malou got up. She pulled up her hood before heading out into the darkness.

DECEMBER 24TH
10:30 P.M.

Chamomile

"Can I get you anything?" Chamomile's mother sat beside her on the sofa with a tray in her hands. "I made chai. With cinnamon and cardamom. And we have cookies."

Chamomile looked down at the large, shapeless blobs laid out on a platter. "Thanks, I'm fine."

"They taste fine enough, even though they don't look so great. You can just break off a corner if they're too big. I made them especially for you."

"Mom. Seriously, I can't eat any more."

Her mother had made Christmas lunch. In their little thatched farmhouse, this always consisted of a mountain of falafel, flatbreads, lamb meatballs with mint, hummus, pomegranate juice, and much more. "Jesus was from the Middle East, after all," Chamomile's mom would always say.

They had done what they always did. Eaten, sung, and swapped presents. Chamomile had given her mom a gift card for some deadly boring store. Usually she would go to a lot of trouble to find something personal, but her mom had hugged her anyway as if she had been given some minor treasure. Chamomile had gotten a new dress—an expensive one. But even though they were doing what they always did, it still didn't measure up to how she remembered her cozy childhood Christmases.

"Here, there's always room for a cup of tea," said her mom, passing her a mug.

Chamomile took a sip. It was both sweet and bitter. Exactly the way she liked it.

"Hey, I know!" Her mom sat up excitedly on the sofa. "Why don't we play cards?"

"I think I'm too tired."

"Yeah, you're right. It's also nice just sitting here watching the flames." She got up to put another log into the wood stove. "Or I could put some music on?"

"Why didn't you tell me that Jens was my dad? You knew I would get him as a teacher at school. Why didn't you say anything?"

Chamomile's mom sank back onto the sofa as if she'd been deflated. "I've already answered this, as best as I can. I thought you were too young, that it would get too complicated . . . and I also couldn't face it, because . . ."

"Because what?"

"Because I knew how angry you'd be."

"Coward."

"You're right. It was cowardly of me. Have you spoken to him?"

"Yes."

"Did you tell him?"

"Yes."

"What did he say?"

"First he was definitely quite shocked. He didn't know I even existed. Now we meet up every so often," Chamomile said, and shrugged. "We drink tea . . ."

"Really," her mother said in a voice that suddenly sounded strained. She looked down at her cup and didn't ask anything else. The log burned away in the wood stove and the wind whistled through the chimney. Outside, it was still raining.

In truth, Chamomile had only met with Jens one time since their first little tea party. He had been very busy with work, so there hadn't been much time. But it had been good. A bit weird, but fine. Jens seemed very caring, though in a faintly awkward sort of way. He asked after her friends; he seemed to be particularly concerned for Victoria (though he hadn't given away any more about her family). He was curious about her plans for the future, and when he heard she was interested in natural medicines, he suggested she apply to study medicine.

But it seemed her mom didn't want to talk any more about her meetings with her father. And that didn't matter. There was something else Chamomile was much more interested in talking about, and she had a feeling it was better to leave Jens's name out of this context.

"Do you want me to braid your hair?" asked Chamomile.

"Would you?" asked her mom, turning to her. "It's a long time since you've done that. I'll go get a comb."

She loosened her long red, sliver-streaked hair, and let it fall down across her back. Chamomile gently started to comb out the snarls one at a time. Usually it just sat in a messy bun at the nape of her mom's neck, but once it was combed out, here in the flickering of the firelight, it was really beautiful. She plaited it in one single braid. Her mom had lain her head on the back of the sofa, her eyes closed, and Chamomile could see her little silver leaf pendant. And the plain leather purse that she also always wore around her neck.

"Do you remember how I always used to play with the things from your purse?" Chamomile asked.

"Yes," her mom smiled, eyes still closed. "That used to keep you busy a long time."

"But I don't think I ever understood the significance of it."

"The purse? It's where I keep all my small amulets and other important things."

"Can I have a look?" Chamomile asked, and sat down beside her on the sofa.

"Yeah, here," her mom said, and lifted the leather cord that held her purse over her head. She opened it and tipped the contents gently into her hand. "This is a little of everything. An amethyst protects against evil spirits, a hare's foot brings luck. And look!" She prodded a small white object.

"Is that . . . ugh, is that a tooth?"

"Yup, it's your first baby tooth. This way, I always have you near me."

Chamomile scrunched up her nose. "That's actually pretty gross."

"And look at this one, this one is really special. Do you know what it's called?" she asked, picking an oval matte-black stone from her palm and placing it in Chamomile's.

"No," Chamomile lied. "What is it?"

"It's a victory stone," said her mom. "My mother passed this on to me, when I was pregnant with you. They help prevent difficulties in childbirth. If the child doesn't want to be born, you place it on the mother's belly. This stone has saved many lives, believe me. And it has been passed down from mother to daughter over hundreds of years. Your grandma helped with lots of births herself, just as her mom did before her. Just as I have."

Chamomile turned the stone in her hand. It was a deep black, with bright little sparkles through it. "It's beautiful."

"You can have it," her mom said.

"No, I can't accept it."

"Yes, just take it. You're ready to have it."

"Well, I'm not planning on delivering any babies anytime soon!" Chamomile said.

Her mother laughed. "No, let's hope not. But you keep it anyway. I never use it. All the young people are moving away from here. There's nobody out here having kids anymore, and those who do give birth in the hospital. It's been a long time since I was a doula."

"Thanks, Mom," Chamomile said. "I'll take good care of it."

Her mom put her arm around her and kissed her on the side of her head. "I know you will, darling."

Let's do it

I think you should really seriously think this through before you make a decision

I already have. Last night I woke up in the park. What would happen if I got all the way down to the tree?

I'm still not quite sure.

You said yourself:
in the end, it's up to me

But what if it goes wrong?

Then it was still my choice.
I'm not a kid anymore.

Okay, if you're sure

I'm sure

DECEMBER 31ST
11:00 P.M.

Kirstine

Kirstine waited on the other side of the moat by the large copper beech. She gave a start when some fireworks went off. The bangs rang out between the walls of the castle, but she couldn't see any people. It was coming from the boys' park. She looked up at the school. A few windows were lit up. Someone was having a party for the few students who were at school for New Year's Eve.

She switched off her phone and put it back in her pocket. Malou had sent them a depressing message. Leah didn't know anything about Zlavko and Trine—if they had been dating. Or she didn't want to tell them. On the other hand, she claimed to have old letters from Trine, and Malou was determined that they would get a hold of them.

Kirstine hadn't given it much thought, as she'd had something else entirely to be concerned about: She had started to sleepwalk. She often found herself waking up, barefoot, out in the park, on the way to the woods. And it often happened after she had seen Jakob. She still had not told him anything, but then maybe she didn't need to. *If this could just work.*

Here he was. Kirstine caught herself hopping, nervously, from one foot to the other. But he wasn't alone. Why was he not alone?

"Good, you're ready," said Thorbjørn's deep voice, as he momentarily mirrored her hops. If she hadn't felt her heart racing so fast, she might have felt more amused by how awkward she and Thorbjørn always were together. Why was he just standing there without explaining why he had brought Jakob along? Goodness knows what he had told him . . .

"Happy new year, Kirstine, or whatever it is you say." The wind caught Jakob's hair—he had no hat on and it was freezing cold.

"Same to you," she mumbled.

"I've told Jakob about the ritual and why it needs to be done," Thorbjørn said. He sounded almost embarrassed, as if he had done something wrong, although he hadn't, in fact. Kirstine only wished she could have been the one to tell him herself.

"Do they all know?" she asked. "All the teachers?"

"No. Only Lisa. She knows the tree. I have had quite a talk with her about it."

"And what did she say?"

"She thinks we should leave it alone." He avoided meeting her gaze.

"I think we should try it."

"Are you sure?" It was Jakob who asked.

Yes, I'm sure. She didn't trust herself any longer. The tree called to her in the night. Who knew what would happen if she got all the way down there? If she lost control of herself and of her powers? She could end up killing herself. Or someone she cared about. *Or else she may kill. Or else she may die.* It must not come to that.

"I'm sure."

Thorbjørn took the lead, heading along the path, over the meadow, and down toward the marsh. Now and then they heard fireworks in the distance, but the noise gradually faded out. At first she hadn't understood why it had to happen on this night, in particular, but now she could see there was good reason. Hardly anyone was at the school, and those who were there were surely drunk and too busy partying, setting off fireworks, and finding someone to kiss at midnight to notice three figures dressed in black heading away from the school into the darkness.

The tall grass hid the earth below, so it was impossible to sense where the ground actually was. A thick layer of ice cracked apart underfoot, and marsh water slurped beneath her soles.

"I set the snares over here in the low bushes," Thorbjørn whispered to them, and signaled to them to be quiet as they approached.

"Argh!" Kirstine stepped in a hole and immediately ice-cold water ran into her boots. When she tried to lift her leg out, nothing happened except that she half toppled to one side. *Great.*

"Take my hand."

She hesitated for an instant before taking off her glove and grabbing on to Jakob's outstretched hand.

"Ow!" He pulled it away again in a flash. She, too, had felt it, a painful current suddenly ran between them. "What—" he whispered, but broke off.

"Sshh!" Her foot should lift now. She pulled and heaved, but it felt as if the hole were closing farther and farther in on her, as if something down there wanted to pull her under. "*Dag, Dag, Dag.*" She muttered the name of the day rune—the rune of daylight and of Balder, the god of light—like a kind of protective spell, and heaved with everything she had. With a reluctant slurp, the bog finally let her go.

"Are you okay?" Jakob reached out a hand as if he was going to put his arm around her, but then stopped the gesture short, leaving it poised in the air. Electricity crackled around them.

"You mustn't touch me," she whispered, and stumbled on, water sloshing around her boot.

"Come here! I've got one!" Thorbjørn's voice was coming from over in the bushes. He spoke softly, perhaps in order to not frighten the kicking animal he held in his grasp. It was a hare. "Hurry. Jakob, get your knife."

Jakob pulled a hunting knife from the holster in his belt and held it out to Kirstine. She stared at it, then looked at Thorbjørn, who had lain the hare on the ground. As he held it down on the ground, its throat was exposed and it was trembling in his hands.

"It should be you who kills it. I think that would be best."

Kirstine stared at the hare. It must have been scared to death. She had killed a person, but she had never killed an animal before. A completely innocent creature. *Come on, Kirstine!*

She took the knife and sliced the hare's throat. Warm blood spurted out in a stream that hit her face.

"Good," said Thorbjørn, relieved. "Good, Kirstine. Now there's just the last part of the plan left."

They changed direction and went into the woods, the hare leaving a trail of blood behind them.

"Do you hear that?" Kirstine tried to keep her voice calm, but did not completely succeed. A loud buzzing filled her ears.

"Yes," said Thorbjørn. "The tree knows you are coming. Jakob, you go just behind Kirstine, and I'll go in front. We'll shield you."

Thorbjørn started to mumble, and Jakob joined in. As they continued, Kirstine got a sense of what Thorbjørn had meant. They were not only shielding her with their bodies, but they were creating a shelter, a little pocket where it felt easier to walk and where the noises were less insistent. Still, it took them nearly half an hour to get near. She could see the tree in the distance, its cold silvery light spilling through between the green branches of the other trees and brightening the dark forest. Thorbjørn signaled for them to stop. It was quiet; the buzzing noise had stopped. Kirstine was shivering. The cold hit her as if she'd just had a duvet whipped off her. Thorbjørn and Jakob had broken off their protective charms, and it left her feeling vulnerable and defenseless.

"Kirstine, I don't like this . . ." Jakob stood behind her, speaking softly. He was so near her, she could feel his breath against her neck.

Thorbjørn turned around and the silvery-white light made him look old and tired. "Are you ready?"

She nodded.

"I'm going with you." Jakob's voice sounded loud in the stillness, and Thorbjørn whipped around.

"No!" he whispered. "It has to be Kirstine and her *alone*."

"But the tree . . . it's awake. It normally needs the ceremony to wake it. We don't know how it will react."

"Exactly. There's a great risk that it will take our presence as some kind of provocation. It is Kirstine it is expecting. It must be her alone—or no one at all."

"I'm ready." She surprised herself with how decisive she sounded.

"Good," Thorbjørn said, and took off his backpack. "I have the wreath, which Lisa has made, here . . ."

Kirstine nodded and unzipped her jacket. She let it fall onto the forest floor where she stood, and with one single movement she pulled off her sweater, stepped out of her boots, and finally stood naked before them. The cold hurt her skin, which shone white in the glow from the tree. She had never imagined this would be the way that Jakob would see her naked for the first time, but she didn't feel shy. There were more important things at stake.

"The wreath," she whispered, and Thorbjørn held it out to her, without looking at her directly. Lisa had made it using mistletoe and ivy. Kirstine set it on her head and reached for the hare from Thorbjørn's arms. Then she left them and walked the last stretch alone. It was quiet. No noises, no tree roots twisting around legs. The rough bracken tickled her legs and the frozen ground gave under her feet, although, strangely, when she stepped into the clearing, she didn't feel cold anymore. The tree was pulsating, glowing more strongly than ever before, and she couldn't tell if it was her own heartbeat she was hearing or if it was the heartwood of the tree itself beating. She continued slowly, very slowly, just as Thorbjørn had instructed her. This ancient ritual had been performed since the beginning of time by countless nameless priestesses who wanted the magical tree to gift them superhuman powers. But Kirstine was no priestess and she didn't want the tree to give her powers—she wanted it to take them back.

As she came to the foot of the tree, she knelt down, holding the hare out before her with her eyes lowered to the ground.

"Accept my offer, and set me free," she whispered. Then she lay the hare down on the ground and took a few steps back. The tree was silent, as were the woods around them. Then the wind picked up, the leaves started to rustle around the forest floor, lifting and drifting across the clearing toward her, and the tree's branches began to tremble. Kirstine spotted some movement at the base of the tree. A root was shifting. At first, very slowly, tentatively searching. In contrast to the silvery tree, the root was black. It slithered across the forest floor, jerkily impatient now, closer and closer to the hare. Kirstine held her breath as the root felt its way to the dead animal.

"Accept my offer, and set me free," she said again. The root wrapped itself around the hare, but with a sudden swish, it cast the animal away. It kept coming, though, faster now, as more roots broke free from the soil, whipping and flicking around blindly, but all coming in her direction. The tree had rejected her offering. It was *her* it wanted. And her feet were frozen to the ground so she couldn't flee.

Kirstine opened her mouth in a silent scream as the first of the jet-black roots curled itself around her ankles, up her legs, and pulled her closer.

"Kirstine!" Jakob was at her side, but the roots had wound themselves around her arms now, too, and finally she was able to scream as they burned into her flesh. Jakob held her tight and worked to get her free, and she caught a glimpse of Thorbjørn, who was flailing at the roots, roaring rune incantations to his left and right while she just screamed and screamed. With a peculiar shriek, the tree finally let her go, and Jakob lifted her up from the ground, squeezed her into him, and started running away. Kirstine closed her eyes and felt herself become limp in his arms.

JANUARY 7TH
10:20 A.M.

Malou

"They say she's in the hospital. That's the second time this school year."

"What happened?"

"I don't know. But I heard that both Jakob and Thorbjørn also got injured."

"It happened on New Year's Eve. Amalie, in third year, was having a party, but nobody saw Kirstine or either of the teachers."

"Maybe they were having their own party?"

"What do you mean?"

"Maybe some kind of ritual? A threesome or something?"

"Eurgh. I feel like I'm gonna puke. You are so disgusting."

"They were up to something, for sure. I also think that she seems really weird."

"Maybe she just really wants to get laid!"

"Hahaha—you'd have to be really desperate to jump Thorbjørn!"

"Man, what a pile of crap you all talk!" Malou slammed the door of the toilet stall open with a bang so that the four girls standing at the mirror all jumped. "There really ought to be a law against this much stupidity all in one place."

The girls gawked at her, wide eyed, but Malou didn't care. In fact, she almost hoped one of them would be dumb enough to answer her back. They looked at each other. Malou knew them well; they were all second years. Asta, who hadn't gotten into the Crows, appeared to be the little gang's leader.

"If you're so fricking clever, then you tell us: What happened to her?" she said.

Malou stepped right over to Asta. "It's none of your business what happened. You'd be better off using your limited brain powers to try and keep up in class—or you run the risk that your little heads might implode with the effort."

"See, you don't have a clue either," she said bravely. But her wide, startled eyes gave away how frightened she was.

"What is your problem? What part of this don't you understand?" Malou took another step toward Asta, who was now pressed up against the sink under the mirror. She could sense the girl's fear, feel her heartbeat. Her blood.

"Malou! What are you doing?" Chamomile stood at the door of the bathroom. "Stop it, you're terrifying them."

"We were just chatting, weren't we?" Malou said without taking her eyes off the girl.

"Malou!" Chamomile pulled at her arm to get her away. "What's going on?"

"I just overheard this clique of innocent little girlies standing here, saying how it's Kirstine's own fault she's in the hospital because she goes around trying to get laid and tries to get it on with all the teachers."

"What?!"

"That's not true, that's not what we were saying at all!" one of the other girls blurted out.

"We were just having a bit of fun, and she came and totally flipped out!" another agreed.

Chamomile put her hands on her hips and shook her head, while giving the girls her most piercingly reproachful "Mom is disappointed" look. A look Malou knew all too well.

"It just makes me so sad when I hear things like that," she said. "Why is it girls act like this with one another? What do you get out of talking about your own schoolmates like that? It doesn't make sense to me."

Asta's cheeks turned pink. Malou was still furious, but she couldn't help feeling amused that, for once, somebody else was getting the brunt of Chamomile's disappointment.

"It was just a joke," Asta said.

"Get out of here, all of you," Malou snapped.

Asta slammed the door behind them when they went. Malou avoided looking at Chamomile and went over to the sink to splash cold water on her face.

"Really, Malou?"

"Was I supposed to just listen to all that crap and not do anything?"

"No, but you were acting totally crazy. That's the last thing you need right now . . ."

"What does that mean?"

"Everyone knows you got accepted into Zlavko's weird club. There's no need to encourage people to think that he's chosen all the students who are . . . you know."

"No, I don't know. What are people saying?"

". . . into dark magic."

"I couldn't give a damn what those idiots think of me. I know they're lying. You know they're lying. Victoria and Kirstine know.

The rest of them can kiss my ass. I'll defend my friends, no matter what."

"Alright, miss feisty," Chamomile said. "Come here." She put out her arm to pull Malou into a hug. Malou felt how her whole body stiffened, but Chamomile put her arms around her and held tight, until she felt heat flow through her body, her muscles relax, and her breath still.

"On you go now, you'll be late for Blood Magic," Malou said at last, and pulled away from Chamomile's embrace.

"You not coming?"

"I can't deal with Zlavko right now, it always ends badly."

"Then I don't want to either. Let's do something else."

"Are you sure?"

"Totally."

Side by side, they descended the empty staircase. Rosenholm was quiet, with classes underway all around them behind the closed doors.

"They were actually right, those girls," Malou said.

"What?"

Malou lifted her hands in the air. "Not about *that*. But about the fact that we have no clue what happened. Kirstine hasn't told us a thing about what she was up to. We don't have permission to visit her, or maybe she doesn't want to see us. We don't even know how badly injured she is! This isn't how things should be . . ." Malou didn't like how vulnerable her voice suddenly sounded.

"In what way?"

"Friends shouldn't keep secrets from one another." Malou paused. "Let's see if we can find Victoria, and then go up and visit Kirstine. I don't care what Ingrid says. We are the closest thing Kirstine has to a family right now, and we have the right to see her."

When Kirstine was finished telling them her story, the dark bedroom fell quiet. Malou shifted her gaze from the pale, thickly bandaged girl and down onto her own nails, bitten to the quick. *Shit, man. This isn't kids' stuff.*

"I still don't think I understand it," Chamomile whispered, staring at Kirstine with an almost pleading expression. As if she hoped Kirstine would tell them it was really all just a joke.

"It's like Thorbjørn told me," Kirstine whispered. "The tree has taken him—Vitus—as if he were a sacrifice, an offering. And in exchange, it bestowed me with some powers, which could cause me to harm others—or myself."

"But . . . what did the tree do with Vitus?" whispered Chamomile.

Kirstine swallowed. "It pulled him down into the earth . . ."

"Shit, that's horrible," Chamomile said, turning her face away.

"It did get him off our backs," Malou said softly, in a desperate attempt to shake off the oppressive atmosphere. "But there's still something that doesn't make sense. What were you doing out in the woods—down by the tree—if it's so damn dangerous for you to go out there?"

"We were trying to perform a ritual to break the bond between me and the tree. Thorbjørn had found a description of it in some old texts. But it went wrong."

"No shit," Malou said, feeling her eyes flick over the bandages covering Kirstine's arms and legs. Lisa had done what she could, but there was no avoiding the fact that Kirstine would be left with scars from the serious burns inflicted by the tree's roots.

"So, what now?" Victoria asked.

"Thorbjørn says it's too dangerous to try again." Kirstine's voice lowered. "But he also says he is frightened that it all will end badly. And the prophecy . . ."

Malou remembered the words Kirstine's twisted form had uttered that night at the ship setting. *Fulfill your promise . . .* They still had time. She shook her head to chase away the heavy thoughts. "We still need to find out if Zlavko was Trine's boyfriend, like the necklace suggests. I have a feeling Leah wasn't telling me the truth about him."

"But how can we find that out?"

"The letters," Malou said. "Trine must have written about her boyfriend in the letters she sent to Leah. If we get hold of them, we'll have decisive proof who the killer is."

JANUARY 10TH
2:14 P.M.

Victoria

It was foggy and a cold dampness hung in the air. Night was already falling, though it had never really gotten fully light. Absentmindedly, Victoria snapped off a twig from the high hedge that surrounded the mud-brown house. When they had come in the summer, the hedge had been green, but now it stood bare and dark in the twilight. Malou reached for the gate and opened it.

"So here come the brave musketeers," Leah cackled as they stepped into the dark hallway. It was so cold inside, they could see their own breath. "Aren't you missing one?"

"She's sick," Malou mumbled.

"I knew you'd be back before long. You're so desperate to know more about Trine, are you not?" she mocked, as she directed them through to the living room.

"Where are the letters?" Malou had sat down in a chair at the table opposite Leah.

"I don't know what you're talking about," she said, and looked up at Malou with a smile.

"Stop that!" Malou said. "You promised me those letters."

"I thought you understood that nothing is for free."

Malou took a deep breath. Her pent-up anger gave Victoria the sense of sitting over a human pressure-cooker that might explode at any given moment.

"But—" Malou tried.

"Argh, you're so boring!" Leah interrupted, her smile now gone. "I don't want to listen to you anymore! Go and sit with her, over there." She pointed at Chamomile, who had kept herself over in one corner.

"Leah . . ."

"Go, I said. Move. I want to talk to her instead. This one here." She pointed to Victoria. "Trine's little friend. Come and sit here instead."

Malou got up angrily and gave the chair to Victoria. She sat down tentatively, trying to hide how little she cared to get any nearer to the thin, shriveled woman who was looking at her with a burning stare. Victoria took the trouble to shut herself off. It was important that Leah didn't see even the slightest crack.

"Tell me a secret."

"What?"

"Tell me a secret, then I'll give you Trine's letters."

"But . . . I don't know . . ."

Leah's energy was overwhelming, and it demanded something of her. *An offering.* She would never let her go until she felt she'd gotten something valuable. But Victoria would decide herself what Leah could have. *Some things were more precious than others.*

"We're not here to tell secrets," Malou said from her spot in the corner. "We're here because you promised me the letters Trine wrote."

"Not before giving me a little company first. Come on, isn't that what you do, foolish little empty-head teenagers like you? You sit around telling secrets and talking about boys. Am I right?" She tilted her head to the side and looked at Victoria, expectantly. "You say you can talk to Trine, but Trine isn't talking to you. Is that not how it is?"

"No, she talks to me, just not as often as before."

"Not so often. Maybe she found out that you have dirty little secrets. Because you do, don't you?"

"I don't understand what you mean."

"Tell me about your first time!" Leah demanded.

"My what?"

"The first time you went to bed with a boy."

"Hey," Malou interrupted. "What the hell has that got to do with anything? And anyway, you can't have relations with boys at Rosenholm."

"Tit for tat," said Leah. "Something for me or no letters."

"It's fine," Victoria said, and forced herself to meet Leah's piercing gaze, which she found was lit by gleeful curiosity. This seemed like a suitable offering. "I haven't . . . My boyfriend . . . We want to wait."

"What is your boyfriend's name?" Leah asked, narrowing her eyes.

"Benjamin."

"And you and Benjamin want to wait. And you love each other, and he is to be your first time, on a bed covered in red roses . . . How sweet." Leah blinked and gave a wicked smile. "Except that you're lying."

Victoria shook her head. "What do you mean?"

"Benjamin won't be your first time, will he?" Leah suddenly laughed. "They can't tell, but I can. Your blood, it's going faster—

just a touch, but still, your pulse increased, your heart beat faster. You're lying!"

"No . . ." whispered Victoria.

"Haha, so this is getting to be fun after all!" Leah gloated and clapped her hands together, but then all at once her expression changed, she leaned in across the table and hissed urgently: "Tell me about your first time, or you'll never catch a glimpse of those letters."

"Victoria, you don't need to answer. It's none of her business!" Chamomile said.

Victoria took a deep breath. The air felt viscous, as if it couldn't be drawn into the lungs. The memory caused a cold yellow light to spread before her eyes. Leah had to be given something, and this was a better option than so many others. But that wasn't to say it didn't hurt. She closed her eyes. But the tears spilled from them nevertheless.

"It was before I started at school. It was with someone I've known for years—his parents are friends of my parents. He's a year older than me, and I'd always been a bit crazy about him. Not so long before I started at school, we were at a party at his parents' place. We drank a few of these drinks that had strawberries and champagne in them—they tasted like smoothies. Suddenly he started being really sweet with me—when mostly he just ignored me, normally. We went up to his room, and then . . . we did it. It wasn't something I had planned, it just happened. Afterward he didn't want to talk to me. He didn't even say goodbye. I felt so stupid, I thought . . ."

"What did you think?" Leah hissed, with her head to one side.

"I thought it meant something. That afterward we'd be together. But he didn't even like me. I didn't tell anyone about it. I wanted to forget about it completely. Shortly after that, I got my letter from Rosenholm, so I didn't need to see him again anytime soon, or so I thought. Until there he was, at the initiation ceremony."

"He goes to Rosenholm?!" Malou blurted out.

"What's his name?" asked Leah. "Say his name!"

"Louis. It's Louis. The one who was at Zlavko's meeting."

"Louis?" Malou said. She raised her eyebrows and looked at her with a sudden interest.

"So stupid," cackled Leah. "You're all so stupid, all of you. So young and stupid—you've got no idea how the world works."

"Oh, and you do somehow?" Malou snapped. "What the hell would a loner like you know about anything at all? And so what if Victoria has slept with someone? So what if she's slept with a hundred people? We're all so past giving a damn. Now hand over the letters!"

Victoria felt Leah's suffocating attention shift from her over to Malou, and it felt as if a heavy weight lifted from her chest, letting her breathe again.

Malou had gotten up and was standing in the middle of the floor of the cold, musty-smelling room, and for a moment Victoria thought she might lash out at Leah.

"Malou . . ." There was a tenderness in Chamomile's voice, and instead Malou sank back down into her chair and took a deep breath.

"Seriously, Leah. We're done playing games," she said at last. "Give them to us now."

Leah shrugged as if she couldn't be more indifferent. She got up from the table and left the living room, and they could hear her heavy, shuffling footsteps as they disappeared up the stairs. Victoria wondered if she was gone for good, but after a while they heard the footsteps returning. When she emerged again in the dark room, she was clutching a pile of yellowed papers in her hand. She chucked the pile of letters onto the table between them with a thud that gave them all a start.

"There you are! Now you see if you can work out who killed her," she said in a tired voice, and turned away to leave.

"But don't you also want to know," asked Chamomile, "who killed your sister?"

"Ha!" Leah muttered. She stopped in the doorway and turned back toward them. "I know that already."

January 10, '89

To my Little T,

Mom and Dad called today and told me you'd run off again. And that you tried to come to Rosenholm. Little Troll—it only makes things much worse when you do stuff like that. Did you get time alone? I hope it has all blown over by the time you get this letter.

Little T, it's not long until you are old enough to start at Rosenholm. You need to be patient until then, and do what Mom and Dad tell you to, so they don't get any more upset with you!

Sometimes I feel like my life only really began when I started at school. And when I met "him." Yes, we are together again—he couldn't be without me either. Guess what: he has eyes like Severine in Blixen's short story. Do you remember when I read that to you? Or do you remember the one about the cat better, the one you read to me through the door? You had only just learned to read, so you skipped all the longer words, but it didn't matter a bit.

Stay strong, Little T! Last time I wrote I was really down, but now I'm flying like a bird on the summer breeze, even here in the middle of freezing winter! Life can change completely before you even know. And one day it will be your turn to fly.

Happy New Year xxx

Trine

JANUARY 11TH
4:44 P.M.

Kirstine

Kirstine propped herself up in her bed. It hurt her to move, due to the deep burns on her arms and legs, and she moaned softly.

"Are you alright?" asked Chamomile. "Should we go?"

"No, no. Read on, Victoria."

Trine's old letters were spread out across her duvet. Victoria read them aloud, one after another. They were all letters from Trine to her little sister, and all written in her last year at Rosenholm, which was also the last year of her life.

"Leah made fools of us," Malou concluded, once Victoria had finished with the last one. "They don't say who her killer was."

"If Trine had known who was going to kill her, she'd have done something to stop it," Chamomile argued. "But you're right, there's nothing in here to prove that Zlavko was her boyfriend. She kept the relationship secret, but at some point, Leah told on her."

"All romantic relationships at Rosenholm are secret," Malou said. "That's nothing unusual. Trine's spirit can't reveal her own murderer because he has managed to keep her quiet, in life *and* in death. But Leah can. *She* can reveal him. And she maintains herself that she knows who did it. Why doesn't she just tell us then? Why should we sit here going through all these old letters?" Malou got up, frustrated, and went over to the window.

"Maybe she wants us to work it out for ourselves?" Chamomile said. "Or maybe she would rather we didn't find the killer. Maybe the letters are a red herring."

"The parents don't sound particularly nice," Kirstine said. Her voice was croaky, and she tried to clear her throat but ended up coughing instead. "What does 'time alone' mean?"

"Getting grounded, maybe? The parents both died a few years after Trine's disappearance," Chamomile said. "Malou's library pal found it in a news article. Suicide—out of grief, surely."

Chamomile was interrupted as a blond woman stuck her head in from outside. "Visiting hours are over!" said Ingrid. "The patient needs to rest."

"We're just going," Victoria said, and gathered up the letters. "Can I take these? I'd quite like to read through them again. Maybe there is still something we can use."

"Yeah, take them," Malou said listlessly.

"Do you know when you're getting out?" Chamomile asked.

"A few weeks at the earliest, they're saying."

"We'll come and see you as often as we are allowed," Victoria said, and carefully gave her a hug before they tiptoed out again.

Kirstine was snoozing when a knock came on the door again. With a little trouble, she managed to sit up.

"Is it okay if I come in?" asked Jakob hesitantly. "I won't stay long."

He sat on the chair by her bed. She noticed him glancing at the thick bandages covering her arms and legs. His own palms were also covered in dressings, and she knew that he, like Thorbjørn, had been burned where he had touched her.

"How's it going?" he asked.

"A bit better," she lied.

"That's good to hear. I was really scared." He smiled a half smile, which quickly disappeared, and Kirstine could see that he meant what he said.

"I was too," she said.

"It looked . . . so violent. At one point, I didn't think—" He broke off and just sat, staring down at the floor. Then she realized he was crying. "Sorry," he said, quickly drying his eyes on his sleeve. "I don't know what's wrong with me. I just didn't know how serious it was."

"Is," she corrected him. "How serious it is. The ritual didn't work."

"No, it certainly didn't," he said. "Why didn't you tell me how bad things were? How dangerous?"

Kirstine shrugged. She had no good reason.

He sighed. "I know it was my decision to be just friends from now on. But you must have known that wasn't what I really wanted, deep down. And after all this"—he nodded to her bandages—"I don't think it's a good idea that we see each other. Thorbjørn has told me how important it is that you don't . . . fall in love."

Kirstine looked away. And what if it was far too late for that? What if she had never managed to suppress her real feelings for him?

"Does Thorbjørn know anything?" she asked without looking at him.

"About . . . about us? No, he doesn't know a thing. If he did, he would never allow me to visit you. And I'm not going to anymore, either, Kirstine. I don't dare. I hope you can understand . . . I just couldn't bear it if something bad happened to you because of me."

She nodded. "I'd like to be alone. I'm really tired."

"Okay." He stood up and crossed the linoleum floor. At the door, he turned back. "Goodbye, Kirstine," he whispered. Then he went, leaving her to lie back down in the large hospital bed.

JANUARY 22ND
6:30 P.M.

Malou

"Come in!"

Malou tried the door and found it unlocked. Zlavko was nowhere to be seen in the little apartment, and none of the other students had appeared yet either. She had been quite on edge about arriving there right on time. Zlavko did not tolerate lateness, but she also had no desire to arrive a single minute early if it meant being alone with him.

"Sit down." Zlavko stepped into the small living room. He was wearing a black T-shirt, his long dark hair was wet, and a smell of deodorant wafted through the room. He had just showered.

"Where are the others?" asked Malou.

"They must be on their way. You are early."

"No. I'm right on time."

"It's not until seven o'clock."

"It said six thirty on the note."

"Ah, well, that explains it," said Zlavko, shutting some books that were lying open on the table. "I might have written the time wrong on yours. I'm sure I put seven on the others. Will you have something to drink while we wait?"

"No thanks. I think I'll pass," Malou said icily. "I've got an assignment to do for Nature Magic, so I don't really have time to get poisoned this evening."

"I was thinking more of a cup of coffee?"

"Thanks, but no."

"Well, how shall we pass the time while we wait? There might be something in my bedroom you'll find interesting."

"Oh, no thanks."

Was that why he had invited her here, before all the others? What the hell did he think they'd be doing in his bedroom?

Zlavko raised his eyebrows and gave her a tired look. "So self-absorbed . . ." he spat out.

"What?!"

"Like all young people, you imagine everything revolves around you. I can assure you, I'm not interested in that."

"Maybe you prefer redheads?" Malou held her breath and waited. She fixed her eyes on his face. Would he crumble, once he understood what she was implying? Or maybe explode?

"What are you talking about?" His expression showed little other than caution and some confusion. "Do you want to see where I grow the *Banisteriopsis* plants or not?"

"What . . . what's that?"

"That potent herb in my plum wine, which you were fortunate enough to taste the last time you were here." He opened a door wide, revealing a dark room, lit only by a weak blue lamp. It reminded her of a tanning salon.

She sighed and went in. The place was painstakingly tidy. Even though it felt strangely intimate finding herself in a teacher's bedroom, it was set up so sparsely it could have been any old hotel room—except, perhaps, from the low futon bed, which was made up so tightly you could hardly imagine anyone ever squeezing in under the covers. Along the wall, there was a large chest made of dark wood. Its many small drawers were engraved with decorative carvings, and on top of it there was a mini hothouse. This was where the blue light was coming from. Inside it were some low, leafy green plants.

"It's a fantastic little herb, as I'm sure you discovered. Although you need to know what you are doing, of course. It can be addictive."

"Yet another reason to pass," she mumbled.

"You seemed to be thoroughly enjoying yourself at the party. Would you deny that?"

"Yeah, for sure, I'd deny it. You poisoned me!"

"Such ingratitude," said Zlavko, shaking his head. "I gave you the opportunity to reach inward for a greater truth than we humans are able to comprehend when our minds are not open. I know you saw something. But you're evading it—you're afraid to let yourself go. Tell me what you saw."

"I didn't see a damned thing. And I'm not afraid!" Malou burst out. But it wasn't true, and Zlavko could always smell fear from afar. The truth was that his talk of addiction scared her senseless. She stood and rubbed her left arm, noticing how the skin on the inner side was so thin and the blood flowed so easily.

"There's no need to be afraid of things that help us gain strength and insight. Not these little plants here or any other things one might use," he droned, and Malou hated how it felt like he was reading her thoughts. His eyes bored into her; they were like two dark holes in his face. "By the way, I'm having a little party this weekend. Maybe you'd like to come? I'm inviting the other Crows as well."

"I don't think I can," she said, looking over toward the door, but Zlavko had her pressed into a corner. "Sadly."

"Yes, that is a real shame," he said, in a voice that was so low it was almost a whisper. "You are otherwise always in school on the weekends, I've noticed."

"Anyone home?" someone was calling from the living room. It was Amalie.

Zlavko smiled knowingly at Malou, as if they had just shared a secret, before he turned and went into the living room. "Welcome. Would you like a coffee?"

"I saw a huge snake, it was winding along the sides of the tent. At first, I thought it was going to swallow all of us up, but then I realized that it was us, that *we* were the snake. We were all snakes. I don't understand it though. What can I use a vision like that for?" Amalie set down her coffee cup and looked up at Zlavko expectantly.

"It's only you who can know that. But perhaps the vision was a reminder that the enemy you fear can be found in our midst? Or that we all carry it within us? That all of us, in the end, are snakes?"

Amalie shrugged doubtfully. "Maybe."

"What about you, Malou, don't you want to share with us your experience at the Yule celebration?" asked Zlavko.

"I puked in my friend's hair," Malou said.

"And before that? What happened then? What visions did you have?" He looked at her, waiting.

"I didn't have any visions," Malou insisted.

"That's a shame," said Zlavko, "but of course, not everyone is able to open up their mind. Louis? Can you tell us what happened with you?"

"Yes." Louis turned his cup slowly in his palms. He'd had a haircut. It sat at his shoulders now, and it suited him. "First nothing happened, but then when the music started playing, I got a feeling like my chest was full of fluttering birds. It was really . . . unpleasant." His voice quivered, and he took a sip from his cup before carrying on. His bold smile had disappeared, and now his expression was serious and focused. Malou studied this new version of Louis with interest.

"I wanted to get them out of there," he continued, "and suddenly I looked down on myself, my chest split open and hundreds of birds flew out. They blocked my vision and all around me it was dark from the thousands of black feathers. For a moment, I thought I was going to have a full-on panic attack, but then suddenly the birds disappeared and there was a person there, where the birds had been. I got the feeling that person was something special. And important . . . That was the feeling I had . . ."

He lifted his eyes and looked directly at her. To her surprise, Malou noticed that she was blushing.

"Intriguing," Zlavko drawled. "It's great that you had the courage to follow the vision and didn't try to reject what your vision had to tell you. I think there are important insights hidden in it, if you dare to follow them. Albert, will you tell us now about your experience?"

"Wait a minute!" Louis followed her down the corridor. "Malou! Wait up . . ."

She stopped and closed her eyes for a second. This here would not do; it would get far too complicated, far too quickly.

"There's something I want to ask you about." He caught up with her by the stairs.

"What?" she asked.

"I meant that, what I said. About my vision. It was you I saw behind all the birds . . ."

"I didn't see any birds. I don't think you should read so much into that vision, or whatever it was. It sounds like a load of bullshit." Her voice sounded strangely reedy in the empty corridor.

"It didn't feel like bullshit. Didn't you feel it?" His pupils were wide in the half darkness.

"I'm sorry, but I can't really remember what happened. And as I said, I was really ill. Was there something you wanted to ask me about?"

"Yes. Zlavko is having that party. I just wondered if you want to go with me. We could go together."

"Victoria is my friend. You do remember Victoria, right?"

"Um, yeah. Of course. Our parents are friends. Why? Is she going to the party too?"

"No. And neither will I."

"Are you sure?"

Malou nodded and turned to walk away. He just stood, watching her go.

"Think about it!" he shouted as she turned the corner at the top of the stairs.

Imbolc-Festival

As tradition holds, we will greet
the coming of spring on February 1 with
the solemn celebration of Imbolc,
for all young women in the second year.

The ceremony will be held outdoors.
We will leave from the school at 10:00 a. m.

You should bring with you:
Sleeping bag
Sleeping mat
Warm clothing

Best wishes,
Lisa and Jens

FEBRUARY 1ST
10:25 P.M.

Victoria

Victoria slipped between bare trunks and knotted branches. Besides the crackling of the bonfire and the soft murmurings of students, it was peaceful, and now and then they heard water droplets dripping from the dark branches onto the dead leaves on the forest floor.

"Really? What is this?" asked Malou, holding aloft a black, slimy thing she had found in her bowl.

"Jelly ear," mumbled Victoria, as she nibbled on one of the thick fungi herself. It was a bit like eating boiled gristle.

"Ick, isn't there anything else in here?" asked Malou, poking around in her soup.

It had gotten dark and they had no other light source besides the firelight. It didn't make the soup any more appetizing when you couldn't see what was in it, Victoria admitted.

"Don't say anything to Chamomile," she said in a low voice. "She did her best."

"Dinnertime, finally," Chamomile said, who teetered over, carrying her soup. "It took forever to get it to light. We really needed Kirstine here. None of the rest of us had any luck with the fire rune, so we ended up using matches, and all of the wood was damp."

Kirstine had not recovered enough yet to come with them. She was still up in Ingrid's sick room and was more or less a shadow of her former self.

"So how's it taste?" asked Chamomile.

"Excellent," muttered Victoria with a slight grimace at the bitter taste spreading through her mouth as she chewed on a root.

"It's hot, at least," added Malou.

"Anything tastes good when you are hungry enough, that's what my mom always says," Chamomile said, and dipped her spoon in the bowl.

"Didn't I tell you that the forest would give to us what we needed?" said Lisa, smiling happily as she slurped her soup. "Suserup Forest is one of Denmark's last remaining original forests. In this spot here, there has been woodland for the last six thousand years. So let's have a look at what the food team found for us." Lisa held up a limp leaf, which she had fished out of her soup. "Who can tell me what sea plantain is a good remedy for?"

"Oh, I know this . . . Is it asthma?" suggested Sara.

"That's right. Plantain is an expectorant and it's good for the treatment of respiratory illnesses. You can also chew the leaves or lay them on wounds or sores, and it enhances the healing process. What about dandelions?" asked Lisa, referring to the bitter, woody roots also in the soup.

"Dandelions are good for skin conditions," Chamomile said.

"Correct. And the roots have also been used for depression," Lisa added.

"Then we should have had some more in here," Malou commented, "because this soup is fricking depressing."

A few of them laughed, and Victoria also had to duck her head a little to hide her smile.

"You do the foraging, then, next time we go on a survival trip in February," Chamomile retorted, and demonstratively stuck another spoonful in her mouth.

"Why exactly do we celebrate the coming of spring in February?" asked Asta, shifting an inch nearer to the heat of the flames. "Isn't it a little early?"

Lisa got up to throw another log on the fire. It hissed and crackled as the damp wood landed on the flames and sparks lifted up into the dark sky. The temperature had fallen now, and Victoria was glad they had managed to get a fire going despite their initial setbacks.

"Let me tell you about Imbolc while you finish eating," said Lisa. The slender, dark-haired woman hopped elegantly onto an overturned tree trunk so she was visible to them all as a dark silhouette against the yellow flames. She was barefoot, despite the cold. "In modern times, we see history as a linear path. We are obsessed with thoughts of the future, of growth, and of how everything gets better or, in any case, changes all the time. Placed in a broader context, this is a relatively recent mode of thought. Our ancestors lived in harmony with nature, as we are attempting to do on this trip. They understood how everything repeats itself. For them, life was not linear, but circular. Spring, summer, fall, winter, and then back to the start again. Sunrise, day, sunset, night, and back to the start again. Birth and death. In the stone ages, people lived here in clearings in the forest. They lived on nature's premise that they were one part of the great circle of life."

Lisa balanced effortlessly on the smooth black tree trunk as if she were some kind of forest elf, exactly at home right there. She looked around at them with her dark, sparkling eyes before continuing: "Imbolc is celebrated between midwinter and spring equinox, and since the Neolithic Ages, it was seen as the time that spring is just a step away: the lambs are being born and the light is returning. Hence the tradition of lighting bonfires at night, as we are doing here. Imbolc is Gaelic, but the precise meaning of the word is not known. Some believe it comes from the Irish 'mbolc,' which means 'in the belly,' and refers to the pregnant ewes. Others say that it is an ancient word for cleansing. Imbolc is also a holy time, when you cleanse yourself, commence a new season, and welcome new people into your circle. It is a time of fertility and a tribute to women and femininity." Lisa let her gaze wander over them, settling a moment on a figure sitting at a distance behind them in the clearing. Jens was barely visible in the darkness, sitting on a tree stump, apparently managing to not freeze, even at some distance from the fire.

"In pre-Christian times, offerings were made at the end of winter to the goddess Brigid," Lisa continued. "She was the goddess of spring, fertility, and healing, and is often portrayed as a triple deity—like the Vikings' goddesses of fate, the Norns, or their European sisters, the Greek Moirai and the Roman Parcae."

Lisa bent down and picked a burning branch from the bonfire. Smoke rose from it after the flames flickered out. Using the burned end of the branch, she drew something on a flat stone that had been lying near the fire, and then she passed the stone around the circle for everyone to see what she had drawn.

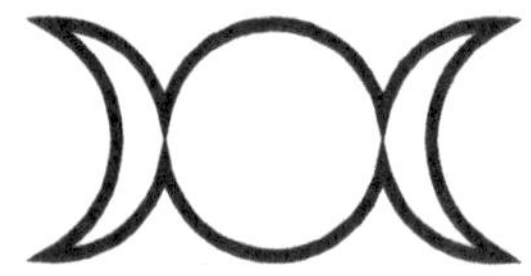

"This symbol is known as the Triple Goddess, or more simply, the Goddess. As you can see, it is like the moon's three phases: waxing, full moon, and waning. The Goddess's three phases are known as the Maiden, the Mother, and the Crone. With Imbolc, we honor the spring, new beginnings, and youth. We welcome the young maidens into our circle, but not before they go through a purification ritual. Here at Rosenholm we celebrate Imbolc with the female students to symbolize your readiness in joining the community of mages. You have completed half of your education, and from now on, more will be required of you. You will have more freedom, but also more responsibility."

"And what if you are not a maiden?" asked Malou.

Some of the girls giggled. Of course they thought Malou was speaking for herself, but Victoria was not so sure, and she suddenly felt quite exposed, sitting there with her back to the vast dark forest.

Lisa hesitated, looking at Malou. "Maiden, in fact, can simply mean a young woman, and that is how it is meant here. It has nothing to do with whether you've made your sexual debut or not. You are all young women, so you are all maidens."

"I've heard that sometimes people have sex in connection with these ceremonies, or something," Sofie said, blushing a little in the light of the fire, while casting a glance over at Jens, who appeared to have noticed nothing.

"Oh, wow, don't you think you've been watching too many movies?" Malou said.

"It's quite alright that you ask," said Lisa with her warm, calm voice. "And it is true, actually, although it doesn't happen quite the way you see it in movies," she added. "There is a ritual ceremony where gods and goddesses come together to release energy.

It can be very powerful, and moving too. Today it is often practiced by means of a ritual where the ceremonial knife, the athame, which is a symbol of masculine energy, is brought together with the cup, a symbol of femininity."

"But is something like that not dark magic?" asked Sofie.

Lisa laughed to herself. "Magic just *is*. It is not evil or good. It just is. It's what we use it for that means something." She stood quietly for a moment before jumping down again from the tree trunk. Then she brought out a little pot of water and sat it upon the bonfire. From the leather pouch she always carried, she took some dried herbs, which she sprinkled into the water, then waited for it to boil. She also sprinkled some of the herbs over the fire while softly reciting something.

"As I was saying, you will go through a ritual of purification this evening," she said, turning to them once the tea was ready. "We start by sharing this tea, brewed using milk thistle, echinacea, goldenrods, and red clover. Take out your mugs."

Lisa went around to them all with the pot. Victoria sipped the tea carefully. She could taste a hint of bitterness and it was herby, but not unpleasant.

"This isn't any kind of hallucinogen, right?" asked Malou, looking skeptically into her mug.

"No, take it easy, the only thing it might do is make you sweat a little," said Lisa. "That's all. It helps the liver, kidneys, and gallbladder to cleanse your body and strengthens your immune defenses. While you are drinking your tea, you can think about the next part of the ritual. At the end of winter, we do our spring cleaning: we celebrate the old and make room for the new. Before you seriously begin your lives as mages, you have the chance to leave behind something of your old life before going to meet the new era ahead. Think about what event, trauma, worry, pattern of behavior, shame, or sadness you could imagine yourself giving up and leaving behind here. Once you know what it is, you may come forward and take a piece of coal from the fire, and then find a stone. On it, you will draw the Triple Goddess symbol on one side, and on the other write something to symbolize the thing you want to leave behind."

Sara raised her eyebrows in surprise, while her sister frowned. Malou was the first one to get up. She took a piece of burned wood from the corner of the fire and a stone from the edge of the fireplace, then went back to sit down.

The rest of the girls sat and thought for a long time. It was completely quiet in the woods, and above them, stars were beginning to appear. One after another, the girls went up to the fire and found stones. Victoria knew the whole time what she would write. Still, she waited until she was the last one to finally choose a stone and write on it, with a shaking hand.

"Good." Lisa nodded to her. "You may all stand. But first take off your shoes and socks."

Chamomile shot her a questioning look before bending down to loosen her shoelaces.

Lisa took the tea off the flames and set it aside. Then she found a large stick on the ground. "Clear the way!"

With a broad, sweeping movement, she swept the smoldering embers of the bonfire so that they were spread out like a glowing orange carpet on the forest floor.

"Please, don't say this is what I'm thinking it is!" whispered Malou. Chamomile had gone pale, and Victoria saw how she grabbed Malou's hand and squeezed it. Victoria felt a momentary stab of loneliness, like an icy jolt in her chest.

"Fire-walking ceremonies are common in many cultures," Lisa explained. "It is a simple but powerful ritual. It symbolizes life's path and reminds us that we have the strength to walk it. It marks the passing from childhood into adulthood." Lisa closed her eyes and took a deep breath. When she opened her eyes again, she started walking.

"Oh shit . . ." whispered Chamomile.

Lisa walked slowly and determinedly, placing her bare feet confidently onto the glowing-hot coals, apparently without getting burned, without glancing down even once. Victoria held her breath and only released it once Lisa had reached the opposite side of the embers.

"Just like that," she said, and smiled coyly at them with a playful glint in her dark eyes. "Now it's your turn."

"I really don't want to," Sofie stammered. "This is even worse than anything Zlavko has ever put us through. Is this even allowed?" She lifted her chin and looked toward the spot where Jens sat, and Victoria half expected him to intervene, but he remained still.

"This ritual is a part of your education," said Lisa. "If you concentrate, you will not get burned. Instead you will get a feeling for how much you are actually able to cope with. You are capable of ten times more than what you believe of yourself. Who wants to go first?"

Victoria looked around at the other girls. Malou stared doggedly into the flames; Chamomile stood with her eyes closed and her head bowed to the ground. All of the girls' anxious feelings were rising like a howling noise in her ears, in the middle of the quiet forest.

"I'll do it," she said.

"Well done, Victoria." Lisa smiled. "Now listen. It's very straightforward. Take your stone in your hand and walk. You should walk like you would on a sandy beach. Don't run, just walk carefully and calmly. As you go, concentrate on whatever it is you want to cleanse yourself of—whatever you want to leave behind out here in the woods. When you get out to the center of the embers, you let your stone drop. Tomorrow, when the fire has burned out completely, we will bury the ashes and the cooled stones at the foot of a tree, and all of it will be left here forever in these woods. Are you ready?"

Victoria nodded. She closed her eyes. Lisa's deep voice rang out in the darkness. She was singing in a strange language, which Victoria didn't recognize; it could have been Gaelic. The song rose and fell, and Lisa's voice sounded strong and vulnerable at the same time. Victoria took a deep breath in, opened her eyes, and took her first step. The dark closed in on her. There was nothing but the glowing light on the ground, the sound of Lisa's singing, her dark eyes across the other side of the embers, and the white stone in her own hand.

Let go . . .

Victoria let her stone fall.

FEBRUARY 2ND
1:32 A.M.

Malou

Malou stared into the darkness. Besides the wind and Chamomile breathing deeply next to her, there was nothing but silence. No, there was also the chattering of her own teeth. That must have been what had woken her. She wormed even farther into her sleeping bag. It was freezing now, and her feet had gone numb with cold. She tried to wriggle her toes down at the foot of the bag, to get some warmth in them. This crappy camping trip swung from one extreme to the other. First they had to walk on burning coals, and now they were lying, getting frostbite on their toes. Her first thought had been to refuse, but when Victoria volunteered to go first and walked over the coals without even hesitating, then Malou couldn't opt out in front of her. It helped, of course, that Victoria hadn't been hurt. She had cried once it was over, but not in pain. Perhaps she was simply super relieved to offload whatever it was her stone symbolized. But what could it be that Victoria carried around so sadly? Apart from her little dose of unrequited love with Louis, was her life not actually quite perfect?

Malou turned so she was facing Chamomile and inched as close as possible for warmth. She could smell her lavender shampoo and feel her warm breath in her face. Her red hair was tangled after a full day out in the woods, and around her neck was the awkward leather pouch she had started wearing. She was looking more and more like a right hippie. Malou rubbed her hands together. *Shit, it was cold!* She could guarantee there would be no more sleep tonight if she had to lie freezing like this. *Blood mages don't get cold.* That's what Leah had said. And if that explorer guy they'd heard about in Zlavko's class could survive in the North Pole, then she could damn well keep warm in a sleeping bag in a Danish forest. Should she try?

She closed her eyes and tried to turn her gaze inward. Blood magic was an instinct, Zlavko said, and even though she hated to agree with that man in any way, shape, or form, she did understand what he meant. There were no recipes in blood magic, no herbs to be blended, no runes or incantations you could learn by heart and reel off. You only had yourself. And your blood. Malou looked deeper inward, trying to feel her heart beating, that huge muscle that compresses itself to send blood out through the aorta, into the major arteries, and farther on through thousands of branches in the lung tissue, where the blood is oxygenated and sent onward around the body. A tingling began in her fingers, and Malou concentrated even harder. Then her feet started to prickle and hurt as the warmth slowly returned, and suddenly she remembered that winter when she'd gotten hit by snowballs by some older boys on the way home from school. Malou hadn't had gloves on, but she'd fought back, making one snowball after another in her bare hands and still launching snowballs after the laughing gang of boys long after they were out of reach. Once home, she had stuck her red, numb fingers directly under the hot tap. At first she had felt nothing. And then the pain came.

Malou took a long, deep breath and opened her eyes. She had done it! She lay still, noticing how the pain gradually eased as the heat spread throughout her body. The muscles relaxed, her heart thumped. And thumped. And thumped. It was beating faster than usual, it was exactly as if she had run a hundred meters at full speed. Why was her heart not slowing down, why was her pulse racing, even though she was now relaxing? Something wasn't right.

Malou unzipped her sleeping bag. The wind had picked up, but it was otherwise quiet in their little camp, with everyone fast asleep tucked in small, haphazard shelters they had built around the fire. She could see the embers, still faintly glowing, and the light of the moon, which, now and then, lit up the dark trees. She felt an inexplicable unease in her body. She was simply burning up inside. *What the hell is happening?* She felt as if there was something that she had to do, and there was no way she could keep lying there. This something was pulling her.

Malou slipped out of the sleeping bag and put her boots on. She had kept all her clothes on when they settled for the night, even her jacket. Before slipping away, she draped her sleeping bag over Chamomile.

She weaved her way between the black tree trunks, taking care not to fall in the thick layer of moss, damp leaves, and treacherous fallen branches that threatened to trip her. Once she was a distance from the camp, she pulled down her pants and squatted to pee. The wind whistled through the trees above her, and at once she was cold all over again. Dark clouds scudded by, intermittently hiding the moon and its silvery-white light. She pulled up her pants again and wanted to head back, but something caught her attention. A glint of light through the trees. Was it just the moon and the clouds playing a trick on her? No, it had been an artificial light, like one from a flashlight. Should she wake Lisa? She wasn't sure it was anything though. Malou hesitated for an instant. Then she left the clearing and went toward the spot she thought she saw the light. She couldn't sleep, in any case, until she had checked if there was anyone out there.

Malou pressed on through the trees. The wind picked up and whistled in her ears. She tried to listen for the sound of twigs breaking, or anything that might point to someone walking around here, but it was impossible to hear over the gale. In the darkness she couldn't find the narrow path they had used earlier in the day, and instead she was stumbling around between rotten stumps and fallen branches. How far had she strayed from the camp now? She'd be better off turning back, as there was nobody here after all. But as soon as she turned, that's when she saw her. Malou gulped a lungful of cold air in one long gasp and opened her eyes wide. The woman came haltingly toward her. She was wearing a long, shapeless coat, which was far too broad at the shoulders for her frail body, giving her a strange appearance. How long had she been following Malou?

"Leah!"

The old woman's white hair flapped in the wind. In her hand she held an unlit flashlight.

"What are you doing here?" Malou blurted out, trying to sound calm, while she switched between holding Leah's gaze and scanning their surroundings.

"Looking for you and your friends," she said, her voice a dry rasp. "It's so hard to get into the school. But I did imagine you'd come out here for Imbolc. I was just about to give up searching for you, but then I sensed you. Maybe you sensed me too? I called you to me. And now you're going to show me where your camp is."

"What do you mean? Why are you here?"

"I finally worked out what it is I need to do. So I can be free."

"Free from what?"

"From Trine, of course!" She sneered. "All these years, and she's still bothering me."

Leah stretched her arm in the air, the one not holding the flashlight. Her sleeves were far too long and covered her hands, but she shook her arm so that the sleeve slid down and revealed what she held in her bony fingers. A long, shiny knife with a dark handle. An athame.

Malou wanted to turn, she wanted to get away, but she was planted in place like a statue, unable to move. Her heart raced, panicking, but her legs refused to respond. *What is going on here?*

"You girls are not going to ruin things for me," Leah said calmly.

Malou's eyes flickered, but she remained frozen, even while every part of her was screaming to get away.

Leah gave a toothy smile and nodded knowingly to Malou. "What's the matter? Are you feeling a little . . . stuck?" She laughed.

Everything inside Malou turned to ice. It felt as if Leah's bony fingers were sliding through her veins and arteries and closing on her muscles so that she couldn't do a thing. Leah had taken control over the blood that flowed in her very veins, and Malou was defenseless.

"Show me the camp," Leah whispered.

"Let me go," hissed Malou, discovering that she still had the use of her voice.

Leah slowly shook her head. She pointed the knife toward her, and to her horror, Malou felt her body taking a step. Forward. Toward the knife.

"No . . ." she whispered.

"Take me to the camp."

"Forget it."

Malou took another wobbly step forward, despite using all her strength to hold her legs still in place. The moonlight caught the knife blade, which was lit up momentarily before cloud again covered the sky. One more step and she would walk right into the knife. She closed her eyes.

"Malou!" The voice was almost swept away by the wind, but it was there.

Chamomile. Chamomile was looking for her. Malou wanted to scream, but her throat clammed up and only a half-strangled moan came out.

"Malou!" Chamomile shouted again, this time closer by, and Malou saw Leah's eyes flicker and felt how Leah's concentration had been disturbed. If she had any chance at all, it was now. Malou fought with everything she had. Her blood fizzed inside her, and she felt as if she was being torn apart. The sweat poured from her, even though she was standing stock-still.

Leah snarled. She could feel it too. Resistance. Malou screamed again, hoping that Chamomile could hear the strange noise coming from her throat. But Leah was too strong. Malou lifted one leg, but still remained where she stood, her leg hanging awkwardly in the air.

"They're coming," Malou said. "They're on the way. You can't take them all on. Lisa, Jens . . ."

"Malou!" Chamomile called again.

Leah's smile had gone. It was her who took a step now, backward. And then another.

"You girls are not going to ruin it all for me," she repeated. Then she turned and disappeared into the dark.

FEBRUARY 4TH
7:30 P.M.

Kirstine

Kirstine pulled her sweater cautiously over her head, taking care to avoid looking at the long red wounds that circled her arms and wrists. Finally they had begun to heal fairly nicely, and Lisa no longer insisted on bandaging them. Kirstine was now also allowed to leave the bed in the medical room by Ingrid's office.

She straightened the duvet and put her last few things into a tote bag she laid on the bed. She had been in here for over a month. She had missed Imbolc—the ceremony marking the transition from girlhood to womanhood. Her transition had been postponed for an entire year. Lisa had talked with her about maybe joining in next year—if she even lived that long. In the meantime, Lisa had only given her something to read up on.

"Knock, knock." Victoria stood at the door. "Can I come in?"

"Of course."

Victoria gave her a cautious hug, but still Kirstine couldn't help let out a moan.

"Sorry. Does it still hurt?"

"A bit. But I'm getting there."

"Yeah, I just thought I'd come get you. I can help you with your stuff."

"This is all I have," Kirstine said, pointing to the bag.

"We've missed you so much. Malou has stolen a tray of muffins and Chamomile is setting up the dorm; it's going to be a little party."

Kirstine hesitated. For a second, all she wanted to do was to hide under the duvet again, even though shortly before that, she'd felt sick and tired of lying in that bed, day in, day out.

"Maybe you're not really up to a party?" Victoria laid a hand on her shoulder.

She shook her head. "I've missed you all too. It's not that, but I don't really want to be the center of attention."

"It's only us four. And you don't need to entertain us or anything like that. Have a muffin, drink some tea, that's all. I've got something important to tell you all."

Kirstine put her hand on Victoria's and gave it a squeeze. "Thanks. And thanks for coming to get me."

"I figured if I didn't, you might not actually come."

Touché. Kirstine looked at Victoria, and her smile was warm and didn't show any sign of offense, even though she had clearly seen through her.

"It just feels a bit much," she mumbled. "Or . . . it's hard to explain . . ."

"You don't have to explain," Victoria said. "I get it."

Victoria held the door for her and they left her room.

"Sometimes it's pretty practical, having a mind-reader as a friend," Kirstine said as they climbed the stairs to their dorm, where the others were waiting.

"I can't read your mind, take it easy." Victoria laughed.

"But you can sense how I am . . ."

"Sometimes. But this was mainly just from knowing you well."

Kirstine paused by a small window on the stairwell, but night was already falling and she could only make out the black outlines of trees against the deep sky.

"They're saying I'm not supposed to go outside," she whispered.

Victoria didn't answer, and Kirstine was grateful that she didn't come out with some cheering comment or try to brush her off.

"It's all so shit," Kirstine said.

"Yup," Victoria said. "Mega shit."

They stood awhile, looking out into the darkness. Then Kirstine turned from the window and climbed the rest of the stairs.

"Here they are! Malou, wave your flag!" Chamomile had hung decorations all over their little kitchen and armed herself and Malou with paper flags. "Welcome back, Kirstine!"

"Thanks," she whispered, and shrunk back as Chamomile wanted to give her a hug.

"It wasn't my idea," Malou said, but she was also smiling at Kirstine and tipped her flag a little while still trying to look like she was only there under duress.

"It's so great that you've come home," Chamomile said, pouring tea and passing around a tray of chocolate muffins. "Now we're finally back together. Everything's back to how it was."

Kirstine nodded but didn't speak. Instead she took a bite of cake, though it felt dry in her mouth and chewing it was an effort.

"There's something important we should talk about," Malou said, looking pointedly over at Chamomile, as if this was something they had already discussed.

"Can't you give Kirstine five minutes?" Chamomile said, quite righteously. "So she can at least eat her muffin in peace?"

"Kirstine also has good reason to find Trine's killer before it's too late, I think?"

"You don't need to go talking about me as if I'm not here!" Kirstine said, putting down her muffin.

"Sorry," Chamomile said, shooting a dark look at Malou. "I'm sorry, Kirstine, you're right."

Malou looked at Kirstine for a sign, and she nodded. "I'd like to hear."

"Leah was out in the woods at Imbolc," Malou said. "She was searching for us, and she threatened me with a knife and wanted me to lead her to our camp."

"Why?"

"She said that she wouldn't have us ruining it all for her. I don't know what that means, but it seemed like she had reached a decision. She said she wanted to be free. Free from Trine. But the worst part was . . ." Malou picked at her chewed-down nails, the only part of her that wasn't perfectly manicured. "Leah took control of my body. She tried to make me do what she wanted. I fought my way free, but . . ."

Kirstine realized that Malou was afraid. Not angry, not irritated, but afraid. And that scared her even more than this unpleasant news itself.

"Don't you think it was just because you got scared, seeing her there?" asked Chamomile carefully. "Maybe you went into shock a little?"

"No," Malou said. "It's like I told you."

"But how do you know?"

"I've felt it before. With Zlavko once, when he did the same thing. Just not as obviously. But I recognized the feeling. She could actually control me."

"Do you think she is capable of killing?" asked Kirstine. The thought filled her with a strange mixture of horror and relief.

Or else she will kill . . . Perhaps the prophecy wasn't about her, in the end. Perhaps it was about Leah.

"I think she's capable of anything at all," Malou said. "Including murder. After what happened in the forest, I can't stop wondering how her parents died. What if it wasn't even suicide? What if Leah forced them to do it, just like she tried to force me to show her the camp?"

"Do we know how they died?" asked Victoria.

"All it said in the paper was that it was suicide," Chamomile said. "It didn't say how they did it."

"Maybe there was a police report," Victoria said.

"Can those be accessed?" asked Malou.

"No, not unless you are a relative of the dead person. But maybe I could try asking my dad. He works at the Ministry of Justice."

"Whatever happens, we can't go to see Leah anymore," Chamomile said. "Not even if she asks us to. She told Malou that she couldn't get inside the school. As long as we are here, we're safe. We need to find a way to prove that Zlavko was Trine's boyfriend, and without involving Leah."

"Yes, about that," Victoria said, pulling out the stack of Trine's letters. "There's something I should show you. I decided to reread all of these. I thought there had to be something we could use. And I found it. In a letter from January." She unfolded the lined sheet and read aloud. "*Guess what: he has eyes like Severine in Blixen's short story. Do you remember when I read that to you? Or do you remember the one about the cat better, the one you read to me through the door?*" She looked up from the letter. "When I read it again, it rang a bell and I managed to find the story."

Victoria brought out a book. It had a scruffy, blue-green cover and on the front, in slim, dark lettering: *Winter's Tales.*

"This is an anthology of short stories by Karen Blixen," she said. "I think we actually read the story about Severine in middle school."

"Really?" Chamomile said. "Why is it important, Victoria?"

"The story is about Severine, who is married to a sailor. He has a figurehead made in the image of Severine. The figurehead has eyes of sapphire. Listen: *And when he came home to Helsingør, he showed his wife these clear blue eyes and repeated to her: 'Now, she is quite perfect. Now, she has your eyes, and you have hers. On the voyage from India, she has seen flying fish flash by only a few feet before her; with these clear blue eyes she has seen the moon in the sky reflected on the sea.'*"

"Severine had blue eyes?" Chamomile said.

"Yup. That's even the title of the story. It's called 'The Blue Eyes.'"

"The one about the cat . . ." Chamomile said, pointing to Trine's letter. "She must mean *The Blue-Eyed Cat*. The children's book Leah read aloud for Trine."

"That can't be right," Malou said, pulling the book over to her. "Zlavko has brown eyes."

"Exactly," Victoria said. "Trine's boyfriend had blue eyes. It wasn't Zlavko."

"But the necklace. We all felt it. It had a connection to him. And he followed you in the woods, Victoria," objected Malou.

"Maybe we made a mistake?" Chamomile said hesitantly. "We had just spoken about him, right before the thing with the necklace, because I was angry he'd given you that stuff to drink . . ."

"But then what now?!" Malou snapped. "So, we just find some guy with blue eyes, or what? That won't be very hard at all, will it, there's so damn many of them!"

"Malou . . ." Chamomile said. "We have to try. We can't just give up."

"If this is all correct, then we're completely screwed," Malou said. "The only lead we have is Leah . . ."

"Whoa, no way," Chamomile said sharply. "I know what you're thinking and it's far too dangerous. We cannot visit her again."

"Maybe *I* can try to see if she's hiding something," Kirstine said, almost surprising herself with her words.

"You!" exclaimed Malou. "The one not even allowed to leave the school!?"

"No, I don't need to go anywhere. I can try through clairvoyance, see if I can get a feeling for whether she's holding something back. Hiding something."

"Can you? Just like that?" asked Malou, sounding impressed. It wasn't like her.

"Yeah, I think so. Since . . . the thing with the tree . . . I often get visions. Some are of things that happened long ago, others are of things happening in the present. I saw you, lying out in the woods, Malou. During the Yule party."

"No way," Chamomile said. "That's really cool, Kirstine."

"Should I try?" She was surprised at her own courage. Or was it foolhardiness? On the one hand, she felt so safe here, in the dorm with her friends around her, and the idea was tempting. She had been doing nothing at all for over a month, and this was making her feel that, despite everything, she wasn't completely caged in.

"Yeah, try it!" Malou said.

Kirstine closed her eyes. The visions she had had until now, they almost always overwhelmed her. They were something she would rather not experience. But now that she was actively calling on them herself and searching for something in particular, she was a little unsure how to go about it. The Viking seeresses often performed seid in connection with a ritual. They took drugs or reached a state of trance via singing and drumming. And they used a special staff. Kirstine had tried using a staff like that last year, but she didn't have one now. She knew, though, that she had the power to do this. She could feel it, deep inside. She was grounded, linked to the earth and the power of thousands of years of Nordic history, and she knew that the tree had given her special abilities.

Normally, above all else, Kirstine avoided thinking about the tree in any way. Its snaking roots, the clicking noises from the earth below it, the trembling branches. Now, however, she allowed her mind to go there, and very quickly she noticed a tingling feeling in her body, a sign she was on her way to another place, and she let herself follow. It was a bit like flying. She saw flashes of the landscape below her, fields, roads, a little grove, a white tower by the sea. Now and then, something would catch her eye, but she knew where she was headed and she focused on that. And then there it was. The house. She was there. She was standing in the living room. It was quiet, she was alone, and she didn't feel afraid. *What are you hiding? What is it you're not showing us?* She repeated the questions to herself again and again. The daylight had fading and it was dark in the house. Kirstine had the feeling that she should get away from there before nightfall, but she stood where she was. After all, there was nothing here that frightened her. *Where are you hiding it?*

It was almost completely dark around her now, but light fell into the room from the kitchen door. Kirstine went in. The kitchen was also empty, and she went through to another door. On the other side was a set of steel stairs, leading up. The steps strained under her feet. She was weightless and took up no space in that place, and she saw it all clearly, as if she were standing on the stairs in that moment. At the top, there was a landing and a single door. She tried the door, but it didn't open. She tried again. She felt very clearly that there was something on the other side that she needed to see. Something important. Suddenly, the still air around her was ripped apart by a scream. She'd been discovered!

The scream continued, splitting her eardrums and making her head ring with pain. Kirstine clenched her fists and pressed them against her ears, until it hurt, but the sound of the furious scream continued. Leah knew someone had gotten into the house, but Kirstine couldn't see her and Leah hadn't done anything to her. Other than screaming at them, to the point that Kirstine almost fainted. Maybe Leah *couldn't* harm her. Kirstine wasn't really there on that landing; she was here in the kitchen at Rosenholm. *Turn back. Get back to yourself.*

At once the scream stopped and she returned to her own body. She was breathless and soaked in sweat, but unharmed.

"She found me," she spluttered, as she opened her eyes to the others' shocked faces. "I don't know how, but she knew someone was in the house."

"Did you see anything?" Malou asked.

"There's a room. Up on the second floor. I'm sure there's something important in there. But I couldn't get the door open."

"Could it have been Trine's room?" asked Victoria.

"Maybe," Kirstine said.

"We need to get into that room," Malou said. "And I'm going to work out how."

Happy birthday, sweetheart!

I hope you celebrated.
Did you get some nice presents?

Yeah, thanks

Good. I'll come by with
mine tonight ;)

Tonight? The girls are
planning a party.

I'll just wait till you can sneak out

It'll go wrong.
You'll get found out.

No, I won't. See you later.
Love you!

Love you. Be careful!

FEBRUARY 23RD
8:13 P.M.

Victoria

The music from the kitchen was loud. Victoria had a glance in the mirror. Seventeen years old. She smiled to herself. A little tentatively, as if she didn't want to be happy prematurely. She certainly hadn't had the best luck with her birthdays in the last few years. Last year she had collapsed out in the snow and could have ended up freezing to death if the other girls hadn't found her. And the year before had been even worse, if that was possible.

"Come on, Victoria. The party's starting now, with or without you!" yelled Chamomile from the kitchen.

"I'm coming!" she answered, and left the turret room, dressed in the pajamas Chamomile said were mandatory if she wanted to join the party.

The kitchen was still decked in decorations—hanging there since the day Kirstine got home—and now, colored fairy lights had been added. On one of the walls, silver balloons were pinned up in the shape of a number seventeen.

"Whoa, oh, oh," sang Chamomile as she danced around in her slippers and scattered confetti across the kitchen table. She was wearing her big sunflower T-shirt, her faded cotton pants, and her red hair was pulled back in a messy bun on top of her head.

"Lovely!" Victoria said.

"Isn't it though?" Chamomile said, and stuck a yellow cocktail umbrella in her bun. Victoria shook her head when Chamomile offered her a turquoise one.

"Shall I serve the nachos now?" asked Kirstine, who was standing at the kitchen door, wearing a pair of old, shapeless jogging pants and a long-sleeved T-shirt.

"Yeah, I made guacamole as well," Chamomile said. "You like it quite spicy, right?" She put the bowl on the table and turned to Malou's closed bedroom door. "Malou, we're starting! And bring the beers!"

"Relax, I'm coming!" called Malou from the room, and shortly after, she appeared wearing a pink robe. She had a plastic bag in her hand. "Smart of me to hang them outside the window so that they're chilled," she said, putting the beers on the table.

"You've got makeup on," Chamomile said accusingly, putting her hands on her hips as she inspected Malou closely.

"I always have makeup on," Malou said without meeting her eyes.

"And that there is not your normal night wear—I've never seen you sleep in that."

"It's a robe, it counts as nightwear."

"What are you wearing underneath?"

"Nothing. Do you want to check? Honestly, it's like living with a prison guard, this stuff."

"We agreed, pajamas on, no makeup."

"That wasn't something *we* agreed. You just decided it. And that was before I found out I was going to another party as well. If I have to go do my face after this, then I won't make it, so can you maybe drop your little reign of terror?"

"I honestly don't know why you've said you'll go to that party. And with Louis. And on Victoria's birthday. Seriously, Malou. As if we don't have more important things to deal with right now. Were you not supposed to be working out how we can get into Trine's room?"

"What do you mean?" snapped Malou. "Have you, by any chance, worked out a way to keep Leah away? Because then I think we should cancel this and get down there right away. As if it wasn't actually your idea to have this party. You said we were needing to enjoy ourselves a little!"

It went quiet as Chamomile and Malou kept staring each other down. It seemed that neither wanted to be the first to look away.

"So here are the nachos . . ." Kirstine said, carefully setting down a large bowl on the table between them.

"Great," Chamomile said huffily, though it was unclear whether she meant Malou's party or nachos. "Well, we're not going to spoil Victoria's birthday, in any case. Sit yourselves down, have a beer, there's more where they came from, and Victoria, I've got an extra present for you."

Chamomile put down what was obviously a bottle, wrapped in colorful paper, onto the table with a slam. Victoria quickly unwrapped it.

"It's a bottle of my mom's homemade blueberry schnapps. It's really good, just wait and see!"

"What about 'Happy Birthday' one more time?" asked Kirstine, her words a little slurred.

"Please. We sang it four times already," grunted Malou, who was still sipping her first beer.

"Yes, let's do it with the instruments again!" Chamomile said, ignoring Malou's complaint. "Kirstine, you choose this time."

"I'll have the uke, then!"

Victoria was happy to clap along this time, while Kirstine and Chamomile sang at the tops of their lungs.

Despite the strained atmosphere between Malou and Chamomile, Victoria was surprised to be enjoying her birthday and had come to have a big grin firmly on her face.

After the fifth rendition of "Happy Birthday" and yet another large schnapps, Chamomile stood up. "Hey, we should really sing the schnapps song!" she said, and cleared her throat before starting to sing, heartily, as if it were the national anthem she was performing. "Haps, haps, we want schnapps!" she reeled off some lines of the bawdy traditional drinking song. "Haps, haps, we want schnapps—cheers!"

Victoria felt a bubble of laughter spreading from her belly right up and through her until she couldn't hold it in any longer. "Hahahaha," she laughed aloud, and clinked glasses with Chamomile, downing another schnapps afterward.

"Seriously, you don't know that one?" asked Chamomile.

Victoria shook her head. "No, I've never heard it."

"Kirstine?"

"Well, we don't drink alcohol in my family," Kirstine said, finishing the drink and then bringing the glass down onto the table with such force that it gave a loud smack. That made Victoria burst out laughing all over again.

"Malou, you know it?" Chamomile said.

"Yes, thanks. I know it all too well," she answered, as she examined the guacamole suspiciously. "Has this got a lot of garlic in it?"

"Yes, sir! And that's why we should all eat some of it," Chamomile replied.

"No thanks," Malou said, leaving the bowl where it was.

"Oh, of course. You can't go out smelling of garlic if you're hoping to score."

"Hey, will there be boys at that party?" asked Kirstine, who was concentrating on scooping up a small mountain of guacamole on a nacho and cramming it all into her mouth. "That's not allowed!"

"Yeah, that's sneaky!" giggled Victoria, who still had that bubbly feeling inside that made everything seem funny.

"Louis says it's Zlavko's party. So he can decide who gets to go. It happens to be taking place somewhere in the school, but school rules don't apply."

"Wow, then I think we need to set up our own club," Chamomile said.

"Yeah, where we make up the rules!" Kirstine said, knocking over the beer Chamomile had given her seconds before. "I don't actually like beer," she slurred, when she saw how it had spilled across the table and was dripping down onto the floor.

"Is that right?" Chamomile said, casting a glance at Victoria while she dried up the mess. "Leave it then."

"But I do like schnapps!" added Kirstine, squinting slightly at her glass, which made Victoria burst out laughing again. "A schnapps club!" Kirstine exclaimed. "We can start a schnapps club!"

"Oh yeah, baby!" Chamomile said, and raised her glass to all three of them. "Then we need a motto, like Malou's club. What is it you all have again? 'To infinity and beyond!'"

"Don't be so dumb," Malou said.

"Tell us what it is, then!"

"I don't feel like it."

"*Corvus oculum corvi non eruit*," Victoria said. "It means something like 'A crow never stabs another crow in the back.'"

"Aha. Sounds like the perfect motto for a band of criminals," Chamomile said.

Malou made a face at her.

"Does it *have* to be in Latin?" asked Kirstine, leaning her elbow into her guacamole. "I don't know any Latin . . . or wait! Is Lego not Latin? And Volvo. Or yoyo . . ."

"I know!" Victoria said. "*In vino veritas.* That means that there is truth in wine. Or, like, how the truth is spoken by kids and drunk people."

"I don't like wine either," Kirstine said, and reached for the schnapps bottle, which was already nearly empty.

"No, we don't even drink wine," Chamomile said. "What about *In schnappsis veritas*? The truth is found in schnapps!"

"Schnappsis!" laughed Victoria. "That's good!"

"And we will always remember the day the club was founded. On Victoria's birthday!" Kirstine said solemnly, and raised her glass again. "Happy birthday!"

"This party is getting out of hand pretty fast . . ." Malou said, who was picking at the label on her beer.

"Where is your party going to be?" asked Victoria.

"I don't know," Malou said. "I'm going with Louis. He's waiting until I'm finished here." She checked her phone. "Actually, I need to go gather my things, so I don't end up late."

"Yeah, you go do that," Chamomile said, standing up. "I think we need to change up the music a bit. Get something more upbeat. Come on, Kirstine, we need to dance!"

Victoria laughed so hard her belly ached at the sight of Chamomile and Kirstine dancing around to some deep reggae beat that

Chamomile had put on. While Chamomile moved perfectly in time with the music and looked like she belonged in a Jamaican dance hall, Kirstine swayed around slowly, her arms raised like a large bird with outstretched wings.

Victoria sat for a while watching, feeling grateful, before she got up and went into Chamomile and Malou's room. Malou was leaning over her makeup case, selecting a few things, which she put into her purse. She had taken off the robe and underneath wore a black evening dress.

"Sounds like it's kicking off in there," she said when she saw Victoria.

Victoria sat down on Malou's bed. It was, as ever, perfectly made, with the quilt folded neatly over the duvet, in contrast to Chamomile's messy heap of clothes, sheets, and pillows.

"I'm sorry I have to leave your birthday party a little early," she said as she rummaged through her handbag, "though I do doubt those two are going to last much longer if they keep drinking schnapps like fruit juice."

"Malou . . ."

"I can't find the lipstick I wanted to wear . . ."

"You were right, with what you said about Zlavko's club. That it's much easier for me to say no. Because I already have so much of those things they're offering . . ."

Malou looked at her in surprise. Then her expression hardened. "You have everything."

"Ha, no . . . not everything." Victoria shook her head. "I said no because I know them. I know people of their type. Their lodges and clubs and special societies. And I know Louis. He's not worth wasting your energy on, Malou. Honestly, keep away from him . . ."

Malou closed her bag and swung it over her shoulder. "Were you in love with him?"

"Yes," admitted Victoria, "I was."

"Maybe you're still a bit hung up on him?" asked Malou. "Or maybe you'd simply rather not see him getting together with your friend? A bit like when my friend got together with Benjamin, right under my nose. It doesn't feel so great, I can tell you that much."

"Malou, it's not that. I'm trying to warn you, but I understand if you find it hard to trust me after Benjamin . . ." Victoria looked down to where her hands lay in her lap. She took a deep breath. "I'm only asking that you look out for yourself, Malou. That's all."

Malou opened the door to the kitchen. "I'm really good at looking out for myself," she said. "You don't need to worry about that."

She turned on her heel and left Victoria alone.

"Oh, here comes the black crow!" screeched Chamomile from the kitchen.

Victoria couldn't hear Malou's response, but she did hear the door to the hallway slamming behind her as she left. She sighed and got up.

Back in the kitchen, Chamomile and Kirstine were still dancing around.

"Oof, now I need that beer, Kirstine. Don't you want something else to drink? Some water, maybe?" Chamomile asked, and sat down at the table, but Kirstine didn't answer. She was still swirling around, faster and faster, her head moshing out of time with the music.

"Do you think she's okay?" asked Chamomile.

"Maybe she was needing to let go a little," Victoria said, watching Kirstine. "She's been shut away such a long while. She must be dying to forget it all for a bit."

"Yeah, that makes sense." Chamomile nodded. "I'm worried we'll soon have finished off your present altogether," she said, gesturing to the schnapps bottle, which was nearly empty. "I'll need to steal another one next time I'm home. We can't very well have a schnapps club without schnapps. What did you get for your birthday from Benjamin?"

"Oh . . . I . . ."

"Whoa!"

Victoria was interrupted by Kirstine, who had clearly tired of dancing and collapsed into her chair. She mumbled something unintelligible.

"What?" Chamomile said, bending over her. "Do you want some water?"

"HAPS, HAPS, HAPS!" shouted Kirstine, spattering Chamomile with drops of spit, while Victoria fell about laughing.

"No more schnapps," Chamomile said. "Have a little water."

"I'm tired," muttered Kirstine.

"Do you want to go to bed? Come on, Victoria, let's help her."

They got Kirstine propped on her feet and steered her into her bed. It wasn't easy, as Kristine was heavy and Victoria was also feeling fairly dizzy, and still couldn't stop laughing as they stumbled into the doorframe and tripped on the kitchen chairs.

"That's it, now you can get some sleep," Chamomile said, placing the duvet over Kirstine once they had finally gotten her lying down. "That's the clever part about a pajama party—you've already got your pj's on."

"Malou wasn't wearing pajamas. That was against the rules," Kirstine mumbled. Her eyes were already closed.

"Who cares," Chamomile said. "Malou just wanted to look good for the party with the boys."

"Malou's sad that she's not as pretty as Victoria," Kirstine mumbled. Immediately, Victoria felt her cheeks flush red and she avoided Chamomile's eye.

"Well, that's life," Chamomile said, and touched Kirstine on the cheek. "Get some sleep now."

"You're not as pretty as Victoria either, Chamomile . . . but you're lovely," Kirstine drawled.

Victoria looked up at Chamomile, horrified, but Chamomile just smiled and smoothed down Kirstine's hair.

"That's the truth," she said. "*In schnappsis veritas.*" She blinked at Victoria.

"I'm not pretty, either, but I've got nice breasts. And Jakob was in love with me, even though I'm too tall," Kirstine continued. Her voice was really soft and slow now. "But I broke up with him before I even got to sleep with him . . ."

Victoria had to cover her mouth to stop herself giggling out loud, and Chamomile repeated, "*Sleep with him!*" in an astonished tone.

"I sometimes think it's a real shame," slurred Kirstine. "I think he would have been really good at it . . ."

"Seriously, that's our teacher you're talking about," whispered Chamomile, pretending to cover her ears, and tears came to Victoria's eyes as she held back her laughter. But Kirstine didn't notice. She was already asleep.

FEBRUARY 23RD
10:30 P.M.

Malou

Forget them. Just forget them.

Malou topped off her nearly nude lipstick and put a discreet brush of golden blush along her cheekbones. She took one last look in the mirror. Earlier, she had actually taken out an ankle-length, lightweight, flowery dress she had recently bought. But when she tried it on in her room, she'd immediately regretted the purchase. *Nope, it just isn't me.* Instead she went for a short, tight dress. It was black and, together with the high-heeled boots, emphasized her long legs. She had pulled her hair back from her face but otherwise left it loose. She packed her makeup bag and nodded to her reflection. *Just forget the others.*

She let herself out of the bathroom near the girls' dining room and went toward the stairs to the floors above. On the way, she met Anne and a few of the first-year girls, but Malou did not stop to chat. Instead she headed up the stairs—not the ones she normally used, but the ones to the boys' rooms on the floor above theirs. When she got up to the second floor, she found Louis waiting for her in the narrow stairwell. He gave a low whistle.

"Good evening, miss," he whispered, and she saw the trace of a smile at one corner of his mouth. They stood facing each other for a moment. Malou was worried at first that he was going to give her a kiss, but he just stood there. And looked at her. Then he smiled. "It's this way," he said, pointing upward, letting her go first.

"I don't think I've ever been up so far before," she commented. "Are we going into the attic?"

"You'll find out in a minute," said Louis, sounding amused about knowing something that she didn't.

"Why couldn't you just tell me where the party's being held?" asked Malou.

"Only Crows are allowed to know. That's to say, full members of the Crows' Club."

"Wait," Malou said, and stopped on the narrow stair to turn and face him. "Are you a member now? Like, fully?"

"That's right," he said. "I'm no longer on trial. Zlavko picked me as a member a few months ago, after the Yule party."

Malou frowned. "Why?"

He smiled again. "I think he thought I was ready. Zlavko keeps an eye on all the aspiring members and picks the ones he wants to let in."

"Who else is in?"

"Not many, so far. Amalie, Albert, and Vibe. But be patient. He'll ask you soon. He definitely wouldn't have invited you to the party if he didn't think you were worthy of it."

"Worthy . . ." spat Malou, turning back to continue up the stairs. "I don't even know if I want to be a member."

"You don't mean that . . ." He squeezed alongside her. "Why?"

"I have my reasons."

"What reasons are they?"

"Firstly, people are talking. They think the club is all about dark magic—that we practice it." She stopped again and turned to him. He was very close.

"Come on, who says that? Have they been to the meetings? Do they know what it is we do? No, right?"

"Why is it only people from Blood or Death who were invited?"

"Because they are the best. Zlavko wants the best students. Do you not think people are just jealous because they didn't get invited?"

"Victoria is not jealous. She turned it down, and she advised me against joining. She warned me about all of it. Including you."

"Did she really? Victoria?" For the first time, she noticed anger in his voice, which rang around the empty stair where they stood, so close they were almost touching. "Why?"

"Maybe because you used her? She was really into you and you used her, and then afterward you never even spoke to her. She told me about it."

"What? That's total bullshit. Is that what Victoria said?"

She nodded. "Yeah, something along those lines."

He gave a cold laugh. "Well, that's pretty ironic. You know Victoria's family is known for their fairly weighty past, right?"

"What does that mean?"

"A long line of dubious mages with a tendency toward dark magic—a very sinister family tree, I can tell you that much. Nowadays, of course, they have reinvented themselves to appear nice and regular—outwardly, in any case."

"Victoria's family? But they're not even mages. She told us that herself on the very first day we moved into school. She's the first mage in her family."

He snickered. "Wow! Did she really say that? She's very creative, you've got to give her that. I don't think I'd be able to come up with such an imaginative lie. Our parents are friends, if you can call it that. Though, my mom and dad are more like hangers-on. I think they were very flattered when Victoria's parents started inviting them to their fancy parties. They are mages, through and through."

"But why would she lie about that?"

"I don't know. Maybe she gets off on lying. It's also not true that I used her. It was more like she used me."

"Victoria used *you*?"

"Yeah. She persuaded me to be her first time."

"Persuaded?" Malou said, crossing her arms. "You could have said no, right?"

"Yeah, and I should have, but she insisted. She wanted it to be me, but if I wouldn't, then she would just find someone else. That was what she said."

"Louis, that doesn't make any sense at all . . ."

"Don't you get it? I became an instrument in some plan or other of hers. She wanted to get her first time out of the way, before she started at Rosenholm. So that her powers would be stronger. So that she would have an advantage she could make use of."

"But . . ." Malou stopped. Her mind was whirling. Victoria was from a family of mages, a family with a shady past. *She* had persuaded Louis to sleep with her. To get stronger powers? Was that why Victoria had found it so easy to contact spirits, even since she began at the school? Is that why she always seemed to outperform Malou across the board? And had she really planned the whole thing quite deliberately?

"I can't get my head around it . . ." she said.

"Victoria is not the person she's made herself out to be, Malou. She's lied to you. I'm sorry if you thought you were friends . . ." He took her hand, but she pulled it away.

"We *are* friends." For some reason or other it sounded more like a question than a statement. Malou glanced back down the stairs. "You know what, I don't think I should go to this party, actually . . ."

"Argh, this is so annoying!" he exclaimed loudly, making her jump.

"What?"

"That we are standing here on the stairs talking about Victoria, instead of being in the party, dancing, getting drunk, and having fun. I really couldn't care about Victoria. This is not what I had in mind, for sure . . ." They stood for a moment, saying nothing.

He took a deep breath. "Malou. Beautiful, fascinating Malou. Can't we just forget this? Can't we forget Victoria for a moment? Should she be allowed to ruin our evening? Come on, let's not give it any more thought. Let's go to the party, have a drink—I'm great at mixing drinks. If you still want to leave after you've tasted my espresso martini, then I'll personally escort you all the way to your door."

She hesitated.

"Okay?" he asked softly.

"Okay."

He smiled with relief. "Come on then."

They continued up the stairs to where they soon heard the muffled sounds of music gradually getting louder and louder. They reached the end of the stone steps and continued up some steep wooden ones. Finally there was an old door, and from behind that, the thumping electronic bass showed they had come to the right place.

"After you," said Louis, opening the door.

The room was big and dark, with sloping walls. There were no lamps, but candles flickered all around, tall, narrow ones in empty bottles or big, thick candles in clusters in bowls. In one corner, she saw a guy she didn't know bent over some mixing decks, deeply focused on fusing the next piece of music with the one before so that the little huddle of students on the dance floor would have no thoughts of leaving it. She caught sight of Amalie and Albert, whirling around, but there was no sign of Zlavko.

"This is the old drying loft. Really cool, isn't it?" said Louis loudly to be heard over the music.

Malou looked around. They were right up in the rafters, and she could see the beams and the inner side of the old roof tiles.

"This is where the castle's maids would hang up the clothes to dry in the olden days," Louis continued. "And they lived up here too. Their old sleeping quarters are still here. You can see them later. First, come and see the bar—I helped build it."

He took her hand and led her down to the farthest corner of the room, where a bar had indeed been built out of old planks and pallets. Some beanbags had been scattered around it, and several people were sitting chatting, as far as the music allowed them.

"Who are these people?" she asked Louis.

"Zlavko invited them," he said, shrugging. "Maybe they're former students. But check out the bar, it's great, right?"

Malou nodded. Both at the temporary bar and at the homemade shelves behind it, filled with bottles of all shapes and sizes. Any kind of alcohol you could think of—spirits and others she had never seen before. There was a huge bowl of citrus fruits, a large bucket of ice with a couple of bottles sticking out, rows and rows of different kinds of glasses, and a large silver cocktail shaker. It must have cost a fortune. Had all that really only been brought in for tonight?

"What can I say, Zlavko knows how to party!" Louis said, and went behind the bar. "So, what can I get you? You can choose anything from any shelf. Do you want to try my espresso martini?"

Malou nodded, grateful she wouldn't have to choose, as the only drink she really knew was rum and cola. She watched as Louis poured various measures of different things into the shaker, mixed it together with ice, and poured it into two fancy long-stemmed cocktail glasses.

"Wait!" said Louis, searching for something. "I know I brought them. It needs to be just perfect . . . Here they are!" He fished some coffee beans out of a jam jar and sprinkled them over the drinks decoratively. "Ready!"

Malou held the glass carefully and took a sip. "Mm!" she said, and nodded approvingly. Louis smiled from ear to ear. It suited him, and she got a sense that all of this had in some way or another been for her benefit. It was a good feeling.

"Hello, you two, are you enjoying the party?"

Malou turned around, feeling her good mood instantly draining away. There was nobody quite like Zlavko for ruining a nice atmosphere. As always, he was immaculately dressed—a midnight-blue shirt, tight trousers, and his glossy hair pulled into a topknot. The knife he insisted on always carrying hung from his belt, and in his hand he held a tall, slim wineglass of something bubbly. "Champagne?" he asked.

Malou lifted her glass to show she had already been taken care of.

"It's great in here," Louis said, popping out from behind the bar and putting his arm around her. Normally she would have shrugged him off, but right now it actually felt pretty nice that she wasn't standing alone under Zlavko's scrutinizing gaze. He nodded without lifting his eyes from her, but luckily his attention was drawn away by a young man who wanted to ask him something, and Malou spotted the chance to slip away.

"Didn't you want to show me the maids' quarters?" she whispered in Louis's ear.

For a second, he just raised his eyebrow in surprise, but then he nodded. "Of course, it's this way."

As they stepped away, Malou caught the young man talking with Zlavko give Louis a quick thumbs-up and a slight raising of his eyebrows. Malou took that to be the internationally recognized sign for *Good job, dude, you've scored!* and she shook Louis's hand off her shoulder, annoyed.

The maids' quarters were at the gable end and were separated from the rest of the drying loft by some basic plasterboard walls.

"We knocked together a few of the other rooms and made a kind of lounge, but we left this here just as it was," said Louis, opening the door to the little chamber. He had picked up one of the candle-lit bottles so they could see in the dark room. Other than an old chest, the room was empty, but the thin walls were covered in moth-eaten, dark red floral wallpaper. Malou tried to imagine how its little gold-and-white flowers might have been the only cheery thing in here for the young girls who had once lived here. There was a small window in the roof, through which they could see the clear, starry sky. Of course the stars would always have been free for them to enjoy as well, even as such poor girls.

"It must have been cold up here in the winter," said Louis, putting the candle down on the chest. "The kitchen maids were better off. They were allowed to sleep down by the fireplace, where it was lovely and warm."

Malou took a few steps back and forward on the ancient floor, which surely creaked, though you couldn't hear anything over the music.

"Did you know there were only male students at Rosenholm in the olden days?" asked Louis. "The only women and girls were all servants."

Malou narrowed her eyes. She hadn't known that. Should she have? Louis seemed to know lots of things that she had never even thought about.

"Young women were only allowed to start studying here in the 1800s," he continued.

"The world is so damn unfair," Malou said.

"Yeah," he said, and crossed over to where she was. "You're right about that. But we can change that. We can make it better." And he leaned down and kissed her on the forehead. A light kiss, like the way you kiss a child. Full of care. It felt good.

FEBRUARY 23RD
11:51 P.M.

Victoria

"So I managed it after all."

It startled her. Victoria hated when he snuck up on her like that. Hated it and loved it. She turned slowly around.

"You managed what?"

"To give you a birthday kiss." Benjamin gently pulled back the hood of her winter jacket. "Happy birthday."

The kiss was tender and slow and it left her more lightheaded than even the schnapps had.

"Come on," he whispered.

They headed away from Rosenholm, from where they could be observed from its windows. The night was cold and still. There was a new moon, and the stars of the Milky Way trailed a glittering band across the sky. A thin layer of snow covered the ground, revealing the way Benjamin had come in. She traced his footprints with her eyes, knowing they would somewhere become paw prints if they followed them in among the trees. Instead they turned down toward the castle garden, where Lisa grew her many herbs and plants. They walked in silence along the narrow paths and looked over the many beds framed by low hedges. Little signs indicated what would grow where when spring arrived.

"You would never imagine Lisa would be such a neat freak," said Benjamin. "Look how perfectly cared for it all is."

But Victoria was not interested in gardening right now. "You promised me a present," she said, leaning in toward him and pretending to bite at his earlobe.

"Ow!" he said. "You'll get it, be patient. Are you a bit drunk, or what?"

"How can you think that?" she said indignantly, holding back a laugh. "I never get drunk."

"What about your party, is it finished?"

"It peaked early. Stand still."

"What is it?"

"I just need to check something. Come over here into the light." She pulled him closer to the greenhouses. One of them was lit with a dull orange light, which colored the snow and made his hair look completely black. She put her hand on his cheek and turned his face gently so she could look at his jawline. Right there, where the muscles of his jaw tightened, whenever he concentrated or was angry or looked at her with those big eyes . . . She had often wondered what it would be like to let her tongue trace over that exact spot. She stood on her tiptoes, and his skin felt warm and a tiny bit salty on her tongue.

"Victoria . . . what are you doing?" He looked at her in surprise. "That tickles."

A broad smile spread across her face. "Where's the present?"

"Okay. Here it is." He rummaged in his jacket pocket and pulled out a small package. "Wait a minute!" he said, pulling it back in to himself. "Listen, I really wasn't sure if this was a good idea. You mustn't be disappointed if it's completely off the mark, but you're also not so easy to buy gifts for . . ."

"That's because I'm so rich," Victoria said, and laughed when she saw how his face fell. "But it's true! How could you ever buy anything that I don't already have?"

He sighed. "Yeah, now that you mention it. Maybe we should just forget about it . . ."

"Never!" Victoria said, snatching the present out of his hands. She tore the paper off. It was a small wooden figure. A wolf. "Did you . . . ?"

"Yes, I made it myself. As a kind of amulet. It can keep watch over you when I'm not around. I don't know, maybe it was dumb of me . . ." He scanned her face anxiously, and in that moment he reminded her more of a dog looking for its owner's approval with its big, searching eyes, as opposed to the wild and free wolf she knew he could also become.

"It's perfect," she said, putting her arms around his neck and pulling his mouth toward hers. Her tongue burned, her body felt both heavy and light at the same time, the blood pounded in her ears as she pressed into him, as if there shouldn't be even the slightest gap between their bodies. Victoria slid her hands under his jacket and he winced lightly.

"Your hands are cold," he whispered.

"Are you cold?" she asked. "You've got such a thin summer jacket on. You should take it off."

"Take it off?!"

"Yeah, I think you're going to have to take it off. Or you'll just be standing getting cold in it," she said, and tried to stop laughing, though his confused expression felt like the funniest thing she'd seen in a long while. "I actually think you'll need to take a whole lot of clothes off."

He stared at her. "But . . . here?"

Victoria nodded, serious now. “We have to.”

“There’s snow!”

“Come on then, we’ll go in here.” She pulled him toward the end of the lit outbuilding and opened the door. It was a kind of orangery, a huge, high-ceilinged greenhouse where Lisa grew all the plants that couldn’t withstand the Danish winter, and that’s why it was heated. Citrus trees, exotic shrubs, passion fruit, kiwi, peaches, figs, and olives grew side by side with smaller insignificant plants that Victoria didn’t recognize.

“Welcome to the jungle.” She laughed and started to unbutton his jacket. “Isn’t it lovely and warm in here?”

“Oh yeah, it’s at least 50 degrees in here.”

“I’ll make sure you don’t get cold.” She took off her jacket and spread it on the floor. “Get undressed.”

He laughed softly and wriggled out of his jacket. Then he pulled his shirt over his head so he stood just with his bare torso. “Is this what you wanted?”

“Yes,” she whispered.

First, she just looked him all over, and then she let her hands run over his body. Over his shoulders, shoulder blades, lower back, and belly. She felt the warmth of his skin on her lips, let her tongue trace over his collarbone, his chest, his neck. He stood with his eyes closed, a deep growling noise coming from his throat. When she undid his jeans, he took hold of her face in both hands and kissed her so hard that it felt like everything melted away and flowed into one.

FEBRUARY 24TH
1:30 A.M.

Malou

"Whoa!" Malou twisted over on her high-heeled boots and fell onto one of the beanbags, with most of her drink sloshing out over her hand. She giggled at herself and took a taste of what was left in her glass. What was it called again? Tom Collins? It sounded like the name of some '80s singer her mother would put on at her parties, but the drink tasted really good in any case, sort of both sweet and sour. Malou downed the rest and let the glass roll on the floor. *Shit!* How was she going to get out of this bean chair again? She looked around to see if there was anyone who might give her a hand, but then gave up and lay her head back instead. She closed her eyes. The room was spinning around her anyway, and maybe she had a few too many samples of those fancy drinks. But it had been fun. Really fun. They had danced. And kissed. But where was Louis now? Had he just disappeared? She needed to find him and say good-night before she left. And he'd also promised he would walk her home.

When she opened her eyes again, she couldn't tell how long she had been sleeping. The music was still on, but quieter now, a slow, heavy rhythm, and there was nobody to be seen. Lots of the lights had burned out and it was dark around her. The party had to be over.

Had Louis just gone without saying goodbye? Had he left her here? She had to get back. Malou rolled out of the beanbag and onto all fours before—with some difficulty—getting to her feet. Right now, she was really glad nobody was around to see her like this. She tottered a little on her heels and thought about taking her boots off, but then she got the hang of them again. Where was her bag? Malou looked around, and the movement made her feel dizzy. Had she left it in the maids' quarters? She staggered toward the rooms at the gable end and was about to open the door to the room she'd stood in with Louis, when something else caught her eye. The door to one of the rooms farther along stood ajar, and light spilled out. Malou went over to the door and opened it. It was something she was going to regret.

Hundreds of candles burned in tall candlesticks. In the middle of the room there was something between a sofa and a bed, made of wooden pallets and mattresses. That's where Louis lay. His torso was bare and his near-white hair shone against the black cover on the mattress. His eyes were closed but he was not sleeping, and a faint smile danced at the corner of his mouth.

Behind him was Zlavko, half sitting, half lying, with his long black hair loose and covering his face, so that at first Malou couldn't see what he was doing. But then he casually swept his hair back and leaned over Louis again, and Malou saw how he was slowly licking up the drops of blood that formed a thin red trail from Louis's throat and down over his collarbone.

Malou turned away and threw up.

PART 4
SPRING

Forget-me-not
"May my image live forever
in your heart."

Please answer me.

At least let me explain?!

You can't go on just ignoring me like this.

PLEASE! Will you give me a chance
to tell you what happened?

I'll give you a chance to go to hell.
Leave me alone.

Guidance support for second years on March 6

The focus will be on career planning, subject choices, and the second-year project.

A schedule showing individual student appointment times is hanging in the canteen.

See you there!
Jens

MARCH 6TH
9:05 A.M.

Malou

I just need to get this over with as quickly as possible.

Malou sat down in the chair opposite Zlavko. He gave her a nod.

"Half an hour of guidance counseling," he said. "But you can take your time. I don't have many students doing their project in my subject."

There were few blood mages, so even though all students were introduced to the subject, hardly any would specialize in it. Which seemed to mean, to Malou's dismay, that Zlavko was not exactly busy.

"And what does Malou want to be when she grows up?" He placed his elbows on the table and rested his chin on his clasped hands.

Malou avoided his gaze. Every time she looked at him, she saw *that* scene before her. She had fled from the drying loft as fast as she could. Louis had seen her, but had Zlavko? Or had he been too busy licking up Louis's blood? Did he know what she had seen? Malou looked down at her hands. She had bitten her nails again. What did she want? Right now, more than anything, she wanted to avoid being involved with Zlavko in any way whatsoever. Unfortunately, she was running out of options. They needed to find a way to get into that room, the one that might have been Trine's. Malou had plowed through tons of books and shady websites but without finding any information that was any use to them. Nothing had gotten her any closer to understanding the powers Leah possessed or how they could be overcome.

"Well, a tongue-tied Malou. That must be a first," Zlavko said.

She took a deep breath. Okay, what did she want to do when she left school? She wanted to become someone, she wanted to have a career and earn money. Have a job, where she would wear nice clothes, and not be dependent on anyone else. Where she could put her special abilities to use to her own advantage. She knew Zlavko could help her with that. He might be creepy as hell, but as long as he wasn't actually a murderer, it was her intention to make some use of him. She came from a family of losers, she had no contacts, she didn't know any important people. But he did.

"I want to be rich."

Zlavko laughed quietly. "If nothing else, at least you're honest. And how do you plan to go about that?"

"That's what you're supposed to tell me."

"Aha. Well, among other things, that depends on how much it matters to you how you earn your money?

Malou thought about it. "I don't want to have anyone else making the decisions about what I do."

"You want to be your own boss?"

She nodded.

"Then maybe you should be self-employed. Start your own business. What about becoming a lawyer? Then you could open your own practice."

"And defend petty thieves and violent criminals? No thanks."

"You decide for yourself what cases you take on. And a powerful blood mage would have certain advantages in a court of law—plus the fact you have knowledge of our world. Now and then, we mages also get in trouble with the law. It would be nice to have a defense lawyer who understood the demands we can be placed under. I could quite imagine that any such lawyer would quickly be in demand in our circles. Of course, you'd need to be good and have what it takes to make it."

"And how do you become a lawyer?"

"I can get you some information about studying law, but right now you would do better to concentrate on your project. What do you have in mind?"

Malou cleared her throat lightly. "I'd like to look into how far you can go to form a special connection with another person, so that you are able to influence their actions . . ."

"Telepathy?" asked Zlavko.

"No, not exactly telepathy, more being able to get them to do things you want them to do."

"You want to learn how you can control another person?"

"I would like to *study* the phenomenon."

Zlavko smiled, revealing a row of neat white teeth. "*Mind control.* Also known as *Impero Spiritus*. A branch of magic that is no longer respected and, in fact, forbidden in many countries, and certainly not something that is on the curriculum here at Rosenholm. So-called dark magic."

"What if you want to research ways of combatting it?" asked Malou. "To protect yourself from it?"

"I don't think that would make a great difference, if you were to ask anyone else. I, of course, hold the view that we shouldn't overprotect our students. They should be allowed to study the world—

the whole world and not just the parts of it we adults deem nice or refined or censored enough for our little ones to delve into without getting their hands dirty. Thankfully, our new principal is not as controlling or fearful as our last one. But you should be aware there won't be any material on that subject here in the school. All books on such subjects have long been removed from our library."

"What do I do then? Find stuff online?"

"No. I mean, you might find something there, but most of it comes from cheesy quacks trying to con people out of their money. But there is another library. A place where they collect all the literature on these special areas of magic. The vast majority of the books were sadly destroyed after the Great Reform, but some were saved. The library also has a vast archive containing research data and the records of various studies undertaken over the years that are no longer considered comme il faut. Have you heard of the Society for Psychic Studies?"

Malou shook her head.

"It's an organization concerned with all aspects of the supernatural. They have a huge library in Copenhagen."

"At the Black Diamond?" she asked.

Zlavko smiled. "No, it is a little more tucked away. In a cellar under Vester Voldgade. It's close to the city's main square," he added. "I can give you the address and a note for the manager, who I know fairly well, and you can arrange a visit yourself. You might find some information on your subject there, if you are lucky."

She nodded. "Fine."

"And, Malou? It would be better to handle this project with a certain amount of discretion. There's no reason to go around telling everyone and anyone about it. Is that understood?"

She nodded again. Zlavko tore a sheet of paper from his pad and wrote an address and a short message on it before he handed it to her.

"Remember to give my regards."

When Malou reached for the note, he pulled it back toward him, just an inch or two, but enough that her fingers only snapped onto thin air.

"What do you say?" he asked, and looked at her with raised eyebrows.

"Thanks," she mumbled, and Zlavko handed her the note.

"You're welcome."

Fricking idiot. Malou shut the door behind her and stuck the note in her pocket. At the very least, he hadn't assaulted her or drunk her blood, and that was always something.

"Malou?"

Louis was leaning against the wall opposite the door she had just come out of.

"Get lost."

"We need to talk!" he said, but it sounded more of a plea than an order.

"Have you been standing outside the door listening for me to come out, like some creepy stalker?"

"What else can I do? You won't meet up with me. You don't answer my messages. I asked Zlavko and he told me when you had your guidance meeting."

"Yeah, I imagine he owed you a favor."

"I'd just like to explain to you what was going on."

"Seriously, I have really, *genuinely*, no desire to hear what you two were up to. I saw plenty, and I definitely don't need any further mental images like what's burned into my retinas!"

"Have you told anyone else about it?" His voice was a little strained, as if it was a great effort to keep it so quiet. He took hold of her arm, and she wanted to pull it away, but she froze when she saw what was in his eyes. It wasn't anger, it was fear.

She sighed and closed her eyes momentarily. Then she shook her head.

"Good." He breathed again in relief. "Good."

"It wasn't to protect you," she said. "I just don't want to have to look the others in the eye and admit they were right all along. That I should have kept myself out of it. Why did you let him do it?"

"Zlavko is sick, Malou. I don't know his story, but lots of blood mages experiment with that stuff when they are young."

"Drinking other people's blood?!"

"Taking in a little part of another person, when that person has allowed you to, yes. It's a strong tool for harnessing your powers and getting them under control. I've heard that's why many powerful blood mages throughout the ages have made use of it. It helps them to focus their powers. Sadly there is a risk of becoming dependent."

"Dependent?!"

"Not so loud," he shushed her, while checking they were still alone in the empty corridor. "Yes. There are ways of keeping the addiction at bay, but deep down, you'll always have that same craving."

"You knew all that, and you still went along with it, willingly? I saw you, you weren't being forced into it."

"That's true. I've let Zlavko drink a little drop of my blood a few times, but I don't take any of his or anyone else's, for that reason. I'm not going to get hooked on it. I did it to help him out."

"You honestly feel sorry for him?"

He nodded.

"That's sick, you're all sick!" Malou said. "I don't want to have anything to do with you anymore."

"Zlavko *is* sick, but not in his mind," said Louis. "He is really afflicted by it, and I helped him. He does so much for us, and he is going to do so much more. What's a few drops of blood, in that bigger picture? For me it doesn't mean anything, but for him it's everything. I wish that you hadn't found out in that way, but I'm not going to be ashamed of it."

"Then why don't you want me to tell anyone?"

"Not everyone can handle it. So it needs to be a secret . . ."

His face darkened, as if the thought running through his mind at that moment really caused him pain, and Malou expected him to start shouting at her. Instead he took a deep breath and looked at her.

"Listen . . . I really want you to understand this. You know the whole thing about all people being equal?"

Malou shrugged. "Yeah?"

"It's a lie. Some people are predestined for something special. And you know that yourself. You've always known that you are somehow special. That's true, isn't it?" He didn't wait for her to answer before continuing, "And you know how I know that? Because it's like that for me too. I've always known it. And I can recognize it in you. I saw it in my vision. We have been chosen. Other people will never understand that. Your friends don't understand you the way I do, so don't go telling them anything. It just causes a bunch of gossip and confusion. That's why we need the Crows. We understand each other. We don't judge, nobody gossips, nobody is ashamed. There's only loyalty. And the freedom to be who you are."

He gently touched her chin and made her look into his bright gray eyes.

"Imagine it, Malou. A place where you are allowed to be completely yourself, where you can develop yourself and reach your full potential. None of that 'blessed are the meek,' none of that stuff about you shouldn't think you're better than anyone else. No, here you can be the real you. The Malou I see is beautiful and strong. Powerful and ambitious. You've got the strength to make whatever you want in life happen. If you stick with me, if you join the Crows and have their support, nothing could stand in your way. I promise you that."

She shook her head. Then she turned and walked away, clenching her fist around Zlavko's note in her hand as she went.

MARCH 6TH
11:25 A.M.

Victoria

"So, Victoria, I'm really excited to hear what thoughts you have." Jens fixed his gaze on her, and as always, she could sense how his intense and charismatic energy filled every room he entered.

"I don't know what I'll do my project on, but I know what I would like to be when I'm finished with school."

"Okay, let's hear it."

"A therapist."

"A therapist?" Jens eyebrows shot up. "Why a therapist?"

"I want to help other people," Victoria said, and noticed the disappointed sigh that her words elicited.

"Yes, of course, and there are lots of different ways of doing that. You have a great talent, Victoria."

"Do I?" She had been expecting this reaction, but nevertheless, she felt annoyed by it. "I can sense how people are, but I'm almost never able to help them get better. Either I can't think of anything to say to them, or I say it all the wrong way. My talent, as you call it . . . I don't think I can put it to any use unless I learn how to help people get better."

"Yes, and that sounds very admirable, Victoria, but also a little . . ."

"Naïve?"

"Yes, naïve," he said, not quite managing to hide his irritation, which Victoria could feel like a tingle on her skin. "What do your parents say about that?"

"I haven't told them."

"Victoria, you have many possibilities here. You have an unusually clear connection to your powers, you are intelligent and studious and you come from a family who will support you to achieve great things in life. Why throw that away? Zlavko tells me that you declined to be a part of the Crows' Club?"

"That's right."

"I think you should reconsider that. The members of Zlavko's club may be students today, but they will be tomorrow's elite. I'm sure that in ten or fifteen years' time, we'll be seeing many of them in important positions. Victoria, you also belong there, with the best students at this school."

"No, you're wrong there," she said. "That's not where I belong. I don't want to be one of the elite. I want to become a therapist and help people. I'm sorry if that disappoints you, but that's how it is."

"You shouldn't apologize to me, only to yourself. You're wasting your potential," said Jens. "Yes, you can sense moods, but your talent is not just that. You have an exceptional connection with the spirit world. You only need to learn to channel that, so you can develop your clairvoyant abilities. I don't think you quite understand how good you could become. If you were willing to take up those extra classes with me again, I'm sure you'd get a real sense of how great you can be. It would be real shame to waste that talent. You could make a difference, Victoria. A real difference."

"I'd like to make a difference for ordinary people."

Jens leaned back in his chair and sighed. "I see." He drummed his fingers a little on the edge of the table. "Then at least you'd need to study psychology in college?"

"Yes, that's what I also thought at first, but that would be too easy."

"Too easy?" He looked at her, quite surprised.

"Yes. I could manage that kind of education. Read books, write essays, sit exams, get good grades. But then what? After five or six years, I'd be out of college again and right back to the very same place I started, without any experience of how to talk to people and help them in practice. No, I don't want to do a long, theoretical education. I'd rather one where I get lots of real experience. *That* would be a challenge for me."

"It sounds like you've made up your mind," Jens said, and his face became all those faces who had looked at her in that same way—her father, her mother.

Victoria took a deep breath. She held it a moment, and as she released it slowly through her mouth she imagined opening a big door in the wall she had learned to build around herself. She was angry. Angry at Jens and angry at her parents, with their critical looks when she didn't live up to their expectations. And she knew that Jens could sense her anger right now. But she could also sense his feelings. Much more clearly now, as she had let her guard down.

"Disappointment, irritation, contempt," she said, looking him straight in the eyes.

For a moment he kept still, but then he frowned as he realized what she was doing. She was reading him.

"Surprise, curiosity, nerves."

"Stop that, Victoria," he snapped.

"Anger, fear, control." As she said the words, she realized she was going in deeper than she normally did. *Control* was not a feeling. It was a thought. Jens's thought. Suddenly, her sense perception disappeared. A wall of energy rose up between them. He had pushed her away and regained the upper hand. They sat facing one another for a time.

"Thank you, Victoria, I think we are finished for today then." His voice was no longer angry and revealed nothing about his emotional state. She got up and left without another word. Only once she was out through the door did she realize they hadn't even talked about what she would write her project on.

On her way upstairs, Victoria took out her phone to check for messages from Benjamin. There were none, but she did have one email. Her heart started racing and she took the last of the stairs two at a time. Luckily the other girls had finished their guidance meetings and were gathered in the little kitchen, around a vase of crocuses Chamomile had picked in the park that morning.

"Did it go well?" Chamomile asked, as she sat down.

"Nope," Victoria said, "but who cares. Look. I got the police report." She put her phone down on the table before them so they could all read it together.

Kalundborg Police
November 16, 1995, 5:15

Two found dead at Solvangen 11, Kalundborg. Police were called after neighbors reported not having seen the residents for a long time. A patrol car visited the address, but nobody answered the door after officers knocked several times. The officers decided to force entry to the house and were able to see for themselves that two people had died there—a man and a woman, both approximately fifty years of age. Both had hung themselves and were still hanging in the living room. Also at the address was the couple's adult daughter, who appeared not to acknowledge the death of her parents. Officers accompanied her from the house and presented her for psychiatric assessment. The attending officers suspected suicide, and a suicide note was also found at the address.

Additional note, November 20, 1995: District medical officer confirms that the couple committed suicide and the police hereby close this case.

"They hung themselves in that living room," Chamomile said as she shivered. "Right there, where we've all sat."

"And Leah did nothing," whispered Kirstine. "She just left them hanging there."

"I think she knew exactly what she was doing," Malou said.

"You mean it was her who was behind it?" asked Victoria. "Imagine killing your own parents . . ."

"It would certainly have been the perfect crime," Malou agreed. "Impossible to prove."

"Leah is so full of hate," Kirstine said, looking puzzled. "She hated her parents, she hated her sister. And now she is the only one still alive."

"But does that mean . . ." Chamomile frowned. "Leah could be the one behind Trine's murder? Is that why Trine wants Leah to say sorry?"

"Trine was killed by a man. That's what I saw in my vision," Victoria said.

"And what about the boyfriend. The one with the blue eyes?" Kirstine said.

"Oh yeah. Forget it."

"Leah knows who he is," Malou said. "At some point, we are going to get that secret out of her."

Victoria got a strong feeling that they were all thinking the same thing, although none of them were saying it aloud. *At some point isn't good enough.* Time was running out for them to fulfill their pledge to Trine, before it was too late. *Before the night that leads into summer.*

Can't we meet and talk it over?

I don't know . . .

I've put that world behind me.
I can't go back.

And that's just the end of it?

We should be able to talk
to each other.

Okay. At the greenhouse.
I can be there around 3:30

MARCH 10TH
3:57 P.M.

Chamomile

"Are you coming, Malou?" Chamomile asked cautiously. "Dance class starts in ten minutes."

Malou was lying on her bed staring at her phone. Chamomile half expected Malou to ignore her, but she lowered the screen for a moment and looked at her.

"I don't feel like it."

"There will be boys there, at least," Chamomile tried to tempt her. As always, all students were expected to practice the formal dances during spring semester, but the actual Spring Ball was only for third-year students. Dance practice was therefore a heaven-sent opportunity to get a little closer to the opposite sex, even though it would be supervised by teachers.

"I don't want to dance with the boys. Can't we just practice together instead?" Malou muttered.

Chamomile smiled and made no reference to how Malou had been very interested in dance practice the year before, when she had danced with Benjamin. Malou had lost interest in this year's lessons as soon as she found out her partner was one very lanky, shy guy with glasses who would blush and break out in a sweat as soon as he saw her. Still, Chamomile was happy. The atmosphere between them had been strained, to put it mildly, since Victoria's birthday and the Crow's Club party. Malou had all but stopped talking to her. It hadn't helped her mood any that she still hadn't managed to contact the secret library Zlavko had told her about, where she hoped she could find out how to stop Leah.

"Hey, can we skip it?" Chamomile asked. "We can go down and see how my St. John's wort seedlings are looking. I sowed a few rows, I'm really hoping they grow well so I can use them in my project."

Chamomile had told Lisa she might want to study medicine and potent plants, but Lisa had advised her to narrow her field and focus on one specific plant in her project. So she'd decided to study the beneficial properties of St. John's wort, which for hundreds of years had been used against depression and feeling down. She was thinking about using it on herself when it was ready—she sure could do with a boost to her mood.

Malou put her phone down. "Hmm . . . okay. Anything sounds better than an hour of getting my feet trod on and that guy's Adam's apple jutting in my eyes."

"Malou!" Chamomile said, shocked, though her mood had already lifted a degree or two.

They took their jackets and scarves and headed to the greenhouses. It was cold and damp still in March, so Chamomile had sown her herbs down in the heated greenhouse, where Lisa had altruistically offered the use of a planter in the farthest corner.

When they stepped into the warm, humid air of the greenhouse, they could hear a male voice that sounded agitated. Chamomile looked at Malou, who raised her eyebrows in surprise and shrugged her shoulders. She gestured with her head and went a little closer. Behind the large, lush fig tree stood Benjamin and Victoria. The two hadn't noticed them come in.

"Tell me, though, what had you imagined?" said Benjamin, frustrated. "You make a revelation like that, and now you expect me to just act like nothing happened, or what?"

"No, I don't. But you could at least try to understand . . ."

"I really can't, though!" he shouted, waving his arms. "I can't understand it."

"But can you forgive it? Even though you don't understand?" Victoria's voice sounded thin and vulnerable, and it pained Chamomile to hear it.

"I don't know . . . I really don't know, I . . ." Benjamin turned and saw them.

"Sorry!" Chamomile exclaimed. "We weren't snooping. We just came down to check on some seedlings I've planted . . . St. John's wort . . ."

"Damn it, there's no getting a minute alone in this place!" he yelled, and turned on his heel. He slammed the door of the greenhouse behind him so that the old glass panes rattled sharply.

"Sorry, Victoria," Chamomile said. "We didn't know you were in here."

Victoria shook her head to show that it didn't matter, but her big dark eyes were filling with tears. Chamomile wrapped her arms around her.

"What were you fighting about?"

Victoria shook her head and hid her face in her hands as she sobbed. "I think it's over."

"No! But why?" asked Chamomile. "Can you talk to us about it?"

Victoria shook her head again. "I just want to be alone for a while." She dried her eyes and pulled out of Chamomile's embrace.

Then she turned up the fur-lined collar of her elegant wool coat and left the greenhouse without saying anything else.

Chamomile watched her go. She could not forget about what Jens had told her: that he worried Victoria might run into trouble. Next time they were alone, she would try to get him to explain what he had meant.

MARCH 16TH
4:15 P.M.

Malou

Malou was walking quickly. An icy wind blasted through the streets and she wanted to avoid her hair getting totally messed up before she even got there. She had taken the train to Central Station and quickly found her way to Vester Voldgade, which was very close by Tivoli and city hall. An expensive address, although the house she was now facing looked fairly ordinary—almost anonymous—certainly in comparison to the elegant buildings around it. If she hadn't been looking specifically for this place, she would have walked right past it without even wondering what lay behind its closed door. A small plaque by the entry system showed she had come to the right place: the Society for Psychic Studies. Malou pressed the buzzer and waited. Nothing happened. She rang again, this time holding it down a few seconds longer. The entry intercom stayed silent. Damn . . . It had taken a long time to arrange this appointment. Far too long. It was already mid-March. Time was running out, and if this trip turned out to be a dead end, she knew what she would have to do. Zlavko would know how they could protect themselves from Leah. He was a blood mage and possessed the same powers. But could they trust him? Malou was far from sure of that.

She pressed the buzzer yet again, this time holding it down firmly, but nothing happened. She was about to turn and leave when the intercom crackled.

"Yes?" said a fuzzy voice.

"My name is Malou Nielsen . . ." she began, but a buzzing noise from the door let her know the person had already opened the door. She pressed the handle down and opened the large, heavy door. As it closed behind her, the noise of the traffic and the city subsided and it fell quiet. It still seemed like any ordinary hallway, neat and well kept but nothing special. There were two sets of stairways. Zlavko had said that the library was in the basement, so she went down. *Bingo.* The next door she came to had a small sign saying *Society for Psychic Studies Library. The library is open by appointment with the manager.*

Malou smoothed her hair down with one hand and grasped the handle. It was unlocked. On the other side stood a man who looked to be around the same age as one of those iron-age bog men. He was pressing a button on the entry system, slowly and hesitantly, but when she came in, he turned to her.

"Is that you?" he shouted, blinking at her. His eyes were a watery gray-white.

"I'm Malou Nielsen," she said loudly, and reached out her hand.

"I can't work this stupid thing," he said, indicating the intercom. "Helmuth Winther."

"I have an appointment. I'm a student of Zlavko's. From Rosenholm. He sends his regards."

"What?"

"Zlavko sends his regards," Malou shouted. The old man nodded, but she wasn't sure how much he had understood. "He gave me this note to give you." She opened her belt bag, but Helmuth shook his head and pointed at his strange eyes.

"I'm seeing less and less now. It's the worst curse of getting old, not being able to read anymore. You should make sure you appreciate your sight while you have it," he said, indicating for her to follow him. It was dark in the cellar. A worn dark-green carpet covered the floor, the ceiling was low, and every space was filled with metal shelves stacked with books. Freestanding filing cabinets lined one wall, interspersed with small tables and desk lamps. In various spots, piles of books had been left out, as if nobody had looked at them in a long time, and on the whole, the place seemed pretty dusty and cluttered. Helmuth continued slowly and hesitantly farther into the library, the whole time fumbling around and holding on to bookcases and cupboards, so as not to lose his balance, and most likely also to help him find his way. Malou imagined he had likely spent so many years in the library, he no longer needed his eyes to navigate the labyrinth of bookshelves.

"Are you familiar with the Society for Psychic Studies?" he asked without waiting for an answer. "The society was founded in 1905. Now, you might be thinking it was me who founded it, but I'm not quite that old! I'm not yet past ninety-six."

Malou laughed politely. She had the feeling Helmuth Winter gave the same spiel to any visitor to the library.

"The society was founded with the purpose of studying and documenting those things that established science dismisses as inexplicable. Which those of us in the know call magic. That includes summoning spirits, telepathy, clairvoyance, healing . . ." He stopped and waited for her. She was a little taller than him; his stooped back must have taken a good eight inches off his original height. He was bald on the top of his head, but a few straggly white tufts still partly covered his rather ample ears. People said that ears never stopped growing your whole life, didn't they?

"Is this for an assignment?"

"Yes. I'm a student at Rosenholm," Malou said, taking care to speak loudly and clearly.

"Ah yes. My own old alma mater. But that's such a long time ago. I was there when Svensson was principal, but he must be long dead. All of them are gone now." He stood still for a moment and looked ahead of him blindly, his bottom lip sticking out like a little child's. Malou wondered if she should say something, but luckily he came back around again. "My hearing is also very poor. More and more, it's only the spirits I can hear," he said, as if he had forgotten who she was and why she was there.

"I'm looking for a book for an assignment," Malou tried.

"Yes, yes." He nodded. "The library is here at the disposal of those who seek knowledge and insight. You can't take the books home with you, but you can read them for as long as you like. I have nothing I need to see to. If you tell me what subject you are interested in, I can guide you toward the right shelves. I may not be able to read anymore, but I do still remember where most of the books can be found."

Malou hesitated. Zlavko had said she should be discreet, due to the nature of the project. "I'm looking for information on magic that is no longer practiced . . ." she tried.

"Aha, maybe you're writing about the Great Reform? Then you should try that shelf on the second row to the right."

"Thanks!" she said, but the old man had already turned away from her and was wandering toward an old oak chair with broad armrests. Malou found the shelf and scanned the spines of the books. They meant nothing to her. What was it she was even looking for? Resolutely, she pulled out a huge pile of books and dumped them down on the nearest desk.

Two hours later, Malou hadn't gotten very much further. The books were about the Great Reform of 1810, when much of the magic now known as dark magic was stopped and forbidden. But they didn't contain many specifics about the banned magic itself.

Malou closed the book she was sitting with and reached for another. She could hear Helmuth muttering something incoherently in the background, but after a few hours in the cellar she had gotten used to his talking to himself now and then. Malou sighed and opened up at a random page, but her eye was caught by something else. As she heaved the book off the shelf, something had fallen out. She bent down and picked it up. It was little more than a booklet, a few pages sewn together down the spine, in a grayish cover with no writing on it. She flicked through it. It seemed to have been typed. It may have been the only existing copy. Her eyes fell on a particular expression.

"No, Alfred, stop it. She'll be going soon."

Malou gave a start and looked over her shoulder. At the end of the row she could still see Helmuth, who was slouched in his chair, talking to himself. He muttered something else she couldn't make out, and she leaned back over the booklet. This looked like a description of the types of magic that were banned around 1810.

"Well, all sorts of people come in here nowadays. Even women and servants, that's just how it is now. That's what the board decided."

Helmuth was obviously sitting talking about her to someone she couldn't see, which felt pretty creepy. She needed to get out of here. Malou shut the booklet, then opened her bag and slipped it inside, before putting the other books back in their places. Helmuth was quiet. Maybe he had fallen asleep. She thought about saying goodbye, but if he was really sleeping . . . Instead she crept toward the door. As she took hold of the handle, she heard the old man's voice again.

"Stealing? Why would she steal, my dear Alfred? Stop that nonsense. I'm certain she is a sensible young woman . . . No, but what do you mean with that, Alfred?"

Malou pulled the door behind her and hurried out onto the street again.

Impero Spiritus

**(NB: Classified as dark magic.
Use with the greatest of care!)**

Impero Spiritus is the ability to take control of another person's mind or body with the aim of directing that person's actions. Also found in this category are, more specifically, the ability to impede, control, or prohibit the actions of another person, the ability to control another person's dreams, the ability to manipulate and summon sensations like pain, fear, happiness, and attraction, and the ability to read thoughts and manipulate minds.

The mastery of Impero Spiritus is incredibly complicated, and it is a form of magic that only accomplished mages can achieve. Furthermore, guidance on many of the old methods has been lost since the Great Reform of 1810. It has been said, however, that founder Nikola Tesla practiced Impero Spiritus publicly as late as 1936, by way of a private arrangement in New York City.[1] Like many other mages who have had success in this craft, Tesla was a blood mage. The simplest form of Impero Spiritus is achieved through the blood and gives

---

(1) According to "Nikola Tesla—The Later Years" by Svenningen and Rosenblom, 1982.

the practicing mage control over their victim's body. The effect is strengthened if the mage has taken in some of the victim's blood. This needs to be repeated regularly, though, for the effects to not wear off quickly, and that itself is inadvisable, due to the risk that the practicing mage suffer from Sangius Servus.
The most advanced practitioners of Impero Spiritus are not only able to control a victim's body and actions, but completely control their mind.

Protection against Impero Spiritus

It has been shown that specially made amulets can be effective if they were made by a powerful mage, but they do lose their effect over time. The best protection against Impero Spiritus is still a victory stone, which, if carried close to the heart, never loses its power.

MARCH 16TH
9:36 P.M.

Chamomile

"Read this!"

Chamomile looked at the little booklet Malou had put on the table between them. "Impero Spiritus . . . I'm not sure any of us need any more spiritus . . ."

"*Spiritus* means ghost," Victoria said, reaching for the booklet.

"How come you know so many Latin words, Victoria," Kirstine asked.

"Private school," Victoria answered bluntly, her eyes still glued to the book. "I'm absolutely certain you've found it, Malou. *Impero* means something about dominating or control, and *spiritus* means spirits, or maybe even minds. So being able to control another person's mind."

"Mind control," Malou said. "Exactly. That's what Leah can do. Have you seen what it says there?" Malou pointed.

Chamomile took the booklet and read aloud: "*The effect is strengthened if the mage has taken in some of the victim's blood . . .* Yuck, that's so disgusting!"

"Does it really say that?" Kirstine asked, going quite pale at the very thought.

"Yup. Lucky that Leah hasn't drunk your blood then, Malou?" Chamomile pointed out.

Malou shook her head. "No, she hasn't drunk it, but she . . . she scratched me on the hand, so that it bled, and after . . . after, she licked her fingers. It was that time I visited at Christmas . . ."

Chamomile brought her hands over her mouth and stifled a gasp. "Yuck, no!"

"You didn't read it all, Chamomile," Victoria said, taking the book. "Listen: *This needs to be repeated regularly, though, for the effects to not wear off quickly, and that itself is inadvisable, due to the risk that the practicing mage suffer from Sangius Servus . . .*"

"What does that mean, that Sangus . . . What was it?" asked Kirstine.

"Sangius Servus," Victoria said. "*Sangius* means blood, and *Servus* is like being a slave to or serving. I would say it was a warning against addiction . . ."

"Aw man, that booklet is just horrible!" Chamomile moaned.

"Yeah, but that's not the most important part," Malou said, and snatched the booklet from Victoria. "Listen to what it says about protecting against it: *It has been shown that specially made amulets can be effective if they were made by a powerful mage, but they do lose their effect over time. The best protection against Impero Spiritus is still a victory stone, which, if carried close to the heart, never loses its power.*"

"What is a victory stone?" asked Kirsten.

"No idea," Malou said. "And what's worse, I haven't the foggiest where you can get hold of one."

Chamomile felt as if time stood still for a moment while she let it settle in, what Malou had read aloud. Could that really be true? Had they had the solution the whole time? She realized she was squeezing the little leather pouch her mother had made for her. So far, it held only one thing.

"I know," she said. "I know what a victory stone is."

"Yeah, well, out with it then!" snipped Malou.

"It's one of these." Chamomile loosened the purse, opened it, and laid the smooth oval black stone on the table in front of them.

"That's a victory stone? Are you sure?" Malou said.

Chamomile nodded.

"Where did you get it?" asked Victoria.

"My mom. It has been passed down through generations of women in my family. It can help with difficult births." For some reason or other, she didn't feel like telling them the real reason she had thought it so important to get a hold of this stone. Jens had told her it could protect those who had made a promise to a spirit. But if they could find Trine's killer before Walpurgis Night, then they wouldn't need it for that.

"It's beautiful," Kirstine said.

"What do we do now?" asked Victoria. "Now that we have the stone?"

"Now," Malou said, leaning in as she looked at the stone, "now we plan how to break into Leah's house and find out what she's hiding up in that room, the one that might have been Trine's. We can still do this, there's over a month until Walpurgis Night. Plenty of time to find Trine's killer."

MARCH 21ST
10:45 A.M.

Chamomile

"Is that you?"

Chamomile could clearly hear Leah's hoarse voice, even from the other side of the high fence that shielded the house from curious eyes. Right now, it was also helpfully stopping Leah from seeing that Chamomile and Victoria stood there, too, hidden, holding their breath.

"Yeah, can I come in?" Malou said, her voice somewhat friendlier than usual, which put Chamomile on edge already, worrying that alone could raise her suspicions.

"You're always coming here," said Leah.

"It's been a long time since I visited," Malou said. "I haven't been here since you chased me out in the woods with that knife . . ."

"It wasn't you I was chasing."

"Who then?" asked Malou.

"I won't give up without a fight. She was here, you know that?"

"Who?" Malou asked again.

"Trine . . ." snapped Leah. "I couldn't see her but I could feel her, clearly. She was there, she was going around in my private stuff like she always used to . . ."

"Are you hungry? I brought lots of food," Malou said.

It was silent for a while. Chamomile shot Victoria a quizzical look.

"Come in then," Leah said, and they heard the door close after Malou.

Chamomile closed her eyes and began to count. When she reached sixty, she opened them again and nodded to Victoria. Then she cautiously took hold of the gate's handle.

MARCH 21ST
10:52 A.M.

Malou

Malou waited while Leah threw herself on the food she'd brought, in her usual way. She ate like an animal. Malou excused herself to get a glass of water and tiptoed to the sink. She held her breath as she quickly flicked open the kitchen window latches.

Returning to the living room, she closed the door to the kitchen behind her. Leah was in the middle of eating the last bread roll they had brought. Malou had hoped it would take her a long time to get through it all, but she'd never seen anyone eat the way Leah did. She was like the fire in that Norse story about Loki, who had to compete in an eating contest—it seemed her hunger could never be satisfied.

"What do you live on, actually, when we're not bringing you food?" asked Malou. Leah looked like someone who never stepped inside a supermarket, but despite her sudden curiosity, Malou immediately regretted her question. She wasn't sure she really wanted to hear the answer.

"I don't need a lot of food. I can get by on very little." Leah chomped noisily into the last lump of bread. Then she hesitated a little. "Do you want to see what I eat?" Her eyes gleamed.

Malou felt her own gaze falter. Why the hell had she asked

anything about food? The last thing she wanted was for Leah to head toward that kitchen and anywhere near the open kitchen windows.

"No, it doesn't matter. Here, have some milk. It's organic!" She poured some into Leah's glass, but a little bit spilled. *Shit*. She hoped Leah hadn't noticed how her hands were shaking.

"First, you're curious, then you can't be bothered at all. I don't know what that's about. No, you should see." Leah stood up. There was something in her commanding tone that made Malou want to give a squeeze on the victory stone, which hung in a pouch around her neck under her shirt. "Come on, it's out in the garden." To Malou's relief, Leah got up and went into the entrance hall rather than the kitchen. Malou followed.

MARCH 21ST
11:03 A.M.

Victoria

"Do you hear something?" Victoria whispered.

Chamomile shook her head from where she was on the stairs, still keeping an eye out for Leah. "But hurry!"

Victoria felt her courage dissipating. They had to find a door into a room. The problem was, there was no door. Or if there was one, it was almost totally barricaded by stacks of cardboard boxes, piles of plastic bags filled with old newspapers, old clothes, envelopes, and typed documents. It would be impossible to get the door open without moving all that junk.

"You'll have to help me," Victoria whispered to Chamomile. "Or else it'll take too long."

Chamomile threw a worried glance down the stairs before nodding and joining Victoria. It was nerve-wracking. Each plastic bag rustled in a way Victoria knew must be audible down below them, and the boxes were so old and worn, she was afraid they might split open in their hands, all the contents hitting the floor and giving them away. Gradually, as they managed to move more and more of the stuff, their cover story became harder and harder to believe. *We just came by because we were curious to see the whole house . . .* It wasn't believable, and especially not now where they were moving around a ton of old cast-off belongings.

Victoria got a fright when a plastic bag ripped, dropping its fill of old papers all over her. She recognized the handwriting from the letters they'd gotten from Leah. It was Trine's writing—all these things must have been hers. Leah had never cleared them out.

"Here, take this!" Victoria passed a box to Chamomile, but misjudged the distance and ended up tipping the box so that a book fell out, hitting the floor with a soft thud. Had they blown it?

MARCH 21ST
11:05 A.M.

Malou

The garden was a wilderness of old shrubs and trees, but Leah followed paths she had created herself through the weeds and withered plants. Around it all was a scattering of large broadleaf trees, and an old swing dangled on a rope from one branch. At the foot of the trees, the first yellow daffodils poked up between the tall, rather shriveled grass. A piece of glass crunched underfoot, and when Malou looked down she saw it came from the remains of an old greenhouse that had once stood there. She wondered if Leah's and Trine's parents had built it.

The sun was actually warm, and a group of little birds were chirping away, utterly oblivious to what a strange woman's land they were living on. Leah stopped by some mature shrubs down in the farthest corner of the garden. She smiled. Not a taunting or sarcastic smile, but with a childlike happiness that left Malou wondering how to react.

"Look!" Leah said, and pointed to the other side of the shrubs.

Malou looked and saw a whole load of cages tethered together—they were more like long exercise pens or runs—and they were full of rabbits. Not like the little, sweet kind you have in a cage in your house, but big, meaty rabbits.

"You eat them?" Malou asked, but Leah seemed not to have heard her. She was pulling a section of the mesh aside so she could reach into one cage that held a lone rabbit. It was enormous though.

"This is Samson," said Leah, bringing the rabbit out. It didn't resist but also didn't seem exactly tame. "He is my prize animal." She giggled.

Malou reached out and patted the rabbit hesitantly. It didn't react at all, didn't even turn its stupid, half-closed eyes in her direction.

"He is the only one with a proper name. The others I call Meat and Blood." She smirked. "They're just meat and blood like everything else in this foul world. But Samson, he is special."

MARCH 21ST
11:05 A.M.

Kirstine

Kirstine walked. That was what she did when she couldn't do anything else. "Why do you pace back and forth like that all the time?" her mother had often asked when Kirstine couldn't settle because she was worried about some exam or essay or even just another awful day at school. But here there was nobody to get annoyed by her endless pacing. She was alone.

Kirstine checked the time. Who knew how long they had been away now? Were they at Leah's house? She stopped, letting her gaze drift over the old wooden floor of the turret room, half expecting to see a worn track on the floorboards where she had been walking back and forth ever since the others had left. Then she sighed, threw herself down on the bed, and reached out for the first and best thing she could read. She might as well do something useful.

You would think that with all the time she had now, being practically locked in at school, that Kirstine would be getting a whole lot of studying done. But the truth was, she had fallen further behind than ever. She plowed slowly through the first few lines. It was a text Lisa had given her about Imbolc, so she could learn a little more about everything she had missed out on.

Imbolc is celebrated between midwinter and spring equinox, and since the Neolithic Ages, people have seen this as the time that spring is just a step away, lambs are being born, and the light is returning.

She read through the words again. There was something here that bothered her. Imbolc marked the coming of spring. It was held between midwinter and spring equinox . . . but what did spring equinox mark then? She picked up her phone and carefully typed the words in.

Spring equinox falls on the 20th of March, when the sun is positioned directly above the equator. It is commonly said that the summer season starts with the spring equinox.

Kirstine sat up. There was a whistling in her ears. No, that couldn't be right. They still had plenty of time, it wasn't yet . . . She gripped her phone tight in her hand but didn't dare call them in case they hadn't turned the sound off and it could lead to them being found out. Instead she sent Victoria a message, though of course she wouldn't be able to look at it right away. Kirstine sat, as if paralyzed, on the edge of her bed. Then she made a decision. She had to stop it from happening.

GET OUT QUICK! YESTERDAY WAS
SPRING EQUINOX—SUMMER HAS STARTED.
WE GOT THE DATE WRONG!
THE PROPHECY!!!!

MARCH 21ST
11:12 A.M.

Chamomile

"If we just move this one, I think we can get through." Chamomile pointed to a large cardboard box and wiped the sweat from her brow with the back of her hand. Her top was sticking to her back. The air was deadly still and the sun shone in through a window in the gable end. It was sheltered and warm, and it wasn't helping that they had to move a thousand pounds of junk without making the slightest noise for fear of a mad old witch coming at them. She nodded to Victoria and they grabbed hold of the box. It was heavy, and she grunted with the effort, but they gradually did get it moved.

Victoria stepped over a pile of old clothes and carefully grasped the door handle. The door gave way and they were hit by a foul smell, something like cat pee. Chamomile grimaced and stepped into the room behind Victoria. It was empty and bleak. The window onto the quiet street was boarded up, the walls were bare, and there was no furniture. A worn carpet covered the entire floor. By the window, there was a large, dark stain, which she had no desire to examine more closely. This had not been Trine's room.

"Now I think I know what she meant when Trine wrote in her letter about 'time alone,'" whispered Victoria.

She closed the door behind her, and the room fell into complete darkness. The ill-smelling air was sickening, and an acute claustrophobic feeling made Chamomile want to tear open the door at once and get out of there. Victoria switched on her phone's flashlight so they could see around them, and when she understood what it was she was looking at, she felt sick. On the inside of the door, around the door handle and on the doorframe, were clear scratch marks. Someone had been desperately trying to get out.

"Will you please just open the door again?" whispered Chamomile, swallowing nervously.

Victoria nodded and opened it up. Then she looked around again. Chamomile followed her eyes while the thought crept upon her: The room was empty. There was nothing here. No secret. It had all been for nothing. She turned to Victoria, sure she would be thinking the same, but her friend was standing, eyes closed, with a focused look on her face, as if she was listening.

"Can you feel Trine?" asked Chamomile.

"No, not Trine, but . . ." Victoria stopped but kept standing there, eyes closed.

"Victoria, we need to hurry . . ." she said urgently. There was nothing to say that Malou could keep Leah's attention for much longer.

Victoria nodded, but it wasn't to Chamomile. She walked hesitantly around, crisscrossing the room. Along the walls. Down in the corner under the eaves, she got onto her knees and felt her way forward. She cautiously pulled up the carpet. It was loose, and she lifted it, revealing some old brown floorboards. The underside of the carpet had left yellow stripes across them. Victoria tested the boards, pressing on them so that they creaked a little.

"Here. Help me."

She showed Chamomile how they could just get their fingers down between two of the floorboards. One was loose. Together they lifted it, and Chamomile stifled a gasp. In a small hollow, there was a jewelry box. It was yellow with small pink flowers on it.

"Take it!" whispered Chamomile.

Victoria took hold of the jewelry box and stuck it under her sweater. Chamomile held her breath, as if she feared the theft would set off some alarm or other. But it was silent.

"Come on!" whispered Victoria. Her forehead glistened with sweat and her eyes were wide. "We need to get out."

Chamomile left the room and, straddling boxes and bags, stepped out onto the landing, inwardly cursing her short legs. At the gable end, she turned to the window and looked out over the garden.

MARCH 21ST
11:13 A.M.

Malou

Leah's seemingly endless talk of rabbit rearing came to an end. Despite the boring subject matter, Malou was glad she had finally found something to keep Leah occupied for a long time. But Leah was not talking anymore. Instead she had narrowed her eyes and looked back toward the house. Malou followed her gaze. Something was moving in the window up on the second floor.

"Trine . . ." Leah whispered. Then she curled in on herself and screamed.

MARCH 21ST
11:13 A.M.

Chamomile

"She saw me!" gasped Chamomile. "Leah saw me at the window. She's down in the garden. We need to get out!"

She turned and began to run down the steep stairs, but at that moment the door at the end loudly slammed shut. Chamomile threw herself at it, hammering on it and rattling the door handle, but it would not open. The steps and the attic's old floorboards began to creak ominously around her.

"Victoria! Come and help me, I can't get the door open!"

A sickening creaking and crashing noise was followed by a shrill scream.

"Victoria!"

Chamomile ran back up the stairs, which groaned and shook under her feet, as if there was an earthquake going on. Victoria was sitting in the middle of the landing in a strange, unnatural position. Chamomile realized one of her legs had sunk into a hole in the floor. The old, splintered boards had ripped Victoria's trouser leg, which reddened with blood.

"I ca-can't get up," she stuttered. "Help me! But be careful!"

Chamomile crept nearer, the floor all the while shaking and buckling under her. With loud tearing noises, strips of wallpaper started freeing themselves from the walls and peeling off in long ribbons, and the boxes of books and papers started to shake.

"What's happening?" she screamed.

"The house, it's attacking us. Pull me up!"

Chamomile grabbed Victoria's hand and pulled, but the floorboard splinters only pushed farther into Victoria's thigh, and she moaned in pain. One of the boxes in the corner fell sideways. Chamomile slowly turned her face to look at it. In the same moment, it opened itself and in seconds the contents were cast out over them. Chamomile threw herself down over Victoria as books, trinkets, and old bank statements rained down on them.

MARCH 21ST
11:15 A.M.

Malou

The scream pierced her eardrums and went on and on, so long Malou feared it would never end. The sound coming from the hunched woman ached with hurt and anger. Finally she stopped. Malou could feel her blood coursing through her body.

"Leah . . ." she tried, carefully. "There's nobody there. Trine is not here."

"I saw her," Leah snapped, still doubled over with her long grayish hair hanging over her face. "She's come to take revenge. And it's your fault! You've wakened her from the dead!" She slowly straightened up. Her twisted fingers were still clutching the huge rabbit, but now it hung lifeless in her hands. Leah looked from the rabbit in her grip and up at Malou. Her eyes were black, as if filled with ancient, hardened blood. "You are going to pay for this," she hissed.

Malou took a step back and came close to stumbling in the thick, dried grass. "No, Leah . . . no . . ."

"Stop there!" she commanded, and Malou felt Leah trying to take control of her. It felt as if her whole body was being held in a huge, relentless, viselike grip. Malou was scared that she had been caught again, that Leah's vengeful rage would enter her veins and paralyze her body, but it didn't happen. Leah couldn't do it. *The victory stone.*

Leah's eyes were wide with surprise. And Malou turned and ran. With a scream, Leah threw the dead animal down and chased after her. Her movements were unnaturally fast, like a cat suddenly pouncing on a bird. Malou ran as fast as she could. Her blood was boiling inside her, and she couldn't tell whether it was from anger or fear.

"Stop!" screamed Leah again, but Malou kept running.

She threw herself through the bushes, which tore deep scratches in her arms and legs. She was not too far from the paved yard and the gate out to the street, but Leah was still close behind her. Malou jumped over a pile of dried leaves and ran on, but suddenly her foot slipped in a hole in the ground and she fell, crashing face first on the grass. A rabbit hole. Malou turned and tried to get back on her feet, but it was too late. Leah stood over her.

"Why are you all doing this? Why are you against me?" she snarled.

"We only want to find out who killed Trine . . ." whispered Malou, as she pressed the victory stone and prayed that it would protect her.

"Why? It doesn't matter now. Trine is dead. Just like my mother and father are dead, just like we will all die. Just like *you* will die!"

Leah screamed again, more triumphantly this time, as if she knew Malou could do nothing in the face of her anger. But before she was able to throw herself at Malou, the ground beneath her suddenly was alight. Leah screamed in fright and pain as flames quickly caught the dry grass and flickered up her legs, forcing her back. Malou crawled away from the fire and got onto her feet. Leah roared like a wild animal, but a wall of fire rose between them, quickly ripping through all the dried foliage and branches. Malou turned and ran toward the house without looking back to see if Leah was pursuing her. She had to get the others out of there.

Malou pulled at the main door, but it was locked, and the kitchen window couldn't be opened either. *What the hell!* Kirstine had opened the door using rune magic on a previous visit when they got locked in. But Malou was no rune mage. She glanced out to the garden. The fire had spread to an old, gnarled tree that stood up against the gable end of the house. The tree had died long ago, and the flames crackled insatiably. Malou couldn't see Leah. She bent over and dug her fingers down around the sides of one of the paving stones in the little yard. It didn't give way at all, but she carried on, until her fingers bled. It didn't matter; in fact, the blood gave her the strength she needed and finally she got the paving stone up. She hurled it with all her strength at the kitchen window, and the glass smashed with a sound that was more like screaming than shattering.

MARCH 21ST
11:18 A.M.

Kirstine

Lightning fast, Kirstine was gripped by the fire. It crackled and roared inside her and she realized she had no control over it. There was no option of her getting it to stop. She held her hands up in front of her, but it was already too late to quell the flames. The scorching feeling rose up through her body. It felt like drowning in fire.

A long, pained scream burst from her, and she collapsed onto her bed.

MARCH 21ST
11:19 A.M.

Victoria

"We need to get out!" Victoria squeezed Chamomile's hand as they ducked together and dodged yet another cardboard box spilling its contents over them. "I'll count to three, and on *now*, pull with everything you've got."

"But your leg . . ." Chamomile shouted. "I can get help."

"There's no time. Look!" Victoria pointed to the window in the gable end. Outside, a tree was ablaze. It's old, crooked branches blazed like torches and reached out over the roof of the house.

"It's burning!"

"On *now*!" shouted Victoria. "Three, two, one. NOW!"

They heaved and tugged, but it was as if the floorboards only gripped her leg tighter, and the sharp splinters stabbed into her leg muscles, causing Victoria to cry in pain and desperation. The crackling of the fire had turned into a roar, having spread now to the roof itself.

"Chamomile, you have to go now!"

"No, we'll go together. Come on, try again!"

"It's no use. We can't get my leg out. If we stay here, we'll both die. You need to go see if you can get the door open, so you can get help."

"Victoria . . ."

The fire's roar blended now with a violent pounding and the sound of a tree splintering. Then they heard an angry curse and rapid footsteps on the stairs. Victoria waited to see Leah's crazed features, but instead it was Malou who appeared on the stairs. She dived toward them, her eyes large and her fingers bloody.

"Victoria's stuck!" screamed Chamomile. "We can't get her up."

Malou threw herself on the floor, which groaned under them like a wounded animal. She pressed her fingers down between Victoria's leg and the splinters of floorboard. Victoria screamed in pain when Malou's hands started to pull and rip up the boards. Her fingers were gashed open but she didn't stop. With a huge groan, the tree outside finally buckled and split into pieces, while the hole around Victoria's leg got big enough for her to lift it out.

"Come on!" Malou screamed. "Stay low to the floor."

They crawled across the floor. The attic was full of smoke, which caught in their throats, and when Victoria looked up she saw orange flames about to engulf the roof beams. They reached the stairs, but the steps crumbled under their feet, and they half slid, half fell down to the remains of the door, which hung in splintered pieces from its hinges. They tumbled into the kitchen as Victoria's leg buckled under her, and Malou heaved her up again.

There, by the sink, stood Leah. Her clothes were burning, the flames licking up her thin frame, but she seemed not to even be aware of them.

"You're never getting out," she said calmly.

MARCH 21ST
11:23 A.M.

Chamomile

Victoria collapsed again, and Malou gave up trying to pull her back to her feet.

"Leah, we need to get out. Come on, come with us!" Chamomile shouted, but the woman stood still as a statue as the fire spread to her hair. At once, the kitchen cupboard behind her opened up, and plates and glasses started flying through the air, smashing and filling the room with razor-sharp projectiles.

Chamomile ducked, looking desperately around her. Leah was blocking the way to the living room and to the broken kitchen window. They were trapped.

"Come on!" she screamed, and pulled at Victoria, who only flopped back down onto the kitchen floor again. The kitchen drawers flew open and cutlery whistled through the air. Malou cried out in pain as she was hit.

"*Come.*"

Chamomile turned toward the voice. It had given her a fright.

"*Come.*"

"Trine?"

Malou and Victoria also turned toward the shape that suddenly stood beside them, untouched by the chaos all around her. The white imprint of a young girl, giving them a friendly smile.

"*Come*," she repeated and signaled with one hand that they should follow her. At the corner she stopped and pointed downward. At first, Chamomile didn't understand, but then she saw it. A ring on the floor—a trapdoor. She lifted it to reveal an old, rickety stairway leading down into a low-ceilinged cellar beneath the house. They quickly teetered down the steps. She got a shock to find herself suddenly standing shin-deep in ice-cold water. The dark water was murky and smelled bad, but over in one corner there was light. A little window, with no pane. Chamomile and Malou supported Victoria from either side, and together they pushed through the stinking water toward the window. Malou jumped up and grabbed on to the window frame, and shouting out with the effort, she managed to throw herself out. She pulled Victoria after her, and last of all, Chamomile.

As they fled the house, the sound of Leah's screaming merged with the roar of the fire and the wailing sirens of approaching fire trucks.

MARCH 21ST
7:47 P.M.

Victoria

"Kirstine?" Victoria popped her head cautiously into the medical room.

A pale figure lay in a hospital bed, only just visible in the gathering darkness. The window was open, and outside a blackbird was singing a melancholy tune, which filled the silence of the room.

"Come in." Thorbjørn sat by the bedside in a strange, depleted pose, as if he'd simply given up trying to hold his huge frame upright in any way. He had not put any lights on, and darkness surrounded him. "She's sleeping now."

Victoria hobbled into the room. Her leg hurt under the dressing Ingrid had applied.

"What happened to you all?" Thorbjørn asked.

"We were riding two to a bike," Malou said. Both her hands were bandaged, and she had a large dressing on one cheek where she'd been hit by a flying knife. She nodded toward the bed. "What happened to her?"

Thorbjørn gave a defeated sigh. "I was hoping you'd be able to explain that to me. When none of you turned up at my class, I went looking for you. I found her lying limp on the bed. What can she have gotten up to?" He turned toward them; His blue eyes were set in dark circles and the worry showed in deep furrows on his face. "And where have you been?"

They stood without saying anything.

Finally he looked down again. "How can I help her if you won't tell me anything?"

Victoria felt a strong urge to confess everything, but a look from Malou made her hold her tongue.

"This is my fault," Thorbjørn continued, as if talking to himself. "I can't help her."

"I'm sure everything will work out . . ." Chamomile laid a hand on his shoulder.

At her touch, he pulled himself together and straightened up. There was a tear in the corner of his eye. "You should get back to your rooms," he said. "Ingrid says she is weak but stable. You can visit her again tomorrow."

"It must have been Kirstine who caused the fire," Malou said when they got up to their dorms. "That was also why it burned so quickly. That was no normal fire. She must have performed seid and seen that I was in danger, so she created that wall of fire between me and Leah . . ."

"She was trying to stop the prophecy from coming true," Victoria said. She could feel the others looking at her, could feel their anxiety and confusion. She would have to tell them about it. She took out her phone and let them read the message Kirstine had sent.

"What does that mean?" whispered Chamomile.

"It means we got it wrong," Victoria said. "It was last night, the night we moved into summer. The prophecy didn't speak of Walpurgis Night but of spring equinox. Trine wanted us to save her sister before it was too late. But we failed her. *Fulfill your promise before the night that marks the beginning of summer. Or else she will kill, or else she will die.*"

"Kirstine was trying to stop it happening . . ." whispered Chamomile. "But it happened anyway. Kirstine killed Leah."

"Damn it . . ." cursed Malou, hiding her face in her hands. "Only, it wasn't Kirstine's fault. Leah made her own choice. And she would have taken us with her if it hadn't been for Trine."

"I don't know if that's going to make much of a difference for Kirstine," Victoria said. "She took another life. It's exactly what she was afraid would happen."

"And Leah took her secret with her," Malou said. "Everything went up in flames. It's all gone."

"I've still got the jewelry box," Victoria said quietly. She had stuffed it under her sweater, just before getting her leg stuck through the floor, and since then it had been in her bag. Now she took it out, sat it on the table, and flicked its single locking mechanism to the side. They all jumped as a simple melody started to play. The thin notes sounded fragile and also strangely familiar. Victoria looked into the little case. It was a treasure trove—a child's gold mine. Little bits and bobs that had been precious to a little girl once. Things you could maybe take out and be comforted by, when you were locked in a bare room. Victoria lifted them one by one and laid them out on the table. There was a collection of pretty feathers, some smooth beach pebbles, a piece of amber, some glossy stickers, marbles, and a little ring with a pink butterfly on it.

"That's it! This stuff is what we risked our lives for?" Malou threw herself back in her seat and ran her fingers through her hair.

"Look, there's something at the bottom!" Chamomile ran her nail around the edge of the case. What Victoria had thought was the bottom of the jewelry box was actually a photograph, lying face down. Chamomile placed it on the table. A young woman and a young man smiled back at them. But the young woman was not Trine, that much was clear. She had dark brows, and long dark hair framed her narrow, distinctive face. She was pretty. Beside her sat a young man, also dark haired. They were sitting close and he had his arm around her. The photo had been taken at a party, bottles sat on the tables, and the flash had given the man red-eye. At the bottom right-hand corner a date was printed in orange type digits: *11/12/92*.

Maybe it was due to the young man's smile that Victoria didn't see it at first. It wasn't a sarcastic or malicious smile, but a true smile of happiness and optimism. She had never seen him smile like that before.

"It's Zlavko . . . !" whispered Malou. "It's frickin' Zlavko!"

There was no denying it. The photo showed a young Zlavko, holding a young, pretty girl with a serious expression and the hint of an enigmatic smile on her lips.

"But then that's . . . It can't be . . ."

"It's Leah," Victoria said.

"But she was so old," Chamomile said.

"No . . ." Malou said. "No, she wasn't actually as old as she looked. We could easily have worked that out if we had thought about it. Leah was younger than Trine. She was maybe 45 . . ."

"Not much older than my mom," Victoria said. "Was she really the same age as Zlavko? How come she ended up looking like she did?"

"If she was Zlavko's girlfriend, then look no further. That in itself would have to drain anyone of the will to live," Malou said, then suddenly stood up sharply. "The necklace! Of course. It *did* have something to do with Zlavko. But it didn't belong to Trine, it was Leah's. She must have lost it that night. She was there, after all. At the Yule party, I saw her."

"The necklace," Chamomile said. "It was Leah's. I should have worked that out. It was so polished."

"What do you mean?"

"Silver oxidizes. Gold is unchanging, but silver gets black when it comes into contact with oxygen over time. If the necklace had been lying in the woods all these years, it would have darkened. But it hadn't. Because Leah had looked after it well. Let's look at it again." She stood up and fetched the necklace, which was in a drawer in their room.

Victoria held it up to the light. The chain was made of several fine strands of braided silver and was relatively thick while also elegant and decorative. The pendant, on the other hand, was smooth and wholly unadorned. It was strange, in fact, given the pendant would normally be the most elegant part—unless, of course, it had some other purpose than looking pretty. Victoria started to think about the lockets people had in the olden days, the ones that often contained tiny portraits. She picked up the pendant and twisted, very carefully. The piece gave a little click, and its two halves fell apart. Inside there was a glass cylinder.

"Wow," Chamomile whispered.

"Can I see it?" Malou said, taking the cylinder. She examined it closely. "Now I think I know why Leah was expelled from Rosenholm," she said. "Do you remember that thing about how you can become a slave to blood? Addicted to it? I think that happened to Leah. And that the school found out. That's why she was thrown out. But the one who got her addicted, he's still here."

"Is that what I think it is?" asked Chamomile, taking the necklace from Malou to study the dark insides of the cylinder.

"Blood," Malou said. "Zlavko's blood."

"But why would Zlavko have wanted to get her addicted to . . . other people's blood?" asked Chamomile.

"Because he is, himself. Zlavko is Sangius Servus. A slave to blood," Malou said.

"Where do you get that idea?"

"I've seen it. I've seen him doing it."

"You've seen him . . . what!?"

"Drink another person's blood."

"What?! But why have you never told us this before?" Chamomile exclaimed, shocked.

"I'm telling you now, alright?"

"But how long have you known that?"

"It doesn't matter."

"Like hell it doesn't matter. What's going on here, Malou? Why are you protecting him? Whose blood was it he was drinking?"

"It doesn't matter."

"Was it yours?"

"What? No! Is that what you think of me?"

"What do you expect us to think? You sign up for his creepy little club, and now you're keeping things from us. Things that could be important for us to understand what happened back then."

"I didn't know that Zlavko and Leah knew each other, did I? And I'm not a member yet, just a candidate."

"And what's the difference, if you're already keeping secrets from your best friends?"

"I'm telling you now, for Christ's sake, am I not?" Malou stood up, placing both hands heavily on the table. She was breathing fast.

Then she sat back down in her seat. "It wouldn't have made any difference, you knowing that. It's got nothing to do with Trine."

"It's got something to do with you, though, Malou. With us . . ." Chamomile's voice shook.

"And maybe it does have to do with Trine," Victoria said, turning the picture over in her hands. "Look at what's here on the back. Isn't that Zlavko's handwriting?"

Malou took the picture and studied the words: *Anything for you. Just not that.*

"Zlavko wrote that to her himself. He said he'd do anything for her," Victoria said, and felt an unpleasant chill snaking over her skin. "Anything, except . . ."

"Committing murder," Malou said. "The whole time we've been looking for Trine's boyfriend. But it wasn't Trine's boyfriend who did it. It wasn't that guy with the blue eyes. It was Leah's boyfriend."

"What do you mean?" asked Chamomile.

"It was Zlavko!" Malou said. "Leah must have persuaded him in the end, or she may have forced him to do it. That's why she has been covering for him. The letters were just a red herring. Leah knew that there was nothing in them that would lead us to Zlavko."

"But now Leah's dead," Chamomile said. "How can we prove that everything is connected in that way?"

"I'll ask him about it," Malou said.

"Zlavko?"

"Yup. I'll ask him about it right now." She quickly stood up.

"No, Malou. Have you lost your mind?" Chamomile looked at her, aghast. "Either he'll lie or he'll get dangerous. Remember what happened the last time you went and accused him of a crime."

"I won't accuse him of murder, I'll just ask him about Leah. Find out if it's true they knew each other."

"But why? Unless . . ." Chamomile frowned and looked at Malou, and it felt like a landslide was set off in Victoria but then it was too late and Chamomile had already spoken the words that she had on the tip of her tongue. "Are you thinking about warning him?"

Malou's face tensed up in anger and, below that, an undercurrent of hurt, but Victoria was not convinced Chamomile would see that now as Malou raged furiously at her.

"What the hell did you just say? You of all people know how much I hate Zlavko, and how much shit I have to take from him every day. Nothing would make me happier than to be able to expose him, if it was him who killed Trine. And here you're accusing me of . . . protecting him?! What the hell are you thinking?"

"Okay, let's say you hate Zlavko. Then I don't understand why you'd rather be with him in his ridiculous club than be with us, your friends."

"I need his club for the connections it can give me. It's my chance. Why can't you understand that?"

"Because you don't need Zlavko and all those little rich kids. You've got us."

"You? The schnapps club? Sorry, but can that get me into the right college after Rosenholm? Get me an apartment in Copenhagen and the right internship? I want to be somebody, Chamomile, and I'm willing to work for that. Believe me, I know what it's like to live a shit life, and I don't want that. I'd rather die."

The two were both standing on opposite sides of the table, and the air was so full of anger and pain that Victoria started to feel faint. Chamomile gave a deep sigh and sank back into her chair.

"You really do want to be one of them, don't you?" she said resignedly, rubbing her face with her hand.

"And what's wrong with that?" snapped Malou. "Yes, Zlavko is sick in the head, but there's also nothing wrong with people who are just being successful in life. Maybe it's because they're really good at something and they're willing to work hard—does that make them bad people? It's a damn sight better sitting in a big, huge box like Victoria's mom than ending up like some loser in a rotten dump out in the middle of a field like your mom, having to treat hillbillies for their impotence and hemorrhoids!"

"You leave my mom out of this!" Chamomile screamed so loudly it made Victoria jump. The kitchen fell silent. When Chamomile spoke again, her voice was cold as ice. "You may well think my mom is a loser, Malou, but she's a good person. I thought you were, too, even though it can sometimes be hard to see it. Now I'm thinking I may have gotten you wrong. Maybe it really is for the best that you just run off to your Crows and leave this to us."

"So that's how it is for you, is it?" asked Malou, glaring aggressively from Chamomile to Victoria.

"Malou . . ." Victoria began.

"Yes," Chamomile said firmly. "That's how it is."

"Fine," Malou said, and turned away. The door closed behind her with a bang. It was only then that Chamomile started to cry.

MARCH 21ST
9:10 P.M.

Malou

How could she say such a thing? Accuse her of being a . . . a traitor, damn it? Malou angrily brushed her tears away. Why didn't Chamomile trust her? How could she believe such a thing, after everything she had done for her, for them?

Malou could hear a group of students walking down from the direction of the great stairs, and she ducked into one of the long corridors, which happened to be empty at the moment of students moving between classes. She closed her eyes and took a deep breath, but the tears kept coming. Her hands, wrapped in gauze dressings like some terrible zombie character in a movie, started to shake, and she couldn't get them to stop again. The sound of Leah's screams as they had fled the house mingled with the sight of Kirstine lying as if lifeless on the bed and with Chamomile's reproachful outburst. Malou buried her face in her hands and let herself sink to the ground.

All of it had been for nothing. They would never get the answers, never be in a position to prove anything, and their promise to Trine would end up consuming them all. Leah was dead, the house was burned to the ground, and if Zlavko was involved in the murder, he would never admit it. Chamomile was right.

There was no point confronting him, and certainly not when she was in a state like this. He would snap her in half, easy as anything. Where should she go then? Malou was used to being alone, but she wasn't used to feeling like this. *Lonely.* She got herself up, dried her eyes, and started walking, but rather than heading to the stairs, she turned back, walked to the far end of the long hallway, and continued hesitantly up a narrow stairway.

After taking about twenty minutes to build up the courage, she finally knocked on the door. A confused-looking boy with tousled hair peeked out at her. He was also a second year, but she didn't know his name.

"Um . . ."

"Louis," she said, hoping it wasn't obvious she had been crying. "Does he live here?"

"Um . . ." The boy looked at her inquisitively. Then he turned and called out. Nothing happened. "I'll just go and find him. You coming in?"

Malou shook her head.

She was almost regretting it and about to turn away when she heard footsteps approaching. Louis opened the door.

"Malou? Is something wrong?" He gave her a worried look. "What's happened? You're hurt . . ."

"No, no, everything's fine," she said, but the tears started again straightaway. She closed her eyes. *Damn it.*

"Come on, we can go into my room," he said. "I live on my own."

Malou followed him through a small kitchen, like the one she shared with her friends, but in reverse, although it was decked out in posters of Spider-Man and the Hulk.

"Magnus is a big Marvel fan," Louis muttered, leading her down the small hallway to his room. He closed the door behind him. "Do you want a drink of something? Water, maybe?"

She nodded. It was nice here. Louis's things were organized, the bed was covered neatly with a thick gray blanket, and his books were on shelves rather than lying in piles all around. Next to a little desk was a large wooden chair. It had a leather cushion and an elegant style, and clearly didn't belong to Rosenholm. The designer lamp on the desk was the same. Louis must have brought furniture from home. Above his bed there was a painting, showing a blurry avenue of large trees leading up to a white main building. It was an old painting of Rosenholm.

Louis came in the door carrying a tray with two glasses and a bowl of chips. "I thought you might be hungry."

"Do all the boys have single rooms?" Malou bit her lip. There were so many things she could have said. That he had a lovely room, that it was good to be there, that it was sweet of him to bring chips. Why did she start off with an attack?

But Louis just smiled. "No, there are only a few of them. Last year I shared a room, but this year my father wrote to Jens to ask if I could get a room of my own."

He wasn't bragging about it, he just stated it as fact. That he had a father who, by writing to the school, could get him a single room.

"Here."

Malou took a drink of water. It was sparkling water, nice and cold. They sat down on the bed.

"Are you going to tell me why you're like this?" He nodded toward her hands.

She only shook her head. "It doesn't matter. It's just . . . I've had a fight with the others. They . . ." She felt her voice breaking.

"They don't understand . . ." he continued.

She nodded and tried, in vain, to stop crying. What the hell was going on with her? "Go on then—just say it," she said.

"What?"

"*I told you so.* Just say it."

"Hey, no. I'd never say that," he said, putting his arm around her. "Listen, I'd rather it was me being wrong and you being right. That your friends would have understood and that your ambitions won't lead to scandal and judgment. It's just that I've seen it happen so many times . . ."

Malou dried her eyes. She must look dreadful.

"Here." Louis passed her a few tissues. At first she tried to just dry her nose, not wanting to sit blowing it in front of Louis, but there was no avoiding it. "Just honk away," he said, as if he had read her mind.

"I'm not normally the kind of person who cries," she said in her defense.

"Really, because I'd gotten the feeling you were a real softie," he said with a smirk.

She shoved him with her shoulder.

"I'm glad that you came to me when you were feeling down, Malou," he said quietly, and he reached out his hand to carefully take her bandaged one in his.

"Me too."

She looked him in the eyes. They were so bright, but the pupils were large and black and held her gaze. Malou waited, but nothing more happened. Then she leaned toward him and kissed him.

House fire

On March 21, a fire at an old villa on Solvangen in Kalundborg resulted in the house being burned down. Firefighters were called in by neighbors, but the house couldn't be saved. Technicians are investigating how the fire started. Nobody appears to have been harmed in the fierce blaze.

April 14, '89

Dear Leah,

How could you do it? How do you even sleep at night now?
I hope you are proud of yourself—you've ruined everything!
How can you be so twisted? Of course, I've always known
you were jealous of me, but I never thought you'd sink so low.
They went to the principal, do you know that? I'm only lucky that
I never told you his name so you couldn't go spreading that
around. He says he's going to leave me. And it's YOUR fault! But
I'm not going to let that happen, I'll need to do something. Maybe
we can run away together. I couldn't bear it if he left me—do you
hear that?
I wouldn't survive it.
I don't feel as if I can call you a sister any longer.
Now you really are alone!

Trine

Second-Year
Project Presentations

Alexandra David-Néel and Nikola Tesla—An examination of the retrospective view of leading blood magicians in the context of the 1810 reform
by Malou Nielsen

To be held in room 209 on
April 30 at 10:30 a.m.

Teacher: Zlavko Kovacevic
Examiner: Jens Andersen

APRIL 30TH
8:15 A.M.

Kirstine

Kirstine put some rolls out on the table.

"Whoa, have you baked breakfast?" Chamomile carefully picked out a roll and spread butter on it.

"Yeah, I figured you should have something to fuel you today," Kirstine said.

"I hate exams," Chamomile said, putting the roll down again. "I don't even know if I can manage to eat right now." She fiddled with something Kirstine couldn't see over the edge of the table.

"Luckily it's not too important an exam . . ." Kirstine tried to reassure her.

"Yeah, but everyone takes it so seriously anyway, as if it was one of the key exams. I'm just so nervous that Lisa will think it's a load of crap, what I've written in my project. I dreamed all night that I couldn't even remember the name St. John's wort and that after an hour of me just standing stuttering, they had to send me out again." Chamomile dropped her head onto her arms and moaned loudly. "I'm almost totally jealous of you, Kirstine."

"Yeah, well, at least I'm getting out of all that," she said, putting teacups down on the table.

"Oh, god, that was insensitive of me to say," Chamomile said. "Can you forgive me?"

Kirstine waved a hand in the air to show it didn't matter. Thorbjørn had read the halfhearted assignment she had written on the work of seeresses, but didn't think that an oral exam on it was a good idea, as things were right now. And she hadn't exactly argued. Just like Chamomile, Kirstine hated exams.

"Good morning," Victoria said as she sat down at the table.

"How can you be so calm?" asked Chamomile. "Aren't you even a bit nervous?"

"Not really, no," Victoria said. "I know Jens is already disappointed in me, so I've accepted that he will hate my project. There's not really anything I can do about it."

"Argh," Chamomile moaned again. "I really hope Lisa isn't disappointed in mine."

"Shouldn't you be careful not to lose that?" asked Victoria, nodding toward Chamomile.

"What? This?" She lifted her hands above the table edge and opened them out palms up. In the right one, she held the victory stone.

"You need to put that away." Victoria smiled.

"Yes, of course. I just feel like it calms me." Chamomile opened the leather pouch she wore around her neck and put the stone back inside. "There you are," she said, and threw Victoria a smile.

Chamomile obviously believed that, simply because they had the stone, their promise to Trine couldn't cause them any harm. She had shown them the book with the description of the stone, though when Victoria had stressed that it said nothing about promises made to a spirit, she had gone silent. She was certain about the matter: the stone would protect them. Where she had got that information from, she wouldn't say.

"Should we ask Malou if she wants anything?" Kirstine asked, and nodded over toward the bedroom. Malou was hardly ever in their rooms anymore, and when she was, it was behind a closed door.

"It's not worth it. She doesn't like food anyway," Chamomile said. "I think I'm going to go look over my notes again. Thanks for the breakfast, Kirstine." She got up and went into the turret room.

Once the three of them had gone—without a single word passing between any of them and Malou—Kirstine cleared up the kitchen. That would kill half an hour anyway. It was frightening, how good she'd gotten at filling the days with nothing. That was actually the worst part of all of it—the way she had gotten used to living like an animal in its burrow. Afterward, she went into the turret room and tucked Chamomile's mattress off to the side. She had been sleeping in there with them for the last month since falling out with Malou.

Kirstine decided to take a shower. As she stepped out, she stopped to look at her reflection in the mirror. She had lost weight over the whole recovery period, but her hips were still broad, and her shoulders too. She straightened up to her full height. Her hair had grown. It reached down to the middle of her back and was the color of damp sand. Scars ran from her ankles and wrists, snaking up her arms and legs. The wounds had healed now, but the scars were still purplish-blue lines. They would whiten over time. In some way or another she liked them, and she had stopped covering them up with long tops and pants. There was nothing to be done anyway—they were a part of her now, and it was time she started facing reality head on. *The harsh realities.* Kirstine had lost control of the fire she had started, Leah's house had burned down, and Leah had died in the flames. They had not managed to save Trine's sister, and they had no proof that Leah persuaded or forced Zlavko to kill Trine. Their only chance was getting him to confess, but none of them really thought that was a realistic option and Kirstine only hoped that Chamomile was right and her stone would protect them all.

She began brushing her hair with long, calm strokes, but then started to feel a little dizzy. The buzzing feeling washed over her and she dropped the brush, letting it fall onto the tiles of the bathroom floor. Seconds later, she, too, fell, hitting the floor with an unpleasant smack. Kirstine struggled to stay conscious. She lay there on the floor, the little white tiles damp with moisture under her naked body. And now images washed over her, even though she was conscious. She could be both here and there at the same time. *Leah, she's here. She is at Rosenholm now. She has the knife in her hand, and she has the intention to kill.*

Kirstine turned her head and struggled to get onto all fours. Leah was alive. The prophecy had not yet come to fruition . . . She had to find the others. She had to warn them.

APRIL 30TH
11:00 A.M.

Chamomile

"Thank you so much," Chamomile said yet again, as she fumbled her things together into her cauldron.

"We are the ones to thank you," Lisa said, smiling and holding the door open for her. "Can you manage all that?"

"It's fine."

Outside, Chamomile said goodbye to Lisa and the examiner, who was a tall, older woman she had never met before. They had a break before their next exam, and it seemed they were going to spend it taking a walk in Lisa's herb garden.

Chamomile was left standing in the empty corridor. She felt her breath slowing and deepening as the satisfied smile spread in her cheeks. Her face was flushed and hot, and her hair was probably now horribly frizzy after half an hour over a boiling pot, but right now she felt happy. It had been a gamble, choosing to defend her written project by making a cure for stress, there in front of Lisa and the examiner, but it had all gone well. She felt a momentary stab of regret, as she had to suppress her immediate instinct to send a message to Malou. Should she write to Jens? She hadn't seen much of him recently, but Chamomile was sure that he would be pleased, and proud, when he heard how well it had gone.

"Chamomile!" Kirstine came rushing toward her.

"Hey!" shouted Chamomile. "Guess what, Kirstine, I got an A! Can you believe that? I messed up a bit at the start, but then . . ." She stopped when she saw Kirstine's expression. "What's wrong?"

"It's Leah." Kirstine panted, out of breath now. "I saw her—in a vision. She's alive, and she's here at the school. I think she's planning on hurting someone!"

"What are you saying?!" Chamomile felt the color draining from her face as an icy chill instead spread through her, and her ears buzzed. *Or else she may kill, or else she may die* . . . "But the prophecy!"

"I know!" Kirstine said. "It still hasn't come to pass. We need to find the others."

"We need to warn the teachers too," Chamomile said.

"Lisa?"

"They've already gone. We need to find Jens."

"But Victoria and Malou . . ."

"They are still in their exams. If you try to find them, then I'll run up to Jens's office."

"Chamomile . . ." Kirstine gripped her hand. "Be careful, please. If you see her, you shouldn't go anywhere near her."

"Okay," she said, nodding. "I'll be careful." Then she turned and ran toward the great stairs.

A few minutes later she burst breathlessly into the main office.

"Jens?" she called, although the room was clearly empty. She ran over to his desk. Maybe there would be something that told her where he was right now, a timetable or exam overview. The desk was covered in small handwritten notes and papers, but she couldn't see anything that would help. Chamomile rummaged feverishly through the piles of paper. It was no use. She'd have to give up finding him and help Kirstine find Malou and Victoria. Then she heard a movement at the door. Someone was coming. Slowly the door handle turned.

"Dad?" whispered Chamomile.

But it was not Jens. It was Leah. She was wearing a long black dress with tiny buttons that ran right up the dress front to the neck. It sat neatly on her thin frame. On one side of her face and neck, she had a sickening, open burn. It was weeping and looked painful, so that Chamomile's first feeling was sympathy rather than fear. The fire had also burned her hair on one side, and Leah's appearance was even more grotesque than it had been before—she was like half a person.

"Trine, what are you doing here?" She turned slowly to Chamomile. It was only now that Chamomile noticed the ceremonial knife in Leah's hand.

Chamomile shook her head gently. "I'm not . . . You . . ."

"I know why you're here," Leah interrupted. "You're keeping an eye on me. You want to make sure I do what you've demanded. You've always wanted to control everything I do."

"Leah . . ."

"But don't you worry. I've come to put an end to it all, at last." She turned to the huge windows overlooking the park. "Did you know that they've made him the principal?"

"What do you mean?" whispered Chamomile, despite her fear of hearing the answer.

"Jens," said Leah. "They've made Jens the principal of Rosenholm."

APRIL 30TH
11:10 A.M.

Malou

"That was really well done," Jens said, shaking her hand. "I know that Zlavko's students are good, but it's certainly not every day we see an A+."

"Thanks," Malou said, and smiled.

"I'm sorry, but I have to go. I have a student defending their project in Spirit Magic now. But Zlavko is going to go through some of the things in the project with you, if I'm correct?"

Zlavko nodded. "Thanks for your help, Jens," he said, and the principal hurried out the door, leaving them alone.

It had gone well, really well. Malou hadn't been totally satisfied with her project. It wasn't the best work she'd ever done, but the exam had gone way better than she could've hoped. Zlavko hadn't commented on her changing her topic from what they originally discussed. Instead he seemed interested in the topic and asked questions about the two great magicians who had been discredited after some of their works were banned. He had seemed happy with her answers, and she was sure he had intentionally asked her things he knew she would be able to answer well. Malou had made her points without hesitation, and when faced with any difficulty, she'd faked it as best she could and steered them toward other areas where she was able to shine. They say that oral exams can be unfair, and there might be something in that. But, for once, the unfairness had gone in her favor.

"That was an interesting assignment," Zlavko said once they were left alone. "And a brave choice of topic. Lots of people would think it too controversial to choose two mages who used that sort of magic. It shows a certain courage and an ability to see the more detailed nuances. And in addition to that, you are a talented and capable mage yourself."

Malou squinted at him.

"Surprised?" A smile played on his lips.

"You think I have talent?"

"Of course. I only concern myself with the best students. I have no interest in the rest. Perhaps you think I'm too hard on you?"

"Um, yeah!" she blurted out.

"That's to push you to be better. Life is hard, Malou. I thought you knew that."

She nodded. "Have you . . . spoken to Louis about this?"

"I speak with all my Crows," said Zlavko, resting his hands fingertip to fingertip as he continued to observe her. "That means Louis as well. I'm ready to let you become a full member of the Crows, Malou. But the question is, are you ready?"

She stared at the table in front of her. It took her by surprise that he brought it up now.

"I can sense that you still do not trust me. I would like to change that. Is there anything you'd like to ask me about?"

Trust and *Zlavko* . . . Those two words didn't hang together in any way, unless they were preceded by a big, fat *NEVER*. Was there something she wanted to ask him about? And could she even get him to reveal something if she played this the right way?

A thousand images flashed through her mind. Zlavko licking blood from Louis's neck, Zlavko giving her a nosebleed and forcing her to hold her hand in ice-cold water, Zlavko saying cheers, Zlavko with his arm around Leah . . . Had he murdered Trine? And in that case, had he fallen victim himself to Leah's powers? Or was he just a cold-blooded murderer?

"Why were you out in the woods the night of the Yule celebration?" She looked him directly in the eyes.

He answered straightaway. "I was looking for her."

"Who?"

"You know who."

"You saw her too?"

"Yes, I did."

"You lied to me!"

"Yes. For your own sake. It was for the best that you knew as little as possible. But now I have the feeling you have already found out a great deal."

"You were her boyfriend," Malou said, part scared of his reaction, part proud of showing off what she knew, as if this too were a part of the exam.

"Correct."

"She was expelled from school, because she was Sangius Servus."

"Correct." The slightest twitch of his eyebrows showed Zlavko was surprised she knew the correct term.

"Just like you."

"Correct," he answered again, without flinching.

"Why did you run after her?"

"I was frightened of what she might do. Leah is not well . . . She hasn't been well for many years. Not since she was thrown out of the school."

"Getting sent away maybe made it worse, but it probably started before then," she added.

"Correct," said Zlavko once more, as if they were in the middle of some quiz.

"With the murder of her sister," she said.

Zlavko hesitated, then opened his mouth to answer, but at that moment, the door opened.

"Kirstine!"

"Malou, come on! You need to come, now!"

"What's happened?"

Kirstine's gaze wavered. "She's here," she said. "She didn't die in the fire. She's here!"

"Leah? Leah's here? In the school?" Zlavko stood up.

Kirstine looked totally shocked.

"He knows," Malou hurried to say. "Is she here now, Kirstine?"

She nodded. "I saw it in a vision. She's broken into the school, but I don't know where she is. She's got a knife . . . The prophecy!"

"Walpurgis Night . . . that's tonight," whispered Malou. She turned to face Zlavko. He had turned quite pale. "We need to find her. And warn the teachers!"

"Chamomile already went up to Jens's office to tell him," Kirstine said.

"He's not there. He has an exam right now," said Zlavko. "You'd better come with me. There's not much time!"

"But Victoria . . ." Kirstine said.

"She's with Jens, it's her exam now. Come on!" he shouted to them, opening the door and running down the corridor.

APRIL 30TH
11:12 A.M.

Kirstine

They sped off, but not in the direction of the teaching rooms. Zlavko led them down a narrow stairwell.

"Where are we going?" yelled Malou.

"Out," said Zlavko. "Jens always tests the students outdoors. At the stone circle."

At first it didn't mean anything to Kirstine. But then she remembered the very first time she had met Jens. On the assessment day, when they had asked the students to look down into a strange little bowl filled with water. The bowl had been standing in the middle of a stone circle.

"Wait!"

Kirstine turned around.

From the end of the corridor they'd just come down, Chamomile came hurrying after them. She was so out of breath she could hardly get the words out. "She was there, she was there!"

"Where? Where was she?" asked Malou.

"In Jens's office. She's looking for him."

"Are you okay?"

"Yes. She still thinks I'm Trine. It's Jens she's out to get. That must be why she followed us to Imbolc. And that's why she's here now!" Chamomile spluttered, paying no heed to how Zlavko was looking at her incredulously.

"Why Jens?" gasped Malou.

"She must be targeting Jens because he is the principal of the school," said Zlavko. "Leah never got over being thrown out of Rosenholm. We need to find them, before she does anything. Come on!"

They left the castle and ran out across the park beyond. The cold spring rain was falling heavily, soaking their clothes in an instant. Its low drumming filled their ears and it was hard to see through the park's overgrown trees. Kirstine could feel the clicking and rustling in the foliage, but for now the tree left her alone. Perhaps it was because they were still so near to the castle. She hadn't been here since the day of that first visit, but she could recognize it all. The narrow path, the trees, and suddenly they were at the stone circle. Jens and Victoria both stood there; they were alone.

"Jens!" Zlavko shouted to him.

Just then, Kirstine spotted a movement out of the corner of her eye.

The knife whistled through the air to the left of where they stood and straight into the middle of the stone circle. Chamomile screamed.

APRIL 30TH
11:15 A.M.

Chamomile

"No!"

Everything was crystal clear. Chamomile could see everything down to the finest detail. The touch of the rain on her face, the jagged edges of bright green leaves on the birch trees, the sound of the knife that hit her, the pressing feeling in her chest, the uneven surface of the cobblestones. A puddle of rainwater had gathered in a little dip in the ground. It was like a miniature lake, spreading out in front of her.

"Chamomile?" Jens said, bewildered.

APRIL 30TH
11:16 A.M.

Malou

"Chamomile!" screamed Malou. "No, no, no!" She threw herself down at her friend's side.

Chamomile lay on her side, the knife on the ground. Leah's knife. Why had she thrown herself in front of them like that? What was she thinking! Malou turned her onto her back. Chamomile stared back.

"Don't worry, everything will be fine, it'll be okay," Malou said, teeth gritted.

"Get away from there!" A maniacal woman's voice cut through the night air, but Malou didn't look up.

"I'm okay," whispered Chamomile.

"Keep still, help is coming." Malou could hear the panic in her own voice. She pulled Chamomile's top to the side to see where the knife had made contact. It had hit her right in the middle of her chest. But . . . where was the wound?

"Malou, I'm okay." Chamomile had a hint of a smile around her mouth. She took her hand.

"But the knife. I saw it . . ."

"It must have hit the stone," Chamomile said, and took hold of the leather pouch round her neck. Malou looked at it. There was, indeed, a nick out of it. Like one caused by a knife thrown with great force.

"The victory stone . . ." whispered Malou.

"Come on!" Jens reached out his hand to Chamomile and pulled her up.

Malou got to her feet and looked around her. Leah screamed again. She shouted at them to go away, but nobody moved. Zlavko stood in front and shielded Jens, Chamomile, and Malou, while Kirstine and Victoria had pulled back to the outer edge of the stone circle.

Leah faced them. Her long white hair looked steel-gray in the rain, and water ran down her disfigured face as she stared at them with wide eyes. "Give me him. Let me finish this. It ends here."

"No, Leah," said Zlavko softly, and his voice was almost gentle-sounding in the patter of the rain. "It's not too late. Come on, let's go somewhere and talk it over. Just us two."

"Far too late," she raged. "Especially for a traitor like you, Zlavko. You promised me you would always be there for me. But you lied."

"I am sorry, Leah . . ."

Malou did not know what sounded the most shocking. The fact he was saying the words, or the fact that he seemed to actually mean them. In that moment, Leah attacked. With an exaggerated agility and speed, which made Malou think of something in a movie being played too fast, she hit Zlavko in the chest, knocked him over, and swiped him in the face, her long nails scraping bloody scratches down over his cheek. He hit back at her, but his swing was strangely halfhearted, and Leah managed to grab hold of his hand. There was a nasty, cracking, crunching sound as she pressed her teeth into the upper side of his hand, tearing back the skin. He screamed in pain, and Leah used that instant of confusion to throw herself at him and sink her teeth into his neck. With a roar, Zlavko shook her off, and she clattered down onto the rain-soaked cobblestones.

Blood was dripping from Zlavko's throat. Leah, too, was bleeding from a gash over one eyebrow, red trails running down over the hideous burns on her face and neck. She smiled contemptuously, showing her long teeth, red now with his blood.

"There was a time when you would rather have died than harm me, Zlavko Kovacevic," she hissed.

He looked as if her words hurt him more than the bloody wounds she had inflicted on him.

"I'm going to have to hand you over to the authorities," Zlavko said, getting to his feet. "You are a danger to yourself and to others." He took a step toward her. "I'm sorry . . ."

Leah laughed and gathered herself like a cat ready to pounce, and Malou saw the strength that was still hidden in her. She was no old woman. She was raw power, bent on revenge, and the blood now dripping from Zlavko's wounds and running in little streams with the rain was adding to her strength. An enemy's blood, given in a sacred place, is a powerful source for those who have no fear of using dark magic.

"Leah . . ." Zlavko tried once more, but it was no use. She had already leaped. But this time, not at Zlavko. It happened so fast none of them had time to react.

"What . . . ?" Jens sank to his knees and turned to look at his back. As he fell onto the dark stones, Malou saw it. The knife, in his back. And the red rose unfurling on his white shirt with frightening speed.

“My knife,” whispered Zlavko looking down at the empty sheath hanging at his side. “She took my knife.”

Chamomile screamed as Leah gave a triumphant howl.

APRIL 30TH
11:19 A.M.

Chamomile

Chamomile placed both hands around the knife. She didn't dare pull it for fear the wound would bleed even more. She began to recite protective and healing incantations. She registered vaguely that there was shouting and screaming around her, but then it seemed like the noises faded into the distance until only the rain was left. A whitish wall was forming around them, and she knew it was spirits who were now protecting them, as she could see Victoria standing statue-like beside them. Her palms were open and upturned, and her eyes were white and empty as she looked upon what Chamomile couldn't see.

Chamomile turned back to her own hands, which were stained red now with Jens's blood. She concentrated like she never had before. Life energy was flowing all around her, in the trees and in the plants. In the animals moving around her, over her, under her. There was so much life here, and Chamomile closed her eyes and summoned all the energy she could, and sent it over into her father, so that he would not die.

APRIL 30TH
11:21 A.M.

Malou

They fought like wild animals. It happened so fast, Malou could barely tell who was who of the two figures dressed in black. For a moment, both of them suddenly became still. Leah lay with her face pressed into the cobblestones, Zlavko forcing one arm up her back and pressing his knee into the small of her back.

"That's enough, Leah," he gasped, tightening his grip. Leah twisted under him, hissing angrily. "Stop now!" he shouted again, and pushed his knee deeper into her back.

Leah sobbed with pain and rage, and Malou saw it coming seconds before it happened. Zlavko loosened his grip—ever so slightly—and Leah immediately took her chance. She tore herself free, and suddenly it was her who was on top of him. At that, Malou threw herself at her. Leah screamed in anger when she had to let go of Zlavko to focus on Malou. They rolled around on the ground, Leah shook her off, and Malou landed hard on her back and winced as the wind was knocked out of her. In the next instant, Leah was on top of her, but this time Malou was ready. She let power from the spilled blood flood through her, and she kicked out at Leah. Leah fell to the ground, but seconds later was back on her feet. She hunched, ready to begin again, but at the same time Zlavko's closed fist thumped against her temple and she collapsed right in front of them.

"*Naud!*" shouted Kirstine. The powerful rune rang through the air and pinned Leah to the ground.

Disoriented, Malou got to her feet, gasping for breath. Leah lay between them. Her eyes were closed and her long hair spread out across the dark, rain-soaked cobblestones. They stood watching her for a moment, but she didn't move. Zlavko had knocked her out.

"I'll take her," he said. "You help Jens."

Malou turned. The milky wall around the center of the stone circle had disappeared. Victoria had collapsed to the ground with exhaustion beside Jens's still form, and Chamomile sat with both hands around the knife in his back. Then Malou felt the sharp claws closing around her neck.

"One step closer and I'll slit her throat!" Leah snarled, her voice so tight to Malou's ear that she felt her breath on her cheek. Blood trickled warmly from where the long nails had dug into Malou's neck and broken through the thin skin. With a shudder, she felt how Leah was feeding off her blood, gaining strength as Malou herself got weaker. She tried to fight against it, but it was useless. Leah was too strong, and soon dark spots started dancing in Malou's vision.

"Let her go, Leah," Zlavko ordered, and Malou could hear the fear in his voice.

"Give him to me!" said Leah, flicking her head toward the middle of the stone circle.

Chamomile looked horrified; her eyes found Malou's and filled with tears. "No," Chamomile whispered. "No . . ."

"Give him to me and I'll let her go," Leah said calmly.

"You know very well we can't do that," said Zlavko.

"Once again, you betray me, Zlavko. But believe me, this time you'll come to regret it, like you've never regretted anything before," said Leah.

"Let me go!" Malou gasped as she noticed Leah starting to retreat, pulling her backward with her.

"No!" Chamomile screamed, looking up from the knife still in her hands, to Malou, and back. "Stop, Leah! Stop her!" she yelled, sobbing.

"If you come after me, the girl dies." Leah sneered at them.

Malou felt the stones underfoot turn to grass. Chamomile screamed her name, the sound jarring in her ears, as her vision faded to black.

"Let me go . . ." Malou begged in a whisper as they reached the forest edge, but Leah just leaned over her and licked a little of the blood from her neck, whispering "Shush, girl, just you sleep now."

APRIL 30TH
11:30 A.M.

Chamomile

"We need to get him straight up to Ingrid!"

Chamomile nodded. Zlavko put his arms around Jens and pulled him up, and together they half carried, half dragged him up toward the school. All the while Chamomile muttered healing invocations that should help stem the bleeding.

"Out of the way!" Zlavko yelled at other students who looked on aghast as their wounded principal was taken to the medical room.

Ingrid was sitting at her desk when they came barging in. "What's happened?!"

"He's badly injured," Zlavko grunted.

"Lay him on the bed." Ingrid went straight to examine him. "Find Lisa and tell her to get up here right away!" she ordered without looking up.

Zlavko nodded and ran out the door.

"You can save him, right?" Chamomile said. "He's not going to die, is he?"

"Quiet, I need to have peace to work. Please go outside."

"But . . ."

"Out!"

"Come on." Victoria put her arm around her and steered her out of the door. At that moment, Zlavko rushed back with Lisa. As they closed the door to the medical room behind them, it fell silent.

Chamomile realized her eyes were brimming with tears. She looked at the other two. "Come on, we need to find Malou."

"But where? We don't know . . ." began Victoria.

Chamomile turned to Kirstine. "You'd be able to see it, wouldn't you?"

Kirstine hesitated. "Maybe . . . but . . ."

"You can, Kirstine, I know you can." Chamomile grabbed Kirstine by her arms. "Where is she? Where's Malou?"

"Will you keep quiet, Chamomile?" Zlavko snapped as he stepped out of the medical room and closed the door carefully behind him. "Ingrid and Lisa need peace to work."

Chamomile let go of Kirstine. Her dirtied hands had left two bloody handprints on Kirstine's worn sweater.

"*Or else she will kill, or else she will die*," Chamomile said, the tears running down her cheeks. "Leah is going to kill Malou!"

"We'll find her before that happens," said Zlavko. "Where could she have run to?"

"I can look for her," Kirstine said.

"Yes, but where!" said Zlavko, frustrated. "That's exactly my point!"

"No, Kirstine means she can use clairvoyance," explained Victoria. "She might be able to see where Leah is headed. She's done it before."

Zlavko looked at Kirstine, as if seeing her for the first time. "Okay," he said. "Let's go in here so we won't be disturbed."

The tall, serious-looking girl closed her eyes. For a moment, she sat completely still, and then her eyes began to flicker under their lids.

"I can see something that looks like a kind of rocky cliff. Green and yellowish," Kirstine said. "And the sea down below. It's a long way down to the beach. And the white tower! I've seen that before. A lighthouse maybe?"

"I know where it is," Zlavko said. "It's not cliffs, but more of a rocky embankment. It's Røsnæs. North of Kalundborg. Leah used to go out there with her sister when they were kids. I should have thought of it."

"We need to get there, right away. Have you got a car?" Chamomile asked, feeling a spark of hope rise up inside of her. Maybe they could still find Malou before it was too late.

"We can take Lisa's. But I don't know if I can drive with this hand."

Chamomile's insides churned at the sight of Zlavko's right hand, which was a bloody mess of torn flesh and broken bones.

"I can drive," Kirstine said.

"You've got your license?" Victoria asked, surprised.

"No, I never passed the test . . ." began Kirstine, but she cut herself off. "Listen, does it matter? I'm telling you, I can drive!"

They all instinctively took a step back from Kirstine. The air around her started crackling ominously with electricity.

"I'll get Lisa's keys. Meet me at the front door," Zlavko said, and disappeared.

"Kirstine . . ." Victoria said cautiously as they ran down the broad staircase to the wide double doors leading out onto the courtyard. "Is it safe for you to be leaving the castle? I mean, can you do it?"

Kirstine took hold of the heavy door handle. "I have to and I can."

Then she opened the door and they all ran out.

APRIL 30TH
11:46 A.M.

Kirstine

Kirstine ran through the rain. The car was right down by the road and they had to cross the park to get there. Her feet crunched on the gravel path. They were a good ways from the woods, but nevertheless, something had awoken around her. The forest was a living being, all the trees connected by their roots beneath the earth, communicating with one another. She could hear the clicking noises from the roots beneath them. She did not know what it meant, but she knew they were talking about her.

"Faster!" she shouted to the others. "Run!"

She sped away from the path and shot across the lawn and between the many rhododendrons, which painted the castle grounds pink and purple in the late springtime. An ancient, gnarled magnolia tree uttered a curious, creaking noise as she passed, and large white petals showered down over the grass as she pulled herself free of a branch that had entwined itself in her hair. The rain got heavier and the ground sizzled under her feet, as if it were simmering. As she ran past the great beech, the first roots broke through the surface of the earth. Behind her, Chamomile screamed as the ground came to life with tree roots. Some were like small black worms, blindly wriggling themselves free, while others were as big as snakes, making quick, short jerking movements in their hunt for an ankle to envelop.

"What the hell!" Zlavko cursed from behind them.

"Keep running!" Kirstine screamed shrilly. "Down to the road! Keep away from the trees!"

"Victoria!"

Kirstine turned. Victoria had fallen. A root had snaked around her leg and she screamed, but the roots quickly released her again. It was not Victoria they were after; it was her. But why? What did they want from her?

As they raced on down the path, little stones sprayed up in the air after them, and the old chestnut tree groaned ominously as they ran. They were nearly at the road. *Come on!*

A rumbling sound made Kirstine look back over her shoulder. *No!* The path behind them was breaking up, splintering like a cracked mirror, and the splinters were coming alive, rising like a wave that threatened to capture them. An old chestnut tree they had just passed gave out a huge sigh and overturned onto the path with an ear-splitting crash.

"Get away from the path!" Zlavko screamed.

But it was too late. The wave reached them and the ground disappeared from under their feet. Kirstine screamed as they fell. It was dark all around them. The earth was black and wet and smelled of life and death at the same time, of roots and of budding growth.

"Kirstine!" Victoria screamed.

Kirstine could not see, she had earth in her eyes, earth in her mouth, she could not move, could not get up. Something was pulling her farther and farther down.

"Kirstine, get them under control!" Chamomile's shout sounded muffled, as if she was already far away. Kirstine felt the pressure closing on her chest as the earth pressed in around her.

Get them under control. What did she mean? As if this were a bunch of naughty kids they were dealing with. She gasped for air and tried to think straight. It was her they were after. It was her the tree had chosen and gifted all these powers to, though she didn't know how she was supposed to use them. The tree had made her strong. Powerful. Why, then, was she lying here in a dark hole about to be suffocated? *Hell, no!* Kirstine felt the electricity fill her, buzzing inside her. The earth gave her magical strength, and that magical strength gave her power over the earth. The rune formed in her inner eye even before it formed on her tongue. That strange jagged parenthesis symbol of the rocky ground, of the solid and unshakable. That which cannot be penetrated or undermined. *Pertra.*

APRIL 30TH
11:52 A.M.

Victoria

"Victoria! Here!" Chamomile reached out her hand and pulled her up. It had gone quiet, but rain was still steadily falling, running down Chamomile's face and hair, which was dark with mud.

"Kirstine?" Victoria whispered. She looked around. Zlavko was lying on the ground gasping for breath at the edge of the huge hole where the path had vanished from under them. Kirstine was not there. "Dig!" she whispered. "*Dig!*"

They threw themselves to their knees and started digging with their hands in the muddy earth. The roots allowed them to do it. There was no more sizzling or creaking from the great chestnut. They scooped up one handful of earth after another, but the rain was making the sides of the hole fall in again, and it was as if they were getting nowhere at all. Victoria searched frenetically for anything, a hand, a strand of hair, but there was nothing but mud and soggy leaves. A deep rumble from somewhere below them made them all stop. The ground shook.

"Step away!" yelled Zlavko.

Suddenly the bottom of the hole opened up and a dark shape was cast out onto the path beside them, like a morsel spat up again after being swallowed by some prehistoric monster.

"Kirstine!"

She gasped for air, coughed, and began sobbing. Tears and the rain trickled pale streaks through the dirt on her face.

"Are you okay?"

She nodded and coughed up a blob of bloody spit. Then she looked at them. "Malou," she whispered. "We need to get down to the car."

They stood up and staggered the last unsteady stretch to the car. Kirstine got behind the wheel of Lisa's little Citröen, Victoria took the passenger seat, and Zlavko and Chamomile went in the back. They'd barely closed the doors and Kirstine was turning the key. The car wheels spun as she floored it and Victoria was thrown back in her seat. Before long, they were out on the main road. She was glad she couldn't see the speedometer from the passenger seat, as Kirstine shifted from third up to fifth gear with the engine roaring, and the windshield wipers whipped from side to side to keep clearing the constant rain. A feathered amulet, which was tied to the rearview mirror, swung perilously from side to side.

"Where do we go here?" Kirstine shouted over her shoulder as they whizzed around a roundabout. She had a wild look in her eyes, and Victoria thought she could feel a crackling energy around her.

"Straight on!" ordered Zlavko from the back, trying to find something he could hold on to with his one functioning hand.

The last part of the route was on narrow, rough gravel tracks, and Victoria's legs felt like jelly by the time Kirstine finally stopped the car with a screech and they got out, bruised and covered in dirt from head to foot.

"I can't see any other cars," Chamomile said. "Leah would have to drive out here . . ."

They looked around, but they were clearly not completely alone. Leah hadn't had such a huge head start, given they'd driven so fast. She had to be here someplace, but maybe there were numerous parking places. Or maybe she wasn't here at all . . . Victoria got a cold feeling in her stomach. Maybe Kirstine had made a mistake? Maybe it was the future she had seen. Or the past?

"Look at this!" Chamomile was studying the long grass surrounding the small parking lot. "Tire tracks. A car's been here. Come on!"

They followed the tracks as best as Chamomile could see them. They followed them right down to a tight cluster of tangled buckthorn and elder bushes.

"They end here . . ." Chamomile said.

"She's hidden the car," Zlavko said, taking hold of a branch covered in large thorns, which looked as if it was growing there. However, as soon as he pulled it, it came loose. The headlights came into view. "Help me!"

Super fast, they uncovered the little black car, which was riddled with scratches after being driven headfirst into the bushes. In the backseat they found Malou. Her long, tightly clad legs lay at unnatural angles, and her blond hair covered her face. She looked like a rag doll that had been thrown into a corner. Had they gotten here too late?

"Malou!" Chamomile screamed. "Malou, we're coming!" She heaved at the car door, but it was locked.

"Get out of the way!" Kirstine said, bashing her elbow through the window so she could stick her arm through and open the door. She lifted Malou from the car and laid her on the grass. She was so pale, it was as if she was already on her way to becoming one of the white shadows.

“Malou, wake up now!” Chamomile sobbed, as Zlavko bent over her and placed two fingers against her neck, just over the bleeding gash Leah had made.

“Quiet!” he yelled. “She’s not dead. But her pulse is very weak.” Then he took his fingers up to his own neck, and Victoria had the absurd thought for a moment that Zlavko was checking his own pulse to see if he himself were alive. But then, when he lightly touched the wound on his own neck and put his bloody fingers to gently touch Malou’s lips, she understood what he was doing. It was the same thing Malou had done for her last year on All Hallows Eve, when a séance had gotten totally out of control. Malou had given her blood to save her. A simple but effective form of blood magic, just as Zlavko was doing now for Malou. She gave a loud gasp as she opened her eyes.

“Where is she?” she asked, gulping for breath.

“It’s okay, you’re safe now.” Chamomile knelt down beside her and wanted to lay her hands on her, but Malou waved her away.

“Leah! We need to find her!”

“Can you walk?” Zlavko asked, holding out his good hand to help pull her to her feet.

Malou nodded. She swayed a little and for a moment seemed she might faint, but Chamomile supported her, and slowly they set off toward the lighthouse Kirstine had seen in her vision.

The scenery was beautiful. Narrow paths ran between green hills, often leading them right to the edge of the rocky outcrop so that they saw the sea below them. The rain had stopped, but as they continued farther out onto the headland, the wind continued to pick up, and the sea became topped with frothy white near the land’s edge.

"The lighthouse," Kirstine said as she pointed. The wind had swept her hair back from her face.

Victoria turned. There, at the far end of the high promontory they walked along, was the white lighthouse.

"Why has she come all the way out here?" Chamomile said to herself, and in that moment, Victoria knew the answer.

"Because Trine is here." She did not know what came first, the realization or the sensation that Trine was present, but suddenly she could feel that she was there, even though Victoria could not see her.

"If we find Leah, let me do the talking," Zlavko said. "You all stay in the background. You shouldn't get near her, whatever happens. Even if I get injured. Do you understand?"

"Wait," Victoria said. "I want to hear what Trine is saying. She's here now."

Zlavko hesitated for an instant, then nodded. Victoria turned her face to the sky and opened her palms upward. She knew that her eyes would be turning white and blind-looking from the outside. But for her it was like suddenly beginning to see.

"Trine, we're asking for your help."

Victoria smiled when a white shape slowly materialized. A young girl stood before her, unaffected by the howling wind that whipped Victoria's muddy hair around her own face.

"Thank you," she whispered, gratefully. "For being here."

The young girl nodded at her as if telling her to continue. Victoria hesitated. Trine did not seem angry or scared. She was happy to be here. This was a good place.

"Leah didn't have anything to do with your death, did she?" Victoria asked, even though she already knew the answer—Røsnæs. She could feel it.

Trine smiled and shook her head.

"What is it you want us to do?" asked Victoria. She closed her eyes and listened to the voice the others could not hear. When she opened them again, she knew that they had their same, normal brown color again, but she was pleased to still see Trine's form standing alongside the others.

"Trine wants the chance to talk with Leah."

"How?" Chamomile asked, wiping the hair from her face.

"Through you," Victoria said.

"Me?"

"Leah thinks you are Trine's ghost. All you have to do is repeat what I say to you. And I will only repeat what Trine says to me."

"And what about the prophecy?" whispered Kirstine.

"I trust Trine," Victoria said. "She knows what we should do."

"If this all goes badly . . ." Zlavko muttered through gritted teeth before waving his hands forward to show they should continue.

They had gotten all the way up to the lighthouse by the time they saw her. She was on the other side, right out at the edge of the headland. The wind was blowing her hair around her face and her dress was half-soaked. All at once, Victoria was able to imagine how pretty she must have been, before she became sick on the inside. She could see all the women she had been, and all the women she could have become. The young, beautiful woman full of life and desire and raging emotions; the grown woman with soft hands who could have held a little dark-haired child; and the mature woman, bitter about what had become of her life.

Victoria felt a sudden tenderness, which didn't come from herself. She turned to Trine. Big white tears ran down her cheeks. It was painful to see a spirit crying. Perhaps because it planted the thought in her that even in death you weren't free from pain.

Victoria nodded to Trine and turned to her other side to give Chamomile a signal. Then she took her hand. Together, they walked slowly through the lyme grass that grew along the outer, sea-facing edge.

"I knew you would come, Trine," Leah said, her voice sounding neither angry nor bitter, but gentle and a little bit hoarse, like the rushing of the wind.

Victoria squeezed Chamomile's hand and whispered the words Trine said to her.

"Of course I came, my sister."

Victoria closed her eyes to concentrate better.

"I want to apologize to you," she whispered to Chamomile, who repeated the words. "I'm sorry, Leah. Sorry that I never saw you. Sorry that I always thought of myself, sorry that I didn't realize how bad things were with you. Sorry that I let you down and left you alone with Mom and Dad."

It was only after saying this out loud that Victoria realized they had misunderstood Trine when she had written *Say sorry* in the steam on the mirror. It hadn't meant *Get Leah to say sorry*, but *Say sorry to Leah from me.*

"I ended up hating you," Leah replied.

"I know that," Chamomile repeated.

"I hated you so much that I was glad when you disappeared. But then everyone kept talking about you. Even though you were dead, it was impossible to silence you. Still, I tried. I knew right away that you were dead, I could feel it. But I didn't say anything. It was my fault that the truth never came out. Do you know that?"

I know, Trine said in Victoria's ear.

"I know," Victoria whispered.

"I know," Chamomile repeated.

"It was me who told on you. It was my fault they found out about it. And I have been tormented by that ever since. I finally understood that I had to avenge your death, if I was to ever have peace. But I haven't managed. I wasn't strong enough. Can you forgive me?"

I forgive you, Trine said in Victoria's ear.

"I forgive you," Victoria whispered.

"I forgive you," Chamomile repeated.

Victoria opened her eyes. Leah stood upright, facing them, in the wind. Then she bent her face down to the ground and wept. Trine nodded her thanks to Victoria and left her side. Slowly, she walked barefoot through the lyme grass that could no longer scratch her until she bled, right over to her little sister, who had turned into a woman, while she herself remained frozen as a nineteen-year-old. She put her arms around Leah, and it looked almost as if the older woman leaned her head onto the young girl's shoulder. There was beauty in it, and Victoria wished the others could see it; she wished that Leah herself could see it too. The two sisters, united at the edge of the world, across life and death. The wind whipped at Leah's skirt. She had gotten dressed up. A terrible certainty gripped Victoria suddenly, as she understood that Leah had prepared herself for this. She had known all along this would be the end. *Or else she will die . . .*

"Leah, no . . ." she whispered, but it was too late.

The figure of the older woman slipped out of Trine's white spirit-embrace. For an instant, she spread her arms out and looked just like a bird about to take flight. But then she fell out over the edge of the cliff and disappeared.

"Leah!!" Zlavko screamed after her.

APRIL 30TH
3:53 P.M.

Malou

Malou was startled when the door to the medical room opened and Lisa came out. Chamomile, who was sitting, crying quietly with her head on Victoria's shoulder, looked up sharply.

"How is it going?" she asked.

"No news," Lisa said, her voice deep and reassuring. "Jens is still stable. He's sleeping now. There's no reason for you to wait here. You've done more than enough. It's thanks to you all that the healing process was started so quickly. It has helped to save his life."

"Come on," Kirstine said, carefully putting her arm around Chamomile. "Let's go upstairs."

"Malou?" Lisa said, and held her back. "I'd like to have a look at that wound."

"It's just a scratch. It looks worse than it is," she said without actually knowing how it looked at all.

"I want to have a look and clean it anyway, to make sure there's no chance of infection. Come with me." Lisa opened the door and offered Malou a chair. On the farthest exam bed, Zlavko was sitting, staring vacantly into space. He didn't even look up when Malou walked in. His hair was plastered to his filthy face, the dark eyes were set in shadow, and his normally immaculate shirt was stained and sticky with blood and earth. His mangled hand lay on a white cloth, and Ingrid was bent over it. Her brow was more deeply furrowed than ever before.

"This is going to hurt, Zlavko. Several of the bones are broken and out of place. I need to reset them if they're to heal well at all."

Zlavko did not react, not even when she started to adjust the broken bones in his fingers, cursing quietly as she worked. His face stayed an unflinching mask, as if Ingrid were merely brushing his hair.

"Let's take a look at you then," Lisa said, looking at Malou carefully with her dark, playful eyes. Malou leaned back her head to let Lisa see her neck better, but instead Lisa placed both hands on either side of her head and closed her eyes. Soon Malou felt a strange heat and a welcome feeling of well-being spreading all through her body as Lisa let her healing energy flow into her. It was like getting into a warm bathtub after a long and cold day, and Malou felt herself quickly relax. Next, Lisa focused on cleaning the cut on her neck, and finally she applied to it a thick green ointment that smelled strongly of herbs, and asked Malou to lie back and relax.

"That needs to be left for a moment," Lisa said, and left the room, but returned shortly after, saying "Ingrid, can you come now? I think Jens is waking."

"I'm finished now, too, but this just needs to be dressed. I'll be back as soon as I can," Ingrid said, and let go of Zlavko's hand, but he didn't even react to that.

It became very quiet in the room, and Malou felt as if she ought to say something. But what? *I'm sorry that your batshit crazy ex-girlfriend threw herself off a cliff and died? What do you say?* It was Zlavko who first broke the silence.

"I should have finished her off when I had the chance. At the stone circle. Then all this would never have happened. But I hesitated."

"She could have given herself up," Malou said.

"She would never have done that. And I knew it. It was me who pressured her to turn on you instead," he said darkly.

Malou instinctively lifted her hand to her neck and got green ointment on her fingers. "Leah could control me," she said. "She did it at Imbolc. She was already after Jens, but I didn't know that. I was afraid it was me she had come for."

"And that's why you had a sudden interest in Impero Spiritus," he stated.

Malou nodded and turned to face him. "And what about you?" she asked hesitantly. It felt as if she was stepping out onto some very, very thin ice, which could break at any moment. "Could she control you?"

Zlavko grimaced, with a real pained expression, and for a moment she feared that the honest, tender hiatus between them was over and would be pushed aside for a return to Zlavko's usual angry contempt. But then he started to speak, slowly, as if he was in great pain. "Yes. She could make me do anything, but it wasn't because of Impero Spiritus."

Malou studied his expression. "You loved her," she whispered, holding her breath. She was certain she had gone too far this time.

"Love," said Zlavko hoarsely, and Malou could not think of a time she had heard the word spoken with such bitterness. "More dangerous and powerful than any form of magic. Yes, I loved her."

"She was very pretty, I've seen a picture of her when she was young."

He gave a short laugh and pressed his eyes closed. "Why is it people are so fascinated by beauty? Such a ridiculously flighty and incidental thing? Eye color, shape of the face, the arrangement of fat deposits around the body. A coincidental mixture of genes, which people place all the value of the world on. I've never understood why that should be decisive in two people's love for one another. I loved her soul, and I will always love her. Regardless of how she looked on the outside. Regardless of how I ended up failing her. Regardless of the fact she is dead . . ."

His voice cracked, and she didn't know what she should do or say. They sat for a while in silence.

"We thought Leah had something to do with her sister's death," Malou said at last, leaving out the fact they had also suspected Zlavko of being in on it with her. "Why did she hate her sister so much?"

"Leah had a great darkness inside of her," Zlavko said, and closed his eyes, as if he was remembering something. "I thought that our love could fill the emptiness deep inside her, but I was wrong. No matter what I did, she could never feel whole, it was never enough for her, even though I gave her everything I had. My blood . . ."

"It was *her* who made *you* . . . addicted," Malou whispered.

"I chose it myself. I knew what the risks were and I don't blame her. But even that didn't help. And the last thing she asked of me, I couldn't do."

"*Anything for you. Just not that*," she quoted.

Zlavko looked up with a start, fixing her with a stare, and Malou forced herself to not look away.

"You wrote that to her, on the back of the photograph. What did it mean?"

Zlavko shook his head and turned his face away. "It doesn't make any difference now. I refused to do it, but I never imagined she would do it herself . . ."

"Her parents!" Malou gasped with sudden realization.

Zlavko looked at her, and she could read the answer in his eyes.

"It was her! And you . . . you knew it!"

He lowered his head and avoided her eyes. "If you knew what those people had put those two girls through . . . I heard about the so-called suicide. It was many years after we had split up, and I never confronted Leah about it. But I knew it must have been her."

"You never said anything to anyone?"

He shook his head. "No, it wouldn't have changed anything. The parents were dead, and Leah's life was long ruined. But maybe I was wrong. Maybe I could have avoided all this, if . . ." He broke off and didn't finish his sentence. "At some point or other I just hoped she would get to a time when she found some meaning in her life. But it was as if the emptiness in her had no limits."

"Some people are just like that," Malou said. "There's nothing you can do. You can't save them, because they don't want to be saved."

He lifted his gaze and looked at her. "Are you not a little young to be so cynical and disillusioned?" A tiny little glint sparkled at her from his dark eyes. "Is it not your role to be hopeful and naïve?"

"And Trine? Who killed her?"

Zlavko shook his head. "I don't know. And I don't believe Leah knew either."

"What about Jens? Why was she going after him?

"Who knows? I don't think Jens had ever met Trine. He studied at Rosenholm long before she did, and he only started at the school as a teacher after she had left. Leah's version of her sister's disappearance changed like the wind. She would always think that she'd discovered the truth this time. Until that truth had been replaced by a new one. Maybe we will never find out."

The door opened. "Jens is awake now, Zlavko. He'd like to talk to you," Ingrid said.

Zlavko got up from the exam bed and stood for a moment with his eyes closed. It was as if she was watching the transformation happen right in front of her. When he opened his eyes again, he was the same old Zlavko: the taunting smirk was back around his mouth, the upright posture, as if it was all a mask he had put back on.

"I've arranged an initiation ceremony for you next Friday. If you're still interested." He reached into the inside of his shirt and pulled something out. It was wrapped in a piece of white cloth, which was splattered in blood and dirt. "I think you should have this," he said without looking at her directly.

Once he had closed the door behind him, she unfolded the cloth to one side. It was a silver knife with a black handle. An athame. *Leah's athame.*

APRIL 30TH
5:30 P.M.

Victoria

"So we have tea," Victoria said, placing the tray down on the table in front of Chamomile.

"Hey, that's my line!" she said, in mock offense. "I didn't know you could even make tea."

"Haha. You'll have to go easy on me if it's not quite perfect," Victoria said, and held out the mugs. Chamomile still wore a towel on her head. They had both taken showers and washed all the mud off.

"Is Thorbjørn still in with Kirstine?" Chamomile asked.

"Yeah. He really wants to hear how she managed to get control over the whole forest, which had decided to bury us alive."

"Yeah, I bet he does." Chamomile shivered. "But her driving was even more terrifying. Unless it was all just to get away from the trees?"

"I actually think that's just how she drives," Victoria said, joining her friend at the table.

Chamomile nodded thoughtfully. "There were some points I was sure we wouldn't come out of it alive."

Victoria smiled. A little piece of all the horrible weight lifted from her shoulders.

The sound of the dorm door opening made them both turn. It was Malou.

"Hi," Victoria said cautiously. "Did you get the cut looked at?"

"It was nothing," Malou said. "But Jens is awake, he's speaking to Zlavko now."

"Ah, that's good," Chamomile said, relieved. "Do you want some tea? Victoria just made it."

"No thanks. So I also had a talk with Zlavko. He didn't know why Leah attacked Jens. Jens and Trine didn't even know each other."

"I don't think we're ever going to understand her," Chamomile said. "Sit down, I'll get you a mug."

"No thanks. I just came to grab some things and I'll be heading out again," Malou said.

"Heading out? Where are you going?" Chamomile stopped halfway to the cupboard.

"Does it make any difference? I . . . I decided to be accepted into the Crows' Club. The members have been allocated some special rooms, so . . ."

Chamomile nodded and pressed her lips together. Her eyes became blank. "If that's what you want . . ."

"It is."

"Well. Congratulations."

Malou nodded and turned to go into the room. Chamomile sat down. Neither of them said anything.

A little later, Malou came out of the room with a stuffed bag over her shoulder and a pair of shoes in her hand. As she got to the door, she paused. "I should never have said that about your mom, Chamomile. I'm really sorry about that, okay?"

"Okay," Chamomile whispered.

Then Malou closed the door behind her.

Large teardrops fell silently down Chamomile's cheeks and onto the table.

"Aw," Victoria said, putting an arm around her. "Never mind, you'll be friends again."

"I don't know about that," Chamomile said, and sniffled. "It looks like she's made up her mind. She's chosen them."

"Let's see if you don't work something out. Malou probably just needs some time, then she'll come around." Victoria stroked Chamomile's back until her sobbing gradually eased.

A bulky figure emerged from the turret room, closing the door carefully behind them.

"Kirstine would like to sleep a little now, she's very tired . . ." Thorbjørn paused as he caught sight of Chamomile crying. "Oh . . . is there anything I can do?"

"It's her time of the month," Victoria said seriously.

"Ah, oh, okay," Thorbjørn mumbled, his cheeks going from pink to red hot in a few seconds. "Well, in that case, I won't disturb you any longer . . . Bye for now."

"Bye!"

Once Thorbjørn had shut the door behind him, Chamomile burst into laughter, sending a spray of spit and tears over the tabletop. "Victoria! How could you do a thing like that? With poor Thorbjørn. The man nearly died just then!"

She laughed. "I don't know, I couldn't help it . . ."

"What are you up to?" Kirstine peeked into the kitchen.

"Victoria was just traumatizing Thorbjørn a little, nothing much else. Listen, weren't you supposed to be sleeping?"

"That's just what I said to get rid of him." Kirstine took a mug and sat down. "So here we are," she said.

Chamomile wiped her nose and dried her eyes. "Yup. The school year's nearly over and we haven't really learned a damn thing."

"We didn't find Trine's killer," Kirstine said. "The prophecy was fulfilled."

"But luckily it wasn't about you," Victoria said. "It was Leah who had plans to kill, and it was her who, in the end, had to die, by her own hand. I thought of something when we were sitting there outside the medical room. I don't know why I didn't think of it before. *The night that leads into summer.* It wasn't by chance that Leah chose exactly that day to carry out her plan and take her own life. It think today must be the anniversary of Trine's death."

"How tragic," Kirstine said.

"But the two sisters managed to make their peace at the end," Victoria said. "Leah got her sister's forgiveness."

"Yeah. And the murder case can still be solved. Now that we have the victory stone, luck will be on our side. It saved my life and it will give us the time we need," Chamomile said.

Victoria looked at her. Sadly, she couldn't quite share her optimism.

"To think that Leah and Zlavko were once together," Kirstine said.

"Yeah. The whole thing was a love story. I would never have guessed," Chamomile said. "A sick, twisted one, but still a love story."

"Are all stories not that, when it comes down to it?" Victoria asked. "Love stories?"

"Maybe."

"Even this one?" she asked, and nodded toward the closed door of Malou and Chamomile's room.

Chamomile turned to her. "You mustn't ask me that, because I honestly don't know. It's all so confusing . . ." Chamomile put her arms down on the table and rested her forehead on top.

"It's okay," Victoria said.

"And even if it was, then Malou has made it quite clear. She doesn't even want to be friends, never mind . . . I must be the unluckiest person in the world when it comes to love. First Vitus and now this."

"At least Malou hasn't tried to kill you yet," Kirstine said.

"Ha! No, so I suppose you could call that progress." Chamomile smiled and shook her head. "How did you both know that? Does everyone know? Does Malou?"

Victoria shook her head. "No, no. I think I just guessed it somewhere along the way . . ."

"I wrote Malou's name on the stone at Imbolc, did you know that?" Chamomile said. "Not because I wanted to be free of her, but I didn't want things the way they were. But it didn't work. Not the way I hoped. Malou is gone, but the feelings aren't."

"Nope," Victoria said. "It didn't work for me either."

"Can I ask what you wrote on your stone?" Kirstine asked.

"I wrote the date of my birthday."

"Your birthday. Oh, was it on your birthday that you and Louis . . ."

"Yes."

"And it was really terrible?" Chamomile asked sympathetically, which would normally cause Victoria to pull back, but this time her care didn't feel suffocating. Maybe it was time to tell them the truth. *The whole truth.*

"No, it wasn't so awful, us being together, but . . ."

"You were pressured into it?"

Victoria nodded.

"By Louis?"

"No. By . . . my family."

"What . . . what do you mean? Your family forced you to have sex?" Chamomile asked.

"They didn't force me, I went along with it. It's hard to explain. It's a tradition in my family . . ."

"A tradition? What the hell, Victoria?!"

"You could also say it's a ritual."

"So, like, a sex ritual?"

"Yeah, but not something where everyone stands around wearing black cloaks and chanting. Even though it maybe was like that once . . ."

"Seriously?!"

"It's been like this in my family for hundreds of years. When you reach a certain age, the eldest in the family chooses a suitable partner from another family. Afterward, you are seen as having reached adulthood."

"Victoria, is your family . . . I mean, is that even legal?"

"I know I told you my family weren't mages, but that's not true. I'm sorry that I lied. I just so wanted to have a fresh start here at the school. The truth is, I come from an ancient line of mages. They don't care about the law. They do what they've always done, even if it's something that's not talked about openly anymore. I was part of the decision that it should be Louis. Not everyone is fortunate enough to be included in that. But even though it was with someone I really liked, it still felt wrong. Deep down, I knew he was just doing it because he felt he should, and not because he wanted me."

"What the hell, Victoria . . ." Chamomile squeezed her hand. "Does Benjamin know about this?"

"Yeah. Benjamin is also from an old magical family, but he refused to have anything to do with all that stuff. He cut off all contact with his family. When he heard what had happened with me, he wanted me to cut ties with my family too."

"So that's what he was angry about?" Chamomile said.

"But you didn't want to do that?" asked Kirstine.

"I love them. My brothers . . . I can't do it. Even if Benjamin thinks they . . . they follow dark magic . . ."

"Do they?" Chamomile whispered.

"I've always known that my family was different, and that there were things we didn't talk about when other people were around, but my parents aren't evil. They do things in a slightly different way. They follow the ancient traditions." Victoria wiped her eyes and looked at them. "What do you think of me, now that you've heard all this?"

Chamomile smiled sadly. "I think that you can't choose your family. You have to put up with what you've got. And you are the last person in the world I'd suspect of being drawn to dark magic, Victoria. I can understand how you couldn't choose to cut off your own brothers and parents."

Victoria nodded. "But now I've lost Benjamin. And sometimes I wonder if I really made the right choice."

She looked at the two of them, and in that moment it was as if she could hear them thinking: *I don't think that you did.*

**An informational meeting
for all first- and second-year students
will be held in the dining hall
on May 27th at 11:00 a.m.**

Attendance is compulsory for all.

Until then!
Jens

MAY 27TH
10:47 A.M.

Chamomile

Chamomile stood stuffing clothes into her scruffy duffel bag when there was a knock on her door. It was Jakob.

"Kirstine isn't here," she said, and carried on with her packing.

"That's not . . . It's just, a letter arrived for Malou," he said.

"She's not here either," Chamomile said without taking her eyes off the pile of clothes in front of her.

"Isn't this her room?"

"Yeah, but . . ."

"Well, will you give this to her?" He seemed annoyed, or maybe he was just in a rush.

"Okay." She sighed, taking the letter and shoving it in her pocket.

"Thanks. And you should all get down to the hall. The assembly is about to start."

Chamomile couldn't stop herself from looking out for her, even though she had told herself to leave it alone. Maybe she wasn't even planning on coming. Maybe she was too grand for assemblies and the like now. Nevertheless, Chamomile had kept her a seat. Just in case.

The whole school was gathered. She could see Thorbjørn, Jakob, and Lisa sitting in the front row, but none of them showed any sign of stepping up to speak. Then the great double doors at the end of the dining hall opened and everyone turned, as if they had been instructed to do so in that way.

First there was Zlavko in a red shirt and black trousers. One hand was still obscured by a discreet bandage, and there was the hint of a smile at the corners of his mouth. He walked confidently down the rows of gaping students, taking long, purposeful strides. Behind him came a group of students, all dressed in black. *The Crows.* Malou entered the hall with the first of them, dressed in an elegant trouser suit and high heels. She held hands with Louis, her blond hair was pulled back from her face in a tight ponytail, and she carried herself tall and proud as she crossed the hall. Not once did she look around at the students, but rather, she kept her gaze straight ahead on the little stage that had been set up at the far end of the large, high-ceilinged room. Finally, there came Jens. He nodded and smiled at the students as he went up to the stage. He was, perhaps, a little paler than usual, but that was the only trace left of Leah's attempt to kill him.

Chamomile sighed with disappointment. It was the first time she had seen him since that day. She had tried to visit him, but Ingrid had turned her away. Chamomile had thought about telling her that she was more than just an ordinary student, but she had been unsure how angry Jens might get with her. Maybe she was also in some doubt about how far he even saw her as more than an ordinary student, given that he hadn't made contact with her himself. The thought that Jens had perhaps already lost interest in his newfound daughter made her sadder than she would like to admit.

The black-clad students had gotten up on the little stage and stood tall, facing the rest of the students, while smiling, complicit, at one another, as if they had planned a funny show that they were about to put on. Jens stepped up on the stage and turned to face the audience . . .

"Dear students. Dear colleagues. It is with great pleasure that it falls to me now to bring to a close my first year here as principal of Rosenholm. A greater pleasure than I'd previously imagined. As you all know, recent events nearly ended so badly that I might not have been standing here with you today. I am very grateful that things did not end that way, despite evil forces having wished me dead. The fact that I am alive today is in great part thanks to Zlavko."

The Crows on the stage all burst into applause, which gradually spread through the rest of the room. Zlavko nodded, a superior smile still on his face.

"I also have Zlavko's diligent students here to thank—also known as his Crows," Jens said, facing the students behind him.

"Why are they getting called out?" Kirstine whispered to her left. "What did it have to do with them?"

Chamomile shrugged and straightened herself up to see everything properly.

"Rosenholm is lucky to have such resourceful, talented, and fearless students." Jens was still standing with his back to the hall, addressing the students behind him. "Many thanks."

Chamomile studied Malou. She was smiling happily, her cheeks flushed. *It should have been her who was Jens's daughter. He would have been very proud of her, he wouldn't have wanted to keep her a secret.* Chamomile couldn't help it. The envy was eating at her like an acid bubbling inside.

"The attack on me was an attack on the whole of Rosenholm. On everything that we stand for," Jens continued, this time facing the hall again.

"I really don't like this . . ." Victoria whispered, frowning.

"Mages have always lived against the grain. In danger. Threatened by a society that doesn't understand us, that is afraid of us or angry or hateful," Jens said. "We are reminded of that now, and that the threat is greater than it has been in many years."

"But Leah was a mage herself," Kirstine objected. "That doesn't make any sense!"

"It is of paramount importance to the school that all students can get an education here without feeling threatened or afraid," Jens continued. "For that reason, we will be introducing further security measures in the coming school year. The first of these we'll reveal right now. Zlavko and his brave Crows have agreed to act as a kind of special security force here in the school. They will patrol the perimeter of the grounds and ensure that no outsider breaks into Rosenholm, and they will make sure that all students flourish and feel safe from danger. If you see something you are not comfortable with, you can go to one of these students, who will report directly to Zlavko or to me. To prepare these students for this sizeable task, the Crows have agreed to give up their vacation—all will stay here over summer to receive instruction from Zlavko and me. You can be reassured that the Crows will be fully trained to undertake the responsibilities we are placing on their shoulders."

Silence fell in the hall. There wasn't a single cough or creak of a chair. Everyone sat with their eyes toward Jens and the black-clad figures behind him. The whole thing gave Chamomile a strange, uneasy feeling in her body. Jens must really have had a scare to want to put Zlavko and his gang in charge of patrolling Rosenholm. Did he really know what he was doing? Or had Zlavko managed to manipulate him for his own gain?

"In order to recognize the special commitment these students are making to Rosenholm, I would like to present them with a small token of the school's gratitude and as a sign of the status they now hold." Jens took a small fabric pouch from one of his inside pockets and turned again to the Crows. He shook each and every one of them by the hand and placed a badge on the right-hand side of their chest. Chamomile squinted to see. *A feather. A feather made of silver.* Last of all, Zlavko received his feather. Jens held his hand for a long time as they exchanged a look of understanding. Then Jens turned back to the hall.

"The Crows are not the only new thing you will experience next year. During my first year, it has come to my attention that there are aspects of the school that need to change. Relics from the olden days, when people didn't believe that students could be trusted to make important decisions. Instead young people were treated like children, who should be instructed, brought up, and it was thought that everyone should learn exactly the same. I would like to gradually move away from that old-fashioned mentality. I fully trust all of you who come to this school. Therefore, the old-fashioned division of girls and boys will be discontinued as of next school year."

What?

A gasp went around the room, and a soft ripple of whispering broke out among the students.

"Instead," Jens said loudly, to be heard over the murmur, "instead, we will concentrate on development. We will take into account that all students are different, that they all have different abilities and should be treated differently in order to all meet their full potential. Rather than separating students by gender, we will separate by ability. You will get much more freedom, but there will also be greater demands on you. You should be prepared to give your best, and together we will build a new, fantastic generation of mages!" The last part, he shouted out across the hall, and the Crows burst out again into a noisy celebration.

Chamomile sat as if she were frozen, while the hall slowly emptied. Jens had been the first to leave, followed by Zlavko, and then the Crows. After that the students all broke into noisy chatter.

"How cool is that?" she heard Sofie say to her sister, as they walked arm in arm past the rows of chairs. "Do you think we'll also share dorms with the boys?"

"That was smart of him," Victoria said softly.

"What?" muttered Chamomile.

"To announce the thing about boys and girls being allowed together now. That's all that everyone will be talking about. The thing about the Crows will sink away completely after that news."

"I don't understand how Zlavko convinced him to do this . . ." Chamomile whispered.

They sat there until everyone else had left the hall. The teachers were the last to leave. Thorbjørn's expression was so dark, he might as well have just received his own death sentence, and Lisa and Ingrid went by deep in conversation without noticing them.

"Come on," Kirstine said. "Let's go up and finish packing. I really don't want to be here any longer."

An hour later, when Chamomile was sitting in the bus, looking out at the blue sky, the bright yellow rapeseed fields, and the gardens with newly budding lilac bushes, she remembered the letter.

Malou's letter. She took it out and examined it. Malou's name was on the front, nothing else. It could be from her mother. Perhaps it was from Louis, but why would he write a letter to her, when they seemed to be together the whole time anyway. Zlavko? Or Jens maybe? Maybe it was instructions related to her new role as one of Zlavko's henchmen and a member of the Crows.

Of course she couldn't open somebody else's mail. That was wrong, and possibly illegal. But one doesn't always manage to do the right thing. Chamomile opened the envelope.

To Malou,

By the time you get this letter, I will be no more. It is a relief, nothing else. I have longed for death for many years. I don't regret it—not that. But there are many other things I wish had gone differently. I regret falling in love, and I regret that I trusted in the one I loved. Above all else, I regret that I never exposed Trine's murderer. I wanted her dead, and when she disappeared, I hid the truth away. I wanted her to be forgotten forever. I didn't love Trine like a sister, but she still didn't deserve the fate that my hatred of her gifted her. That is what I regret the most of all.

Before I close my eyes on this despicable world for the very last time, I will try to atone for my wrongs. I want to avenge Trine. I want to get retribution for all the young girls who have met the same fate she did. If I fail in this, then that will become my greatest regret of all. In that eventuality, I hope you will do what I didn't have the strength to.

I enclose the last letter Trine sent me.

May you have the strength to do what is right.

Leah.

April 30, 1989

Dear Leah, dear sister,

my own little Troll,

I didn't think I would be able to forgive you, but I can't be angry with you any longer. We must not part as enemies. This is the last letter I will send you. From now on, I must live in hiding—but I'm prepared to do anything for love's sake! I'm sure you will understand one day.

I have also written to Mom and Dad and told them the truth. It will come as a shock to them, but I comfort myself with the thought that their anger can't touch me anymore. Maybe I'll come back and we can be united again. Shortly, I'm going to meet him, and we're going away together. I'm sending you this photograph, so you can see for yourself how happy we are with each other. I take my leave of you now. Forget me not, dear sister, and keep my image in your heart always, until we meet again.

With love,

Trine

There was a photograph in the envelope, and Chamomile felt as if a wave was engulfing her, pulling her down into a deep darkness, as she came to understand what it was she held in her hands.

Trine had put the photo of her and her boyfriend in the envelope and sent it, with the letter, to her sister. Leah had read it and ripped the photograph in two. The half with Trine in it, she must have shown to her parents, and it had been used in the investigation and printed in the newspaper. But the other half, she had hidden away. The whole time, Leah had known who Trine's boyfriend was.

Chamomile stared at the photo. The man's blue eyes stared back. The blue of *her* own eyes.

He had been so interested in Victoria. So apparently concerned about her. But in reality, he was afraid. He knew that Victoria could speak with spirits. With Trine's spirit. He was afraid that she would disclose who he was. It was him who had scared Trine away, it must have been.

And what else had he done, without her noticing? Suddenly the thought went through her like an ice-cold gust: What had he gotten *her* to do? She grasped at the leather pouch around her neck and tipped its contents into her open hand. The same shape, the same weight, but the stone was gray. He must have known that her mom owned a victory stone, and he had seen his chance to manipulate Chamomile into getting it. Now it was gone.

She grabbed her phone.

Malou! Get yourself out of there.
It was Jens. It was Jens who did it!!!

EPILOGUE

He looks proudly out over the world that is now his own. The dining hall is empty and the students have left the school, but when summer is over they will return again. It fills him with a buzzing sense of expectation.

The woman is dead, the last witness—one he hadn't even known existed. Nobody can touch him anymore. Especially now that he has the stone, which he has dreamed of for many years.

He thinks about her. About Trine. What a pity no one will ever know the fate that befell her. A fate that deserves the highest acknowledgment. The same fate as all the others, of so many before her, a long line of young women, wandering as white shadows through the centuries. And more of them will follow. That is what he is thinking about as he looks out over the empty hall. Then he turns and walks out into the sunshine.

Find out how the mystery started . . .

Gry Kappel Jensen
Roses & Violets
On sale now!
ISBN 978-1-64690-012-1

Four girls from four different parts of Denmark have been invited to apply to Rosenholm Academy for an unknown reason. During the unorthodox application tests, it becomes apparent this is no ordinary school. In fact, it's a magical boarding school and all the students have powers.
Once the school year begins, they learn that Rosenholm carries a dark secret—a young girl was murdered under mysterious circumstances in the 1980s and the killer was never found. Her spirit is still haunting the school, and she is now urging the four girls to find the killer. But helping the spirit puts all of the girls in grave danger . . .

Find out how the mystery and drama concludes . . .

Gry Kappel Jensen
Nightshade
On sale Fall 2025
ISBN 978-1-64690-014-5

After two hectic years at Rosenholm Academy, Kamille, Kirstine, Victoria, and Malou have found out who killed Trine—the spirit who has been haunting the school. But nothing is over yet as the girls find out that the darkness runs much deepr than they first thought, and little by little they must solve the riddle that rests deep in Rosenholm's walls . . . before it's too late!